Sunnie's Rainbow

by

D.H. Barbara

Visit Lakeville online at
http://www.dhbarbara.com /

Follow on Twitter
@dhbarbara1

Find Lakeville on Facebook!
www.facebook.com/DHBarbara

Acknowledgements

Foremost, I thank my God and Savior, Christ Jesus, and I pray that the words I have written and the storyline herein are edifying, entertaining and enjoyable.

My biggest thanks to Detective Kevin Doheny of the Bergenfield, NJ Police Department. He endured scores of silly emails, read rough drafts of scenes and answered the most ridiculous questions for me to ensure that Officer Tom Jacobs was as true to life as possible. Kevin is married to one of my best friends in the whole world—I owe thanks to Lynda for letting me "borrow" him.

Many, many, many thanks to Anne Siglin. She keeps me on my toes, and she knows why. I may send her some Klick-Klacks. ☺

Thank you to the many who read rough drafts, suggested and critiqued, and above all, encouraged and made me laugh when I sometimes wanted to cry. The Woupies and the fellow writers at Keeping the Course, and of course those of us who reside in a small corner of the internet dubbed "Looneyville." you are the best!

Enjoy the story!
Blessings,

Barbara

To all the men and women who serve this country, be it on homeland or foreign soil, God bless and protect each and every one of you.

To the families, no matter if they endure odd hours or long deployments, God's grace and mercy.

Especially to the wives of all our fine men, thank you for your selfless spirits. May the Lord's peace always hold your hearts. Thank you.

I APPEAL TO YOU THEREFORE, BROTHERS, BY THE MERCIES OF GOD, TO PRESENT YOUR BODIES AS A LIVING SACRIFICE, HOLY AND ACCEPTABLE TO GOD, WHICH IS YOUR SPIRITUAL WORSHIP. DO NOT BE CONFORMED TO THIS WORLD, BUT BE TRANSFORMED BY THE RENEWAL OF YOUR MIND, THAT BY TESTING YOU MAY DISCERN WHAT IS THE WILL OF GOD, WHAT IS GOOD AND ACCEPTABLE AND PERFECT.

ROMANS 12:1-2

Chapter 1

Her arms laden with four overflowing bags of toys, Sunnie exited the store heading in the direction she thought her Miata was parked. She stopped for a brief moment, certain her car had vanished from the crowded parking lot. Relief flooded her—with frustration following close behind—when she spotted it behind an enormous work van. Sunnie huffed as she continued on, knowing she'd never be able to see around it when she pulled out. Once she placed the bags in the small compartment behind the driver's seat, she peered around the vehicle to make sure the parking aisle was empty.

Sunnie rummaged in her bag for gum—a much better habit than her former 'pack-a-day' habit. Before pushing a CD into the player, she unwrapped two sticks. The car filled with loud Christian rap music as she shifted into reverse, bopping her head to the beat. Seconds later her head bopped off the windshield as the sounds of breaking glass and mangling metal drowned out the music.

She rubbed a spot on her forehead, then turned to see what had hit her. Attached firmly to the bumper of her car was the sleek black nose of a police cruiser. The urge to swear came swiftly. Sunnie pounded the steering wheel a few times as she prayed to fight off the struggle she was now winning more often than losing. She added a request for patience and a good attitude before opening the door.

Emerging from the cruiser was a tall officer sporting a light frown. He pulled his sunglasses up, resting them on the top of his closely cropped, brilliant red hair. Sunnie immediately observed two things: he possessed a strong, broad build and the frown became an amused grin.

Before she could form a coherent thought, his deep voice called in a somewhat surprised tone, "Sunshine Young? Is that really you?"

Taken aback, Sunnie fumbled her response. After all, it was entirely possible he had quickly run her plate number.

"I...well, I don't believe I know you, Officer...?"

"Jacobs. Tom Jacobs. We graduated Lakeville High together. You were in my senior English Lit class and Geometry. Aced them both, too, if I remember correctly."

Sunnie filed through her usually bright mind, but couldn't come up with the

9

reference. "I'm really sorry, Officer. I, umm...well, I..."

"You just backed out of a parking spot doing about eighty-five, creaming an official town vehicle in the process." Officer Jacobs held his amused grin.

"I was not going that fast! Besides, you weren't there a second ago!"

The grin deepened. "All right, sixty. Where are you off to in such a hurry? Didn't you look? Though you couldn't have possibly seen around the back of this." He waved a hand at the irksome van.

"Of course I looked! You. Weren't. There!" Sunnie turned away with an exasperated breath to get her information out of the glove box. She fleetingly wished she kept an emergency pack of cigarettes in there as well. *Today*, she thought, *would be a good day to start up again*.

Sunnie started as a shadow loomed over her. The pleasant, deep voice asked, "What are you doing, Sunnie?"

"*Duh*. Getting my information. Isn't that what I'm supposed to do, Off..."

The sneer got lost somewhere in her throat; she was not prepared to be looking directly into the clearest and brightest blue eyes she had ever seen. The amused expression returned.

"Yes, Sunnie. It's exactly what you are supposed to do. Thank you." Officer Jacobs nodded slightly, taking the paperwork from her trembling hands before returning to his car.

What is WRONG with me? Sunnie reprimanded herself. *I hit him, and I'm getting all...*

Flustered was the correct term, but Sunnie shrugged it off. She turned to say another silent prayer, and took a deep breath. She walked to the cruiser and leaned on the open door, peering into the car.

"Listen, Officer Tom, I'm really sorry. Sometimes my temper gets the better of me. I'll behave myself now," she offered, smiling the amazing disarming smile she possessed. It was immediately imprinted in his mind.

"I appreciate it. I rarely hear an apology. I usually hear worse; trust me. Now, we do need to be getting you a tow."

"A tow? Why..." Sunnie's question trailed off as she turned to view the damage. The nose of the cruiser was almost to her rear tire and the trunk on the driver's side was completely crushed. The damaged tire seemed to be dangling from the mess at a strange angle. Sunnie uttered the first thing that came to her mind.

"Jude's gonna kill me."

Officer Jacobs stepped from the cruiser. "Jude? Your brother? It's not his car," he stated in a bit of confusion. He'd just run all of her information and *Jude* Young had not shown as the owner of the vehicle.

Sunnie shook her head, eyes still on her beloved Miata's now-crumpled body. "Oh, no—car is mine. He's a bit protective of it, though. Jude works at Vince's Garage, in town. I'll call him."

"Yes, I know. We take all the department's cars to Vince's. Jude's a great kid—he's in my Guard unit. I didn't realize you were related."

"Great. That's great. Excuse me a second; I need my phone," Sunnie said with unconvincing cheer. She reached into her car far enough that her shirt rose a bit and Officer Jacobs was afforded a clear view of the elaborate Celtic knot tattooed across the small of her back. He quickly returned to his car to better concentrate on the accident report.

Sunnie reappeared with her phone by her ear. As she adjusted her shirt, she glanced around at the gathering crowd. She called to several bystanders, "Don't you have other things you need to be doing? Go on, shoo!"

Eventually, Jude answered. "Hey, Sis. Listen, some of us do work during the day, ya know. What's up?"

Sunnie placed her hand over her eyes, praying for sisterly patience. Jude and Silas frequently referred to her real estate business as her lack of a job. "What. Ever. Punk. Listen, I need a tow."

"What? Sunn, are you okay? What happened?" Sunnie grinned at the change in tone of Jude's now-matured voice. It reminded her of their late father, although she'd never heard that hint of protectiveness directed towards her from him. Only aggravation and anger.

"Easy, big fella. I had a little fender bender in the parking lot. At the toy shop."

Sunnie didn't hear a response right away. She surreptitiously watched Officer Jacobs tapping away on a screen in his car while she thought through her senior year classes. Why couldn't she remember the arresting face, or those irresistible eyes...

Jude's voice brought her back from the halls of Lakeville High School. "Okay, Sunn, I'll be there with the wrecker in ten. Don't move! Are you hurt?"

"No, punk, I'm fine. I'm sure you'll see me." She hesitated before adding, "I have a Lakeville Police cruiser in my trunk."

"You hit a cop? *A Lakeville cop?*" Jude's voice rose an octave. Possibly two.

"Huh, yeah. Funny thing, he says he knows you. Officer Jacobs? Tom Jacobs." Sunnie removed the phone from her ear just in time. Jude was beside himself at this news.

"You hit who?!? Sunnie! Of all the cops in the world, you hit my sergeant? I'll be right there!" Jude didn't say goodbye or wait for Sunnie to respond.

Sunnie shook her head, quickly deciding to call her mother before Jude did. Somewhat relieved that Rob answered, she explained the situation and thanked him for his willingness to pick her up. Sunnie turned to find Officer Jacobs waiting behind her when she ended the call.

"Is everything in order?" she asked, realizing she needed to say something instead of stare. Sunnie was unnerved over feeling so...unnerved. *Maybe I did hit my head harder than I thought.*

Officer Jacobs pulled his sunglasses down from his head. "All is fine, Jude is on his way—I heard the radio call." He handed her a metal clipboard. "Did you hit your head? You've got a mark, there."

A strong hand lightly brushed her forehead. He seemed satisfied when she mutely shook her head; words were completely lost at his touch.

"Please review that and sign the bottom. Can I offer you a ride home? You must be late for a birthday party. One of yours?" He pointed to the bags behind Sunnie's seat.

"Oh, umm, yes. I mean, not really. No, thanks. My stepfather is on his way, so long as it's okay for me to go with him. I have a slew of family...younger siblings, nieces and nephews."

"Well, I doubt any are for Jude." After another glance at the bags, he asked, "Which sister is married?"

"Oh, they both are. Storm and her family are in Europe, at a mission camp somewhere. Autumn is here in town. Her husband runs the chiropractic clinic on

Orchard and Main." She mentioned her mother's remarriage and their subsequent second family, unsure why she kept blathering on. She tore her gaze from his to concentrate on the report.

Officer Jacobs nodded, seeming interested in her family history before commenting, "You know, I always thought you ran away and got married."

A much too loud and forced-sounding laugh emerged from Sunnie as she handed the clipboard back to him. "Oh, not me! I ran away to school. I stayed upstate a while, in real estate. I came back to town a few years ago. No kids...or husband," she added over the rumble of a large, black tow truck.

"That's a shame, Sunnie Young. Damn shame," he said seriously before turning to clear the parking aisle for Jude to pull over to the accident site.

Sunnie removed the bags from the car while Jude greeted Officer Jacobs. He shook his head at her in a dismayed fashion, which she answered with a put out tongue before thinking better of the action. Jude ignored it and went to examine the damage, while Officer Jacobs chuckled at the show of familial affection. The sound sent a shiver up Sunnie's spine even in the heat of the day.

Once her car was secured on the flatbed, Jude pulled Sunnie aside. "Sunn, are you sure you're all right? Do you need a ride home?"

She unconsciously rubbed her forehead. "No, I called Mom. Rob should be here any minute. Thanks, though."

Jude hugged Sunnie quickly before shaking Officer Jacobs' hand. "See you over the weekend, Sarge."

Sunnie watched forlornly as Jude pulled away with her car. Relieved to spot Rob driving up the now-crowded aisle, she waved and signaled him to wait for her. She picked up her bags and turned to Officer Jacobs.

"Thank you. Again, I'm sorry. I guess you have all you need?" Sunnie smiled, disappointed his eyes were hidden behind the dark sunglasses again.

Officer Jacobs nodded. "If I need you, I'll find you."

Disquieted by his comment, she turned to run to Rob's car; Officer Jacobs' gaze followed her movements until they were driving off. "Damn fine woman," he said to himself with a wave to Rob.

"Who's your friendly officer, Sunnie?" Rob asked as they drove out of the lot.

"That is so. Not. Funny, Rob! I wish I had a cigarette! Just one! Did you tell Mom?"

"Of course." Rob overlooked Sunnie's grumble. "She said you can use her car until yours is repaired. Was it bad?"

"Sure it was bad! I hit an officer—who happens to be Jude's unit commander or some such thing—who insists he 'knows' me from high school. How much worse can it be?"

Rob laughed, agitating Sunnie's already frazzled nerves. "What is so funny?"

"I was asking about your car. Not your officer."

When he glanced at her, he could see she was visibly flustered. Sunnie was a strong and confident woman, not given to bouts of diffidence. Her next statement interested him.

"He isn't mine. I just hit him...that's all," she insisted, crossing her arms in a posture that indicated the discussion was ended. Rob drove them to his house in amused silence.

Sammie looked out over the deck to the play area Rob had created for the children with Jude's help. Aina played happily in the sandbox, filling then dumping out her bright pink pail. River, the newest family addition, was at Sammie's feet in the car seat carrier, asleep after a meal.

Aina abandoned the pail at the sound of Rob pulling in the driveway, excitedly running toward the car. Piercing shrieks of "Daddy! Daddy!" emanated from her tiny body, turning quickly to "Sunnie! Sunnie!" when Aina spied her getting out of the car.

Sunnie caught Aina mid-run toward Rob and grabbed her mid-stride. "Hey! Where's my big hug? You see him all the time!"

The small girl wrapped her arms around her neck in a surprisingly strong hug. After placing a kiss on Aina's smooth cheek, Sunnie released her to greet her Daddy. She climbed the deck steps, and sat heavily by her mother.

"Are you okay, Sunnie? Jude says it was quite a hit." The concern on Sammie's face made Sunnie bite off a tirade about her brother.

"Did he call the paper, too? I'm okay, Mom. More frustrated with myself than anything else, really. There was a big van blocking my view—I should have been more careful. I got rather snotty with the cop, to top it all off."

"Sunnie, you know better. Jude said something about knowing him. Who was it?" Sammie watched a look of consternation flit across her daughter's face. Sunnie had made so many strides in her relationship with God the past few years but there were times when her old nature still bubbled close under the surface.

"His name is Tom Jacobs. He's apparently Jude's squad leader, or whatever it is they're called in the Guard."

Rob arrived on the deck steps with Aina on his shoulders. "Is that who he was? You hit Sergeant Jacobs?" He received a glare from Sunnie and headed into the house under the guise of getting something to drink, chuckling as he walked through the French doors.

Sammie reached to rub her daughter's shoulder. "You'll be fine, Sunnie. Jude says they'll know by the time he gets home about your car. He should be here soon. He has to leave for base tonight."

"Great. He can really yell at me. I could tell he wanted to take my head off before." Sunnie snickered at the memory of the look on Jude's face when he pulled up in the huge tow truck.

Rob and Aina returned, placing a glass of tea in front of Sammie. Deciding a change of subject was in order, she asked Sunnie, "How's the house sale going? Any buyers yet?"

"Someone did call, wanting to see it, but they never showed up. I'm sure it'll sell soon, though. The price is right. I still think it's...."

Sammie held up her hand to forestall the repeated argument. "I know, Sunnie. I know, it's too low. I just want it to sell. I told you, keep your commission and split the rest with everyone. Just pay whatever taxes or fees you need to pay out of it first."

"Mom, you should keep something. You grew up there...it's your house," Sunnie forged ahead with the dispute. She thought her mother should keep something for herself from the sale, although her mother's past generosity had helped all her siblings.

"I don't need it, Sunnie. You all invest it in something. I want you all to have it," Sammie insisted. With a resigned sigh, Sunnie sat back in her chair. At times she wondered if her mother was aware of how much money was at her disposal. Rob had enjoyed a good laugh when she confessed that she used the corporate computers to investigate him. He assured Sunnie any concerned daughter would have done the same.

Another gleeful shriek from Aina announced Jude was home at the sound of his huge truck rumbling the ground. Sunnie asked her mother if she had ever done that as a child, rubbing her now-deafened ear.

"It's a girl thing," she assured Sunnie. "You all did. Used to drive your father crazy," she whispered.

Sunnie felt certain her father's annoyance was with her existence, not the innocent shrieking. She found it hard to forget the hurts at times, even though she'd forgiven him.

Rob let Aina down once Jude appeared at the steps to run and leap into the air. He had no trouble catching Aina in his sturdy arms. Aghast, Sunnie turned back to her mother, "Do you let her do that all the time?"

"Yes, Sunnie, we allow her to do anything she wants, don't we Rob?" Sammie teased, tossing her husband a wink.

Sunnie rolled her eyes. "Well, I just don't know that I'd trust Jude to catch her every time."

"I'd definitely drop you, Sunn. It might improve your driving skills," Jude countered while carrying Aina up the steps. After a round of face-making at Sunnie, he sat with Aina on his knee.

"You came out lucky, Sis. It's all sheet metal damage and one new tire. Nothing bent in the frame or axle. It's still going to take some time to fix. Sarge's car gets first dibs on the body man."

Sunnie threw her hands in the air. "That is so wrong! I need my car!" She slapped the table. "The Lakeville police have plenty to spare! What am I going to do? I have properties to manage!" she argued.

"I guess next time you'll actually LOOK behind you before you back out of a spot," Jude retorted. He turned his attention to Aina. "Come on; help me pack my bag! I have to go play with my friends this weekend!"

Aina clapped her hands before climbing from Jude's knee. She ran to the door and stretched, not quite able to reach the handle. She waited for him to open the door and they went off together.

Sammie quickly diffused the storm brewing on Sunnie's brow. "Sunnie, you can use my car. Don't worry. We have Rob's, the truck, the Camaro. We have a surplus of vehicles here." She looked pointedly at Rob.

He pulled a face. "I told you; I am not selling the Camaro! I'll consider selling the truck. River may need it, though." He grinned down at the sleeping baby, paternal pride welling in his eyes.

"River won't need it next week, Mr. Revell. You men and your trucks! You are so exasperating!" Sammie bantered affectionately with Rob. He chuckled, then closed his eyes to enjoy the sun beating down on his already well-tanned face.

Sunnie wondered if she'd ever feel comfortable enough with a man to enjoy as close a relationship as they enjoyed. It wasn't a pressing desire: just a fleeting curiosity. Sunnie didn't envision herself as the married type. Ever.

Jude returned with Aina following dutifully behind, wearing his cap and sunglasses. Sunnie snickered at the sight and snapped a picture on her phone before he retrieved his gear. He kissed the top of Aina's silky hair. Turning to Sammie, he kissed the top of her head also.

"See you on Monday, Mom. Sunn, I'll try to get them to start your car soon as possible."

Sunnie grinned to him, understanding he would do his best for her. "Thanks, Jude. Let me know if you need anything. All the insurance information is in the glove box."

After shaking Rob's hand and kissing his older sister, Jude left the deck. He tossed his duffle bag into the passenger side of the truck and performed his cursory inspection. He waved once more before pulling out of the drive.

"I better get going too, Mom. Thanks for the loaner."

She took Sammie's keys and thanked Rob once more for picking her up. After hugging Aina, she transferred the bags to her mother's car then waved to everyone on the deck. Sunnie drove across Lakeville to her building, thankful that she'd heeded the Lord and moved home.

Chapter 2

After showering away the leftover annoyances of the afternoon, Sunnie changed into her favorite yoga pants and sweatshirt. Once her wild mane was vigorously toweled and combed through, she picked up the mail from the table before walking to the office.

She sorted through the stack as her computer came to life. "Garbage, bill, garbage, ugh, more GARBAGE!" she exclaimed as she tossed several envelopes in a trashcan. Silas's name caught her eye when her email account screen blinked on. She placed the remaining mail in a basket on the desk as she sat.

Quickly disposing of the SPAM before opening his note, she wondered how he enjoyed living in Philadelphia; she got on best with him of all her siblings.

HEY, SIS!
WHAT'S THE DEAL ON G'MA'S HOUSE? IS IT ZONED FOR BUSINESS? LOOKING TO OPEN UP A BAKERY/COFFEE SHOP TYPE PLACE IN LAKEVILLE. IF YOU HAVE ANYTHING WE CAN LOOK AT, I'LL BE IN TOWN SUNDAY. THANKS! LUV, SI

"Who in the world is 'we'?" Sunnie asked herself as she typed out her reply.

HEY PUNK#1,

I HAVE ONE APARTMENT AVAILABLE HERE, YOU CAN LOOK AT IT. THE STORE DOWNSTAIRS IS IN NEGOTIATION. I'LL LET YOU KNOW ON THAT. I'D HAVE TO CHECK, BUT I DON'T THINK G'MA'S HOUSE IS ZONED COMMERCIAL. THERE'S ALWAYS EXCEPTIONS IF YOU THINK IT MAY BE USEFUL. I'LL HAVE SOME THINGS TO SHOW YOU. SEE YOU SUNDAY.
LOVE, SUNN

Sunnie scanned her database for workable properties. On a whim, she investigated the zoning of her grandmother's house. If Silas was serious about purchasing it, she'd do a more thorough job. She printed several spec sheets before turning the computer off for the evening.

Sunnie made a cup of her favorite herbal tea before she ascended the wrought iron spiral stairs in her room. The typical flat rooftop of the building's era made the perfect area for a patio. The rooftop garden, complete with latticework fencing to hide the mechanical aspects of the building, was her private haven: her labor of love to herself after working so hard to refurbish the old building. She enjoyed watching the sunrises and sunsets from her unique vantage point over Lakeville.

Swinging slowly in one of her hammock chairs, she enjoyed the cooling evening breeze. An unexpected, light feeling fluttered in her stomach as she recalled Officer Jacobs' bright smile.

"No, Sunshine. You will not go there," she chastised herself, deciding a routine of yoga stretches would clear her mind. Once that was accomplished sufficiently, she bid Lakeville a goodnight, before going back inside.

Silas met Sunnie after church in front of their grandmother's house with his mystery business partner. Expecting a friend of the masculine persuasion, she was surprised by the elven girl sporting white spiky hair. Sunnie was positive bright yellow tips adorned one side. The style showcased enormous green eyes that sparkled joyfully, all the more when focused on Silas. Sunnie swallowed her sarcasm in order to discover her relationship to her brother.

"Sunn, this is Wynter. We'd like to settle back here, open up a good breakfast bakery-type deal. Coffee, teas, baked goods, maybe quiches. Wynnie's still working on the menu, right?"

The look of pure devotion that passed between them made Sunnie envious–and a tad nauseous.

"Gram's would not be the best option for you. It's sitting on the edge of commercial zoning, but they don't want anything like that in here. Only doctors, offices, lawyers. No food vendors. Do you still want to look?"

Silas pondered for a minute, looking down at Wynter. They both shook their heads. "Nope, we'll pass. Too bad though, I think it would be a sweet deal. Where to next?"

Sunnie handed them the spec sheets on four similar properties. "If none of those are suitable, we'll end up at my building. Personally, I think it would be your best option. A shop close to what you're describing should be in the town proper. An added bonus is the apartment upstairs. Plus—" a wicked sisterly grin spread across her face, "—I'd be your landlord."

Silas feigned fear, forming a cross with his index fingers. Wynter playfully batted his arm. "Oh, Si Bear, she's nice. Don't be mean to your sister!"

Sunnie contained her eye roll as she walked to her mother's car. "We'll go through them in order. You know the way. See you at the next stop."

For various reasons the other listings were incompatible with Silas's needs, bringing them to Sunnie's building. Wynter loved the location, the apartment, and the large, empty storefront. Sunnie listened to them discussing minor details until hit with the realization that she'd have to refuse them the apartment. The fact that they were not married, coupled with an almost holy fear of what Sammie would say, brought Sunnie back to the situation.

"How soon are you wanting to do all of this, Si? What are your plans? Do you have or need financial backing?" Sunnie hedged, hoping to hear Silas answer that they were planning on being married in six months. Next week would be even better.

"We've got the bulk of our startup money. I was hoping Gram's house worked out so I could use my share as the deposit. With what you want as security, we'll be good to go without the bank. Soon as we can sign the papers, we'll start building the shop. What about the other dude interested in the space?"

Sunnie waved her hand impatiently. "Si, how about a wedding date? Other dude or not, I can't rent you the apartment unless you're married. You know I can't. For more reasons than Mom would have both our heads. I hate to rain on your parade here, but...what's so amusing?"

Containing the snickers, Silas turned to Wynter.

"Well, Wynnie? Want to get married?" he asked with an imperceptible wink.

"Si Bear, I'm already married. You know that."

Losing all semblance of control at yet another nauseating gaze between them, Sunnie burst out, "You're what? And you are planning on living with my brother? I think not! Silas, are you out of your mind? I'm trying to be open here, but honestly! What are you thinking? You can't live with a married woman! You can't...Silas Adam Young, what are you laughing about?" she demanded, hands on hips in a stance that should have made Silas quake with fear and not peals of laughter.

"Didn't I tell you, Wynnie? I wish I had the video. You should have filmed it on your phone, babe," he gasped, wiping tears from his eyes on the back of his hand. "Sunnie, we are married. We got married two months ago. Only Jude knows; I called him that night. I begged Wynnie to go along with me, because I just knew sooner or later you'd blow a gasket. It was great." Silas crowed, his fit of laughter subsiding.

"You. Got married. To her." Sunnie pointed to Wynter. "You haven't said anything to anyone yet, why? Are you having a baby?" Sunnie shot Wynter a quick look of appraisal, not seeing any obvious signs.

"Of course not!" Silas bristled. "When we met, we knew we wanted to be together. We went out to Atlantic City and got married. No big deal, right?"

Sunnie had no pleasant reply. "And Mom?" she asked, eyebrow arched in disapproval. As Silas's face registered discomfort, Wynter turned from him.

"I told him to tell her right away. Now it's going to look like we've been hiding something instead of how wonderfully romantic it was! I told you that would happen!"

Her annoyance with Silas evaporated as she recalled their elopement to Sunnie. "Oh, you should have seen him! He begged me to go with him. Swore he wouldn't be able to live another minute without me. We called my brothers to meet us and off we went! It was wonderful."

Silas's face became a superb shade of magenta. "Wynnie, let's not share that with Mom, okay? In any case, Sunn, we're cool, all right? How soon can you know about the store? We'll take the apartment no matter."

Sunnie looked back and forth between them; she knew her brother well enough to know he wouldn't lie about something of this magnitude. She allowed his attempt to change the subject gracefully.

"Well, *Si Bear*," Sunnie emphasized, enjoying great sibling satisfaction as Silas flushed pink again. "I'll call the other interested party first thing tomorrow to find out his plans. You, though, little brother—you will be speaking to your mother before I will allow you to sign a thing. Understood?"

They nodded to each other in agreement, their smiles mirror images. Sunnie's warm smile was turned to her new sister-in-law.

"Welcome to the Young family, Wynter. How about we go out to dinner, my treat? I'd love to hear this whole romantic tale. *Especially* if it embarrasses Silas more."

Wynter thanked her profusely, reaching up on the very tip of her toes to hug Sunnie around the neck. She wore a somewhat triumphant grin the remainder of the evening.

Sunnie's initial thoughts about Wynter were dispelled over dinner. She was bright, articulate and the perfect cushion for her brother's buoyant personality. They made a wonderful couple. She hugged them both goodbye in front of the restaurant. Walking home under the stars, she found herself wondering for the second time that weekend if she would ever meet "the" man.

Chapter 3

Sunnie waved to Victoria from her seat across the sanctuary; she had been as good a friend to her as she'd always been to Sammie. When she moved back, Victoria dragged her to the large place of worship kicking and screaming. After glaring at her throughout that first visit, Sunnie settled into worshipping at The Tabernacle.

Feeling refreshed in spirit, she picked up her coat and Bible from the seat next to hers and started out of her row. She ended up walking straight into Officer Tom Jacobs in the aisle. He laughed when he saw who had practically knocked him over.

"Nice to see you again, Sunnie. Good to know you walk as safely as you drive."

Sunnie's quick temper faded as those clear blue eyes danced with mischief. A smile broke across her face. "Thank you. I didn't know you came here."

"I usually go to the early service. I wanted to take Pastor Paul's class this semester—he's a friend of mine from school. It's promising to be a great study. Have you been through Romans?"

Sunnie recalled Rob asking her the same question several years before. "Just a read through, not an in-depth study."

"I'm sure you'd enjoy it. He meets in the classroom down by the gym. Maybe I'll see you there next week. Have you gotten your car back?"

"Jude says mine should be ready next week. I'm looking forward to it. My mom's car is fine, but it's not mine." Sunnie tried not to pout, taking the question as a reminder to cultivate that oh-so-elusive fruit of the Spirit, patience.

"I'll be sure to alert the station. Watch for a silver Miata speeding out of parking spots in reverse." Tom winked, easing the embarrassed flush that was creeping into Sunnie's cheeks. She adopted an air of annoyance as she started walking away.

"Officer, I told you that I looked. I will consider your invitation to the Romans class. I hope you have a nice day."

Tom wondered if she was truly upset until he saw the gleam in her own eyes when she glanced back at him. They waved goodbye as she walked down the steps of the balcony, Tom hopeful he'd see her in the class the following week.

The Lakeville Police Department was located in a small historical building in the middle of town with a larger, modern addition hidden behind. Multiple garages in back housed the squad cars, P.A.L. paraphernalia, parade barriers, and other annually used contraptions. Officer Tom Jacobs pulled his Jeep into his designated parking spot and glanced toward the garage to see his newly repaired squad car.

He strode to the building looking forward to having his own car back, even though he had enjoyed partnering with a colleague for the duration of the repairs. Tom headed towards the locker room after clocking in. He was greeted by Officer Anthony Penziotti's familiar call: "Jake, my man!"

He shook hands with a swarthy-looking officer as tall and broad as himself.

"Hey Penzi. Got my ride back, I see. Can you handle cruising Lakeville alone?"

"Man, you know I can. Check out that new bakery in town. It's in that old refurbished building on Maple. Cute chick at the counter with white spiky hair." Penzi wagged his heavy eyebrows.

Twice divorced, Officer Penziotti had changed little since their high school years. While his ex-wives had more colorful descriptions for his philandering ways, the divorces were blamed on his romantic nature, according to his telling.

"Do you ever see a chick who you don't classify as cute, Penzi?"

Penzi held his hands out in a gesture that asked *what can I say?* "I am a chick magnet, man. You should come out with me one night, Jake. You need some lovin,' I can tell. I get the pick of the blondes though—you know I love the blondes."

Tom shook his head, laughing deeply. "Penz, both of your former wives are blondes. Why don't you try a redhead?"

"Good idea, Jake. You busy tonight?" He waggled the heavy eyebrows in Tom's direction. After a friendly wrestling match, the men were off on their respective rounds. Deciding to take Penzi's advice, Tom steered the cruiser in the direction of Maple Street to get some coffee and see what they offered in the way of muffins.

The window of the new establishment showed the name Wynter Delights in a bold gold font and displayed a hand-printed sign offering free samples of pastries and coffee. Inside was bright and open, with an old-fashioned diner counter to one side of the cash register. The six stools were all filled—the last one with the fine shape of Sunnie Young. Tom laughed to himself, seeing that they were destined to keep running into each other. He walked towards her while taking in the shop, stopping just behind the stool she was sitting in.

"Loitering?" Sunnie heard a deep voice in her ear. She turned, laughing when she saw Officer Jacobs.

"Me? Loitering? I would say that it's you who is stalking me, Officer." Sunnie smiled, taking in how the deep blue uniform complimented the clear blue eyes.

Tom felt the flush on the back of his neck. "Ma'am, stalking is against the law. I must obey the law," he said, saluting Sunnie.

"Let me get you some coffee. What sort of sweets do you enjoy? My brother has the best selection of muffins," Sunnie gushed. She hopped off the stool to lead Tom to the coffee bar and poured some rich, dark liquid into a bright green paper cup.

"This is your brother's place? Nice work! It opened fast. Penzi told me about it this morning."

Sunnie pulled the cup back. "Penzi? Tony Penziotti? Please tell me you arrested him!"

Tom laughed heartily as Sunnie offered him the cup; her expression hovered somewhere between surprise and revulsion. He added cream to the steaming brew.

"Sorry, no. He's on the force—I'm surprised you haven't seen him around. I don't know that you'd remember, but we played football together in high school."

A light went on in Sunnie's head so bright Tom should have seen it.

"You! Now I remember! It's been driving me crazy! Homecoming game, sophomore year! You were with Penzi when he attempted to ask me out!"

"I remember it well, Sunnie. I believe you said something about preferring a goat to a hairy greaser. Penz was devastated for days. You must have been the only girl in school who turned him down."

"Ugh, the thought of him as a cop in town makes me queasy. Silas! Over here!" Sunnie called, catching sight of her brother with a tray full of bite sized pieces of their fare. Silas walked around a small queue at the register.

"Si, this is Officer Tom Jacobs. He's Jude's, umm, head guard dude."

Silas offered a hand to Tom. "Oh, hey! You're the dude Sunnie hit. She's a menace. You should have locked her up, man." He dodged her attempt to stomp on his foot. "Anything for you, on the house. And not just because Sunnie hit you. Nice to meet you." They shook hands before Silas went back to greeting customers.

"Head guard dude?" Tom asked when he turned back to Sunnie, the twinkle in his eyes pronounced.

"Sorry, I'm not good with those military terms," Sunnie felt color rising in her cheeks. "Let me get you something, I'm sure you can't stand in here all day and chit-chat. Penzi is probably out flashing the high school gym class." She turned to go behind the counter, wishing away the unsettled state she found herself in once again.

She pulled two enormous muffins from the case. When she whispered something to Wynter, Tom received a bright smile and quick wave before she served the next customer in line.

Sunnie returned, handing Tom a bag. "That's my sister-in-law, Wynter. Here you go. Chocolate chip and a healthy whole grain. My two favorites. Spread the word! Si needs the business."

"Let me try a bite before I leave." Digging into the bag, he broke off a piece of an unseen muffin. Sunnie was reminded of a wine taster as she watched Tom sample the morsel. "Whole grain, with pistachio. Hint of almond. Exceptional. Tell your brother I said good luck. Maybe I'll see you here again, too."

"Quite possibly. I do own the building." Sunnie laughed at the surprised look on Tom's face. "Go tell Penzi that one. And tell him I said 'eat your heart out.' "

He chuckled as he pulled his wallet out of his pocket, "That's just pure evil, Sunnie Young. Pure. Evil. But I'll tell him. You can be sure I'll be back."

He smiled a goodbye to Sunnie and walked to the register. He dropped a large bill into the tip cup with a friendly wave for Wynter. Sunnie resumed her seat at the end of the counter, watching as Tom crossed the street to his car.

Once the morning crowd died down, Wynter bounced over to the empty stool next to Sunnie. "Can you believe that? I'm bushed already! Who was that red-haired cop? He was nice looking. Do you date him?"

Sunnie laughed, "Oh, Wynter! You make me smile. No, I don't date. That was Officer Jacobs. He's the cop I hit a few weeks ago. I almost knocked him over in church yesterday. We seem to keep bumping into each other." That jogged something in Sunnie's mind. "Can you save me one of those whole grain pistachio muffins? I'll need one for Sunday."

"Sure, Sunnie. Take some tonight when we close and freeze them. They hold up well. You only want it frozen a few days."

The bells on the door jingled, and Wynter turned toward the sound with a smile. "Oops, there's some more customers. Thanks for staying with us today! I know it means a lot to Si Bear." Wynter hugged her before zipping back behind the counter.

Sunnie spent the remainder of the day in the shop. Silas's plan to close at three o'clock changed to four-thirty. After helping them with cleanup, she took the two remaining whole grain muffins up the stairs with her. Carefully wrapping one in plastic and foil, she placed it in the freezer. She stuck a bright note to the door, not wanting to forget Officer Tom's muffin come Sunday morning.

Tom spent a long, quiet day looping the town of Lakeville. At the end of the day, he found Penzi admiring himself in the rear view mirror of his car.

"Hey Penz! I stopped at that coffee shop. You'll never believe who I ran into. An old friend from high school."

"Hope you got her number this time, Jake," he remarked lazily, then resumed grooming himself.

"Sunnie Young."

Tony Penziotti stopped mid-comb, his head turning toward him so fast Tom thought his wide neck might snap.

"THE Sunnie Young?" he asked, making sure he'd heard Tom correctly. When Tom nodded, he let out a whoop. "Yee-haw! She still hot as all get out?"

"Didn't notice," Tom lied, disliking the lewd look in his friend's eyes. He enjoyed the usual camaraderie that went on, but Tom drew the line at commentary on the various visual pleasures women offered.

"You must be dead, Jake. She was smokin' hot in high school. Unless now she's all fat with eight kids or something. Where'd you see her at?"

"She was at the coffee shop; she owns the building. She remembers shooting you down in high school."

The uncharacteristic jibe escaped before Tom stopped himself. Penzi guffawed at the memory.

"Well, if I happen to run into her now—ba-bing. She won't be turning Penzi down. All the better, we both have more–*experience*. There's benefits to being mature and single, ya know," Penzi laughed.

Tom shook his head at the audaciousness. "Penz, you are truly demented. I hope I'm there. I gotta see the repeat of Penzi's Down." There was a lingering hopeful tone to the jest that Penzi missed.

"Keep dreamin,' Jake. I'm heading to The Corral. Come with me."

A tavern that had been in Lakeville since before the town incorporated, The Corral was the police hangout next to the station that Tom rarely patronized.

"Meet a nice gal; have a great night!" Penzi let out a coarse laugh, winking as he started the vintage Firebird.

"Thanks, I'm heading home. See you tomorrow." Tom waved off the invitation, as he normally did. He watched Penzi drive away, hoping he wouldn't run into Sunnie—wherever he was off to now. He left the lot, thoughts of Sunnie's smile on his mind as he drove toward home.

Chapter 4

Sunnie listened with interest to Pastor Paul Edwards' outline of the Apostle Paul's missionary journeys; although, she was disappointed Tom did not make the class. After the session ended, the energetic young pastor made a beeline to greet her.

"It's nice to have you in class, Sunnie. Your name is familiar. Do you have a sister?"

"I have three, though you wouldn't know the youngest. You probably know Storm. She's married to Steven Reiger."

Paul nodded with a genuine smile. "Yes! That's it. Wonderful wedding, wonderful couple. You mentioned you're friends with Tom?"

Sunnie paused, wondering if pastors were nosey or just trying to get to know people. "I hadn't seen Tom in quite some time. We recently...well, I ran into him just a while ago. He invited me to the class."

"I'm sure he's around the campus somewhere. He mentioned that he's on duty this weekend. Usually he's out by the west parking lot. Again, nice to meet you, Sunnie. I have to run, I have my own duties." He shook Sunnie's hand, gathered his books and belongings and dashed from the room.

As Sunnie walked to the balcony stairs, she looked out the massive foyer window. A police car sat by the west side entrance. Pausing at a table, she scribbled a note on the muffin bag and proceeded out the door to deliver it.

A loud whistle stopped her in mid-stride.

"Yo! Sunnie Young. Lookin' fine, girl!"

She was startled to see the face of Tony Penziotti when she turned towards the offending commentator. She tossed her head, walking away with a bit more speed in her step while Penzi laughed at her retreating back. His mirth faded quickly when he saw she was on her way to Tom's patrol car.

Slowing herself so she wasn't out of breath when she arrived, she shook off the ill-feelings seeing Penzi produced. Setting aside thoughts of kicking him in the shin, she knocked on the trunk of the cruiser.

Tom stepped from the car as she walked to the driver's side. "Did Penzi just wolf-whistle at you? I heard him all the way over here. I'd be happy to set him straight. For you, of course."

"I was thinking more along the lines of a swift kick, but I doubt either would do any good at all. Thanks, though. You missed a good class. Paul is a great teacher."

"I completely forgot I pulled the weekend tour. I wouldn't have left you sitting alone." They stood in silence by the car, Sunnie feeling a bit awkward.

"Well, here. This is for you," Sunnie handed Tom the bag, her cheeks the slightest tinge of pink. Tom peered into the bag. He looked back at Sunnie with a grin.

"Whole grain pistachio?" Sunnie nodded. "Thank you for thinking of me."

"Sorry I didn't think to bring you some coffee. Well, I figured you'd have it in class..." Sunnie fumbled, wondering what it is about this officer that made her lose the edge of her confidence and caused rapid rising of her blood pressure.

Tom broke off a piece of the muffin. "I do need some coffee, though. Come on, I'll walk back with you. You'll catch the beginning of the sermon." Tom placed the bag on the seat of the car.

Once he and Sunnie parted ways in the foyer, Tom went to the small room behind the kitchen. The congregation provided a veritable feast for the ministry staff every week, and in turn, they invited the policemen on duty to partake of the bounty. Tom filled a cup, added a touch of cream, and looked over the selection of breakfast casseroles and sticky buns. The thought of the muffin awaiting him in the car produced a wide grin before he left the room.

Penzi and his partner were getting ready to leave when Tom came through the large glass door. He lifted his cup in greeting. "Nice move, Penz. I never thought to whistle at a woman at church before. I'll have to add that to my repertoire." The smug look on Penzi's face made Tom want to hurl the cup at him.

"Hey, man, what can I say? The chicks love it, no matter how *religious* they are," Penzi joked as the other officer snickered.

"I understand why there's at least two former Mrs. Penziotti's. Let me clue you in on something. This church—this is my church. Have respect while you're here. No matter if I'm here or not. *Capiche?*"

"Ooo, big, scary Jake!" Penzi waved his fingers at Tom. "Are you sure it's not *who* got whistled at that ruffled you? She's lookin' fine, man. I think I'll be hittin' that coffee shop more often." Penzi waved as he drove away, leaving Tom frowning after him.

Tom turned the radio on to listen to the end of the service once he settled into the car. When he picked the bag up, he noticed Sunnie's email address and an offer to send him the notes from class written on one side. With a light chuckle, Tom tore the message from the bag and placed it in his wallet.

Sunnie switched on her computer after dinner to read business emails and prepare her schedule for the week. An email from Tom spurred her to sort through the rest quickly, flagging two for the morning, before opening his.

HI SUNNIE,
THANKS AGAIN FOR THE MUFFIN, IT WAS A NICE TREAT. I'D LOVE PAUL'S NOTES, I WASN'T AWARE HE WAS GIVING THEM OUT. I'M SURE I'LL SEE YOU AT THE SHOP DURING THE WEEK.
HAVE A GOOD NIGHT,
TOM

Sunnie quickly typed a reply.

HEY TOM!
PAUL DIDN'T GIVE OUT NOTES. IT'S MY OWN SPIN ON WHAT HE SAID. I'M HAPPY
TO SHARE THEM, THOUGH, IF YOU'LL EXCUSE MY LACK OF BIBLE KNOWLEDGE. I'LL
SEND THEM IN A BIT.
SUNNIE

A little over an hour passed as Sunnie transcribed her notes and added a few questions she had. She uploaded the document to another email and smiled when she hit send.

"I have written authorization for this information. This has always been good enough. What's the issue?" Sunnie argued with the woman behind the high counter. She'd been at Town Hall for over an hour, attempting to procure data on a property for a prospective client.

"I'm sorry, Miss Young; the policies have recently changed. You must have either a notarized power of attorney or the owner himself with you. I cannot give you what you have requested."

She smiled sympathetically as she attempted to go back to her work, but Sunnie was persistent in her quest.

"The owner hired me; I am his legal representative. You're telling me I need a power of attorney for this now? Why weren't people notified about the change?" Sunnie slapped the file folder on the top of the counter.

The woman peered at Sunnie over her glasses. "I'm sorry, Miss Young; I'm not certain when the new policy was put in place."

"What is it—*exactly*—that you do to earn a paycheck?" Sunnie snatched the folder back, turned away from the woman, and shoved open the heavy glass door to the office.

Now what? Sunnie fumed to herself by a water fountain in the marbled hallway. A few moments of cooling down caused Sunnie to berate herself over her ill temper. She prayed as she started out of the building, wondering how long 'Old Sunnie' would hang around.

Sunnie laughed to herself as she rounded a corner. She saw Tom in the foyer of the old building speaking with a stout man in a pin stripe suit. They parted, the stout man placing a cigar in his teeth before disappearing into an elevator. Sunnie waved to Tom, thinking to herself, *I know I should know that man.*

"Hey there. I was just thinking of emailing you back," Tom said as Sunnie walked toward him. "Thanks so much for those notes. Did Paul really talk that much?"

They continued walking together to the large, ornate entry doors of the building.

"Probably not. I was never good at outlines. Sorry if it was too long."

Tom held the door open for Sunnie, breathing in a spicy hint of patchouli as she passed him.

"No, not long at all. I was going to reply and hopefully answer some of your questions. Are you busy right now? I know a great coffee shop in town–my treat." The easy smile appeared.

"I think I know the one," Sunnie replied with a smile of her own. "That would be great. I'm getting nowhere fast here. I have to go home and fax my client—well, my perspective client. Who makes the ridiculous, ever-changing policies in this town?"

Tom chuckled, "Probably the council. There are certain things that they have no say in—those come from county or state. There's also the federal things they need to uphold."

"You seem to know a lot about it. I'd love the mayor's ear for just five minutes. Who is the mayor, anyhow? It seems to me that I should know," Sunnie mused, trying to recall his name. She knew he'd been in office a while.

"Did you see the man I was talking to?" Tom asked, the irony lost on Sunnie at the moment.

"I see him often when I'm here—was he the mayor?" He nodded. "He's always howling at some poor soul," Sunnie added acerbically. Tom's polite chuckle turned into uncontrollable laughter.

"Wait, why were you talking to him?" Sunnie asked Tom warily.

"We just got back from lunch."

Sunnie's eyes widened.

"Also known as Pop, by me. He's my father." She thought for a moment, made the name connection. With a flush of pink, she snickered.

"I'm sorry, Tom. I would have never...oh my! How about we meet at Si's in twenty minutes? That gives me time to extract my foot from my mouth and fax my client."

They arrived next to Sunnie's car and Tom opened the door for her, his easy smile in place. "I'll be there. No worries about my father. He'd be pleased that you said that. He loves cultivating his 'tough' image."

Sunnie nodded as she entered the car. "See you at the shop," she said through the window. Tom watched her drive away, still chuckling over the comment.

Sunnie faxed the client about the snafu at Town Hall as her notes churned from the printer. Once changed from her business suit into jeans and a soft sweater, she collected them and headed down the stairs to meet Tom. He was already settled at the counter, sipping coffee and chatting with Wynter.

They smiled to each other as Sunnie took a stool beside him. "What did you print? The Constitution of Lakeville?" Tom pointed to the sheaf of papers in Sunnie's hand.

"My notes...I didn't realize it was seven and a half pages. I told you outlining is not my strong suit." Sunnie's cheeks felt warm again. Wynter grinned over the counter, not at all unhappy about being forgotten. She went about coffee shop duties as their conversation continued and they became unaware of customers coming and going.

"It's fine; I was fascinated by what you picked up. Look here," Tom scanned the pages, and pointed out a question. "Not many people would have picked up on that. Don't forget, Paul has a Catholic school background as well as Protestant seminary. I think he probably has a unique view that many don't get from one or the other exclusively."

"So, I'm right?" Sunnie tried not to be distracted by the killer blue eyes—not an easy task.

"I would say so. Ask Paul, in any case. I'd like to hear him expound on that point."

"I will," she assured him, completely absorbed in the discussion about ancient Rome, as well as Tom's charismatic presence. They stayed at the counter talking, laughing, and sometimes arguing until the last customer of the day had gone. Silas walked past them to flip the 'Closed' sign on the door.

"I hate to interrupt, especially when Sunn is losing an argument—" he said, returning to their place at the counter.

Sunnie swatted at his arm. "I'm sure you must have other things to do on a day off, Tom. I'm sorry to keep you all day. You go; I'll help Si," she offered, amazed and disappointed that the afternoon had escaped them.

Tom thought a minute. "I'll go, but only to return with a few pizzas. It's the least I can do, considering I took up a stool all afternoon. Silas, what's your pleasure?"

Silas gave Tom a thumbs-up. "Dude, 'Meat Lover's' all the way. Wynter likes plain. Sunnie is the problem, though."

Tom turned to Sunnie. "Why? No, don't tell me—you're a vegetarian? I suppose you do yoga too?"

Sunnie tossed her head, insufficiently conveying annoyance. "Yes, Officer. I do eat mostly vegetarian, and I enjoy yoga. Now hurry back. I'm starving." She encouraged him with a light-hearted shove off the stool. She disappeared to the kitchen to find a broom.

"Sunn, I don't think we've ever been on a double date. This should be interesting," Silas mused after locking the door behind Tom.

Sunnie stopped sweeping and leaned on the handle. "Date? This isn't a date, you goof. We're having pizza. Get a grip, Si. You know I don't date."

"Sure. Whatever, Sunshine. We'll go up to our place. A bit more cozy, wouldn't you say?" Silas winked. Sunnie protested a tad too much.

"You are twisted. Go help your wife; I'll clean in here," Sunnie pushed Silas towards the kitchen, frowning at the smug expression in place when he walked away and went back to sweeping the floor more vigorously than needed.

Sunnie returned from the broom closet to see Tom through the door, waving one arm, the other loaded with pizza boxes. They enjoyed talking more over their casual dinner until they both noticed Wynter attempting to hide a wide yawn behind Silas's shoulder.

"Sorry, you two. I'll bet you're up at the crack of dawn. We should do this again soon, but not so late. Thanks for letting me take up your whole day." Tom stood to take his leave.

Silas stood also, shaking Tom's hand. "No problem. Nice getting to know you better. Thanks for the pizza. We haven't had the chance to go enjoy one in a while."

"I'll walk down with you, Tom." Sunnie announced before she turned to hug Wynter. "Thanks Wynn. Si, if you need me tomorrow, call...I have nothing lined up."

They said good night and Tom picked up the empty pizza boxes from the table.

Silas turned to Wynter when they had gone, smiling softly at her sleepy form on the couch. "Come on, baby. Let's get in bed. You'll be more comfortable. What do you think, huh? Sunnie likes him."

Wynter grunted an agreement, resting her head on Silas's shoulder as he picked her up off the couch and carried her to their room.

After tossing the pizza boxes, Tom and Sunnie stood beside the Jeep. A small span of uneasy silence went by before Tom broke it. "I enjoyed the day, Sunnie.

Would you be willing to send me notes again? I'm on Guard duty this weekend."

"Oh, sure. I'll try to keep it to four pages this week. Thanks for dinner—that was nice. You didn't need to," Sunnie brushed a stray curl from her face. Tom had thought of doing that exact thing.

Another short silence occurred. "I'd like to keep in touch, email-wise. Do you mind?"

"Sure. I'd like that, too." She glanced at the building, then back to Tom. "I'm going to head on up. Thanks again."

Sunnie smiled, and then turned to walk across the lot to the back steps. Once she disappeared through the door, Tom got into his Jeep thinking an email relationship would be interesting.

Chapter 5

The following weeks became a blur of emails, followed quickly by instant messaging. There always seemed to be something to talk about in cyber space, even if they had just seen each other at church or in the coffee shop.

On a luscious crisp day, a mysterious instant message took her attention from scanning the property base.

TSJake445: LOOK OUT THE WINDOW
SunnieYoung01: *WHAT?*
TSJake445: LOOK OUT THE WINDOW
SunnieYoung01: *TOM, YOU'RE WEIRDING ME OUT....*
TSJake445: I AM NOT, YOU ARE DYING TO SEE WHAT'S OUTSIDE ☺
SunnieYoung01: *FRONT OR BACK?*
TSJake445: FRONT

Sunnie sped through the apartment and out her door to the windows in the hallway. Tom was on the sidewalk leaning against the Jeep; a trailer filled with bundled hay was attached to the back. She waved when he looked up from his phone, signing that she'd be right down. She hurried back to the apartment to get her keys.

"What in the world are you doing towing around hay? And how did you instant message me?"

Tom held up his phone. "I've got connections. The hay is for home. I thought you might want to come for a ride. See some horses. Get some fresh air instead of staying cooped up inside staring at a computer screen."

"Horses? You have horses?" Sunnie was intrigued.

Tom shrugged casually. "Sure. Doesn't everyone?" He laughed at the look of irritation on her face.

"No! Where do you live? No property *in* Lakeville is zoned for horses." Sunnie had searched that client request frequently enough to know.

"Oh, but there is! I live in Lakeville and we've always had horses." Sunnie rolled her eyes and made an impatient sound. "So, are you game?" Tom asked.

33

She eyed the trailer and looked back to Tom's confident expression. She turned back to the hay. After another moment's mental deliberations, the wonderful smile broke across her face.

"Okay. I'm game. Come back up with me a minute so I can turn off the computer and grab my bag. Am I dressed for horses?" She stared down at her bare feet, rag-tag jeans and oversized Penn State sweatshirt she had donned earlier.

"Sure, you look great!" Sunnie's cheeks flushed at his enthusiastic answer. Tom continued with a grin, "I would grab a pair of sneakers, though. Lead the way."

She pointed out the refurbishing work that had been done as they climbed up towards the top floor. They waved to one of the tenants, an elderly woman with a garbage bag in hand. After introducing Tom, Sunnie insisted Mrs. Butler leave it in the hall for her to take care of. The woman smiled, looking relieved that she didn't have to go down steps with a bag.

"I tried to get her to move to the first floor. She's so sweet, but she wanted to stay put. Even with the dry wall dust flying. I really should have put in a garbage chute. Even I hate dragging my garbage down the steps. That and a laundry chute would have been great," Sunnie concluded, fumbling with her keys.

"You did a great job on this, Sunnie. Are all the apartments like Silas's?"

She smiled her thanks as the keys finally managed to do their job. "All but mine. I have the whole floor. Come on in—you'll see."

Sunnie tossed her keys on the table by the door before walking to the office. Tom took in what he could see from the entry, amazed at the open space and size the apartment had. "This is quite spacious. I like how you designed the kitchen and living room."

"Thanks," Sunnie called from the office, noting that Tom had not followed her through the apartment. He showed respect for her space; she liked that. After ducking into her room, she emerged in a less raggedy pair of jeans, better fitting sweater and blue Converse. "Okay, I'm ready. Let's go! Do you want to get something from the shop first?"

"Sure, a coffee sounds great." Sunnie made a face, and Tom laughed. "I take it you aren't even a casual coffee drinker."

Sunnie shook her head. "Not since high school. That's when I started yoga and eating more vegetarian. Do you remember a guy named Kyle? I can't remember his last name—he taught a yoga class after school. It was really great. It was around the time I was straightening out my head. It helped."

They remembered to toss Mrs. Butler's garbage bag before stopping in the shop for coffee. Tom dropped a bill in the tip cup and waved before walking out the door.

They drove west through the wealthy neighborhood that Victoria lived in to the outskirts of Lakeville that was surrounded by lush state forest. Sunnie was surprised to realize that they seemed to be headed toward the country club.

"I didn't know there were houses out here," she called to Tom. The drive in the Jeep was fun, although it made conversation difficult. Tom's deep voice rang through the open vehicle with ease.

"There aren't any. Only ours. My grandfather sold the land to the founders of the country club. We still own the land on the other side of the road."

Sunnie's face showed her confusion. "I thought that was all state forest. There's a house back in there?"

Tom nodded as he turned on the blinker. "It's hard to find. We like it that way, especially during election season."

"I guess it would keep the crazies at bay. I don't even see where...oh! I never noticed this!"

The drive resembled a state road into the forest, a rather natural break in the tree line. A quarter-mile in, Tom exited the Jeep to remove a massive chain barrier with an ominously worded sign about private property.

The trees around them cleared to an enormous vista in the middle of the forest. Along the drive to the right stood a two-story log home. Beyond, Sunnie could clearly make out a stable, fenced paddock and several horses grazing contentedly in the fall sunshine. To the left was a wonderful open space with fading grass that looked like the perfect spot for another log home.

"Tom! This is incredible! I can ride? I always wanted to ride a horse!" Sunnie sounded as excited as a small child at a fair.

"Sure we can. I know just which horse is good for a beginner, too." Her enthusiasm confirmed Tom's intentions had worked.

"You should have said we were going to a ranch," Sunnie mentioned, taking in the paddock and stable.

Tom laughed at the phrase. "It's hardly a ranch, Sunnie. We have land and a few horses. We don't live in Texas, and you'd be hard pressed to find a ten-gallon hat around here."

"Well, it's a ranch to me. The house is wonderful! I love log homes."

"Grandpa Jacobs built it. We added the modernized kitchen and top floor. The front of the house is fairly rustic. We did some work on the bedrooms and bathrooms, making them more modern and insulated. It was a great project. My mother loved it."

Sunnie saw a shadow pass over Tom's face at the mention of his mother. She was about to ask about her when he pulled up to the house.

"Here we are. I'll pull back later to unload that hay." He reached in the back of the Jeep, taking two water bottles from a case before they exited.

As they walked the path to the stables, Tom pointed things out to Sunnie— where his favorite hiding place was as a child, the path to the creek that ran on the south side of their land. "There are trails all through the property and a shooting range way out back. We can ride to the tree house. It's not far."

"Tree house? You still have a tree house?" Sunnie was fascinated that Tom had lived here his whole life; she never felt that secure. She almost envied it. She could see it in the way he walked, his stride relaying confidence that this would always be his home.

Tom nodded with a wry smile. "Pop refuses to let Roy take it down. Says the grandkids need it."

"Who is Roy? A ranch hand?" She grinned when Tom chuckled at her question.

"Sunnie, this is NOT a ranch. I suppose Roy is a ranch hand of sorts—more of a caretaker. He handles things that either my father can't take care of or I don't have time for. The horses need plenty of attention; neither of us can do it all. He and his wife live right over there." Tom pointed to a smaller log home, hidden from view of the drive.

"How long have they been with you?" Sunnie asked while they made their final steps to the stable.

"Just about ten years now. They're a terrific couple. Pop treats them like his own. When he meets someone he likes, he takes care of them." Tom spoke of his father with great affection. Sunnie felt a pang of envy again. She shrugged it off, determined to enjoy the day.

They entered the stable where a very large, ruggedly built man was rubbing down a beautiful black horse. His sun-bleached hair and deeply colored skin spoke of many hours out-of-doors in all weather. He looked up from the horse's flank when he heard them, delighted to see Tom.

"Tom! Good to see you, man!" Roy's voice boomed, causing the horse he was near to shy a bit. "Easy there, Beau." He spoke quietly to the horse as he rounded his haunch to greet them. Looking to Sunnie, he held out a ham-sized hand.

"Roy's the name. Good to meet a friend of Tom's."

Sunnie took the huge hand offered, amazed at its gentleness as they shook.

"This is Sunnie Young," Tom offered. "Thanks for taking care of things while I've been so busy the past few weeks. I stopped at the feed store to pick up a load of hay. I'll stow it later on."

Roy waved away the praise. "Just doin' my job, Tom. I'll take care of it. Are you ridin' today?"

"Sunnie's never ridden before," Tom mentioned.

Roy nodded his understanding, still holding Sunnie's hand in his. "So, Picasso?" Tom confirmed with a smile. "Good choice. I'll get him set up while you take care of Beau. He's ready for a jaunt. He must have known you was comin'."

Roy let go of Sunnie's hand and walked to another stall where a smaller horse was chewing on some hay.

Tom walked to Beau, rubbing his nose and quietly speaking to him. The large head nudged Tom's hand, expecting a treat.

"Not yet, fella." Tom slapped the neck that was wide as a small tree trunk. "We're going to the tree house. We'll have something when we get back." He turned to Sunnie. "Do you want to go over by Roy? Get to know Picasso a bit?"

Sunnie nodded, awed by the enormous animal, who was much larger than Sunnie expected a horse would be. "Have you had Beau long?"

Tom nodded. "About as long as Roy's been here. He was born here, too. The last foal from my mother's horse." That hint of lament tinged Tom's answer. He disappeared around Beau, returning with a saddle, blanket and assorted equipment.

Sunnie watched as he placed the blanket on Beau's back and smoothed it, all the while speaking soothing things to him. He expertly lifted the saddle over the blanket, continuing to smooth underneath as he reached for the cinch. Tom's ease around the animal was apparent; Sunnie was beginning to hope she didn't fall off her ride.

She decided to walk over to see the progress Roy was making with Picasso. Sunnie gasped when the horse turned his head toward her. His eyes were almost the same icy blue as Tom's. His face was mainly white, with deep brown patches around both eyes. He had a short black mane, and his various markings were both inky black and deep chestnut brown. His black tail flicked with excitement as Roy cinched the saddle and adjusted the stirrups.

"I'll probably have to adjust those again for you, Miss Sunnie. Grab a helmet from over there." He pointed across the stable to a shelf where several helmets were stacked. "Just like a bike helmet. Find one that's snug."

Sunnie walked to the stack of helmets. She picked a silver one while goggling at one that resembled a top hat. Tom joined her, reaching for a well-used helmet from a peg on the wall next to it.

"The top hat is my father's. It fits his style."

She grinned before taking her eyes from it, placing the helmet she chose over her wildly curly hair. "Is this one good?" He stepped closer to check, adjusting the chinstrap with a gentle touch. They stared into each other's eyes a moment before Roy called out, "So, you ready?"

"Ready?" Tom asked Sunnie, smiling at her eager nod.

They walked back to Roy, who had reins in hand. Tom helped Sunnie mount up on Picasso, and Roy adjusted the stirrups for her. He handed her the reins, explaining how to hold them—when to pull gently and when not to.

"Now, if you feel skittish at all, you hand them over to Tom...he knows how to handle Picasso. I'm sure you'll do fine; you look like a natural on a horse." Roy waved to them as they slowly rode out of the stable. "Have a good ride. See you later."

They headed down a well-ridden trail. There was much to see, and Sunnie wanted to take it all in. The horses ambled along, Tom keeping Beau in pace with the older horse. They rode close to twenty minutes before they came to a small clearing. The tree house was nestled in the branches of an old, sprawling oak on the opposite side. Well-worn pieces of wood nailed to the trunk forming the ladder made Sunnie laugh. Some were crooked, and one had STOP painted on it in faded red letters, obviously in Tom's immature hand. The walls were weathered with time, but sturdy. The tree shaded the top perfectly.

"What a great get-away," Sunnie breathed.

Tom agreed with a quick nod. "It always has been. Building this is one of my favorite memories. Pop would come out and make some suggestions, pound in a few nails...but it was Mom and me who finished it." Tom had a melancholy expression about his face once again.

"Your mom sounds like someone I would have liked to know, Tom. I can't imagine my mother nailing wood into a tree. My father, either." Sunnie frowned. Jackie? Building a tree house?

"I'll bet you would have liked her. I'm sure she would have liked you. Let's let the horses graze a bit while we scope out the tree house." Tom dismounted Beau, securing the reins to a small tree. Beau shook his head and whinnied, getting down to the business of grazing. Picasso snorted in answer.

Sunnie laughed at Tom's eagerness. "Well, Officer, I need a bit of help... The tree house I'm sure I can handle." She pulled the helmet off her head and hooked it onto the horn of the saddle.

"Swing your leg around. That's it," Tom coached. Sunnie extracted her foot from the stirrup, none too gracefully. Tom caught her before she hit the ground. She swept her hair out of her face.

"That wasn't so bad," Tom assured her. "You'll get used to it. But you never take the helmet off until your feet are on the ground. Please." Tom let go of Sunnie's waist to secure Picasso's bridle by Beau's before removing his helmet. Something in the request caused her heart to ache.

"Come on, up into the tree!" Her annoyance over her poor dismount evaporated at Tom's boyish grin. She followed him to the trunk and started climbing. Seven slats later, Sunnie was standing in a five-foot-by-five-foot roofless haven in the giant oak.

Tom pulled himself through the hatch. Standing next to Sunnie, he pointed down the path. "See there? That's the rest of the riding path. It goes down to the creek and back up and around to the back of the house. If you take it north, you'll be at the shooting range. We can go that way if you want, but it's longer."

He pointed a different direction, resting his hand on Sunnie's shoulder, "If we go this way, it's a shorter loop back to the stable. It's up to you." Sunnie allowed him a moment for his hand to linger.

"When did you get taller than the walls?" Sunnie asked, turning so it was natural for Tom to drop his hand. If he was disappointed, it didn't show. The breeze wafted the scent of Sunnie's hair to Tom. He breathed it in before answering.

"High school. I was one of those guys who had a late growth spurt. Suddenly one summer, I could see over the walls. I was almost devastated."

"I can understand that. Did you always go to Lakeville? It's weird that I don't remember you at all until that fateful homecoming day."

"High school, yep. I was in Catholic school for elementary."

They both stayed quiet for a few moments, looking out over the wall of the tree house. Sunnie felt peaceful in her spirit, like nothing she had ever felt before—it was strange and exhilarating. She took in a deep breath, letting it out slowly. Tom's arm stole around Sunnie's waist. This time she didn't move away.

"What happened to your mom?" Sunnie asked quietly. Tom dropped his arm and moved to a corner of the tree house, looking as though he always sat in that exact spot. She followed, sitting beside him. "I'm sorry; I'm morbidly curious," she added, wrapping her arms around her knees.

"It's fine, Sunnie. I've mentioned her a few times now." He picked up a leaf and examined it momentarily. "She was breaking a horse and he tossed her. It was a freak accident. Long before all the safety gear. Mom was a maverick...she would never have worn a helmet anyhow." His face displayed a range of emotions.

"It happened the summer we graduated high school. Penzi and I were planning on the Army before entering the police academy. After the funeral, I signed up for the Guard instead. I didn't want to leave my father. She was a fine woman." He smiled at Sunnie. "You remind me of her a bit. She had very strong opinions about things, too."

His smile deepened as her cheeks tinged light pink. "Don't be embarrassed about that, Sunnie. It's a good thing."

"I think I get myself into some trouble, you know? Like the woman at the town hall. I brought her a box of cookies in apology. Sometimes I have a hard time with what's a strong opinion as opposed to sarcasm. Or just plain selfishness."

"Well, I enjoy it." Tom's honest statement caused that slight rise in blood pressure once again. Sunnie decided to change the subject before she put her foot into something she wasn't quite ready for.

"Tell me about Catholic school, and why a decent guy like you is friends with Penzi." Tom glanced at her with widened eyes before he laughed deeply.

"Penz. We're not as close as we were in high school. I was involved in church by the time he came home and started the Academy. We lost contact while he was doing his tour of duty; we reconnected when he came on the force. It's a casual friendship at this point. A habit."

He recounted his time in Catholic school giving the nuns a hard time with Paul. Sunnie was disappointed when Tom looked at his watch and declared it time to start back. Riding along the creek, Sunnie enjoyed the continuing tour of his childhood play areas, best spots to skip rocks, and where he broke his arm in the sixth grade.

Sunnie's dismount was a bit more graceful, and she remembered not to remove the helmet until she was off Picasso. After delivering the trailer of hay, they left to bring Sunnie back to life within Lakeville city limits. It was near dusk when they pulled behind the building.

"Thanks, Tom. That was so much fun. Much better than what I should have been doing." Sunnie unbuckled her seat belt and turned slightly to face Tom across the gearshift.

His smile was open. "Glad I saved you from a mundane day of tapping on keys."

"Actually, it was a mundane day of laundry and bathroom scrubbing *after* I tapped the keys. Sometimes I envy my Mom. She likes all this house maintenance stuff. I'd rather hire the gals that clean their house twice a month."

"So? Why don't you?" Tom asked.

Sunnie glanced curiously at Tom. "That doesn't bother you? A woman admitting she doesn't enjoy house chores?"

Tom shrugged. "Should it? I don't know that anyone really *enjoys* it, Sunnie. Even I clean a bathroom, run a vacuum, and do my laundry. It's just what needs to be done."

Sunnie looked thunderstruck. "I never thought I'd hear a man say that. The woman who marries you will be lucky, Officer. Thanks again for a great afternoon." She exited the Jeep quickly, wanting to slap herself on the forehead. The last thing she wanted was to get involved, even if it was with someone as wonderful as Tom Jacobs. As Sunnie climbed the stairs to her apartment, she realized it might be too late to worry—or care.

Chapter 6

The main gymnasium at Lakeville High School was filled to capacity for the annual basketball game featuring the police department versus the fire department. The majority of the townsfolk happily paid their entry fee to the successful fundraiser. Tables laden with donated goods were available for sale; this year included one representing Wynter Delights.

A ripple of nostalgia tickled Sunnie as she finished setting the table. She glanced at the time displayed on the scoreboard; there was time to spare. She turned to Silas.

"I'll be back before the game starts. I'm going to take a quick walk."

As she left the gym, a pair of eyes followed her; the thoughts behind them held no good intent. Penzi excused himself from the crowd of policemen he was talking with and walked through the same door that Sunnie exited.

The hallways, which seemed vast and enormous when she attended the school, now struck her as small and confining. After wandering up and down a few corridors and past her old haunt–the school library–she started back towards the gym lost in memories. An unwelcome voice brought her quickly back to the present. The smell of expensive, overused cologne filled the air as Penzi caught up to her.

"Whooo, look who's walking the halls! Looking for your locker?"

"Maybe I should lock you in one, Penzi. At least the women here would be safe from that toxic aftershave." Penzi smirked and leaned against the wall, successfully blocking her from stepping away unless she stepped into him.

"Where you goin' in such a hurry? I haven't seen you in ages. We must catch up over dinner once we whip the fire boys. I know a nice, intimate place—best Italian in town." Penzi grasped Sunnie's hand, lifting it to his lips.

She yanked it away. "I think not," she insisted hotly, hoping that was enough of a rebuff. She became further revolted when he reached to fondle a lock of curls that was falling over her shoulder.

"Young, come on! You, me, and a bottle of deep red wine. Imagine the possibilities." He pulled the long strand to his nose, inhaling deeply.

"The only possible scenario is that Tom would arrest me for first degree murder," she countered, slapping his hand away. She stepped to one side to make an escape before he decided to do something more foolish, such as attempting to breathe. He was about to block that move when a voice called from behind them; the most welcome voice Sunnie had heard all day.

"Hey Penz, what's taking you..." Tom fell silent as he took in the scene, focusing upon the look of faint panic in Sunnie's eyes. She visibly relaxed as he strode toward them, casting a withering look in Penzi's direction. The glare was returned as Penzi removed his arm from the wall. He planted his feet and folded his arms across his chest.

"Tom! Stop by Silas's table. I'll put together a bag of your favorites!" She walked around Penzi and hurried away, calling over her shoulder, "I'll be sure to wash my hands first."

Tom watched to be certain Sunnie arrived at the gym door unmolested by anyone else. Deciding by her reaction not to make an issue—this time—he turned back and stared at Penzi for a long moment before suggesting, "Let's go change. The team's been waiting."

Penzi's answer was low and full of challenge. "Not to worry, Jake. I'll have a date with her by game's end. You'll see." They returned to the locker room with a strained silence between them.

Sunnie ducked in a bathroom to wash her hands, dismissing the feelings of contamination while fervently thanking God for sending Tom when He did. Returning to the gym proper, she found Silas and Wynter chatting with several firemen at the table. She took her place with them, pushing away the remnants of bad feelings over the encounter.

The announcer opened up the festivities by introducing the firemen, each player by name and position. They hammed for the cheering crowd as they lapped the court before taking up their places at the bench on the far side of the gym.

Sunnie listened for Tom's name when the policemen were announced. Her gaze fell on him as he jogged past, returning his quick wave. She took in the well-defined muscularity that the basketball shorts and Lakeville PD t-shirt showed to great advantage. She stifled the urge to hit Penzi with a chunk of muffin as he passed the table.

The game proved to be exciting with the score tied at the final period. The scramble to the basket for the tie breaking point as the buzzer sounded had the whole gym on their feet. Tom, face full of game-winning concentration, faked a shot before passing off to Penzi. He made a spectacular jump shot right into the hoop. The crowd went wild as Tom and Penzi clapped each other on the back in congratulations while the firemen booed them.

The announcer thanked the crowd, reminding the audience that the proceeds went to the benevolent funds for widows of the officers and firemen. As Sunnie listened to the cheers, the full impact of the funds being collected settled on her. Tom had a dangerous job, here in Lakeville and in the National Guard. Although Jude was in the Guard, she assumed the risks involved were minimal. A new appreciation formed for the services her brother and Tom performed.

Sunnie felt a tap on the back while she helped Wynter box up the few remaining platters. She turned to see Penzi, sporting a confident smile on his face. She backed away a bit before speaking, the aftershave aroma even stronger now that the game was over.

"Nice jump shot, Penzi. You're the toast of the game. Why aren't you chasing those doe-eyed young girls over there?" Sunnie pointed to a group of young women who were whispering together, eyes on Penzi. None looked to be over twenty-one, if that. He glanced over and they all tittered before putting their heads together to whisper.

"I'd rather chase the more experienced women, Sunnie. Bigger challenge and the benefits more than make up for the work."

Sunnie was so repulsed by his insinuation, she turned away. Penzi caught her arm, gripping it uncomfortably.

"Let go of my arm, Penzi. Or you'll lose yours," Sunnie insisted, attempting to shake off Penzi's hand.

"Sunnie, I know you like me. I can feel the heat. We're natural, you and me. Let's go get a drink, some dinner and see what happens from there."

Disgust didn't register high on Penzi's stud-o-meter. Sunnie finally rid her arm of his hand. "I'm not interested, Penziotti. I wasn't interested in high school and I'm certainly not interested now. In fact, I'm less interested now. How did you ever make it onto the police force?"

Penzi grinned slyly before he turned his attention to Wynter. "How about you, baby? Drinks, dinner and see what else happens?"

Sunnie was about to lose the infamous temper she had worked hard to tame when Silas appeared behind Wynter. His arm found its way around her shoulders.

"Officer, that was a great jump shot! Come by the shop, my wife will make sure you have what you need on Monday." Silas turned away, leading Wynter toward the truck. Sunnie folded her arms and watched Penzi slink away.

Once everything was unloaded from Silas's van and put away, Sunnie went up to her apartment, making sure that her door was securely locked. She even locked the bathroom door while she showered. She laughed at herself while she toweled her hair.

"Who would have thought Tony Penziotti would give me the willies?" she asked her reflection.

After a long session of yoga to praise music, Sunnie shut the lights and snuggled into her bed. She proceeded to toss for hours before giving up on sleep. Escaping from the warmth of the covers, she filled a cup with cold water before retrieving her laptop from her office.

She retreated to the warm bed as it whirred to life. To her surprise Tom's name blinged in the instant messenger window, while she surfed a few auction sites for vintage jeans.

TSJake445: ENJOY THE GAME?
SunnieYoung01: WHAT ARE YOU STILL DOING UP?
TSJake445: WHAT ARE YOU DOING UP? ☺
SunnieYoung01: COULDN'T SLEEP, THOUGHT I'D SURF EBAY...MIGHT FIND SOMETHING INTERESTING...IT WAS A GREAT GAME! I DIDN'T SEE YOU AFTER ☹
TSJake445: I HAD TO RUN, I WAS ON DUTY
SunnieYoung01: WHAT??? THAT'S CRAZY! HOW COULD YOU WORK AFTER THAT GAME?
TSJake445: LOL, IT WASN'T THAT BAD...I GOT HOME A WHILE AGO, SO I'M WINDING DOWN

Thinking about the reason the game was played, she typed the next response while fighting the urge to become teary-eyed. She was glad they did not engage their webcams.

SunnieYoung01: I HOPE YOU ARE CAREFUL
TSJake445: I AM...IT'S PART OF THE JOB
SunnieYoung01: I'M GLAD THAT IT IS...I'M GOING TO BE PRAYING MORE FOR ALL THE OFFICERS

She pondered a minute while sipping some water.

SunnieYoung01: EXCEPT PENZI *EVIL LAUGH*

Tom sat back against his pillows, laughing at her answer, although he felt a certain obligation to tell her she should pray for Penzi no matter what. He smiled when her next comment appeared on the screen.

SunnieYoung01: HE'S A...I CAN'T SAY...HE HIT ON WYNTER! IN FRONT OF SILAS! OKAY, I'LL PRAY HE STAYS FAR AWAY FROM ME, IS THAT ACCEPTABLE?
TSJake445: 10-4
SunnieYoung01: ARE YOU ON DUTY TOMORROW?
TSJake445: YUP....TOMORROW EVENING
SunnieYoung01: WANT TO HAVE BREAKFAST?
TSJake445: IS THIS A DATE?
SunnieYoung01: LOL, I DON'T DATE....I JUST WANT COMPANY FOR BREAKFAST
TSJake445: I'M CRUSHED
SunnieYoung01: NO YOU AREN'T ☺ MEET AT DAILY TREAT? 8:30?
TSJake445: HMMM, 6 HOURS...I'LL BE THERE
SunnieYoung01: SEE YOU THERE

Sunnie wondered what had possessed her to ask him to breakfast. Hugging a fluffy pillow after putting the computer on the night table, she fell asleep thinking about Officer Tom Jacobs.

Tom and Sunnie pulled into the lot of Daily Treat simultaneously five hours later. She had her hair swept up in a large barrette, her curls cascading down her back. He waited for her by the Jeep, thinking she looked fantastic dressed in a simple red sweater and jeans and no makeup at all.

Sunnie smiled when she met Tom, rolling her eyes when he asked if she locked the car. His outfit choice masked the muscularity she had observed at the game. She recalled that under the loose fitting jeans and denim shirt was a powerful body, one that her active imagination shouldn't be lingering on. Sunnie prayed, firmly closing the door on those thoughts as they entered the restaurant.

A waitress showed them to a booth by a window. Sunnie declined coffee, ordering cranberry juice and a club soda. While Tom added a small amount of cream to his coffee, Sunnie mixed the cranberry juice and club soda in a third glass.

"Why don't you ask them to mix that?" he queried before sipping his coffee.

"Because they won't. I've asked. Did you stay up all night?" He looked well rested. Fabulously so.

"No, I went to sleep and I'll probably sleep a bit more, later. Nights aren't as hard because it's night. Days are somewhat normal. Evening tends to throw you off. When I get home, Pop isn't up, it's too dark to ride and I'm not big on much of what's on television. Usually I'll hop online a bit or watch a movie while I eat. Somehow, I always draw evening tour right before I go on Guard duty. I sleep a lot when I get home to make up for it."

The waitress returned, smiled, and topped off Tom's coffee before leaving to place their order with the kitchen. Sunnie continued the conversation once the she walked away. "I couldn't sleep last night. I thought I'd surf Ebay. I usually can find some sweet vintage jeans or something."

"You really buy clothes off Ebay? Aren't you worried they won't fit?"

Sunnie gushed about several pair of designer jeans that she found before she stopped, laughing at the absolute lost look on Tom's face.

"Sorry. I think it's fun. Better than dragging around to every small shop in twenty miles like Vic does."

"Who's Vic? Old boyfriend?" Tom teased her, chuckling at her look of impatience.

"*Victoria's* a family friend. I lived with them a while when I moved back. They go to The Tabernacle. My sister Storm is married to their son, Steven. They're in Europe with a mission organization they were both very involved with in college. I think I have a picture on my phone..." Sunnie pulled out her phone and scrolled through the photos. It took a few seconds to find what she wanted.

"Here, they're at...one of those castles over there." Sunnie handed her phone across the table. Tom studied the picture.

"You don't look much alike. There's a family resemblance, though. I would never have put Jude as your brother, even *with* the same last name. Jude resembles her more."

Sunnie took the phone back and scrolled to the recent picture of Aina in Jude's hat. Tom laughed, taking in the small girl's smiling face. "That's Aina. I don't have a picture of River or Autumn."

"Are unusual names a family trait?" Tom handed the phone back as the waitress served their breakfast. She carefully set down all the plates laden with food. Sunnie watched her scurry away, thinking she was probably afraid Tom would order something else.

"Are you really going to eat all of that?" Sunnie indicated the pancakes, eggs, sausage, bacon, and toast the waitress placed in front of him.

"Are you really going to eat all of that?" Tom pointed to Sunnie's plate, boasting an oversized omelet of egg whites and a bowl of fruit. They both laughed in surrender before bowing their heads in a silent prayer; Sunnie's was quick and a bit self-conscious. She watched Tom cut into the stack of pancakes with gusto before answering his questions.

"I'll probably eat at least half of this and yes—my Mom is wacky. I love her, but she's wacky. I mean, who names their kids like this?" Sunnie shook her head, hoping Tom understood.

"I like it. Aina—doesn't that mean grace or joy?"

Sunnie's eyes widened, "Yes! How do you know that?"

Tom grinned between bites of sausage. "My mother was Irish. Can't you tell?" Tom pointed to his bright red hair. "She was born here, but her parents were from Ireland. She had the slightest accent. And the same color hair."

"I'm surprised you know the meaning of Aina's name. It's not common. None of us have a common name. Not something I'd do if I ever have kids." Sunnie poked at a grape in her fruit salad.

"Why not? It's memorable. Not just another Tom."

"Exactly! Do you know what it was like growing up with a name like Sunshine? With sisters named Storm and Autumn? And now we have a River? What was my mother thinking?" Sunnie attacked her omelet.

"What would you name your kids?" he ventured, wondering why the choice of names bothered her so much.

"I never thought about it...I just know they wouldn't be freaky hippie names. What's so bad about Tom? Or Dave? Sue. Nice and normal."

"Well, there's always about ten Tom's and Dave's. Usually double on the Sue's. How do you keep them straight? I like your name; it fits you. You're unusual."

Sunnie slapped her fork on the table so hard Tom jumped in his seat. "See? Do I have to be *unusual*? That is all I ever hear! 'Oh, how can I forget beautiful Sunshine?' 'Oh what an unusual name.' Do you know what it's like for someone to want to know you only because of your *unusual* name? Not because they want to get to know what kind of person you really are."

Customers who overheard the outburst went back to their own breakfasts once noting the expression Sunnie wore. Tom put his fork down and reached across the table for Sunnie's hand.

"Hey, I'm sorry. Topic of names is over. What else do you want to take my head off about?"

Sunnie studied his face—so serious, but humor lit his eyes. How could she be mad at him? Why she went off like that, she couldn't pinpoint. Most people would have left her sitting there. She hesitantly returned a grin, and Tom released her hand.

"Sorry, Tom. See what I mean? Despite the handle, I'm not always so sunny. Tell me about your shift last night. What creepy criminals are lurking in Lakeville?" Sunnie hoped that was safe enough to discuss.

"First, you need to use correct terminology. It's a tour. It was the usual. Chasing drug dealers out from behind the high school, making sure no one is in the parks after sundown. One older man who swears that every night someone is breaking into his house. Nothing exciting." He chuckled at Sunnie's wide-eyed stare. "Really. That's all."

"Drug dealers? I didn't think..." Sunnie stopped, remembering her own wild-child days as well as her father's. "Have they been around a long time?"

Tom shook his head. "Every few years there's a new crop. It's not the same guys we knew in school."

"You knew the drug dealers in school?" Sunnie's incredulous whisper carried to the woman in the booth next to them. She shot them a disapproving look while Tom laughed off her comment.

"We all knew them, Sunnie. I can still name them. None of them are around here anymore."

"You're probably right. I just wouldn't think that you..." Sunnie stopped before she said something else completely foolish.

"Because I'm such a goody-goody? Just like the name thing, Sunnie, cops also have real lives. Some of us didn't make good choices all the time. Some of them still don't. People are people. When my mom died, I had a rough patch, but I got over it. I had it later instead of in school. That doesn't mean I didn't know all about what was going on. You'd have to be blind not to."

Sunnie pondered that while they finished breakfast. She laughed when Tom finally pushed his plates to the side of the table. The woman at the next table had developed a full-blown glare.

"I cannot believe you ate all of that!" Sunnie still had half an omlette and her fruit.

"I'll work it off around the stables. Thanks, and can we have a take-out container please?" Tom said to the waitress as she dropped the receipt on the table. "That's the only thing I don't like about this place. You can't linger." Tom nodded at the door, where several people were waiting for tables. "Let's go; we can quibble over the bill outside."

Tom stopped to apologize to the woman, offering to pay for the breakfast they had disrupted. She fussed, insisting it wasn't necessary. She bid them a cheerful good day when they walked away after the waitress boxed the remains of Sunnie's meal.

Sunnie handed Tom several bills to cover her share as they walked to her car. "You're quite generous, Tom. Why did you offer to pay for her breakfast?"

"Because she looked lonely. I'll bet she's in there every day, all by herself." Tom took in Sunnie's slight frown. "It doesn't hurt to be kind. Aren't we supposed to be?"

"I suppose," she mumbled. What she really wanted to know was how to let her old self go completely. Sunnie would not have offered that kindness to a stranger.

"It's hard for you, isn't it?" Tom asked when they stopped at Sunnie's car.

"Yes. It is. Sometimes I wonder if I'll ever 'grow up' into what God wants me to be. I've been me so long. People like you make people like me annoyed—you know that?"

Tom grinned at Sunnie's exaggerated annoyance. "Well, look at it as iron sharpening iron. Thanks for the annoying breakfast company. I hope I can annoy you again soon. Have a great day frustrating others." Tom leaned over and placed a friendly kiss on her cheek before walking towards his Jeep.

Sunnie watched him until he drove out of the lot, thinking about what he had said. She got in her car, searched for gum, then turned up her radio before she drove across the town to look at a home that she was contacted about selling. She tried hard not to annoy or frustrate anyone the rest of the day.

Chapter 7

"Pop, did you get those tickets yet?" Tom asked his father the following morning as he poured coffee.

Stuart glanced up from his paperwork, his brow furrowed. "What tickets, son?"

Tom smiled with affection at his father. Stuart was a great mayor, involved with virtually every event that happened in Lakeville—so long as he had a note about it. Tom sat at the sprawling table in the kitchen, looking over the reams of paper Stuart had spread over it.

"Sorry, I shouldn't have bothered you about it now. What's the boggle this week?"

"Low-income housing," he answered, sweeping his hand over the table. "There's a property on the east side of town that someone wants to develop. As in homes—not apartments. That new real estate firm is involved. The one that refurbed that old building in the middle of town. Don't you go there for coffee?"

"Of course. All of us go there when our tour is in town. I know the owners."

"Oh? Good folks?" Stuart's interest was always piqued over the people who did business in his town. "I should stop in there. I haven't had the time yet. Who is it?"

"Sunnie Young owns the building. Silas—Sunnie's brother—and his wife Wynter own the coffee shop." Tom waited a beat for his father to make the connection. It didn't take long.

"Oh ho! This is the same gal you've been dating?" Stuart nodded, pulling a cigar from a pocket somewhere on his person. "That's good. You need a good, strong gal with a good head on her shoulders! Like your mother. Do she and her brother partner?" Stuart puffed the cigar to life.

"No. Sunnie owns the building, and Silas rents from her. She owns Young InvestCorps. She sells and manages other properties in town."

"She's involved in your church too?" Tom nodded. "Well, why haven't you brought her around? I'd like to meet this Sunnie. She's sharp. Makes a good argument for the housing." Stuart tapped the papers with his index finger.

"I'm sure she does. She grew up over there. I'd like to bring her around, but she's a little skittish on the whole dating thing. She's a friend, Pop. A good friend." Stuart's brow furrowed again, the end of the cigar turning bright red, a sure sign that he was about to go on a tirade. Tom deftly rerouted the discussion. "What about those tickets? To the race?"

Stuart's face brightened. "Of course, Tommy! Got them weeks ago. They're at the office. Great seats right on the start/finish line. Should be a great race this year—got a good crop of new drivers. Are you going for the whole weekend again?"

"Not this year. I'm asking Sunnie; I can't ask her to spend the weekend. Just the race."

Stuart chuckled, his sense of propriety not being quite the same. "Whatever you say, Tommy. Remind me tomorrow, I'll bring them home. It's not for another month or so. Why don't you bring Sunnie around for dinner one Sunday?"

"I'll ask her, Pop. I'm sure she'd love to ride Picasso again."

"I thought you just told me you're not dating? When was she here?" Stuart's eyebrows rose to his hairline. Tom got up to replenish his coffee and scan the fridge.

"A while ago. You were on a business trip. Didn't Roy tell you?" The furrow in Stuart's brow grew deeper. "Relax, Pop. Really, we're just good friends. I'll see if she wants to come by next weekend; how's that?"

Stuart grumbled a bit about not being informed about things in his own home before consenting to the following weekend. He resumed his perusal of the proposal with renewed interest.

Tom pulled bacon, eggs, and cheese out of the fridge. Placing them on the counter, he called to Stuart, "Do you want an omelet?"

Stuart grumbled and shook his head, consumed with the paperwork before him. Tom started the bacon frying, and by the time he was done cooking, Stuart lifted his gaze from the table.

Tom placed a plate in front of him before sitting with his own. He bowed his head, silently thanking God for all He had given him, especially his father.

Stuart dug into his omelet as if he hadn't eaten in weeks. They chatted about the day's plans, a comfortable relationship between them evident. It had been the two of them alone for a long time. As Tom loaded the dishwasher, he pondered what Stuart might think about him having a serious relationship.

Sunnie sat at her mother's kitchen table, reviewing the low-income housing proposal one last time. When she rolled up the treatise, she nodded to herself, feeling fulfilled. Everything seemed in order for the council meeting several weeks away. If she could secure the deal, it would give Sunnie not only a great reputation in the town, but a tidy sum of money in her bank account.

Delighted to see Sunnie when she awoke, but complaining of hunger, Aina insisted on helping her big sister make lunch. When the remnants of peanut butter and honey on whole grain toast had been cleared from the table—but not quite off Aina's hands and face—they went out to the yard to play. Amazed by what a three year old could get into, Sunnie plunked a rather dirty Aina into the swing.

"Aina, maybe we should take a bath before Momma gets home." Sunnie suggested.

"No. Me play. Me only take bath when Momma is home," Aina informed her, kicking her feet in an effort to go higher than Sunnie was willing to push her.

Sunnie frowned. *Shouldn't a three-year-old listen better?* she thought before employing a different strategy.

"Won't Daddy be upset that you're so dirty? Let's go take a bath; you can put on a pretty dress once you're all clean!" Sunnie smiled, making this idea sound like a party.

Aina frowned. "Push higher, Sunnie! Me go higher!"

This is getting nowhere fast, Sunnie mused in frustration. She stopped the swing and scooped Aina up in her arms. "Okay, missy. We're going to go clean up. Momma will be tired, and she'll have to make dinner. Let's surprise her!"

Aina agreed surprises were a good idea. "You take bath with Aina. Bubbles, we play in the bubbles."

Sunnie made the assumption Aina understood that she would be splashing outside the tub. Sammie, Rob and River arrived in the kitchen in time to hear her startled scream. Taking two stairs at a time, Rob entered the bathroom to the sight of Aina standing over a soaking wet Sunnie with a bucket. He called down the steps for Sammie to hurry with a camera.

Sunnie stood up, sedately requesting Rob watch Aina as she left him laughing in the bathroom. Sammie steered Sunnie to her room, handed her a robe and pointed her to the master bath. Moments later she emerged in the robe that was far too short.

"Mom, I can't run around your house in this! It's nowhere near decent! Doesn't Rob have a robe I can use?"

"I'm sure he does, Sunnie. I just don't know where that would be, offhand. Let me get River settled down. Leave the clothes in the bathroom; I'll bring them down in a bit. Sit down and tell me what possessed you to put Aina in the bathtub."

She carefully sat on the edge of the bed, pulling at the hem of the robe to attempt covering her thighs. "We ate peanut butter and honey sandwiches, Aina played in the sandbox and had sand all over and then she picked a tomato...."

"She didn't eat it, did she?" Sammie asked while rocking River to sleep. Sunnie shook her head. "What was the problem?"

"Well, I didn't want you to come home to a mess..." Sunnie stated, realizing how silly that was at the moment. After setting River in the crib and taking Sunnie's clothes to the dryer, Sammie returned to dig Rob's robe from the back of the closet.

Sunnie appeared downstairs after switching robes, following her mother's voice into the kitchen. "This is so much better. Thanks, Mom. I think I need one of these...where'd Rob get it?"

"I'm not sure, Sunnie. I haven't seen it in a while. Rob doesn't use it much." Sammie laughed at Sunnie's wrinkled nose. "Really, Sunnie...we are married, you know."

"Eww, Mom! That doesn't mean I need to hear about...stuff. Can I do anything to help?"

Rob called a request from the living room for Sunnie to dry the bathroom floor.

Sammie grinned before declining. "No. Thank you for watching Aina. Did you finish reviewing your proposal?" She continued dinner preparations as Sunnie described the land, the housing that would go on each tract, and how the developer would keep the costs down.

"I'm praying it goes through, Mom. It'll be good for the town and good for me. The parcel is over by the old house. Do you remember the family who had the big old house on the other side of the tracks?" Sammie nodded. "That's the property my client bought for the project."

"I think it will be wonderful, Sunnie. Does Tom know about it?" she dropped casually while placing a tray of sauce and cheese smothered chicken cutlets in the oven.

Sunnie shrugged, "I don't know, Mom. I don't consult him on these types of things."

Sammie smiled a knowing mother's smile. "I thought maybe since his father is on the council..."

"Mom! His father IS the council. Even if I wanted to ask, I just couldn't. I don't think it would be right."

"Why don't you invite Tom for dinner? Jude would love to see him, and I'd like to finally meet him."

"What?!? Not tonight?" Sunnie exclaimed. What had gotten into her mother? To her relief, Sammie shook her head.

"No, on Sunday. You're coming, yes?" Sunnie nodded. "Invite him along. You know there's always enough."

"Well, he may have duty...be on tour this weekend." Sunnie hedged. "I'll talk to him later. I'm going to go check my clothes." Sunnie went to the laundry room, hoping the discussion of Tom's weekend plans would not resume upon returning.

Rob entered the kitchen, peeking in the sauce pot approvingly. He smirked at Sammie's grin. "What are you up to, Mrs. Revell? I know that look."

Sammie replied with a wider smile, "I'm getting a pot of water for pasta, Rob. That's all. I think we're having company for dinner Sunday."

"Other than the usual crowd? Did Sunnie meet somebody?" Rob pulled the pot from Sammie's hands and started running the water into it.

"Yes, Rob, remember? Officer Jacobs?"

Rob laughed at the air of innocence Sammie retained. "I knew it. You're matchmaking. I should warn her." Sammie shushed him when Sunnie walked past, warm clothes in hand.

"I am just having a day of observation. That's all," she insisted before turning the water off. Dinner proceeded without further discussion of Sunday guests.

Sammie sent Sunnie home with a dish of pasta, chicken parmigiana and salad. She put her serving in the fridge and put the kettle on the stove. Changed into a pair of cozy pajamas, Sunnie went to the office to power up the computer before making a cup of tea.

Several emails later, she went back inside to find her phone. She started when it rang in her hand. She decided a personal ring tone was in order when Tom's name scrolled across the ID screen.

"Hi, Tom. I was just getting the phone to call you."

"Really? You tell me why first." Sunnie heard him chuckle.

"I was babysitting at my mom's today..."

"And you live to tell the tale. Bravo." Tom smiled at the picture formed in his mind of Sunnie playing with the small girl from the cell phone picture.

"I can handle a three year old." She tactfully omitted the bathtub incident. "In any case, we're all having dinner at Mom's on Sunday; I thought you'd like to come along." Sunnie held the phone away and looked at it when Tom laughed. "Why is that funny?"

"Because, Sunnie, I was calling you to see if you wanted to come out here for dinner next weekend. Pop would like to meet you. He's had his nose buried in the low-income housing proposal for days now. Plus, I thought it was about time for riding lesson two. Unless you'd prefer a shooting lesson."

"Oh, I'd love to ride again! Guns—no thank you. I'm not sure about meeting the Mayor though." Sunnie bit her lip as she rummaged in a desk drawer for some gum.

"Sunnie, he's my father. He's not always *Mayor Jacobs*. He's very impressed by your eloquent stand for low-income housing."

She stood straight up, almost dropping the stick of gum she'd finally found. "Are you kidding?"

"I am not. I'd love to come with you on Sunday at your Mom's. Jude and Silas will be there?"

"Of course. What's the matter? Afraid to meet the Young women?"

"Quite the opposite, I'm looking forward to meeting your mother. I want to see how much alike you are."

Sunnie laughed, thinking how very different she was from Sammie. "You're funny, Tom. I am nothing like my mom. At. All."

"We'll see. So, this weekend, your family, next weekend mine. Sure sounds like we're dating. If you ask me."

Sunnie almost swallowed the gum. "No, we aren't. You know that. I like you fine, Officer Jacobs. Don't make it complicated."

"Whatever you say, Sunnie. For now. I'll see you tomorrow, probably. I'm on that side of town."

"Okay, Officer. I'll make sure there's a muffin for you." Sunnie smiled. She did enjoy Tom's company and the easy way they could talk. "Have a good night."

"You too, Sunnie. Goodnight."

Chapter 8

Tom and Sunnie took their seats in Sunday school after greeting Pastor Paul. She pulled out her notebook and pen as Tom lightly advised her to keep the notes to a minimum of five pages. She grinned, sitting back in her seat as Paul started the lecture on Paul's missionary journey.

Sunnie introduced Tom to the Reigers after service, and they passed some time in conversation before excusing themselves. Penzi was outside leaning against the fender of the cruiser, waving traffic out of the crowded parking lot in a bored manner. Perking up at the sight of Sunnie in her Sunday best, his eyes narrowed when he realized that she and Tom were leaving together.

After a quick stop at the grocers for salad fixings, they were on their way to dinner with the Youngs. Sunnie wondered if this wasn't a good idea. She'd rather not give her family wrong ideas about them. She wasn't so confident that there really were any *wrong* ideas. Tom caught her intensive mien and laughed.

"What are you laughing about?" Sunnie asked while pointing out a turn to make.

"Obviously, you are wondering what your family is going to think. You aren't that hard to read, Sunnie. What do you prefer? Do you want them to think we're involved or should we make it clear that we are only friends?"

Sunnie mulled the question briefly before surprising Tom with the clearest answer she'd give him to date. "We're certainly more than friends, aren't we? I think they'll see it for what it is. That's fine with me. Is that fine with you?"

"Fine by me. I'm waiting on you. Why don't we talk about it when I'm not driving, on duty or skydiving?" Tom suggested as they turned into Sammie's driveway.

"I'll try not to avoid the subject. Maybe. I can't promise I won't. Tom?"

Tom shifted into park and shut the engine. Sunnie's expression was open—something Tom had not seen before. It was heartening, especially as she leaned over the gearshift to place a quick kiss on his cheek.

"Thanks," she said quietly, holding his eyes before taking the sack of groceries from the back seat. She exited the vehicle before anything more could be spoken.

Sunnie made the necessary introductions to the various adults and children running about. Aina immediately climbed on Tom's knee. While she shredded lettuce into a bowl, Sunnie listened to Tom patiently answer each question Aina fired at him pertaining to horses.

Wynter joined Sunnie at the counter. "I thought you weren't dating him?" She whispered to Sunnie over the bowl of lettuce.

A hint of pink showed on Sunnie's cheeks. Slicing a cucumber into the bowl, she answered with an attempt at nonchalance. "I guess I changed my mind."

"I like him. I'm glad you changed your mind." Wynter whispered back, adding diced bell peppers. Sunnie smiled, glancing over at Tom again. He was now involved in an animated discussion over law enforcement with Jude and Rob.

"We'll need to eat at Vic's house when Steven and Storm come back. Unless I can talk Rob into an addition," Sammie joked to her daughters and daughter-in-law as they set the table.

They all giggled; everyone was well aware all Sammie would have to do is ask.

"If you keep having more babies, Momma, you'll need a bigger house," Wynter commented. Sunnie saw the sad look in Sammie's eyes—her last pregnancy had been hard—before answering.

"The Lord is certainly bringing me more in other ways, Wynter. I'm very glad He brought you." The reply sent her into a fit of giggles and hugs. "I'll leave the baby bringing to the younger Young women now. How's that?"

Wynter blushed and rushed from the room under the guise of getting more forks. Autumn followed to gather the children for dinner.

"I've never seen her embarrassed before, Mom. Nice one," Sunnie laughed. "I like her. I'm glad Silas found her."

"Me too." Sammie paused, placing the last of her flatware down. "Tom is quite nice. Is it serious?"

"Get right to the point, Mom." Sunnie rolled her eyes. She thought a minute. "Maybe. Sort of. Best I can do. Is that awful of me?"

Sammie placed the final napkin down. She could see Sunnie cared for the officer she brought to dinner, more than her daughter was ready to admit. She deliberately asked, "I guess that depends on how Tom views it. Is he willing to allow you to be sure?"

"I think so, Mom. I hope so. He seems to be able to handle the Young crowd at least." They glanced in the kitchen to the men gathered around the table, eyeing the stove as the discussion turned to sports.

"He does blend in well. Let's go get the food. Thank you for that salad. It looks wonderful." Sammie hugged Sunnie on the way back to the kitchen. Twenty minutes later, everyone was around the table holding hands while Rob prayed over his family, biological and grafted in.

As serving bowls were being passed, Rob asked, "Tom, was your grandfather's name Gregory Jacobs? I'm thinking I may have met him when I was looking for land when I moved here a thousand years ago."

"Yes, that was him. Were you interested in the land that's now the club?"

Rob nodded. "It was too much, though. Too much land. I opted for the parcel here. He was a character."

"I understand he was. I'm sure he advised you on how terrible the land here on Elm was. I think he was feuding with the owner for years because he wanted it when he first came here."

"Your family must know Vi's. The MacDougall's."

"Sure we do. Say, wait." He turned to Sunnie. "As in Victoria? That I met this morning?" Sunnie nodded. "I didn't realize she's a MacDougall. Yup, we go way back, way before me, at any rate. My grandfather ran against Mayor MacDougall. Lost every time. Pop finally won once her father was no longer in politics."

"Sounds very hillbilly to me." Sunnie commented while sprinkling her salad generously with garbanzo beans.

"You can tell him that next weekend."

An abrupt halt to all conversation came. Sammie, as did everyone else around the large table, looked at Sunnie, curious about the comment. She flushed slightly, kicking Tom's ankle under the table. His wince was well hidden in his forkful of pot roast.

"Tom's father is interested in my low-income housing proposal. He asked Tom to have me over. No. Big. Deal."

Both Silas and Jude snorted into their dinner plates.

"Only Sunn would think it's 'no big deal' to meet the mayor. Just like it was no big deal that she ran into a cop." Jude remarked, safely across the table from his sister's heels. Sunnie tossed a bean at him. Aina scolded her about playing with her dinner.

"I'm sure you'll be your charming self, as always, Sunnie." Rob offered. "Your proposal is very good. I read through it."

"Did you? Thanks. It's the first time I wrote something like that on my own. At Weston, I had resources and help. All that technical jargon throws me off." Sunnie felt bolstered.

"I can't see the council vetoing it, unless someone has other ideas in mind."

Tom nodded before asking Sunnie to pass the salad.

"My father says so, too. As far as I can tell from what he's said, it should go through. Sunnie's got nothing to worry about. Can I have that dressing?" Tom handed the bowl back to Sunnie, reaching for the bottle of dressing. Sunnie held it back, her eyes wide.

"You didn't tell me that."

"You didn't ask," Tom retorted as Sunnie slapped the dressing bottle into his hand.

Sammie and Rob shared an amused look across the table before she stopped several children from throwing beans at each other. Including Silas.

Tom, Silas and Jude flipped a quarter for the last dinner roll. Sammie excused herself to nurse River, and Rob announced the men would clear the table.

"What we need is a hoop and a ball." Tom said, passing Jude with a stack of plates. Jude laughed.

"I know you have a ball in your Jeep, Sarge. We don't have a hoop, though. You'd school us all, anyhow."

"Dude, no way would I get on a court with you! I was at that game!" Silas called from his job of loading the dishwasher.

"We can go over to the club," Rob suggested. "I'm up for a game."

It was quickly decided that Autumn and Sammie would stay behind with children needing naps. Jude shook his head, muttering about being slain as he went to change.

Tom dropped Sunnie at the club before driving up the road to his house. She and Wynter had a table and chairs set up courtside by the time he returned, outfitted for the game. Paul dropped from the game quickly, joining them to cheer after requesting a large pitcher of water. One spirited hour later, Silas and Jude came panting to the table as Rob and Tom finished the game one-on-one. Rob eventually shot the winning basket.

"You should play with us, Rob. You rock," Tom invited. Sunnie handed him a glass of water.

Rob chuckled, wiping his face with a spare towel from the club. "Ha! Not a chance, Tom. I've been to those games; you guys are lethal. Sorry I missed this year's game; I hear it was a good one."

"It was a great game, Rob," Sunnie agreed as she poured Tom a refill. "Silas did pretty good, sales wise too."

Wynter nodded. "The firemen liked the freebies, though. The policemen are more generous." They all laughed, relaxing a while before it was time to return for dessert.

"Are you always ready to play ball?" Sunnie asked as they drove back toward Rob's. Tom laughed, pointing in the back of the Jeep.

When Sunnie turned, she spotted a ball, some clothing, a towel, and a case of water. "I guess you are," she said, turning back with a small grin. "Well, you've made a life-long friend. Rob loves to play, but doesn't always have the opportunity.

"I'll give him my number. I'd be happy to run over to play if I'm home. What do you do for fun?"

"Yoga."

Tom glanced at her while shifting. "Come on, you must enjoy something...else."

Sunnie shook her head. "Nope, I like to watch. Specifically NASCAR. If there was a race on right now, I'd be screaming my head off at home, not watching you sweat on a basketball court." She noticed Tom's grin. "What are you up to, Officer?"

"I'm wondering if I should tell you that I have tickets to the Pocono race."

Sunnie's jaw dropped. "You have what? And you weren't going to ask me?"

"Honestly, I'm not certain if that constitutes a 'friendly day at the race' or a 'date.' Care to enlighten me?" He quickly protected himself after shifting, as Sunnie had taken the towel from the back seat and proceeded to hit him over the head with it. "Sunnie! I'm driving!"

"Humph, driving. You are...extorting. That's what you're doing, extorting! I should have Penzi arrest you." Sunnie huffed, crossing her arms. Loud silence followed.

Tom broached the subject before they arrived. "Sunnie, I was teasing you, you know. But would officially 'dating' be that bad?"

"Would taking me to the race *as a friend* be so bad?" Sunnie countered.

Tom shook his head, sighing in mild exasperation. "No, Sunnie it wouldn't be so bad. It would be very nice, though, as a date." Tom pulled into the driveway. "So, do you want to come? Friend?"

Sunnie searched Tom's face before she answered. "Sure. I'll come. Thanks for thinking of me. I won't even ask how you knew I enjoyed racing. I think you know too much about me sometimes."

"I'd like to know why you feel the need to avoid dating." Tom held up his hand to Sunnie's protest. "It was just a comment. Let's go enjoy dessert. Let me know when you want to get back to your car."

Tom opened the door to get out after shutting the engine. Sunnie started to say something, but her courage wilted. She stepped from the vehicle and followed Tom back to the deck without further comment.

Chapter 9

Tom headed to the locker room after signing in, receiving a cool nod from Penzi instead of his usually enthusiastic greeting. He was in a thick discussion with several other officers coming off tour. Once that was done, he called to Tom across the locker room.

"So, Jake, what's with you and Young? I thought she didn't date."

"She doesn't. We're friends."

He crossed the room, stopping at the bench in front of Tom's locker. Looking as though he were about to impart the ultimate in relational wisdom, he placed his foot on the bench and leaned forward.

"Jake, Jake. Didn't you learn anything from me? She's playing you. All this 'I don't date' crap. You can tell me; she's hot, yes?"

With a slam of his locker, Tom turned to face his long-time friend, attempting to give him the benefit of doubt over his intentions.

"I am telling you this one last time, Penz. Sunnie and I are friends. Period. If there was anything more, I wouldn't be discussing it. I trust this is the end of the morbid fascination you have with my love life."

Penzi spat out a laugh. "Jake my friend, you need a love life. I've been trying to tell you that for years, my man. Now you've got the hottest babe in this burg in the palm of your hand, and you're just friends? Forgive me if I don't believe you."

Penzi stood up to his full height, eye to eye with Tom. "Since you aren't dating, give Sunnie my number. If you can't handle her, I surely can."

Before he could turn away, Tom's fist connected squarely with his jaw.

Caught off his guard, Penzi sprawled against the lockers, barely on his feet. He glared at Tom as he righted himself, wiping the back of his hand across his mouth. He spit blood on the floor next to Tom's foot before striding from the room. Tom lowered himself onto the bench, dropped his head into his hands, and prayed for forgiveness.

Sunnie opened the door to the shop and breezed in, taking a seat on her favorite stool. Once the crowd dissipated, Wynter joined her. "Did you have a fight with Tom? You seemed upset after we got back from the game."

Sunnie considered how nice it could be to have a "girl chat." "Not really, Wynter. Can you come up after work? I have a ton of stuff to get done, and I really don't want to talk just now. I'll make a stir-fry."

"I'd love to! Si Bear can handle cleaning alone once. I'll see you later." Wynter went back to the register as several customers filed in and filled coffee cups.

After spending the afternoon on her own pursuits, Sunnie went to the store to pick up dinner ingredients. As she picked over the green beans, she felt a tug on her sweater. She found Penzi's lopsided and unwelcome countenance leering at her.

"Run into a truck, Penzi? Remove your hand from my clothing."

Making certain she couldn't step away, he continued to finger the soft yarn. After a lascivious sweep, his eyes settled on hers. "I'm always happy to help you with clothing, Sunnie—especially getting out of it. We need to get together. You are way too uptight. That means only one thing. Jake ain't taking care of business to your satisfaction. Give me your number, and I'll be sure to take that edge off."

Fighting the urge to scream and claw at his face, she smiled. "Got a pen?"

Penzi reached across the aisle and snatched a Sharpie from the unsuspecting produce clerk. Sunnie turned Penzi's hand palm-up and began writing. When she was done, she folded his fingers closed.

"See you later, Penzi." She gave the clerk his marker back and turned from him.

Impure thoughts of all manners in mind, he watched her walk away before opening his hand. Imagining the look on his former friend's face when he bragged upon his conquest, his own face fell when he read the rude comment Sunnie had written in lieu of her phone number.

Sunnie watched from behind a display of cookies as Penzi stalked out of the store. She argued with herself over what she wrote, finally deciding that the act of protecting herself was a good time to ignore the Biblical admonition about coarse talk.

Thinking about the incident in the security of her kitchen, she debated calling Tom while she prepared the stir-fry. She decided against it. When she let Wynter in, she set aside all distressing Penzi-based thoughts.

Sunnie and Wynter gabbed about many things over dinner, but not until they were up on the roof with hot tea did Wynter introduce the subject of relationships.

"Sunnie, I think you really wanted to talk about Tom. What's wrong? Isn't he treating you well?"

Sunnie swung in a hammock chair, a reflective giggle cutting through the dusk. "No, Wynnie, he treats me very nicely. Almost too nicely. I don't know. It's me, not him."

With an earnest look, Wynter asked, "Don't you treat him nice?"

Sunnie considered the question honestly before answering. "I hope I do, Wynnie. I try to. Let me try to explain; I've never had a decent relationship. It's always been friendly or physical...never an in-between. I really like Tom. I don't want to blow it, but I'm afraid to let him get too close. I don't want to have to stop seeing him."

"Why would you have to not see him?"

Sunnie's thoughts flashed to Tom on the basketball courts and stopped right there. "Because I don't think I'd be able to fight it, Wynnie. And I really don't think I want to get married. I don't know. How did you fight it?"

"Because we knew it was the right thing. That's why we eloped. You know neither of us had ever..."

"Okay, stop. Too much info." Sunnie insisted, wondering if this girly chat was really all it was cracked up to be.

Wynter giggled. She sipped her tea before continuing. "You did ask, Sunnie. The very first time I met him, I asked Jesus if he could be the one. We got to know each other quickly. We were able to give ourselves to each other completely. You can't do one without the other."

Sunnie envied the contentment in Wynter's voice.

"But, how, Wynnie? How did you know Si wouldn't smash up your heart into a billion pieces? He didn't have a great role model on marriage fidelity. Didn't that scare you?"

"Not at all, Sunnie. Silas is devoted to God. It doesn't matter how your father behaved. Tom's relationship to God is what matters. If a man is devoted to God, he's going to treat you the way God wants him to. Not the way he saw when he was raised. I'm so sorry that your dad hurt you so badly."

Sunnie sat back and looked up at the sky darkening, puffing some stray curls out of her eyes as she pondered Wynter's words. "And you knew Si wouldn't be like this. Because of his relationship with God. You know something Wynnie? You are amazing. I'd like to be so comfortable with myself and my faith."

"How long have you been a believer, Sunnie?"

"Not long. I fought it for a long, long time. I blamed God for my father beating my mother—for his drinking and whatever else he was into. For him leaving us. He tried to hit me once. That was the first time he left. Because Mom wouldn't let him hit me."

She fought the welling tears, struggling against the tightness in her throat before continuing.

"Everything was so empty—work, relationships. My secretary invited me to her church for Easter service. No, it was a missions thing. It was so different. The people there, they cared. I never got that at Mom's church. I probably didn't want to. When I started going there, I thought I was staying in the city forever. But when Mom got married and had Aina...I felt like..." Sunnie hesitated again, pulling a deep breath.

"Like you were missing important things." Wynter filled in. "I think that's beautiful, Sunnie! God drew your heart back to your home. Were you able to forgive Dad?" Wynter asked as though she had known Jackie, had been through the pain with her.

She nodded, allowing the tears their way. "I don't always feel like I did, though."

"I understand. I don't always feel all warm and fuzzy with my dad either. But, that's not my job. To forgive and to let it go is my job."

A knock interrupted the discussion, followed by Silas calling for his wife.

"I'm up here, Bear!" Wynter called back. Sunnie watched her expression change when Silas appeared. He and Wynter shared a loving gaze before he breathed out, "Man, I miss you."

She rose, turning back to Sunnie with a small grin. "Thanks for dinner." She picked up her empty cup. "You don't mind if I run along, right?"

Sunnie glanced at Silas, whose resemblance at that moment to a lost puppy was striking. She laughed as she wiped her eyes; it had been a good talk after all.

"Of course not. Thanks, Wynnie, I appreciate all you said."

Silas winked to his sister. "You can borrow her *almost* any time. Have a good night, Sis."

She watched Silas fold Wynter into the crook of his arm when they turned to leave. *Completely. They completely belong to each other.* Sunnie stayed up on the roof for a long time, thinking and praying.

Pulling into The Corral's gravel lot, Tom searched for Penzi's car. Once he spotted it in the far corner he parked, determined to make amends with his friend. He walked to the door of the ancient building that had been there long before the town hall stood next to it. Inside was loud and dimly lit; sawdust scattered across the floor and the old wood paneling spoke of age.

Allowing his eyes to adjust to the light, Tom observed the patrons after he ordered a soda. A few older men sat at the bar nursing tankards of beer, younger ones congregated around a pool table. In a corner with a bottle of something hard in front of him, Penzi sat broodily watching the pool game. He put his foot on the chair next to him as a clear statement that he wanted to be left alone when he spotted Tom at the bar.

Tom approached and pulled a chair from another table. Penzi continued to watch the pool match, intent on ignoring him. Tom drank half of his soda before speaking.

"Penz, I'm sorry I lost my temper this morning."

He looked to Tom with much more than annoyance in his gaze. "You came here to tell me this? Go away, Jake. I'm in no mood for gentlemanly discussion. If you wanna continue the chat from this morning outside, fine. Otherwise, blow." Penzi spilled some of the amber liquid on the table while pouring it into a shot glass.

Tom finished his soda and set the glass on the table. "C'mon, Penz. Let me drive you home."

A chair was kicked towards him, and a loud stream of swearing filled the air. All activity ceased as the patrons looked at the officers.

Tom rose, then walked to the bar. The bartender watched him warily as he pulled his wallet from his pocket.

"Make sure he gets a cab, please? And call so that someone from the station takes his car over." He placed cash on the bar to cover the request.

The bartender nodded before he pocketed the money. The game resumed, as did the discussions among the others. After a final look back at Penzi, Tom turned to leave. When the door to the bar closed, Tom heard a bottle shatter against it.

Chapter 10

The ensuing week at work was a test of how many eggshells Tom could avoid stepping on if Penzi was nearby. When Friday finally made its appearance, he cleared his locker out thinking the next week couldn't possibly be worse.

Penzi stepped in front of him, offering a hand. "Jake, sorry man. Thanks for the ride home the other night."

Tom took his hand tentatively and nodded. "No problem, Penz."

He watched as Tom continued to clear out his locker, an odd expression on his face. He folded his heavy arms over the equally heavy chest. "Yeah, no use trashing a lifelong friendship over a broad, right? Especially Young." He stated dryly.

Tom held his temper and changed the subject. "Right, Penz. When's the next pick-up game? I'll make sure to be there."

Penzi snickered, leaning against the lockers. "Jake, you've been my friend, what? Since first grade? Take my advice. Drop her. I'm sure there's plenty of nicer girls in that church you go to. Ones with no history, you catch me?"

"Penz, lay off it."

Penzi let out a sardonic laugh. "Okay, Jake. Remember when she tears you up and spits you out that I warned you. You're too soft hearted for the likes of her. Pick-up game—Sunday. You'll be there?"

"Not this week. Plans. With my father." Tom turned back to the contents of the locker, but not before Penzi saw the flash of his annoyance on his face.

"I'm sure you'll make the next game. Tell ol' Stu I said hello. Later." Penzi sauntered away.

Tom shut the locker with force. He leaned his head against the door, praying to curb his ill feelings before he left. Penzi tracked him as he left the room, calling a goodbye over his shoulder to whoever was left.

"Why does my seeing Sunnie eat at him so much?" Tom asked aloud in the Jeep as he drove home. He wondered if her refusal to go out with him years ago damaged his psyche in some way. He debated all of this in his mind as he drove home, looking forward to a good long ride on Beau.

The smell of the stable, the hay and the horses wiped away Tom's concerns. He saddled Beau, secured his helmet, and swung up into his seat. Steering Beau to the familiar path, he allowed him his head at the beginning.

As Beau leaped the creek, Tom felt his own head clearing, resolving the turmoil of the past week. Tom dismounted at the tree house, then climbed into his sanctuary. In the same corner he sat in since the age of eight, Tom prayed over his feelings for Sunnie and his shaky relationship with Penzi.

He returned past dark and spent time giving Beau a good rub down, fresh water and hay. His mind was much more settled and his spirit peaceful when he left the barn.

"Hey, Pop!" Tom called as he walked through the house to his large room. Stuart observed him from his spot in the living room, grinning as the smoke rose from his ever-present cigar. He was looking forward to meeting the woman who put the new, confident spring in his son's step.

Sunnie tapped impatiently on the table waiting for her mother to answer the phone. Just as she was about to hang up, Rob answered.

"Hi Rob, where's mom?"

"I'm fine, Sunnie, thank you for asking. Your mother is putting River down. Hang on a minute." Sunnie made several faces at the phone.

A muffled conversation happened before her mother came on the line. Sunnie plunged directly into her problem, "Mom, I think I have a wardrobe emergency. What would you wear to meet Mayor Jacobs?" She stared out the window, looking down on the eyesore that was Silas's green van.

"Aren't you spending the day? Are you riding again?"

"Well, yes. But Mom, he's the MAYOR."

"Sunnie, you are going there as Tom's guest. It's not a board meeting. Wear your favorite comfortable jeans and that pretty green sweater you have. That color is nice on you."

"Mom, that sweater is lame and Tom has seen me in it already. Not that it matters."

Sammie grinned. "It must matter a bit, sweetie, if you're asking. I think you should relax and enjoy yourself. Be you, Sunnie. That's what Tom enjoys."

"HOW do you know that, Mom? You've only met him one time." Sunnie's exasperation level was high. It seemed everyone in her life—except her—knew how she felt about Tom.

"That was enough. I was hoping he'd be by again soon. Rob enjoyed the basketball game."

"Maybe, Mom. I've got to go buy something to wear now. Maybe. Ugh, I'll go look in the closet. At least I know what to wear to the race."

Sammie hung the phone up, laughing. To Rob's enquiring look, she simply answered, "She has got it bad."

Sunnie looked into her closet, dazed by the choices.

"I have too much clothing!" she announced to the empty apartment. She started to weed through it all in an attempt to keep her mind occupied with things other than meeting the mayor and her obvious attachment to his son.

A knock brought Sunnie out of her closet and across her apartment that was now strewn with clothing on every available surface. When she opened the door, Silas looked around the apartment curiously before announcing, "Tom is downstairs. I wasn't sure if I should send him up or not. Do you want me to?"

"What? Si, are you crazy? Go tell him I'll be down in a minute." Sunnie hastily shoved Silas out the door. She hurried back to her room where she just as hastily shucked the battered T-shirt she'd been wearing. Selecting a blouse from Pile A, she ran a brush feebly through her wild mane before giving that up as a lost cause. Her attempt at nonchalance when she entered the shop caused Silas to hide his laugh in a bite of a stray cookie.

"Hi! I wasn't expecting to see you today. What are you doing in town?"

Tom flashed the lazy smile that made Sunnie's heart do several small flippity-flops. "I had an errand to run so I thought I'd stop by. Make sure you don't back out of meeting Pop."

"Oh, I'm ready. Why would I back out? Plus, I get another riding lesson, right?"

"I was just checking. I'm sorry I haven't been in touch too much this week. It's been—strange. I should have dropped an email, at least."

"Yes, you should have," she said airily as she sat. "Isn't it up to the man to do that sort of thing? In normal relationships, I mean."

"Oh, is that what we're in? A *normal* relationship?"

Sunnie exhaled loudly and dropped the flirty banter.

"That's much better. The real you appeared. Do you want to ride with me out to the house tomorrow? After church?"

"IF I come, I can certainly manage to drive there myself, *Officer*. Excuse me now, I need to get back to...what I was doing." Sunnie turned, leaving Tom to sip his coffee alone.

"Just wear jeans, Sunnie. He's only my father," he called to her as she walked out the door. He laughed when the heavy glass door slammed.

Walking out front in time to witness Sunnie's exit, Silas called out, "You break it, you buy it!" He filled a cup with coffee before joining Tom.

"I hope you realize what you're getting yourself into," he said.

Tom's grin spread. "I can handle it, Si." He gazed back at the door Sunnie had slammed shut. "She's really something."

"Yup, she is. We've been trying to figure out what for years now."

Tom rose from the stool, tossing his cup in the receptacle before walking through the door Sunnie had just slammed. He chuckled over Silas's parting comment the whole ride home.

Tom joined Sunnie in the Sunday school class, disregarding her attempts to avoid him. At the end of class, he picked up her Bible from the desk. "You look great."

Her attitude dissolved as quickly as a snow cone on a hot summer day. "Thanks," she breathed as they started walking out of the classroom.

"I'm glad I decided to ride with you after all," Sunnie said when they arrived at the Jeep. His light chuckle caused the now-expected rise in blood pressure. She was glad for the distraction of listening to part of the church service on the drive across town.

Tom heard her intake of breath when he turned into the long drive toward the house. He pulled the emergency brake once they stopped in front of the rustic front porch, assuring Sunnie a final time that his father was harmless.

"Relax, Sunnie! Remember, he likes to bluster. But he's a big softie." He offered a reassuring smile before exiting the Jeep.

Sunnie opened the door, startled to find someone standing there waiting for her. The man smiling up at her bore no resemblance to Mayor 'Tough-as-Nails' Jacobs. Dressed in faded jeans, work boots and a flannel shirt with the sleeves rolled to the elbow, he smiled while clenching a large cigar between his teeth.

"Well? Are you coming down from there? Son, I thought you said this girl was feisty!" He extended his hand to Sunnie; she was riveted to the seat in speechless awe.

"She is, Pop. Give her time. She's only ever seen you at work." Tom gave his father a good-natured slap on the back. Stuart laughed, a deep belly laugh, his full head of wavy gray hair bobbing.

"I see. I shall be on my best behavior. Come, now."

He turned back to Sunnie, who had finally taken his hand. The fact that she was almost a full head taller than he did not phase the florid faced man. With an air of authority, he led her through the front door of his realm. Tom trailed behind them, a wide grin on his face; this was looking to be a very interesting day.

"Now, Sunnie, I understand your profession allows you to frequently be about the town hall. You aren't one of those trouble-making environmentalists too, are you?"

As Stuart eyed her—part scowl, part smile—she immediately recognized the humorous glimmer Tom shared. He placed himself in front of a massive stone fireplace, one foot propped on the hearth and an arm leaned on the mantle. The house smelled of leather, cigar smoke, open air and cedar. The easy, casual atmosphere reflected the owner. Well lived-in and comfortable. Sunnie was smitten.

"You own Young InvestCorps. You refurbished that building on Oak Street. Great job! That needed to be revitalized! It's a wonderful old building. I'd love to come see it."

Sunnie's face flushed. "Well, you're welcome any time, Mayor Jacobs..."

Stuart laughed again, the hearty sound filling the room. "Sunnie! You are a guest of my son! It's Stuart, please. But!" he held up a finger, "Mayor Jacobs if you see me in town." He threw her a huge, roguish wink.

"Do you ride, Sunnie Young of Young InvestCorps?"

"Are you offering lessons, Mayor Tough-As-Nails of Lakeville?" Sunnie shot back.

"It would be an immense pleasure, but I must man the grill for dinner. I'll let Tommy take care of that. He says you've already had one lesson. Did you like it?"

Sunnie's nod was enthusiastic.

"That's a good girl!" Stuart boomed. "Now, come, sit down. Tell me all about how a young, beautiful woman got into such a cutthroat business."

He led Sunnie to a huge, overstuffed leather couch. "Get your gal something to drink, Tommy. You'll have her back in a bit."

Tom settled in a matching chair after bringing Sunnie a glass of water. Both men listened with interest to her quick resume of her career at Weston Acquisitions and what brought her back to Lakeville.

"Excuse me for now, Sunnie. I must tend to dinner. I can see I'll enjoy our discussion of the housing proposal later." Stuart nodded before he left the room. Sunnie smiled to Tom before taking a drink.

"So? Do we get to see the horses now?"

"You can't wait for that second lesson, can you?" Tom rose. "Let's go; we have time for a nice ride."

Sunnie followed him from the living room through the family room. Over that fireplace was a large portrait of a beautiful woman. As he had said, they shared the same brilliant red hair. Tom stopped in front of the fireplace, gazing a moment at the portrait. A warm—yet sad—smile appeared before he spoke.

"This is Mom. Claire, this is Sunnie. Now you've met the parents. Let's go see Picasso. I think he was jealous yesterday when I rode Beau without him."

Tom hooked his arm around Sunnie's shoulder before walking out of the sliding doors to an enormous deck. Stuart was fussing about a grill the size of which Sunnie had only seen on television food shows. He turned when he heard them come out.

"Heading for the stable?" Tom and Sunnie both nodded. "Have a good time, now. You know where the helmets are, son."

"Yessir. What time should we be back? Are Roy and Maisey coming up for dinner?"

"Remind them. You know there'll be more than enough. About 4:30 I should guess. Just in time for a beer before dinner. Sunnie, you're not a vegetarian, I trust?"

Swiftly debating the wisdom of admitting her preferences, Sunnie smiled endearingly.

"It smells wonderful! I can't wait!"

Stuart's hardy laugh sounded again. "You're a natural diplomat, girl! Maybe you should consider running when I step down." He winked to them and turned back to the grill to tend what looked to be a whole side of beef.

As they walked down the steps toward the stables, Stuart glanced up from the grill. He grinned, chewing the end of his cigar. "That's a fine woman, Tommy boy," he said to himself. "Damn fine woman. Just like your mother."

Tom and Sunnie strolled down a well-worn path to the stables. His pace was fluid, the peace with his lifestyle inviting. A small sigh of contentment escaped Sunnie as she took in the sights. The trail wound along the far side of the corral where large sunflowers grew against the rail fence.

"What wonderful flowers!" Sunnie paused, lifting a hand to the enormous head of one in the cluster.

"Beau and Picasso think so. The other horses don't bother with them much." Tom headed behind the stable, to Roy's house. "Let's just let them know what time to be at the house."

Almost on cue, a small dark haired woman stepped out of a door and onto the deck. Tom waved to her. "That's Maisey. She's part Choctaw Indian. She rides bareback. It's amazing to see."

Sunnie had never met any woman with hair so silkily straight and jet-black. She assured Tom she'd never miss one of Mr. Stu's barbeques and sent them on their way with bottles of cool water.

Sunnie paid careful attention while Tom explained how to saddle the horses, eager to learn all. Taking the same helmet she had last time, Sunnie secured it under her chin. Tom helped her with the mount again, impressed with her effort.

"If I didn't know better, I'd swear you've been out here practicing."

"When will I be able to do it that easily?" Sunnie asked when Tom smoothly swung up into his seat on Beau.

"When you live here and ride every day," came the casual answer. "We'll go down the path around the creek this time. It'll be a longer ride, but we'll end up at the house. How'd you do last time? Were you sore?"

"Nothing that some stretching didn't take care of. When can I run?" Sunnie laughed with Tom, realizing it was a silly question.

"You can allow Picasso to gallop when you feel reasonably comfortable with him. I don't suggest it today. Do those stretches really help?"

"I can show you some. It's really good for clearing the mind. I ignore all the eastern mumbo jumbo."

Tom noted to himself that it kept Sunnie in fine shape. "You really haven't ridden before this? You seem very natural on Picasso."

"Not even a pony ride when I was a kid. It's something I've always wanted to do. I'd love to be riding across an open plain somewhere. Maybe Colorado. By all those red boulders."

"California. On the beach at sunset," Tom suggested.

"Oh, yes! That sounds great. What about...."

The first part of their ride was spent envisioning exotic destinations to ride, becoming more extravagant as the trail wove on. Picasso and Beau were outrunning evil sheiks in Arabia before they stopped by a flat rock next to the creek so the horses could drink and nibble the grass.

"This is the most fun I've had all week. I'm really happy that you're here, Sunnie. Catch!" Tom tossed Sunnie one of the water bottles he stashed in Beau's saddlebag. Sunnie easily caught the bottle; she stuck out her tongue before she sipped the cool water.

"Okay, so you can catch. Big deal, I want to see you shoot a jump shot." Tom teased, sitting on the ground next to the rock.

"Not on your life. I told you; sports are for spectating, not playing. You never told me what day the race is, you know. It's a good thing I follow the schedule. We'll have to leave pretty early. I'll drive."

"What? Why? Can't hack three hours in the Jeep?"

"It's my turn. Unless you also teach me to drive a stick."

"Jude never showed you? I'm surprised."

"I wasn't around. Busy being...well, just busy. Staying away." She brushed away the unsavory memories of her life before moving back to Lakeville. Confiding in Wynter was a far cry from divulging her pre-Christian life to a man she was developing deeper feelings for.

"If you really want to learn, I'll show you. Yes, we'll leave when it's still dark. We've got pit passes..."

"No way!" Sunnie's excited squeal interrupted, and Tom laughed.

"Yes way! This is just one of the perks of your father being the mayor of a town in Penn State. Pit passes, seats on the start/finish line. Should be quite a day. Another day I'm happy you agreed to spend with me."

"I like spending time with you, Tom. I'm sorry the other day I was so..." Sunnie floundered for a word to describe her behavior.

"Weird?" Tom offered.

"Yes, weird. I was kind of uptight about meeting your dad. And I hadn't heard from you all week."

"I am sorry about that, Sunnie. I had a really strange week. Disagreements with a co-worker. That strains the whole squad. Does it matter that I thought about you every night?"

Sunnie's face flushed deeply pink. "Yes. It matters," she said so quietly Tom almost missed it. In more typically Sunnie-like fashion, she asked, "Should we be getting back?"

"Must you always do that?" Tom questioned, brushing some dirt from his jeans after he stood.

"Do what?" She pulled her hair away from her face to put the helmet back on.

"Redirect the discussion. I'm just curious. It happens only when I bring up the topic of 'us.'" Tom turned, the clipped reply revealing the frustration he felt. He eyed the horses as they drank from the creek a few feet away.

Sunnie walked to him, hesitant to open up too much, yet knowing she must. She placed a hand on his arm, bringing his attention back to her.

"I like being with you. I like that I can be real with you. That this—" Sunnie pointed between the two of them, "—isn't complicated. Is that enough for you? For now?"

Tom's gaze on her face was overwhelming; he held her eyes for some time before his softened. Relief replaced the tightness fear had brought to her throat.

"For now, Sunnie. It's enough for now."

Chapter 11

Stuart observed his son and guest riding up to the house, and a smile split his face. As he sipped from the frosty glass, he heard Roy snicker. Placing his cigar back in its proper place he turned to the large man and his wife.

"You got that look, boss. Like you just won another election." Roy pronounced before enjoying another sip from the chilled mug.

Stuart waved his hand in the air, smugly rearranging his face. "Just admiring a woman who looks splendid on a horse, Roy. Like your Maisey."

Maisey waved her hand at the cigar that pointed to her. "You weren't, Mr. Stu. You was planning. I seen that look too."

An indeterminate sound emerged from Stuart before he rose. "I better get the boy a beer now. Roy, help Tommy get the beasts back to the stable. Well, Sunnie, enjoy the ride?" Stuart called out over the deck.

"More than I expected, Stuart, thank you. You may have a permanent weekend guest."

"You're more than welcome. Now, sit while they bring the beasts back. Beer, Tommy boy?"

"Just one, Pop, I'm driving later."

Stuart nodded. "Of course, of course. You, Sunnie?"

"No thank you, Stuart. Iced tea or water is fine for me."

"Sunnie! You don't drink or eat beef? How in the world did Tommy find you?" Stuart teased from the grill. Sunnie glanced to Maisey with a *how did he know?* look.

She shrugged. "He just knows things, Miss Sunnie."

"Oh, please, don't call me that," she pleaded with a wave of her hand. "Just Sunnie is fine. Stuart, I gave up drinking long ago. As for eating beef, how did you guess?"

"Sunnie, it's more about what you don't say than what you do. Politics 101. I asked you if you were a vegetarian, and you said that what I was cooking smelled wonderful. You didn't answer." Stuart smiled, watching Sunnie laugh at herself. "Do you eat chicken? I have plenty of that inside; I can throw some on right now."

"No, please. It's fine. I'll be fine. Don't go to any trouble."

Sunnie's plea fell on deaf ears as Stuart marched into the kitchen, returning with a plate of marinated chicken. Stuart placed it on the grill, then went back for Tom's beer. Once he was satisfied that all was well, he sat to take a long pull from his glass. As he puffed the cigar, Sunnie could see the tranquility he held with his household.

"Stuart, which horse do you ride?"

His deep chuckle resonated in Sunnie's heart—similar, yet more matured than Tom's.

"All of them, but I favor Knight. He's our other black horse—Beau's sire. Buttercup is Maisey's. She's the smaller brown. Roy's Mercury rounds out the family horses. We currently have two boarding for friends. Life without a good woman by your side, and a good horse to ride isn't worth living. Eh, Maisey?"

"Now, Mr. Stu, you know what I think. Without the Great Spirit, life is nothing."

Stuart nodded. "Of course, Maisey, of course. But, I stand by my motto. Ah, here they are. Come, sit. Got you a beer, Tommy. Just a few more minutes, and we'll be enjoying dinner. After dinner, we can discuss Sunnie's proposal. I'm looking forward to hearing what you say about it."

Tom tossed her a wink before he sat. She held a giggle before turning to Stuart.

"I'm looking forward to discussing it, Stuart. That's the neighborhood I was raised in."

Stuart returned to manning the grill. "So Tommy tells me. We'll save all of that for later. Roy, take this plate, thank you. Maisey, don't forget that potato salad; there's the girl. Tommy, here's Sunnie's chicken..." He had everything expertly and quickly plated.

From the meat, starches, and not one vegetable present, Sunnie knew she was in a fully masculine domain. She didn't tire of wondering exactly how much Tom would fill his plate, and was not surprised that the enormous Roy surpassed him. She noticed Maisey, though petite in stature, could compete with their capacity for ribs.

Sunnie had not yet finished the piece of chicken she had as Tom and Roy were filling their third plate of ribs. Stuart enjoyed his steak and was back to contentedly puffing his cigar. While Tom and Roy decided to race through their last few ribs, Sunnie got up to bring her plate in the kitchen and get more iced tea. Stuart followed her inside.

"Don't eat much, do you?" Stuart commented.

"That was my usual," Sunnie replied, deciding he wasn't all that gruff, as he wanted to sound. "What do you want to know about the proposal?"

Stuart smiled, punctuating the air with the cigar. "I knew I liked you. Let me go get the paperwork. Clear off that table so we can spread it out, have a good look." Sunnie smiled after him as he strutted off, shakily pouring more iced tea before she returned to the deck.

Stuart emerged with the proposal and attached community plans. He spread them over the large table. He sat with his hands folded over the spread of his stomach, looking expectantly at Sunnie.

Before Tom's eyes, Sunnie transformed into a sharp businesswoman who eloquently presented the positive aspects of the housing project to Mayor Jacobs. He had to shake himself of the image that had formed in his mind—Sunnie dressed sleek, black business attire, hair tamed back in a twist—so he could pay attention to what she was saying.

Stuart nodded, grumbled, threw out a few negatives, which Sunnie countered.

He stabbed the plans with a finger after dramatically sweeping the proposal aside. "Tell me why this property is the best spot." Stuart was intent on getting to the reasons in Sunnie's mind.

"It needs to be reclaimed...the acreage alone is worth triple what my client paid. The house that's there has needed to be taken down for years."

"Then why the interest in low-income housing? According to you, he's sitting on a goldmine."

The onlookers observed with interest as Sunnie's face turned stormy, not an attitude normally—nor with success–projected in Stuart's presence.

"Have you ever lived anywhere but here, Mayor?" The sharp tone caught Stuart off-guard. He shook his head, focused on her cool stare.

"I suppose your father didn't have to struggle to buy all this wonderful land you call home, did he?"

"No, but I fail to see how..."

They all jumped as Sunnie's hand came down on the table. The startled look on Stuart's face produced a quickly stifled guffaw from his son.

"That's the trouble with politicians, no matter if they reside in Washington or not. When is the last time you toured the old high school? Do you know what that complex is like? It's dirty, it needs repair, and they hardly have any place for the children who live there to run and play. Thankfully it's not a drug haven, but that's due to your excellent police force." She afforded Tom a quick grin.

"Hard working families live there, Mayor Jacobs! And some of them would like to live in a bit more space to call their own. With a small down payment, and some of their own laboring, they can own a home—a small home—but one of their own. Don't content citizens make a happy town? That housing project that the council is so proud of is a tragedy waiting to happen if something can't be done. That needs complete revamping, but you can't kick families out to do the extensive work that needs to be done. It's a Catch-22, and this community would alleviate some of that burden. As the families move out, you can repair apartment by apartment."

Sunnie knew she had their rapt attention—all of them. She took the opportunity to question Roy and Maisey.

"If you didn't live in that wonderful log cabin, would you be able to afford a home in Lakeville?" Roy chewed his lip, but Maisey shook her head.

"No, Miss Sunnie. I seen the prices of them houses when we moved here. I'm sure they be way higher now."

Sunnie turned back to Stuart. "I'm sure that you are most generous with them, but point still being, if housing was not part of their employment package, they couldn't work for you. Because they couldn't afford to live here. I'm not talking about people you don't want in your town. I'm talking about people who already live in your town, probably work in your town, and want a chance to stay in your town."

"One question, Miss Young. Who gets the homes? Legally, we have to open it up to surrounding towns." Stuart's cigar waved in the air, the curling smoke forming a cloud above the table.

"No! Not at first!" Sunnie insisted, becoming animated. "You can hold a lottery. I knew it would be an objection, so I did some research. The people *of* Lakeville get priority on the lottery for up to half of the homes. It's not many in reality, but it's a start. You are assured that some of your people stay in town. You are also allowed to screen every application and deny dangerous felons, child predators, and the like. It's tricky, but it's in the law. You can do it." Sunnie satisfactorily sipped her iced tea as she sat.

"I told you she was feisty, Pop," Tom said with propriatory pride. He laughed when Sunnie flushed pink.

"Sunnie, we need you on the town council. I'm sure Tommy told you that this is already a go. I'm honored to have heard you speak about it personally. I will assure the council that it's a very well thought out plan. Thank you."

Stuart smiled as he rose, setting a look on his son. "You keep this one around a while." Sunnie flushed several shades of red.

"Maisey, sweet Maisey, would you make some of that extraordinary coffee you excel at? We'll need to go over your employment benefits soon, too, I see." Stuart left the deck with the paperwork.

Maisey left the table to start coffee. She turned to Sunnie first, "That's high praise from Mr. Stu. And that's a good plan." Sunnie nodded her thanks, waiting for the heat to dissipate from her cheeks.

Roy stood up with a stretch. "I gotta go rub them horses down; you all have a great evening. Very nice to see you again, Miss Sunnie. Glad someone around here can keep Stu on his toes." He slapped Tom on the back. "I'll win the next rib contest." He strolled off the deck, heading to the stable whistling an old country tune.

Tom turned back to Sunnie, "If you walked into that council meeting, they'd do whatever you said."

"Stop. Was I too...too..." Sunnie couldn't decide what word to use.

"Eloquent? Passionate? How about powerful? Impressive; I like that too. You were wonderful." Tom reached to Sunnie's hand. "He was all for it. He really wanted to hear what you had to say. I'm glad you didn't back down from your conviction over it. Unfortunately, I need to get you back home now. I have the early tour tomorrow."

As they walked through the house, Tom called, "I'm taking Sunnie home, Pop. I'll be back in about an hour."

Stuart was gazing at Claire's portrait, a smile softening his features. He turned from the fireplace, the smile still in place. "It's been a pleasure, Sunnie. I hope to see you around more, both here and at town hall. You'd be a wonderful council member. You should seriously consider a place in the town's political map."

His face glowed when Sunnie placed a kiss on his cheek. "Maybe I'll run against you some time. Thanks, I had a great day."

Once they were out of earshot, he turned back to the portrait. He exhaled deeply, speaking to the woman who silently smiled down at him.

"She's a fine, fine woman, Claire. You'd like her. I'm glad he found someone like you." He waved to the portrait as he turned to pour himself a cup of coffee before retiring to his office.

"Wow, it got chilly!" Sunnie exclaimed when they stepped from the front porch. Bounding back up the steps, Tom returned from the house with his police department sweatshirt. Sunnie pulled it over her head and thrust her hands into the pocket on the front.

"If you ate more meat, you wouldn't be cold." Tom said, turning around to back out of his spot.

Sunnie snorted. "If I ate a quarter of what you eat, I'd be enormous. Your father didn't have to go to any extra trouble. Pasta salad would have been enough for me."

"I warned him you didn't eat beef. He wanted you to have a good time. I'm sure you'll have a nickname by the next visit." Tom assured her before hopping from the Jeep to remove the driveway chain.

"Well, he'll be seeing me a lot. I plan on a riding lesson every weekend. Unless you aren't home."

"Glad to. I won't be here next weekend; I have Guard duty. The week before the race, I'm gone all week. That still gives you five or six lessons."

They discussed the housing project in more detail as they drove. Too soon for Sunnie, they were sitting in the Jeep behind her building.

"I had a great time, Tom. Your father is wonderful. It's going to be strange, watching him strutting down the hallway next time I'm at Town Hall." Sunnie laughed at the image. Stuart wasn't as tough as he wanted his constituents to believe him to be.

"I told you he's all bluster. His whole 'image' thing is weird for me sometimes, too."

They sat in silence for a few minutes before Sunnie reluctantly opened the door. "I should let you go. You will call this week, right?"

Tom nodded. "If I can't, I promise to email. I'll walk to the door with you." He opened his door to get out before Sunnie could protest. He put his arm around her shoulder as he had earlier in the day. They stopped at the door so Sunnie could get her keys out.

"Thanks again," Sunnie said quietly. Mesmerized by the sincerity and trustworthiness she saw in his eyes, she willingly swayed to him when he pulled her close to kiss her goodnight. Before Sunnie could fully enjoy it, it was over. It was not possessive or demanding. It was sweet and romantic, leaving her hoping that it was not the last one she would receive.

Chapter 12

The promise to call or email did not disappoint. They sometimes came earlier than Sunnie cared to function, and every night there was an email or silly e-card.

When hit with a wave of malaise Saturday, she realized it was due to Tom's absence. After a session of online shopping that included a small gift for him, Sunnie retreated to the couch with a thick book. As the light dimmed, she realized she had forgotten about the weekly ritual of hallway sweeping. With a glance at the time, she flipped her phone open to call Wynter.

"Hi Wynnie. Listen, I'm not cleaning today. Don't worry about it...No, I'll do it on Tuesday; I have to get to a meeting on Monday...No, really...Thanks though. See you tomorrow at church." Sunnie put the phone down and contentedly continued reading.

Sunnie's eyelids soon lost the battle against the fading light and involved plot line. A fire truck roared past the building late in the night, startling Sunnie from her sleep. The empty feeling returned as she sat up and listened to the sirens drone to silence. She prayed fervently for the safety of the men before she rose to check her email, hoping for a message from Tom. A wave of peace enveloped her when she saw his name on the Inbox list.

HI SUNNIE,
BUSY WEEKEND. JUDE SAYS HELLO. LET'S HAVE BREAKFAST MONDAY.
TOM

Sunnie's hand went to her throat before hitting the reply button. Typing quickly, she thanked God Tom could access his email from his phone when she pressed "Send."

TOM,
I HAVE A MEETING ABOUT THE HOUSING PROJECT ON MONDAY, I CAN'T MISS IT. HOW ABOUT TUESDAY FOR A LATE LUNCH? HI TO JUDE. PLEASE BE CAREFUL, I REALLY MISS YOU.
SUNNIE

"What a waste!" Sunnie groused as she drove home from the meeting. So much time had been spent arguing over minutia of the houses themselves and not the project. Replaying the more annoying points of the meeting, she drove through a stop sign. When the lights appeared in her mirror, she suppressed the one word she still struggled with as she pulled to the side of the road. The embarrassed smirk—how silly to be stopped by the officer she was dating!—turned to a scowl when Penzi emerged from the cruiser and swaggered towards her car.

"So, Young, you think because you're dating Jake, you don't have to obey the law? Tsk, tsk, tsk. I'll need your info, please." Penzi had a perverse smile of pleasure about his face. Well aware that she'd knock him off his feet, Sunnie shoved her door open. He agilely avoided it.

"Just write me a ticket, Penzi. I am giving you nothing." Sunnie leaned against her car with her arms folded.

He took a long look from her head to her feet, taking in the short black skirt and matching bolero jacket, fitted silk blouse and dark hose. Lingering on the heels a moment, his eyes made their way back to Sunnie's face. Sunnie tugged the jacket tighter about herself.

"Always dress so—stimulating—when you work?" Sunnie puffed her hair from her face and turned the other way. She jumped at the touch on her arm. "I see Jake hasn't explained the intricacies of a traffic stop. I need your information, Ms. Young, so please lean back in that car and get it. Take your time, so I can enjoy the rear view of that fine skirt."

Walking to the other side of the car, Sunnie opened the door and slipped in, the swift movement affording Penzi a view of her head only. Hands trembling, she pulled the required paperwork from the glovebox. She vented her indignation by slamming the box and her car door shut.

Penzi took the paperwork from her. "Careful, Young. I'll have to arrest you for resistance. I'll check this out. Don't go away." Penzi smiled smugly before returning to the police car. She was washed over with a sudden relief that this was the middle of the afternoon on a fairly busy road.

She watched Penzi strut back to the cruiser before leaning on her fender. He returned in a very long few moments, with her paperwork and ticket in hand. She snatched the clipboard and signed the ticket before thrusting it back at him. He grinned, removed the needed papers, and placed the clipboard on her roof. He held the information and ticket out.

When she reached for them, he pulled it back, pulling her arm along with them. Sunnie's stomach flipped at his touch on the sleeve—not in the happy way it did when she saw Tom.

"We can work this out, Sunnie. Just tell me when...I have the address." He snickered at the panic that showed in her dark eyes. "Don't let me catch you again, especially at night. I'd hate to have to search your car...or you." He let the papers go and left her to ponder that alarming thought.

Back in the driver's seat, she waited for him to drive by before slowly pulling away from the curb. The urge to shred the ticket came and went quickly as she drove home at a whopping 25 MPH.

"This is Sunnie Young," she snapped before checking the ID screen on the phone, still seething from the run-in with Officer Penziotti.

"Good afternoon. This is Officer Jacobs." Tom replied in his best police-business voice.

The deep tone relaxed Sunnie, and she was able to laugh away the remaining nerves. She had already decided not to enlighten him about her traffic stop and arranged with Silas to pay the ticket first thing the following morning. "I'm sorry. It's been...well, it's been a day."

"Just checking to see if we're still on for lunch tomorrow. I'm meeting with Paul earlier, so I'll need to get home and back."

"Why do you need to go home after a meeting with a pastor?" Sunnie asked as she poured hot water over a chamomile tea bag.

"We're playing ball; I'd rather go home and change at least. Unless you won't mind me showing up in shorts and a sweaty shirt."

Not at all! was her honest answer, although she voiced a completely different thought. "Thanks. Where are we meeting?"

"We didn't decide. That was the other reason I called. What do you feel like? Burgers?"

"Yes! Big old burger smothered in bacon." They both laughed. "How about pizza? We can both get what we want."

"Only if we enjoy it in the park in town. How does that sound?"

Sunnie considered that. She liked walking through the big park in the town center, but rarely took the time to sit and enjoy things. "Sure. It's a date."

Several beats of silence went by. "An official date? Did I hear that correctly, Sunnie?"

Sunnie snickered. "Yes, Officer. An official date. I think I can handle it." Sunnie paused a moment. "You know what that means, right?"

"You tell me." Tom answered, wondering what was on Sunnie's mind. He laughed at her final response.

"That means you buy. Goodnight."

As the ball bounced off the backboard and through the hoop, the few teens that were watching the one-on-one match cheered Tom's skills. He waved to them as he walked toward Paul at mid-court.

"Aren't they supposed to be in a class?" he asked, wiping sweat off his forehead.

"Game point, your ball."

Paul panted out a laugh. "It's a study period for them. Don't think I don't know what's happening around me, Jacobs. Ready?"

"Go for it, Edwards."

Paul's aggressive efforts failed to stop Tom from shooting the winning basket.

"Nice one, Officer Jacobs!" an overenthusiastic boy shouted.

Paul pointed a finger of warning to Tom's fan club, threatening extra memory verses if they spread the news of his defeat. They scurried from the gym as a bell for class sounded.

"Gotta love teens," Paul chortled before drinking down the remains of his bottled water. "You should work with the youth, Tom."

"We've been through this, Paul. My work and Guard schedules don't give me the time I need to devote to them. Maybe at some point, but not now."

"You seem to have the time to devote to other things," Paul said as they descended the stairs leading to the parking area behind the building. At Tom's sideways glance, Paul provided, "Sunnie?"

Tom's wide smile spoke more than his answer. "Oh. Yeah, Sunnie."

"That's all? 'Oh, yeah?' Come on, Tom. I know you. How serious?"

"Depends on her, Paul. All indications are to take it slow. So, slow it is."

"But?"

Tom opened the back of the Jeep and tossed the ball in. He pulled a bottle of water from an open case.

"Nothing. She wants to take it slow. That's all. Keep it 'uncomplicated,' as she would say."

Paul leaned against the bumper. "Are you taking the necessary steps to stay pure?"

Tom gagged on his water. "Don't be shy, Paul!"

Paul laughed, watching Tom wipe his mouth with the edge of his t-shirt. "Believe it or not, teens are not the only sector of the population to succumb to sexual temptations. For them it's usually a matter of 'forbidden fruit.' For adults who have been involved in previous relationships, it's more a matter of wanting it all, at any cost. Don't give yourself an occasion to test my theory. I wouldn't be a very good friend—or pastor—if I didn't make sure all was above board."

Tom nodded. "I know. I appreciate the words of wisdom. I'll admit, studying through Romans while developing a relationship is...challenging."

Paul pushed off the bumper. "It's challenging no matter what you're studying. I need to get back, or I'll be pastoring at the local grocery store. Call me when you're free for a rematch."

They parted, Paul to the church offices and Tom to drive home for a shower before meeting Sunnie. Along the way, he considered the differences Paul pointed out in relationships.

"We can handle it. I'm sure we can," Tom assured himself.

Sunnie decided to walk to the pizzeria, better to enjoy the mild weather. After ducking into a storefront to hide from the police cruiser slowly driving up the road, she giggled at herself. Ignoring the unease over Penzi's misguided attentions, she continued on the way. As she approached the door, she sniffed the wonderful aromas of spicy sauce, pepperoni, and garlic. Hearing the familiar beep of Tom's horn, she spun to wave. Tom returned the gesture as he drove past her to find a parking spot.

"What is going on in town today? It's so busy!" Sunnie commented when he finally reached the pizzeria.

"It's a nice warm day. Everyone wanted to get out I guess. Come on, let's order quick. We can catch up after." He smiled before leaning in to place a kiss on her cheek. Swinging the door open released more mouth-watering scents into the open air. They chatted lightly while awaiting their order. Tom paid when it was called and took the two boxes off the counter to carry to the park.

The block-long-and-wide area was the hub of Lakeville. At the very heart was an enormous pitch pine, the town's premier Christmas tree. The surrounding area included cement tables, benches, and trash cans strategically placed between. Some tables held embedded chess boards, although none were being used that afternoon.

"There's no wildlife here, right?" Sunnie asked before sitting at the table they'd chosen, looking suspiciously at the large tree. Tom opened the top box to inspect the contents before handing it across the table.

"Why? Afraid of squirrels?"

"Not funny. Yes, I am. As well as other creepy stuff that lives in trees. Do you have your gun?"

Tom chuckled at the serious look on Sunnie's face. "I can't say. That's one of those cop secrets. The TV ones always have theirs with them, right?" She caught the wink before they bowed their heads. She forgot all self-conscious thoughts when he looked up and smiled.

"How was your meeting?" Tom asked, pulling out a slice of pizza that more readily resembled a meatball sandwich.

"Boring as hell," Sunnie answered. Realizing what had popped out, she rephrased her reply. "Umm, sorry. Quite boring. I tapped two thousand eighty-seven times."

At Tom's quizzical expression, Sunnie explained. "A bad habit I developed at Weston—probably at Penn State. When a class or meeting got boring, I would tap my pen on the table. Now I can gauge how boring it is by estimating taps."

"Maybe I'll try that next time we have a meeting. No, I think I'll do that while sitting at the sign, on radar duty. That will be a good one."

"I knew you guys had to do that! How boring! I hope you at least listen to the radio."

"Depending on how many people speed past, it can be boring. It's boring to even discuss. Tell me more about the meeting. Or, what you did after."

Sunnie took a long drink of her water, formulating how to get around the traffic stop debacle. "I just went on home; I had to get laundry together. I had to clean today; I didn't do it on Saturday. I was caught up in a book, but I fell asleep on the couch."

"Sounds like a great book. Why don't you hire a service to clean the building?"

"No way! Costs too much and I'd have to watch them anyhow. Wynter helps me. I did hire someone to do snow removal, though. I'm not that crazy."

"Really? Who does it?"

An engaging smile emerged before she nibbled the slice. The obvious answered purred from her lips: "Jude."

"Wow. I should have seen that one coming. Here I thought you'd hire some professional person from town, and you've enslaved your brother. I really didn't miss out on anything being an only child."

"Are you telling me you wouldn't plow for your poor sister, who may hurt her back if she shoveled?" Sunnie put on a very thick and inept southern accent, including batting her eyes for effect. It took Tom several moments and gulps of iced tea to recuperate from laughing.

"I hope Jude didn't fall for that one. I can more easily envision you threatening him."

"That is more like it," she admitted. Lunch was finished and Tom pushed the boxes to one side of the table. When he reached across to take Sunnie's hand, he chuckled at her anxious glance about the square.

"Sunnie, I wish you'd relax. It's not like we're having a wild make out session." Sunnie puffed in annoyance, but didn't pull her hand back from Tom's. "No one is paying any attention to what we are or are not doing. Do we have some sort of rules about dating that I'm not aware of?"

"Well, no. Not really. Did we decide we were officially dating?" Sunnie asked innocently enough.

"You're confusing. Did we need a declaration? Would you feel better if I got on my knee and asked formally?"

"Tom! Don't you dare!" Sunnie looked around again, scandalized.

"I can't believe that would bother you. Explain it to me." It was a sincere request, one she knew he wanted to understand. It was unfair not to attempt to.

"I'll try, although I'm not sure I can. Maybe, since I was a bit of a wild child way back when...I don't know. It just seems weird to be in the middle of town innocently holding your hand." She blew an errant strand of hair from her face. "I guess you'll just have to deal with my quirks, Officer, if you want to officially date."

Tom's answer was lost in sudden screeching, followed by Sunnie leaping from her spot on the bench and cowering behind him. Pizza boxes flew through the air and the next thing Tom knew Sunnie's fingers were painfully dug into his shoulders. All Tom saw when he looked around—hand on his holster—was a gray furry animal scurrying to the tree.

The high-pitched voice in his ear would have caused him to laugh but for the note of complete terror it held. "What is that?!? Can't you shoot it? It nearly bit me!"

Rearranging Sunnie's position, he managed to tuck her under his arm. He tried to soothe her trembling: she really was frightened!

"It was only a baby, Sunnie. A baby possum. It's probably looking for food. Let's get going; I'll walk you home. I'll even treat you to a cup of Silas's world-famous tea."

No longer concerned about anyone misconstruing their behavior, she clung to Tom as they left the park. She remained in his secure embrace until they reached the shop. Once Tom settled her at the counter and made her tea, she began to unwind. Silas emerged from the kitchen to greet them.

"Si! Do you know there's wild animals at that park? I may never go there again!" Sunnie proclaimed. Her voice still held a tone of the panic she'd felt.

"Wild rabbits?" Silas joked.

"No, it was some ugly thing with a ratty tail. Tom wouldn't shoot it. Some big brave cop he is." Sunnie rolled her eyes.

"Yes, I can just shoot up the town square because of a possum. This is not the wild, wild west." He looked to Silas, expressing male confusion. "It was only a baby."

Silas was trying to show a modicum of sympathy. "Did Sunnie tell you she got bit?"

"No, she left that part out. She just screamed and hid behind me."

Sunnie shuddered. "It was disgusting. Yes, when I was small, my stupid father thought it was fun to feed the squirrels. When I tried, one bit my finger. Right here. See?" Sunnie vehemently pointed to a spot on her index finger that looked exactly like the rest of the long, slender digit.

Deciding it was far better to agree with Sunnie at this juncture, Tom nodded. "Sure. So, what happened after that?"

"I freaked. Went to the ER with my father. Rabies shot. That was before all the recent research, whatever. It hurt and I was only a kid. My father made fun of me for days after. I hate squirrels."

She raised her eyes in disbelief to Silas when he decided to change the subject to her undisclosed traffic ticket.

"Hey, I paid that ticket for you. Here's the receipt," he said, reaching into the deep pocket of his work pants. The threat of his quick demise on Sunnie's face changed the course of the discussion. "Uh, maybe I left it in the back..."

He quickly walked away, leaving them staring at each other oddly. He did not have long to wait before the explosion.

"What did you get a ticket for?"

Sunnie squeezed the tea bag in her hand, deciding that talking about squirrels wasn't all that bad. Intent on keeping the ticket a mystery, she shrugged. "Nothing."

"If it was a ticket for nothing, why did you pay it? What happened?" Tom put his cup down, concerned.

"Nothing happened! My goodness, what is with the police in this town? I went through a stop sign...no big deal. No one was even coming the other way. It was a stupid oversight, and I got a ticket and paid it right away. Isn't that what you're supposed to do?" Her voice had taken on the quality of hysteria it had earlier.

Tom frowned. "Sunnie, why are you so upset? Is that all it was? Who stopped you?"

"Certainly no one as nosey as you!" she shot at him, to his stunned surprise. "Thanks for the *wonderful* day, Officer."

Tom abruptly rose to leave. "Wonderful it was. Our first official date and fight. Thanks, Sunnie. It's been a blast." He threw his empty cup away and called his thanks to Silas as he stalked out.

Silas returned in time to see Sunnie hurl her cup after him.

"Dude. Glad there's no one else in here. Thanks, Sis. I live to mop up tea off my clean floors."

"Oh, shut up, Si. I'll clean it. Stop being so whiny. I should let you...why did you mention that ticket? I asked you to go pay it so Tom didn't find out. And this is why I should not go out with men. Ack!"

After listening to Sunnie's disjointed tirade, Silas went back to get the mop. She snatched it from his hand to start cleaning the mess she created.

"You are bizzaro, do you know that? What else would you like to destroy in here?"

She looked up, thrust the mop into his hands, and stormed out of the shop. Silas hoped Tom was prepared for Sunnie's strange moods.

Chapter 13

Over a week had gone by since Sunnie had spoken to Tom. She assigned him a ringtone, which didn't prevent her from continually checking her call list to see if she'd missed one from him.

Sunnie's pen tapping on the desk during Sunday school echoed the senselessness of the argument they had. The thought *Why can I not keep my temper?* gave way to *I should have told him.*

At the end of Paul's lesson, Sunnie started to gather her notes when Tom walked past her. They looked at each other a moment. Tom handed her a folded paper, nodding formally once she took it from his hand. She stared after him as he walked away before opening the note; she stifled her laugh at the content.

TOTAL: 3562. WOULD YOU LIKE TO RIDE THIS AFTERNOON?

Sunnie hurried from the room, eager to find where Tom had gone. Slightly disappointed he didn't wait for her, she entered the large sanctuary to locate him. She walked down the aisle and excused herself to step past three other people in the end of the row, wondering why he had to sit in the very center of the building. She waited until he was done praying before quietly asking, "Mind some company?"

He stood with a smile that set off the silly little cartwheels in her heart, gesturing to the seat next to his.

They shared an embrace before apologizing at the same instant. They laughed while he helped her remove her jacket. He draped it over his arm before they sat.

Somehow standing together—worshipping—melted away all the aggravations. When Tom slid his hand into hers during the sermon, she had to hold back fresh tears. There was something intimate and beautiful the gesture contained. When the service ended, they walked together to Tom's Jeep

"Do you want to ride with me?"

"Not yet. Follow me back to my place. I need to change. I'll ride with you from there. Did I really tap that many times today?"

A wry grin spread over his face. "I counted every single one. I haven't a clue what Paul talked about today. I think we should keep that to ourselves though." He winked, unlocking the door. "Are you parked close?"

"I'm just over two rows. I didn't see you when I pulled in."

"I was late. I was playing ball last night with Penzi and the other guys. Anyhow, I'll meet you there."

"Okay. See you in a few minutes," she called, walking to her car. The drive home was consumed with trepidation that Penzi informed him of the traffic stop. Several moments of greeting Silas and Wynter when they arrived distracted her from the growing concern. The discomposed feeling she had when filling the teapot with water had nothing to do with Tom's presence this day.

Determined to explain the whole absurd situation to him before the teapot whistled, she puffed her stray hair from her face. She walked back into the living room where Tom was seated, scanning through the church update.

"I'll be right back...I'm going to change." Debating the pros and cons of relationships as she pulled her jeans on, the awareness of the need for honesty settled. Securing her unruly hair on the back of her neck with a clip, she left the bedroom prepared to face Tom's feelings on the matter, whatever they might be. He was pouring hot water into the mugs when she returned.

"So, what do I do with tea? Sugar?"

She reached to the cabinet to get down a jar of organic honey. "No, silly. Honey goes in tea, although I like this one fine without it. Don't you dare think of putting milk in it."

"Okay, I guess I'll manage. You show me, so I'll know for next time. It smells like oranges."

"It's a citrus blend, but heavy on orange. I think you'll like it." Sunnie spooned in a liberal amount of the thick golden liquid while Tom watched her. "There. That should keep you happy."

"This should keep me in a coma. Thanks."

They returned to the couch with their steaming mugs in hand. "Tom, I need to tell you about this ticket," Sunnie began. The frown appearing on Tom's face shot a dart of pain into her heart.

"It would have been better if you told me when it happened, Sunnie. But, go ahead," he stated quietly.

"Penzi told you, didn't he?"

Tom nodded, but didn't expound. She continued with her version of the event.

"The meeting was over and I was distracted. I blew the stop sign on Wisteria. I wasn't going fast." Tom's eyebrows raised a bit. "Really! I wasn't! I didn't even see the car until the lights were flashing. I was hoping it was you, even though I was embarrassed. Instead, Penzi got out of the car. This isn't the first time I've had an incident with him."

She recalled the grocery store confrontation, wanting to clear all secrets between them. She sighed at the finish, "Really, he is so..." Sunnie stopped, biting her lip.

"I know all too well how he is, Sunnie," he gruffly assured her. "He enlightened all the guys playing about the stop—particularly the outfit you had on. In vivid detail. How angry you were and how you refused him your paperwork. He was having a great time recalling the whole thing."

Sunnie dropped her head into her hands, her face a shade of pink Tom had rarely glimpsed on anyone. "That's why I asked Silas to go pay it for me. I didn't want you to know about it. I especially didn't want to run into him at the station. I should have known he'd tell you. I wish he'd stop bothering me. Did he tell you what he said?"

Anger flickered in Tom's eyes. "He did. I wasn't as amused as he was. Sunnie," he moved her hands from her face, gently turning her towards him. "He's out of line. I need you to tell me anything he says to you from now on. I made it clear to him not to bother you anymore. Please do not keep things from me."

"I should have told you right away. I'm so sorry."

"I don't understand why you didn't go right to the station and report him. He's harassing you, and if any other woman reported it..."

"That's just it, don't you see? I'm not 'any other woman,' I'm...your...well, girlfriend." She tripped over the phrase, giggling at his expression. She returned to the gravity of the discussion at hand.

"I was upset, I didn't want you to know, and I made a bad call. You're absolutely right; if any co-worker at Weston would have said half of those things to me, I would have gone right to Mr. Weston."

"It *was* a bad call. I'll let it slide only this once. I'm sure my warning to him was enough." He held her eyes long enough for her to see he was serious before he cracked the terrific smile. "At least it got you to admit we're a couple."

Glad that Tom's pleasant demeanor returned, she turned back to her tea. "I had a really nice day until the rabid possum showed up."

"I promise—no possums while riding. What do you want to do for dinner?"

"Dinner? We didn't even have lunch. I don't know. Can't we decide when the time comes?"

"Sunnie, I have the feeling going out with you is going to be quite the challenge. We can grab a burger on the way back. There's got to be some place around that makes soy burgers."

Sunnie wrinkled her nose. "Those are disgusting. We can stop at the store and make much better burgers. I'll get ground turkey and good, whole grain buns. Stop making faces at me...you *will* try it." She laughed when Tom imitated her nose wrinkle.

When they returned to Sunnie's later that evening, they stayed in the Jeep talking. Despite the newer commitment to their relationship, the debate raging in Sunnie's head—invite Tom upstairs or not—distracted her from the discussion at hand.

"Sorry Tom, I zoned out. What did you just say?"

"I thought you looked spacey. What were you thinking about? If it's that I'm boring, don't tell me."

"You are the least boring person I know! I love spending time with you. I can actually have a conversation with you, and I know you really listen. It's amazing all the stupid things men say to women. They don't really hear what they say."

"Women aren't much better when it comes to that sort of thing. One woman I dated a while back wanted to get married. After one date. It was kind of scary and that did not last long."

Sunnie suppressed a desire to ask who it was. "Not one man ever asked me to marry them. Not that I wanted to marry any of them, anyway." Sunnie mentally cringed. Why was she talking about marriage? "I think we better not continue this. I have something for you." Sunnie pulled a small box from her bag and handed it to Tom. He pulled out a small, beaded figure.

"What is it?" He asked, holding it up to inspect.

"It's a car angel. Let me show you." After fussing with it to make sure it was hanging properly from the rear view mirror, she pointed to the box. "There should be a prayer in there too. For safety. I'm sure it was specifically for policemen."

Tom looked at the angel now gracing his mirror, sparkling in the glow of the security lights on the back of the building. He removed a paper and read the prayer out loud:

"*Lord, I ask for courage; Courage to face and conquer my own fears... Courage to go where others will not go. I ask for strength; Strength of body to protect others....Strength of spirit to lead others. I ask for dedication; Dedication to my job to do it well...Dedication to my community to keep it safe. Give me, Oh Lord, concern; For all those who trust me...And compassion for those who need me. And, Please, Lord, through it all; be at my side.*"

All he could say once he read the prayer through was, "Wow. Thank you, Sunnie. This is...thanks."

"I'm glad you didn't laugh. I was afraid you'd find it kind of cheesy." Sunnie offered, not certain what to say to the wave of emotion.

"That's why I like it. How about I walk you all the way up the stairs tonight?" Agreeing with a sigh, she opened her door. Sunnie thought that her days spent with Tom ended much too soon. She thrilled that he took her hand before climbing the four flights.

"I have that crazy midday tour this week. I'm not sure how much I'll be able to come by." Tom did not miss her disappointed eyes before she looked down to their clasped hands. "More than likely I'll sleep all day next Saturday. Let's make plans to spend the day Sunday again. I'll even make sure there's ground turkey in the fridge."

Sunnie lifted her eyes back to Tom's. "It's a date. I have a busy week too. The council is meeting on the housing project and I have two other perspective properties to view. Even so...I think it's going to be a really long week."

He lifted a hand to her face, "I'll call. Text. Email. You'll be tired of me by the time Sunday comes."

Tom was certain he heard Sunnie whisper "Never," before he kissed her goodnight.

Chapter 14

"Who in the world?" Sunnie said to herself when she reached for her phone. She'd just stepped from the shower and the phone slipped from her wet hand back to the bed. She practically dropped it again when a booming voice demanded, "I expect to see you shortly, Sunnie girl!"

Floundering for an answer, Sunnie mentally ran through her schedule. "Stuart, I'm sorry but I have no idea what you're referring to?"

"The council meeting!" Stuart bellowed. "Sunnie girl, you must be here! I've been telling these men about you. You need to make an appearance."

She swallowed the panic that had risen; board meetings had been her way of life at Weston, but it had been well over three years since she'd attended one.

"Sunnie, are you there?" Stuart's inquiry brought her back to the now.

"Stuart, I wasn't prepared to attend," she stammered honestly. Regrouping, she asked, "What time is it? What should I bring with me?"

"Just you, Sunnie girl. The proposal is here; all I ask is that you come. It will be good to walk the final steps to see this come to fruition. I'll meet you in the foyer of the town hall in an hour."

Sunnie stared at the phone in her hand for only a moment before she dove into her closet to choose an outfit. Once she was satisfied with the mirror, she headed to Lakeville Town Hall.

Excitement built as she walked through the heavy doors, remembering the days when she thought Lear jets and champagne were all she needed. The amounts of money she'd seen exchange hands at times was staggering. She knew well why the real estate moguls she'd dealt with enjoyed their extravagancies, thriving on the game of chance they played.

Stuart smiled, observing Sunnie's statuesque form entering the doors. "You are a vision, Sunnie girl! I'm glad you were able to make it. Come now, let's get upstairs." Stuart took Sunnie's elbow, guiding her to the elevator.

"Thank you, Stuart. I'm still a little stunned you called me. I wasn't expecting to be able to sit in on the vote. I'm curious to see how it all works."

Stuart punched the 'Up' button, and just as quickly the 'Door Close' button. A clerk whose arms were laden with papers tried to catch a ride. The doors shut on his distraught face. Sunnie tried to smile an apology; Stuart didn't notice.

The elevator doors opened to a large domed foyer, ornate with gilded pillars and scrolled woodworking on the ceiling. The echo of Sunnie's heels sounded as they walked to a large conference room. A bound copy of her proposal lay at each seat around a large table, and the development plans were displayed in the front of the room.

Stuart led Sunnie around the table to a seat next to his. Obviously his: an ashtray sat on top of Stuart's copy of the proposal. Sunnie glanced at him with a grin.

"Exactly how do you get away with smoking in here?"

Stuart belly laughed, the rich tone carrying into the vaulted foyer.

"My dear, I know all the right people. Ah, here's one of them now..." Stuart greeted a tall man who was obviously one of the eight council members. The attitude of wealth oozed into the room as the rest of the men arrived, all nodding politely to Sunnie before gathering to talk among themselves.

Sunnie extracted her notepad and pen while observing the good-old-boy network at work. She jotted a few notes while she awaited the start of the meeting.

The tall man who had arrived first called across the table as he sat for the beginning of the meeting. "You never lose your eye for good looking secretaries, Stu. I don't believe we've had the pleasure?"

"I knew that if one of you were going to put his foot in it, it would be you, Darren. Gentlemen, this is Miss Sunnie Young, author of the proposal before you. She's here by my personal invite. I'm certain she'll be happy to quell any lingering fears."

Stuart introduced each man, including the abashed Darren MacAfee. Sunnie smiled politely—and a bit disarmingly—at each of them.

"So, let's bring this all down to brass tacks, men. This is a good proposal, and it's good for Lakeville. It reclaims property that taxes have been lax on. In fact, it will bring them up again. Useable land, going to a good use. So far, there has only been one voice of dissent. The people want it."

Stuart sat back in his chair, hands resting across his small potbelly. Sunnie was reminded of a hungry lion eyeing a watering hole full of prey. General statements of approval went back and forth across the table between the members. Sunnie eyed Darren MacAfee. She knew by his bearing that he was the lone dissenting voice. He didn't disappoint once the chatter died down. He cleared his throat and stood.

"You all know why I don't like this. I do not believe that this will bolster the tax rolls, nor the general atmosphere of the town. In fact, I firmly believe that this will open the door to all sorts of characters that we do not want or need in Lakeville. I stand by my nay. No offense to you, Ms. Young. Bringing a stunning woman to the meeting—no matter who she is–will not change my mind."

"Darren, really now. Sunnie worked hard on this, and I felt it would be advantageous for her to..." Stuart was stopped mid-sentence by Sunnie's hand on his arm. The surprise on his face turned to a grin. He extended his arm, inviting Sunnie to counter the man who was now glaring openly at her.

Sunnie turned to face him. "I should only take offense if it was truly meant, mister..." Sunnie glanced down quickly at her notepad. "MacAfee. Exactly what sort of characters are you referring to? Hard working people who would enjoy a home to call their own?"

Darren MacAfee sniggered. "Come now, Miss Young. I'm sure you're aware of the undesirable element we've been able to keep at bay here. We'll have to allow people as far as Philly to be able to apply for housing. We have more than enough low-income housing right across the tracks from that parcel of land. A shopping mall, doctor's offices...hell, even another church would bring better revenue than more lowlifes."

Sunnie gathered her thoughts and rose; the men ceased all conversation as she walked to the map. Finding the area she wanted, she pointed to a spot on the opposite side of the railroad tracks from the building site.

"Darren," Sunnie's use of first name threw him, and caused more than a few snickers among the rest. "Do you remember the explosion that happened here? Just about four years ago?"

"Of course I do, the whole town does. Probably a meth house—and good riddance." He nodded, a smug smirk on his pasty face.

"Far from it. There was a gas leak...a woman was almost killed. She raised her family in that home, family who all have become well-adjusted citizens of Lakeville. One is in the National Guard, one owns a building here in town, one owns the new bakery and coffee shop on Maple. The families on that street are all hard working, if not affluent."

She faced the skeptical man, "Where in Lakeville do you live?"

"By the country club. I fail to see what that has to do with things." Darren grumbled. Sunnie turned back to the table, looking at each man.

"It matters a great deal. Have you ever been through the low-income housing? Do you know anyone on 'that side' of Lakeville? I was raised there. Among the lowlifes—that is what you said, isn't it?" Her gaze was unapologetic. Darren MacAfee gazed back, annoyed that she was not backing down.

"Those lowlifes work hard, love their families, and shop in this town. They send their children to Lakeville schools. Worship in Lakeville churches. The few true lowlife people that are in this town are taken care of by the police force."

"There's nothing that would be better for this town than this community!" Sunnie walked back to the map. "Thirty-five sweet homes. That's thirty-five more families to live, raise their children, shop and worship in Lakeville. That would be at least ten families moved out of the old high school, with their apartments able to be repaired and revitalized. That's ten happy tax-paying families. Happy to pay a bit more taxes so they can own a small piece of Lakeville."

Stuart's mouth quirked in a small grin when he nodded to Sunnie. Taking his cue, she looked around the table, meeting their eyes with a small smile, including Darren MacAfee's.

"Mayor Jacobs, I appreciate the chance to be part if this meeting. Thank you for hearing me out, gentlemen." Sunnie walked back to the seat she had been in to gather her belongings.

Stuart leaned forward, whispering an invite to wait in his office. She nodded to the men at the table once more before exiting the room.

One of the men asked Stuart, "Exactly *who* is she again, Stu?"

"That there...that's the future mayor of Lakeville." Stuart answered with a smile.

Sunnie paced the office that reminded her of the log home she had come to love. Questions rang through her mind as the men across the hall debated: Did she make an obsolete argument? Should she have taken on Darren MacAfee, which obviously alienated him from the project more?

A sound broke her pacing. She realized it was the ringtone she had assigned to Tom as she reached for her bag to answer.

Before she had a chance to say a word, he demanded, "Where are you?"

Sunnie decided this must be the tone Tom adopted for the purposes of interrogation. She glanced at the time, seeing it was close to when Tom had to be on duty.

"I'm at the town hall. Your father invited me to sit in on the meeting over the housing proposal. I got to..."

"So you're fine. You've been there. You're fine."

Sunnie frowned, not enjoying this particular form of banter. "Yes, I am fine. Tom, what's the matter?"

He breathed a deep sigh. "Nothing now. I'm sorry to be short. Are you going to be there long?"

"At least until they finish the voting. I'm in your father's office right now."

"Please wait there for me. I'll be there in fifteen, maybe twenty minutes. Please, Sunnie. Stay there. I'm glad you're fine—I'll explain when I see you." Without so much as a goodbye, Tom was off the line. The time to contemplate his attitude was minute since Stuart swept into his office with an enormous grin.

"Sunnie girl, you are a natural! I knew I needed you there today! You shut that old windbag down and did it with style! I would offer you a cigar if I thought you'd take one!" Stuart broke out his lighter and puffed away until the end of the cigar would have lit the room. He sat down happily in his chair, casually blowing a smoke ring in the air.

"They voted unanimously. It's a go, starting next month. You should have one happy client, Sunnie. Yes sir. You are a natural."

"Stuart, why do I have the feeling that you just set me up?" Sunnie smiled across Stuart's desk. He failed to look innocent. "You did, you old sneak! If I wasn't so fond of you..."

Stuart waved his hand. "Now, now. No harm. It's the way the game is played, my dear. We could have spent hours in that room arguing with MacAfee and the vote would have been 7-1. Enough to pass, of course, but with dissent. I do not like dissent."

"No, I don't suppose you do. Thanks for the civics lesson. It's not good for the nice side of town to think badly of the not-as-nice side. I know there are problems, but the people who have them aren't only the low-income people."

Stuart agreed. "I understand that, Sunnie. Sometimes others need to be shown the light. I don't know how you kept your temper in there."

"Lots of deep breathing and prayer. I keep telling Tom that yoga is good for stress..."

Sunnie's dissertation on the merits of yoga ended with Tom entering the office. Without regard for his father's presence, he quickly crossed the room and gathered Sunnie in a fervent embrace.

"Yes, well—we'll finish that discussion another time, Sunnie. You fill Tommy in on the details of your triumph. I'll see what those men are up to..."

Leaving a trail of smoke behind, Stuart grinned as he walked past the couple and out of the door, closing it firmly behind him.

"Tom, what in the world is wrong with you? I told you I was fine...what's the matter? I can't believe you..."

He answered Sunnie's inquiry with a kiss that sent her mind reeling. Once satisfied with her response, he loosened his hold on her and led her to Stuart's chair. He situated himself on the corner of the desk, keeping a hold on her hand.

"I'm so glad that you're all right...didn't you hear your phone?"

Sunnie could only gape at Tom as he recalled the morning. "I heard over the scanner about a massive accident where you were going to look at properties. It was bad, Sunnie. Fatalities. Involving a silver Miata."

She squeezed his hand, understanding his angst.

"I've been calling and calling. I tried the shop, then the station. That's when I realized I don't know your plate number."

Pausing for a breath, Tom finally smiled down at Sunnie. "I'm sorry, but that's one thing I never, ever want to contemplate again. I'm so glad that you're fine. Very glad." The visions of her crumpled car faded from his mind.

Sunnie stood and tenderly put her arms around him. "I'm sorry you were worried about me. I'm fine...better than fine, now."

"Me too. I have to go clock in, but first I'll walk you out. Tell me about the meeting."

Several of the men were gathered in the hallway talking town business with Stuart, Darren MacAfee among them. He eyed the couple with a grim expression as they walked away hand in hand.

Chapter 15

Sunnie's trip to the mailbox several days later was rewarded by the appearance of an envelope bearing a fat commission check for her work on the housing project. Forcing herself to smile at the young mother and her two small children next to her, she sat at the counter in the coffee shop. She slit the envelope open, ignoring the other mail that had fallen from her hand. She goggled at the amount before planning an impromptu shopping excursion.

The small boy handed her the discarded mail and she thanked him with the largest cookie Silas had to offer. After insisting that Silas charge her for their coffee and treats, she bolted up the stairs to get her bag. She returned to find her bank book so she could make a deposit.

When the check was secure and her account balance reflecting the impossibly large amount, she called Tom to plan a dinner date. His enthusiastic agreement assured her their relationship was in a good place. The day couldn't have gone any better.

At home, she went about putting her newest purchases away. Satisfied with the state of her living space, it was time to get ready for their dinner date. Sunnie spun in front of the mirror when she was dressed, assured that Tom would be happy with the image reflected. With a light heart, she decided to walk, better to enjoy the balmy evening. It was already spattered with stars as she turned the corner to meet Tom.

He waved as she approached, while continuing his discussion with a man Sunnie thought she recognized. As she drew closer, she saw it was Darren MacAfee, from the council. Sunnie held in the groan, her light mood evaporating with the glare she garnered.

"Hi Tom. Hello, Mr. MacAfee." She greeted him politely—if warily—regardless of the cold stare.

"That's right; you met at the council meeting." Tom looked between them, wondering at their tight expressions. Sunnie told him they had words, but surely not enough to cause this much tension.

He turned back to Darren MacAfee. "It was nice to see you, Mr. MacAfee. We need to go get a table, it's busy in there tonight." He offered a hand to the man as a parting gesture.

Darren MacAfee took Tom's hand, shaking it slowly as he continued to scrutinize Sunnie. His eyes went wide with recognition, and he dropped his hand as though stung. "Young! Your father is John Young? Married to Sammie Slessor?"

Sunnie's stomach clenched. This was the situation she dreaded: discussing her parents–especially Jackie–with those who held no good memories. That much was apparent by his abrupt hostile stance.

"Yes, Mr. MacAfee, they are my parents." She turned a pleading look to Tom, "Please, let's go in..."

"I'm surprised, Ms. Young, that you seem to be so–normal. One would expect him to have spawned a passel of drug addicts. Your mother should have left him to rot in that rehab place he went running off to. His claims of a changed life never rang true, not to me; once a loser, always a loser."

Sunnie caught a breath, stunned by use of the same phrase she heard all her life from her grandmother. When Darren MacAfee looked from Sunnie to Tom, an ugly expression spread across his face.

"But of course, I see how the low-income housing proposal got through Stuart. Sleeping with the mayor's son helped that slide across the desk with no questions. The proverbial apple theory holds true, I suppose."

Before Tom was able to form a retort, Sunnie stepped forward and slapped Darren MacAfee across the face.

"Just to keep you informed, you complete imbecile, my father died clean and sober and took care of my mother in the end. As for my personal relationships with Tom or Mayor Jacobs, that is none of your damn business!"

People on both sides of the busy street stopped to observe the strident argument. Darren MacAfee continued as Tom pulled Sunnie back from their face-to-face stance.

He jabbed a finger to Sunnie, his face turning crimson. "This is exactly what I expect of trailer trash like you." He turned the finger to Tom. "I will see you at the station tomorrow when I press assault charges against your girlfriend, Officer. Have a wonderful dinner." He sneered before stalking down the street.

Sunnie started after him, "Trailer trash? I..."

"Sunnie. Shut. Up!" Tom demanded, pulling her toward the parking area behind the restaurant.

"What?" Sunnie turned, yanking her hand from his. "Shut up? Did you hear him?"

"Along with all of Lakeville. Come with me. Now!" He frog-marched Sunnie behind the building to the parking lot, releasing her when they arrived at the Jeep. He unlocked the passenger door and swung it open.

"Get. IN."

"No." She countered; her dark eyes were crackling with anger.

Tom's eyes widened with surprise. "Get in the Jeep, Sunnie. Now," he commanded, eyes narrowing.

"Don't use your *official* tone with me, unless I am under arrest!"

"Would you rather have this argument here—in the parking lot?"

"Are you telling me that you agree with that...that absolute jackass?" She waved a hand in the direction she last saw Darren MacAfee walk.

"That's irrelevant at this point. Do you know that if he does press charges, I'll have to testify? AGAINST you, Sunnie! Someone so quirky about hand holding in public should be just as quirky about public brawling."

Sunnie's foot stirred up dust as she stomped the ground. "I cannot believe you! As though I would allow anyone to speak to me that way!"

"And you handled it so well! Do you want a ride home or not?"

Sunnie kicked the door shut with all the strength she could muster.

"I want nothing from you. Ever."

They glowered at each other a moment before Sunnie walked away. He frowned after her until she disappeared. The little beaded angel that she had given him glittered in the glow of the streetlights when he entered the Jeep. Tom yanked it down and considered tossing it out the window before dropping it in the back seat.

The promising evening ruined, Tom went home to shovel horse stalls. Sunnie stormed into her apartment and vigorously scrubbed the bathroom until it gleamed before collapsing on the bed in tears.

Both were certain the other was to blame for the argument, although neither was certain exactly how it had escalated.

The following morning—as promised—charges were filed against Sunshine Ellen Young: battery and verbal assault. The result of a heated debate with Stuart was Darren MacAfee vowing to protest the housing development at every turn.

A call to the squad room informed Stuart that his son was out of the building. A call to the booking desk ordered the clerk to hold the charges filed. Stuart swept from his office, barking to his cowering secretary that he would be out indefinitely.

Perched on her favorite stool, Sunnie was attempting to alleviate the headache she was afflicted by with herbal tea. The hard and embarrassing truth of their argument kept Sunnie up long after she had a gleaming shower. She rose to the bait MacAfee had thrown to her, humiliating Tom in the process. For a second time, her impulsive anger caused a rift between them.

"Hey Sunn," Silas called from the register. "Is that Mayor Jacobs?"

Dread filled Sunnie's chest as she spun to look out of the window. Stuart was striding across the street, purposefully heading to the coffee shop. Her first inclination to bolt out of the back door was replaced by the Siberian option. Pushing both aside, she arranged her face into what she hoped was a pleasant smile when he pushed through the door.

He exclaimed over the success of the shop, pronounced the coffee Silas handed him best in town and gushed over Wynter's adorable factor before turning to Sunnie. The same storm she provoked in Tom's eyes the night before looked to be brewing in Stuart's. Struck by how the two resembled each other, she offered a weak smile.

"Tommy says you did quite the overhaul on the building. I thought I'd take up your invite for the grand tour."

Overwhelmed by the visit, neither Silas nor Wynter sensed the tension between Sunnie and Mayor Jacobs. She led him through the kitchen to the back stairway. Floor by floor, Stuart inspected the work Sunnie had done. They spoke to Mrs. Butler for five minutes before arriving in Sunnie's living room.

"Stuart, I don't know what to say...I am so..."

He held a hand up to quell the apology. She contritely closed her mouth.

"Explain exactly what happened. Leave no detail out."

Stuart chuckled when Sunnie recounted the slap. "Damn fool," he muttered rubbing his chin. "Tommy was there the whole time?"

Misery tinged the affirmative answer.

Stuart's expression softened as he patted Sunnie's arm. "I'm sure you and Tommy will smooth this over," he assured her, noting her tear-filled eyes. "Darren is another matter entirely. He's accused me of favoritism in the past, but this is a new low even for him. I will work on getting him to drop these absurd charges."

Sunnie started, her mouth dropping open.

"Yes, he filed first thing this morning. I have it on hold, Sunnie, don't you worry. I'll get this sorted out before long. I do want to apologize for what he said about your father. He is a representative of this town, and he should behave in a more appropriate manner as such."

Deep-rooted anger with Jackie welled up in Sunnie's heart. Would she never be rid of his legacy? "My father was no Boy Scout, Stuart. Some people enjoy reminding me of that fact."

Stuart waved his unlit cigar in the air. "No, he was wrong. As are the charges."

New mortification brought pink to Sunnie's face. "Stuart, I can't ask you to..."

"You haven't. Now, I need to be getting back. Your brother and sister-in-law seem to have a good following already. I like that. Good for the town. I'll see myself out. I want you not to worry about any of this. I'll see you soon?"

"I...well, I hope so. Thank you, Stuart." Sunnie hugged the man before showing him out. He waved as he descended the stairs, searching in his jacket pocket for his lighter. She heard it click before he was on the next flight. With a sigh, she closed the door. She walked slowly across the room and sank onto the couch to pray for the opportunity to reconcile with Tom.

Two torturous weeks had gone by since Stuart's visit. Sunnie had not heard from Tom; her call went unanswered, and she had no news of the charges on file.

Sunnie found a seat in the sanctuary as the praise band played through their first song. Breathing deep, she cleared her mind of the strife as the music swelled. She raised her hands in praise, eyes closed, allowing God's peace to pour over her once she placed all the concerns she carried at the Cross.

From the balcony, Tom regarded Sunnie as he worked to place his own hard feelings in their proper perspective. Although the excuses seemed to sound reasonable—he was on duty, arrived home later than usual—he knew he was remiss in not returning Sunnie's call. He bowed his head to pray, leaving his pride at Jesus' feet.

When the service ended, Sunnie chose to leave instead of mill about to fellowship. When she turned to walk from the seat, Tom was waiting on the end of the row. He held his hand out and nodded in the direction of the parking area. The relieved smile on Sunnie's face, as well as the hand she eagerly offered, set his mind to rest about their relationship.

Her heart soared at the feel of his hand in hers again. The hard part was coming, though. Sunnie feared it would be the last time she held Tom's hand.

She laughed as they got closer to her car, seeing Tom's Jeep parked right next to it. He grinned sheepishly as they reached their vehicles.

"I'm sorry that I didn't call you before I left, Sunnie. I shouldn't have left this unresolved. I hope you can forgive me."

"Tom, you have nothing to apologize for. I, on the other hand, have a boatload. I'm sorry that I embarrassed you. That I made such a scene...you have every reason to be annoyed with me."

"Annoyed doesn't cover it, Sunnie. I was furious."

Distressed, she looked at the ground, awaiting the final goodbye.

"Sunn? Look at me." She lifted her gaze. "I was furious. I'm not now. What I am is sorry."

Even as the pounding fear that he would drive away and forget about her beat in her chest, she replied, "I'm sorry too. Would you...can you forgive me?" Consolation, in the form of his smile, arrived.

"Of course, Sunnie. And you? You forgive me?"

"You didn't do anything, Tom."

"Yes, I did. I shouldn't have ignored your call. I especially should not have gone away for a week without speaking to you," Tom explained again.

"Yes. Of course I forgive you."

"I need you to do something for me." Tom looked embarrassed, reaching his hand in the pocket of his khakis. He pulled out the angel. "I was hoping you'd put this back. She's been riding around in the back seat a few days."

He held to out to Sunnie. She examined the somewhat mangled figurine. It looked so small in his large hand. She lifted it carefully, straightening the wings before placing it back onto the rear view mirror.

They stared at it a few moments before Tom broke the unease surrounding them. "Would you like to go to dinner today?" The invite was hopeful.

"No. I'd rather go get Chinese takeout and go home to watch the race. We've got to get in practice, you know. If we're still going."

"Sunnie, there's no way I would go without you. Go call the order in. I'll pick it up on my way over after I run home to change. The place on Birch Street?"

"Of course. There's none better."

Knowing they needed some time to rebuild, Tom offered, "How about asking Silas and Wynter to join us. Does he like racing?"

"He prefers college football. Are you sure you can handle more psychotic Young behavior?" Sunnie asked, only half in jest.

"I wouldn't miss it. I'll see you in about an hour." He hesitated only a moment before leaning in to kiss her cheek. She waved as he drove away, then pulled out her phone to tap out a message to Silas before driving herself home.

Chapter 16

Stuart shoveled the ceremonial first load of dirt for the ground breaking at the housing site. After the festivities concluded, Sunnie cautiously approached Darren MacAfee. Staying at a discreet distance, Tom kept a wary eye and ear on the discussion.

"Mr. MacAfee? May I speak with you, please?"

Clearly not wanting to stop for a chat with Sunnie, he glanced about before resigning himself to it with a shrug. His desire to ignore her was clear to all who had heard her call to him.

"What can I do for you, Miss Young? Please! That's close enough." Darren MacAfee held his arm out as a warning for Sunnie to keep a distance.

"Mr. MacAfee, I want to apologize. I'm sorry about my behavior the last time we met."

All available ears perked up at the apology. Taking his time to chew over Sunnie's words, he looked her in the eye after a glance in the direction Tom and Stuart were standing.

"Completely unacceptable behavior, young lady. You should be ashamed. I'm certain your *mother* didn't raise you that way."

Refusing to allow the anger to boil over again, she clenched her teeth before nodding. She had done all she could do to soothe the man's damaged ego.

"You're right, Mr. MacAfee; she did not. I do hope you can forgive me. I assure you it will not happen again."

Darren MacAfee held his hand out to Sunnie. When she moved forward to accept his hand, he did not lose the opportunity at one last jab.

"I still don't like this idea." He waved his arm around the project site. "Let me tell you, Miss Young; just because you are sorry does not mean I will drop the charges. A lesson in personal responsibility seems to be in order. A lesson your father didn't learn."

"Of course. You do what you think best, Mr. MacAfee. If it should come to that, I will see you in court, ready to answer for my behavior. I hope you have a pleasant day, Mr. MacAfee."

They quickly dropped their hands and turned away, both relieved the distasteful moment had passed. Stuart stalked past Sunnie, determined to have a final say. Tom's arm about her shoulder led her away from the site towards the Jeep.

"I wish your father wouldn't worry about this. What will happen? I mean—I wouldn't go to jail?" She cast a nervous glance over her shoulder to see Stuart waving his arm and a cloud of smoke billowing from his cigar.

"Do you have a record?"

Sunnie poked his ribs with her elbow. "Of course not! But he's a council member. Does that matter?"

"It shouldn't. You might have a hefty fine. I know Pop has been sitting on it, hoping he would have changed his mind by now. It's been a while."

"Not long enough," Sunnie said under her breath as they reached the Jeep.

"Let's get some lunch. We can make plans for July 4th. It's my first one off in years and I want to have some fun! What do you usually do?"

"Vic's party. Although without Steven's fireworks, it's just not the same. I was hoping Si would bring some this year."

"Didn't you see enough fireworks at the race last weekend?" They recalled the high points and results of the event as they drove through town.

"What do you want?" he asked when they pulled up to the old Dairy Queen. Ignoring Sunnie's faux-vomiting, he left the Jeep to place an order while she fiddled with the radio stations. She shook her head when he returned with several bags of food and hopped out to hold them so he could open the back gate.

Tom pulled food from the bags, handing Sunnie an order of onion rings over her protestations.

"These are—by far—the most disgusting things I've eaten since the race."

"You've got to be kidding. You didn't even finish that chili dog!"

Sunnie rolled her eyes before sipping her thick shake. "I had you to finish it for me. I don't understand how you stay in shape when you eat the way you do,"

"Who says I'm in shape?" Tom asked while unwrapping his second cheeseburger.

"Just because I like things to stay uncomplicated between us doesn't mean I don't appreciate things, Officer. I notice you dress nice on Sundays. I love how you look in uniform. When I watch you play basketball, you're always so focused on the game you never notice the women watching you."

"Get real, Sunnie. What women watch me? Name one." As she rattled off the names of several women at the last game, crimson creeped up Tom's face. Sunnie giggled before taking another onion ring.

"Sorry to embarrass you, Officer. I hope you can keep your concentration at the next game. You're a nice looking man...of course women look." She could continue about his broad shoulders or how much she looked forward to his kiss goodnight. Before she lost herself in thoughts of far more passionate situations, she redirected the conversation.

"So, basketball. You played football in high school. When did you switch?"

This was one time he didn't mind Sunnie changing the subject to something sedate.

"Police academy. They had a great team. I always liked it in high school, and it's easier on the body than football ever was. Pop wouldn't have cared if I played either or none, but he enjoys football. Penzi played, so I tried out. No big deal."

"Okay, Mister All-American," Sunnie teased him. "If I remember correctly, you won that homecoming game."

She tossed an onion ring at him when he unconvincingly swooned over her bad memory, mentioning he was also MPV their senior year. As they laughed, Sunnie pulled her legs into the Jeep and tried not to act as though a hideous wild beast had just walked up to them.

"What's wrong?" Glancing around the tailgate, Tom spotted squirrels digging in the garbage cans. He tossed some French fries at them, and they scattered.

"You didn't have to do that. I know in my head they won't come over by us. But, thanks." Sunnie smiled. "Are you going to come to Vic's with me on the fourth?"

"Sure. I must protect you from squirrels. One condition." He grinned when Sunnie tossed her head and turned her back on him. Her false annoyances amused him.

"I'd love to go out to dinner when I get back from Guard duty. I'm on a week after the fourth. A nice, sit-down dinner, dressed to the nines. What do you think?"

"Nothing's stopping you from going out to dinner." Sunnie laughed when Tom's mouth dropped open. "Oh, that was good, I got you."

A determined expression crossed Tom's face. He put his remaining fries down and stepped from the Jeep. Before she realized what he intended, he pulled Sunnie from the back and dropped to one knee.

With a firm grip on her hand, he looked into her started, pink face. "Sunshine Young, would you do me the honor of being my dinner companion one week after the date of July four? Please excuse my boorish behavior, but your incomprehensible beauty has taken away my senses."

"That was the worst British accent I've ever heard, YES! I will go with you; now please get up before someone sees you!" Her face was seven shades pinker than it ever had been.

Tom rose and kissed the hand he was still holding. She pulled it from him, mumbling over his lost sanity as she busily stuffed their garbage into bags. He held a satisfied grin on his face when he took the bags to throw them away. Sunnie remained in the Jeep, lest a renegade squirrel returned.

When they arrived at Sunnie's, Tom walked her up the stairs with the usual plan in mind. In an unexpected change of pace, Sunnie pulled herself against him in an intimate embrace when he leaned in to kiss her goodnight. With colossal effort, he interrupted the tantalizing moment.

"Assuring I won't forget you while I'm gone?"

Admitting what she enjoyed in their relationship ignited the spark she'd been trying to keep snuffed. She'd give him more than something to remember; the time had come to show him how she felt.

The vampish smile that appeared sent warmth up his spine to the tips of his tightly curly hair. She leaned forward, so close to his ear her lips brushed the lobe when she whispered.

"Do you want to...stay a while?"

Tom stepped back to lean against the wall, towing Sunnie along. The movement did not deter another ardent embrace, broken only long enough for Tom to murmur an acceptance to the invitation. He was more focused on caressing the area he knew a Celtic knot lay hidden under the thin cotton shirt.

During a pause for breath, Sunnie glanced on the floor, looking for her discarded pocketbook. They both stiffened when a voice behind her sounded.

"You dropped it by the door."

Sunnie spun around, releasing the arms that were locked around Tom's neck. He dropped his hands to his side and stood straighter as they both worked to compose themselves under Silas's scrutiny.

"Hey...Si. Why...what are you doing up here?" she asked, bending to retrieve the purse.

"I heard you come in, I need to talk to you about installing something in the kitchen. I didn't realize you'd be–occupied."

He and Tom engaged in a brief and uneasy staring contest before Tom cleared his throat.

"I better go, Sunnie. I'll keep in touch."

Feeling defiant, he kissed her one more time before nodding to Silas. Sunnie watched until his bright hair disappeared in the stairwell. She turned a hot gaze to her brother.

"Install whatever you need, Si! You don't need my permission!"

"No. I don't suppose I do."

She stopped digging through the bag long enough to realize Silas knew exactly what was happening and felt a rush of relief that he stopped it from going farther than it should have.

In the Jeep, Tom was staring at the angel, replaying the situation several times before letting loose a long sigh.

"That was close, Lord. Too close."

July fourth dawned characteristically humid for Lakeville, with a perfect evening for firework viewing promised. The party was in full swing by the time Sunnie and Tom arrived. After they ate and played several rounds of volleyball, she took him to walk the grounds of Victoria's massive property.

"I used to love walking out here early in the morning," Sunnie said as they headed away from the crowd. "Except for a random squirrel, it's beautiful back here."

Tom put his arm about Sunnie's shoulders. "It's nice. A bit too manicured for me, but nice. It needs a creek—something wild."

They walked quietly a bit, enjoying each other's presence. They were a good way away from the party, when Sunnie had the overwhelming urge to ask a question; it was out of her mouth before she thought better of it.

"Why didn't you marry that girl?"

Tom stared at her curiously before answering. "I was just out of the Academy. It was supposed to be a casual date. I wasn't looking or ready to get married at that point."

He stopped, his arm dropping to grasp her hand in his, wondering if Sunnie would allow the discussion to get beyond the surface. As usual, she attempted to shut it down as quickly as she had brought it up.

"I'm sorry, that was...well, it's not my business."

"Don't you think about getting married someday?"

"Married? Please! Do I seem like a marrying type of girl?"

"Of course. To the right man. One who will appreciate you as you."

"Well, if you meet him, let me know. Let's get back. It's starting to get dark. I don't want them to miss us." Sunnie turned to walk back the way they had come.

Tom pulled her back, into his arms. Every thought was erased from her mind at the feel of his lips on hers. Different from the sweet and safe kiss that she knew, this demanded a response to the unspoken question. She struggled with her own desires a moment before supplying the answer.

The intake of breath–his breath, her breath, their breath together–pushed the thin wall of propriety to the limit. Somewhere, something in Tom's mind was telling him this was not the time or the place; they had averted this once already.

Someone called his name, although it could not have possibly been Sunnie. She was otherwise engaged.

"Sunnie? Tom! Where are you guys?" The unwelcome voice belonged to Silas.

He must have some kind of annoying brother radar, Tom thought. It might have been wishful thinking on Tom's part since he was reluctant to let Sunnie go, but Silas sounded a good distance from where they were.

She heard the call, Tom knew. He felt the change, subtle as it was, before she pulled away. This was not the proper moment to demand she marry him—to let her know that he, indeed, was the man. In their current level of fervency, it would not have appeared remotely sincere. He looked deep into her eyes as Silas called to them again.

"You're gonna miss the fireworks!"

"You heard him," he said, releasing her from his arms.

"I've had all the fireworks I can handle for one day," she said in a husky whisper before starting back.

Tom hung back several steps to regain himself, a task not easily completed with the hidden tattoo striding down the path in front of him. The problem–he knew–was try as he might to forget it, his mind could call up the image as easily as a blind man could read Braille. The bigger issue–which he steadfastly ignored–was that he did not *want* to erase it.

Chapter 17

Tom arrived at Sunnie's fifteen minutes early for their date, chalking up his nervous energy to the box in his pocket. He planned on talking with her on a more serious level, no matter how many times she tried to divert the subject. He felt confident that she would open up to him—that he could coax her beyond the fears she clung to.

"Okay, Officer. Let's roll," he encouraged himself after spending three and a half minutes drumming the steering wheel. With sunflowers in hand, he stepped from Stuart's luxury car, squared his shoulders, and strode toward the building.

Upstairs, Sunnie crammed six rejected dresses back into the closet after choosing a peach silk she was certain she hadn't worn to church—at least not since they'd been dating. She juggled several pair of nylons until a knock made the decision for her—none. Quickly stuffing them back into a drawer, she hurried from her room. Uncertain why this date unsettled her so, she took a few deep breaths before answering the door.

Tom, always attractive, looked exceptionally handsome. The gray suit accentuated and advertised every muscle in his arms and shoulders, and one glance at his broad smile and killer blue eyes screamed, "Perfection!"

"Come on in," she remembered to say as she stepped aside.

"You look great, Sunnie. That's a terrific color on you." Tom held out the sunflowers. "I rescued them from Picasso and Beau."

"Thank you...I do love sunflowers." The transforming smile appeared. "I should have something to put them in. Let me take care of these, and I'll get my shoes. Where are we going that we have to leave so early?"

"All I'm telling you is that I have Pop's car. He insisted that I 'could not take a fine woman like Sunnie girl on a date to the mystery place in that contraption.'"

Sunnie laughed at his parody of Stuart. With the florals in their proper spot, she disappeared to her room for one last perusal in the mirror.

"He actually complimented the color...no man does that!" she told herself in the mirror before sliding her shoes on and picking up her bag from the end of the bed. He was so unlike any man she'd ever been out with. Certainly none had kissed her so thoroughly as he had at Victoria's. The rush of mixed emotions that stirred momentarily took her breath.

Pushing at an imagined stray hair, she attempted to force those thoughts from her mind, knowing they would lead to the place she was afraid to enter, yet eager to arrive at. They refused, lingering as she flicked the light off and returned to the living room.

"Ready. Where are we going?"

Tom held the door open for Sunnie. "I am not telling you. It's a bit of a ride, but the scenery is great along the way."

They waved hello to Mrs. Butler on their way out. She waved at them, murmuring about what a handsome couple they were.

"No, we aren't! The Parkington?" Sunnie cried as she spotted the immense luxury hotel appear on the horizon. "Tom! My mother still raves about this place, and it's been over two years since she's been here. Are we...what are we doing?"

"Dinner and dancing. I hear they have a glorious garden to walk through. Lights, quiet spots, the works. Whatever you want to do."

"Oh, I'd love to stay overnight. Mom says they have the most amazing Jacuzzis in the rooms. Just the thought of waking up in those beds..." Sunnie clapped her hand over her mouth. "I mean...well, I didn't mean...Tom, I may not talk the rest of the night."

Sunnie didn't see the flush creeping up his face as he turned into the drive. As Paul's words of wisdom popped into his head, Tom prayed for soundness of mind as he pulled up to the valet. He dismissed the not-unpleasant images that projected themselves into his mind's eye.

A sign announcing a Glenn Miller-style orchestra was prominent in the ornate atrium, music from one ballroom drifting through the grand foyer. Tom led Sunnie to the luxurious main dining room, gave the maître d' his name, and in moments they were seated in front of an enormous window with a beautiful view of the garden.

"Tom, this is so...so wonderful," Sunnie breathed while Tom held her chair. She turned back to him, her face glowing. "We must walk through that. By the time we finish, it should be dark."

"I told you, Sunnie, whatever you want. Pop says they have great steaks here. I assured him you wouldn't touch it," he added playfully as he sat. Their waiter appeared, introducing himself as Marco. He handed them menus while ticking off ten assorted specials and took their appetizer order before leaving them to decide dinner choices.

"Tom, I can't remember half of what he said," Sunnie commented. She closed her menu and handed it to Tom. "You order for me."

"Me? I don't see tofu anywhere." Tom looked dubious.

"I'll eat whatever you order, with a good attitude. I can eat steak."

Marco returned with their tray of appetizers. As Tom recited their order, Sunnie lost herself in the music from the ballroom. Once Marco left, Tom moved his chair over and took Sunnie's hand. He bowed his head and prayed a short, touching prayer over their dinner and evening.

"Now tell me how you do that." Sunnie said, while she placed one of each morsel on small plates.

"Do what?"

"How do you sit in a room like this—with all the people around—take my hand and pray as though we were alone?"

Tom shrugged. "I just do."

Sunnie shook her head. "You are so frustrating."

"Because I prayed before we ate?"

She sighed before nibbling at the mushroom on her fork. "No...because it's so easy for you to do. I never feel like anything is that easy. Maybe I think too much."

"It gets easier. When you're alone with Him, isn't it easy?" Tom watched her over the plate, ignoring the enticing aromas.

"Oh, sure! It's the only time I ever feel like I can be me...I can be who He made me to be. I can laugh, cry, sing, dance..."

"So, why is it hard to be you in a more public place? It gets easier as you grow. It doesn't bother me to thank God for my dinner, and if it bothers someone else, well, that's between them and God. Not me."

"I want to be more like you, Tom. Not afraid to be me. Silas always calls me his 'tough big sister.' I guess that's how I was for so long, it's ingrained."

"I remember, Sunnie. That was a long time ago. It's part of you. I told you; you are unique."

Sunnie frowned. "I believe you told me I was *unusual*, not unique, Officer."

Tom laughed. "See? That's what I mean. You really aren't afraid to be you. It's becoming the new you that you aren't as comfortable with yet. It'll come."

She pondered the discussion while Marco cleared the plates from the table. He placed steaming crocks overflowing with melted cheese in front of each of them, then left them to their soup and privacy. Sunnie looked at the crock, then at Tom.

"This is my favorite soup, you know. How do you do this every time?"

"I told you, I observe. Maybe it's an occupational hazard. Of all the choices, this made the most sense when I thought, 'What would Sunnie want?' Unless you feel better if I said I had special mind reading powers."

"Just what I need, to be dating an alien. I'll let you know when I need a mind meld, thank you."

Tom grinned, admitting that people called him worse things than an alien, causing Sunnie to giggle. They enjoyed the course mostly without conversation. When Marco came back to clear their table, he had a single pink daisy in hand. He presented it to Sunnie, commenting that she was his most beautiful patron of the evening, and she simply must have this small gift. Sunnie thanked him, blushing wildly while he cleared the table.

"I told you." Tom said while she fussed with the water glass and the flower.

"Well, that was, hmm..."

"Unusual. Out of all the women in this room, Marco brought you a flower." Tom took her hand. "At least he knows who the most stunning woman in the room is."

"I'm slightly suspicious that you paid him." Sunnie changed the subject, as she often did. "I'm not sure how much more I can eat. I hope there's not a lot more coming."

Tom squeezed her hand before he let go, allowing the opportunity to pass. "I'm sure you'll manage fine. Promise me one thing. Enjoy dessert."

"I love dessert! Why wouldn't I enjoy it?"

"Most women don't—or at least won't admit that they want to or enjoy it. Just more of your unique personality. Here comes Marco. I'm sure you'll love it." Sunnie decided if it was a raw steak on a skewer she would love it because he assured her that she would.

She gasped in surprise when Marco set a large plate before her, piled high with vegetarian Paella, topped by grilled artichoke hearts. Tom's steak and shrimp scampi sizzled on the hot plate before him, the aroma of garlic filling their table.

When Marco sauntered away, Sunnie took Tom's hand. "Thank you so much! This looks wonderful...like way too much, but wonderful!"

Tom was pleased with the look of pure delight on Sunnie's face. He would be more pleased if he could steer the discussion the way he'd intended and decided that dessert might be a good time.

Sunnie was still trying to pick out the vegetables by the time Tom had finished his plate. She surrendered her fork to the table. "I do not know how you eat so much and where you put it all. I hope I can enjoy dessert."

"You will; you'll see." He waved to Marco. He made his way over to their table. "Marco, I have a request."

"Anything, Mr. Jacobs. What can we get you?" He bowed, his smile genuine.

"Nothing now. We're going to dance and walk the garden before dessert."

"Naturally. Would you like your dessert on the garden patio?"

"Perfect—thank you, Marco. I'll let you know when we're ready for the garden. Ready, Sunnie?"

She nodded, taking her daisy from the table.

The band was in full swing as they entered the ballroom. Many of the couples were elegantly attired, men in tuxedos and women in vintage ball gowns. They observed the dance floor before joining the crowd, enjoying several more lively numbers.

"You are wonderful! I'm not much for some older stuff, but this is fun." She exclaimed during a break between songs. The next song cued and Tom held Sunnie closer as they spun to "Moonlight Serenade."

"I could dance with you all night." She sighed happily, leaning fully into him as the music drifted through the room.

"If you let me, I will," he breathed in her ear. Recalling her thoughts on public displays of affection, he assumed the night would end in a row if he dropped to his knee on the dance floor. Finding the right moment to propose was becoming a larger challenge than he thought it would be.

The lights dimmed, and both entertained thoughts about the soft beds and jacuzzis Sunnie had mentioned earlier. Applauding from the dance floor brought their attention back where it should have been.

"How about that walk?" Tom suggested. Sunnie looked disappointed, but agreed. After stopping by Marco, they were through the doors onto an elaborate terrace with a view of the whole garden walk. They set out to see it up close, being introduced to an explosion of roses and twinkling lights along the way.

Marco appeared as they walked to a table at the end of the cloistered footpath. He presented them with two plates laden with bubbling chocolate cake, and the cheque wallet. He smiled broadly and exited.

"Tom, what is this? I've never seen this before." Sunnie turned the hot dish around to look at it from every angle.

"The Parkington Chocolate Volcano. Dessert was easy to pick. Everyone loves chocolate." Sunnie's answer was a smile.

No opening appeared for Tom to steer the conversation the way he hoped. He determined to have Sunnie's attention focused on the subject at her place; he would not allow the night to end without it.

Picking up his fork in one hand, he reached for her hand with the other. She entwined her fingers in his, giving him a glimpse of hope that his request would be positively received.

Chapter 18

"What a beautiful night! Thank you so much, Tom."

Tom leaned against the wall while she unlocked the door. "Mind if I stay a while? I'd really like to spend more time with you, Sunnie." *The rest of our lives, if only you'd agree*, he almost added.

Sunnie glanced over, the ice blue eyes taking a bit of her breath away as they always did. "I'd like that. Come on in."

She dropped her keys and bag on the table. "Would you put some water on for tea? You know where everything is. I'll be right back."

Draping his jacket over a chair, Tom pulled at his tie, loosening buttons as he rehearsed a proposal. In the kitchen, he pulled two mugs from the cabinet, filled the kettle, and opened the cabinet to peruse Sunnie's tea vast selection. Being so diverse in choice, he turned to ask about her preference. Instead, he lost all sense of what he was doing when he saw her standing at the other end of the counter.

Sunnie had changed to an alluring summer dress. More than alluring. She looked downright dangerous for any man to be alone with–especially accessorized by her sultry smile.

"What's the matter? Stumped by tea overload? Here, this one is great for a late night mug."

She stepped closer, reaching across him to retrieve a brightly colored box. The now-familiar scent of patchouli from Sunnie's loose hair was heady. It was difficult to curb the rush of thoughts that entered his mind with no effort.

Tom turned off the flame under the whistling pot. "Sure, Sunnie. Whatever you say; you're the tea expert. Maybe you should put on something—different."

The suggestion was weak, at best.

Sunnie was confident she achieved the desired effect. From the moment he held her on the dance floor, her battle was surrendered. It was now her mission to break down his resistance.

"I like this dress. Don't you like it?" Tom turned from the mugs and looked into her dark eyes.

"I do—that's the problem. I like it a bit too much," he answered in a tone as dangerous as the dress. "Sunnie, I want to talk about us. Your outfit choice is—" He worked on some mental regrouping. "—distracting."

Sunnie ignored the comment and picked up a mug. "Let's sit. I'll put on a CD and we can talk."

With only a brief span of hesitation, Tom followed her into the living room. The back of the dress, or lack thereof, had more of an effect on him than the front. The tattoo he failed to purge from his mind was on vivid display. Concentration was going to be a turf-war he might not emerge from victoriously, if at all.

"So, what are we discussing?" Sunnie asked, sliding close when he sat.

While his fingers lightly played through the ends of Sunnie's curls, a feeble warning to leave sounded through his mind. He was too entranced by the smooth skin of her shoulder to pay any mind to it.

"Discussing?"

"You said you wanted to discuss...something." She pulled the knot of his tie loose, allowing the cool silk to slip through her fingers.

The vestiges of propriety Tom held on to evaporated as he pulled Sunnie into his arms. Intensity quickly built, and Tom whispered his proposal—a different one than planned. With no hesitation, Sunnie accepted, leading him to her bedroom.

The pleasant sense of drifting experienced when waking from a deep sleep flowed quickly away when Tom's eyes opened. Rolling over to glance at his watch, contrition set in as he took in the time and place. A frustrated breath involuntarily emitted as he laid back and threw an arm over his eyes. The realization of their actions hit Tom full force.

Oh Lord! How did I let this happen? This was the very hurt he had wanted to spare Sunnie.

He dressed while Sunnie was in the shower. He thought to run downstairs for coffee, but just as quickly discarded the idea. It would be obvious to all that he had spent the night. He would not compromise Sunnie any further. Instead, he went into the kitchen to put on water for tea.

While Tom agonized in the kitchen over boiling water, Sunnie struggled in the shower. She was certain her actions had destroyed their relationship. She would not allow herself to believe Tom was in love with her, no matter how many times he'd declared it the previous evening.

The memory of the night mortified her; how could she have given herself over to him so willingly, and with so much abandon? She painfully understood, all too late, exactly why she should have heeded the still, small voice. The roar of the raging fire had drowned it out.

The satisfaction she felt when she woke up dissolved into embarrassment and shame as choice verses from Proverbs filled her mind. She was not feeling attractive as she raced to her room to get dressed. When she finally emerged, she couldn't decide whether to retreat and never face Tom again, or sit weeping at his feet and beg his forgiveness.

Tom sensed her indecision, breaking the awkward moment with a smile. He patted the couch, inviting her to join him. "Hi there; I made you some tea."

She hesitated before approaching the couch. Unsure of what to expect, she sat by him, her dark eyes registering doubt. Tom covered her hand with his, feeling it tense at his touch.

"I hope you can forgive my lack of control last night. Please believe that I did not want to stay to take advantage of you. I'm very sorry."

"Tom, I...Well, I'm a bit confused. I should be the one apologizing to you. It was my intent, from the minute we left the restaurant last night. Please, listen to me. I need to get this out right now, or I'll never be able to."

She turned her attention back to her cooled tea, spilling a few drops onto her jeans. She willed her hands to stop trembling before she replaced the cup.

"When I moved back and started attending The Tabernacle, I finally understood so much of what living as a Christian meant. I was happy to give up unproductive things: smoking, drinking, bad language. I still need to work on that last. I honestly never gave physical relationships any thought. I never thought I'd meet someone. Even if I did, what safer place to deal with it than in church?"

She stole a glance at Tom. He seemed to understand, so she continued.

"I enjoy things with you, being in a relationship that I never thought would exist for me. I can be *me* when I'm with you. Like my mom and Rob, my sisters—even Silas and Wynter. There's something deeper to it all. I think it hit me this morning. It's their relationship to God first. That's what makes them different."

This is what Tom wanted—what he had been hoping would happen the previous evening. It seemed Sunnie was finally opening up. He squeezed her hand as an encouragement to continue.

"I'm not sure what to do in a normal relationship. This...well...last night...was the next logical step for me. I was tired of fighting it, and now I ruined—us."

"Sunnie, we both..." She looked away as understanding of her odd behavior dawned on his face. Tom saw the wall go up; she was pushing him away again. He wasn't going to let her without a fight.

"I wish you would have told me sooner. I've been having the same struggle. I should have known not to give us an opportunity to stumble." Paul's advice rang too clearly in his head. "Nothing is ruined in my mind, Sunnie."

She stayed silent. He started to offer a solution he thought would be adequate.

"We'll have to be more cautious now, of course..."

"Don't say whatever it is you were going to say, please! I can't be *careful* with you, not now. Another time I would have invited you to stay—move in. I understand why that's not possible now. I don't know what to do now, and it's all my own fault."

She left Tom an opportunity to make a clean break. His answer was one she was not prepared to hear.

"Be my wife."

As Sunnie sputtered and coughed on the tea she was drinking, Tom got up from the couch. From his jacket pocket, he pulled a small box. Once he was assured that Sunnie was fine, he placed the box in her hand.

"I bought this weeks ago. Last night, my plan was to talk about all these obstacles that bother you, give you this, and ask you to marry me. You've got to know that I love you. I think we have a good thing—good enough to make permanent. Sunnie, I want to know. What are you afraid of?"

Sunnie leaned back on the couch with an impatient sigh. How could she explain that while her heart pounded wildly whenever they were together, she was afraid? She knew how painful deeper relationships were. It would be especially hard now, after last night.

"Tom, it's all so..."

"Complicated." Tom finished the aggravating sentence that belonged to a tired argument. "Don't say it. Life is complicated. Do you remember what Paul said a few weeks ago? About moving forward, out of the comfort zone you're in?"

Sunnie scowled. "He was talking about ministry, not personal relationships. Don't twist his lesson to fit your argument. Besides that, I—we—I just complicated it times a thousand."

Shame, followed by pain, crossed Tom's face.

"As far as that specific 'complication' goes, I told you I am sorry. I should have known better, been able to stop when it was going too far. I should have left the minute I saw you in that dress."

Tom paused to clear from his mind the memory; he already failed at that once and it had gotten them to this point. He couldn't carry that in his head or his heart.

"Please don't use that as an excuse. I understand now why you fight with me so often. It keeps you safe, so we can't get too close." Tom's frustration was vented. "Truthfully, Sunnie, you make it very hard for a man to love you."

Sunnie waved her hand. "Tom! Don't. You don't have to declare undying love to me because of last night."

"Because of last night?" Tom spat, conveying the sting he felt from her rebuff. "I thought you would know me better than that by this time. I wouldn't tell you I love you 'just because.' It's no excuse, but it's the truth."

"Tom, I told you that it's not your fault." Sunnie weakly argued.

"Yes, it is. So, what's it going to be, Sunnie? I do love you. That's more than enough for me. No matter what is going on around us, regardless of anything past."

The answer she wanted to joyfully shout stayed locked behind her wall of fear and doubt. "I'm not sure, Tom. I enjoy being with you. More than anything. I just don't know if I can make it...let it be...more."

When Tom looked away, she knew she broke his heart. Her own wasn't faring all that well. The tears almost came when he turned back.

"You *can't*, Sunnie? Or you *won't*? That's a big difference." Tom rose, pulling her from the couch. With a gentle smile he pushed a loose curl back from her face—the one that always seemed to be there. His hand lingered at her chin a moment before he went on.

"I want a life with you. Married, children, growing old together. The whole thing. I want you to be by my side for life. Will I never, ever hurt you? I can't promise you that. I know what I can say—that I wouldn't purposely hurt you. I didn't want to hurt you last night. I know I did, and I am so sorry for not being a better man about it."

Tom leaned forward, kissing Sunnie as he always did. The wonderful, romantic kiss. This time it felt like goodbye—forever.

"This is up to you, Sunnie. You seem to be bent on staying safe. Safe is lonesome. Very lonesome. When you decide to open up your heart, I'll be waiting." He walked across the room, gathered his jacket, and paused at the door. He turned back. "I hope it's not going to be a very long time."

Tom closed the door quietly when he walked out. Sunnie's confused and hurting heart heard it slam. The box was still unopened in her hand. Would she really allow him to walk out of her life? Could she leave all the fears behind to allow Tom into the places she never allowed anyone?

She put aside all the things she knew were right and manipulated—no, she had blatantly seduced the only man she ever cared about. Sunnie closed her eyes, too miserable for tears to come. The man she could be happy with; the one she could trust and love completely walked out of her door. Now what could she do?

Silas glanced at the brilliant sky before he tossed the bags into the dumpster. He saw Tom as he was turning to go back inside but the greeting he was going to call died in his throat. The unbuttoned shirt flapped in a light breeze, and he carried the jacket over his shoulder. Tom was headed to the car that had been there overnight.

His first reaction—to meet Tom at the car and pound him into sausage meat—gave way to the need to speak to Sunnie post haste. He stalked through the kitchen to scan the shop occupancy. The breakfast crowd was gone save one lingering customer at the counter.

"Wynnie, I'll be back in a few. I need to go see Sunnie." He pulled off the green apron and tossed it on the workstation.

Wynter followed him into the kitchen, seeing an expression on his face she wasn't sure she had ever seen. "Si Bear, what's wrong?" She called to him as he walked out, cringing when he punched the dumpster as he strode past it.

Sunnie found Tom's tie buried between couch cushions as she straightened the room. If it hadn't been for insistent pounding on her door, she would have dissolved in tears. She answered, Tom's tie still in hand.

Silas's scowling stance—complete with arms crossed over his chest—was reminiscent of the angry father she remembered so well.

"Si! What's wrong?"

He brushed past her. "Listen, Sunn, I don't care if he's an officer—next time I see him I may break his face. Tell me what happened." He paused to control his anger. "Did he force you?"

Outrage to match her brother's appeared on Sunnie's face. "Like it's your business, Si! How dare you assume what's happened here! You aren't my father!"

"I saw him, Sunn. I know. Strutting out of the building half undressed, parading his conquest out in the daylight. Like you're some cheap piece of trash. I won't have him treating you like the town slut!"

Sunnie laughed bitterly at Silas's remarks. Her little brother, defending her tarnished honor.

"Gee, Si. It's just amazing how you've assumed the blame is all his. I'm a big girl, capable of making my own choices. No matter how poor they may be. Maybe I lured him upstairs and seduced *him*." She turned from him and sat on the couch, wadding up the tie in her hand unconsciously.

"I've seen that he can't keep his hands off you! He's a Christian man. He shouldn't be taking advantage of you!" Silas countered as he followed her across the room.

"If that's all you wanted, Silas, you can go. I have things I need to do. Please don't bother yourself about my reputation. Tom hasn't ruined it any more than I have in the past." Sunnie's voice broke. She wondered if that was good enough for a confession of her sins.

"Si...please just go. I really don't need you banging on my door, acting all Jackie-like. It's very annoying. I had enough of that when he was alive. Never being *good enough* for him. Now I'm not good enough for you either. Or Tom. Please go away. Don't you have cookies to bake or something?"

Silas sat down on the couch next to Sunnie. Whatever had happened, he could see she was not handling it well. He saw the box on the table and reached for it, opening it before Sunnie thought to stop him. He stared at the ring Sunnie hadn't looked at, eyes wide with surprise.

"Sunn! Are you going to marry him?"

She looked over at the box. Snuggled in the velvet was a slim white gold band with a single flawless blue diamond—as clear as Tom's eyes—perched in the prongs. She'd never have the chance to look into those wonderful eyes again. Sunnie pulled it from Silas's hand and tossed it across the room with a howl of misery. "Please get out of here!"

Silas didn't budge from the couch. Once she composed her emotions, she pleaded with him, "Keep this to yourself, please? I mean it, Si...no Mom, no Jude. I have to think on this. I'll try not to...well, I don't really know. Did Wynter make muffins today? I'm pretty hungry."

Silas smiled, knowing his sister did not want to discuss things further. The anger between them diffused, and an understanding settled in.

"You know we have them every day. You coming down or calling in a delivery?"

Sunnie hugged Silas around his neck. "Thanks Si. I'll come down in a few minutes. Do me another favor?" Sunnie wiped her eyes on the back of her hand. She looked so vulnerable, so unlike the 'tough big sister' he used to know so well.

"Sure, Sunn. Anything."

"Would you pray for me? I don't know how I feel. No, I do know, but I'm afraid to feel like I feel. Ugh, Si, go away. I'll be down soon." Sunnie shoved him, and Silas rose from the couch.

"You know you've changed...no, let me start again. The Lord has changed you so much, Sunn. I always loved you, but getting to know you—the you that's in Jesus—I really LIKE you now. I can see that you're happy, Really happy for the first time in a very long time. Don't let old feelings over Dad, or anything else, keep you from Tom. There's nothing so terrible that happened that couldn't be made right. Whatever this was..." Silas paused. "Whatever happened, Sunn, God knows. And forgives. Don't forget that. See you at the shop. I'll save your favorite stool."

"When did my little brother grow to be so wise?" she pondered after he closed the door. She shook her head and unraveled Tom's tie from her fingers, smoothing it out as she did. It mirrored Sunnie's fears over their relationship...beyond repair and smoothing over.

She looked in the vicinity she had tossed the ring box, finding it under the entertainment center after getting on her hands and knees. Sunnie placed it on her nightstand on top of her Bible. She had much praying to do, but not at that moment. She needed to try to enjoy a muffin with her brother.

Chapter 19

Deep in contemplation over the morning's events, Tom did not notice his father as he walked up the steps.

"Had a rough night, son?" Stuart called from the swing. He took in the disheveled appearance without further comment.

Tom glanced over and paused with a hand on the handle of the front door. "More like a rough morning. I'll be out in a few. I need to wash up and grab some coffee."

He was back twenty minutes later with a cup in hand. He sat on a chair across from his father, sipping his coffee in silence. Stuart was not one to wait for details to be offered.

"How was the date? Service good? Did Sunnie girl enjoy it?"

Tom nodded with a distracted air. "Yeah, Pop. It was a great date. It's a nice place, thanks for getting the reservation. Sunnie had a great time. She did."

Stuart pulled a cigar out of his shirt pocket, and bit off the end. Tom watched him—puff, puff, puff until it was lit, knowing he wouldn't get away without a better explanation. He knew the look of expectation on his father's face.

"Sorry. It was a really great date. Dinner was excellent and so was the dancing. It was the 'after' part that got dicey. We went back to Sunnie's, and things..."

Tom let out a great breath as he raked a hand over his head. "I asked her to marry me."

Stuart's elated grin faded fast at the expression on his son's face. He understood all too well how Tom was felling at that moment.

"Sunnie's a spirited girl, Tommy. One thing's certain—she cares about you. A blind man would know that. Give her the space she needs, boy. She's well worth the wait. Just like your mother." Stuart's voice softened at the mention of his late wife.

"I know, Pop. I just hope Sunnie doesn't take as long as Mom did. I don't know how you waited so long for her to decide to marry you. Was it really almost ten years?"

Stuart chuckled. "It was, son; trust me. I can recount every moment of it. I knew she was the best thing in my life. I wasn't going to throw that away. I waited because your mother was worth it. If you're smart—and I know you are—waiting on Sunnie to come around will be the right thing to do."

Tom thought on that as he got up. "I'm going to go out a bit, Pop. I'll be back before dinner. You need anything in town?"

Stuart shook his head, "Not a thing. I'm going to take a ride on Picasso. He needs the exercise. I'll see you later on, Tommy boy."

Stuart watched him walk away, his heart heavy for the pain he knew his son was carrying. As Tom drove away after making a brief phone call, Stuart asked God—with whom he'd had a turbulent relationship since Claire died—to make Tommy's way easy and his burden light. Then he snuffed out the cigar. It was time to ride Picasso.

When he parked in the crowded lot at the church, Tom instinctively looked at the beaded angel in the rearview mirror. A wave of guilt came, as though she was warning him that speaking to Paul would be betraying Sunnie.

"No, it isn't," he insisted to the small figure. "I need the spiritual input. There's too much already twisting in my mind."

The angel swayed, offering no further wisdom. Tom snickered at his paranoia before leaving her to meet Paul in the gymnasium. He waited on the sidelines as the dodge-ball game Paul was involved in ended. When he paused to acknowledge Tom, he was tagged out. A group of junior high boys booed him in good fun when he left the floor.

"What brings you out on a glorious day like this when you have off? Where's Sunnie?" Paul caught the look of anxiety on Tom's face. "What's wrong, my friend? Tell me what's happening."

They sat in Paul's office most of the afternoon. Tom relayed the evening, his intentions once they arrived back at Sunnie's and how it had gone awry. He was appropriately discreet, shouldering the blame.

"Paul, I'm not happy that I allowed it to get out of control. Especially after talking to you about it. I thought we'd be above that—at least be able to stop it from escalating."

Paul pulled his battered Bible across the desk and opened it to quote a verse. Tom recited it in his mind as Paul read aloud.

"*'For I do not understand my own actions. For I do not do what I want, but I do the very thing I hate.'* Romans 7, verse 15."

"Oh, wretched man that I am," Tom mumbled. He knew exactly where Paul was stopping next toward the back of the book. Tom echoed it aloud before Paul was able.

"*'If we confess our sins, he is faithful and just to forgive us our sins and to cleanse us from all unrighteousness.'* That's why I'm here."

"You can confess to me all day long, Tom. Have you really gotten into it on your own with God? Asked Him to forgive you?"

"Of course. I spent half the time Sunnie was in the shower praying and the other half chastising myself."

Paul appeared satisfied, so Tom went on.

"Sunnie seems to think this destroyed everything. I assured her it didn't. I left the ring with her—I told her to call me when she's ready. I don't know if I should have said more. Stayed until she either agreed or tossed me out."

"Sunnie cares for you, Tom. But, it sounds as though she has some baggage she needs to work through. Let her have the time. What was her response when you asked forgiveness?"

"I'm not sure. She didn't really say anything, except that it was her fault somehow. I'm not even sure she believes that I do love her. She's so afraid, Paul—I don't understand it. I really have tried to. I think she'll use this as an excuse to call it off. The thought that I caused it is killing me."

Tom's voice was raw, and he drew a ragged breath before continuing.

"I know it sounds dramatic, Paul, but I feel as though I violated her. I'm not only a Christian, but an officer of the law. I'm not supposed to do that. I hurt her—unintentionally—but I did. How can she trust me again?"

Paul leaned forward, grasping his friend's arm. "You need to trust God to work on Sunnie, not you. It's all in His hands. It sounds as though you've done all you can to restore yourself to a right relationship both with God and Sunnie. We should pray; give it all to God. Trust Him, Tom. You know you can."

Tom nodded, swiping his hand across his eyes before they prayed together.

Tom held his breath as he stepped into Wynter Delights. Relieved that Sunnie was nowhere to be seen, he waved to Wynter before walking to the coffee bar. She returned it with her always-chipper smile. He poured his usual, biding his time while she waited on the other customers at the register.

He approached once the other customers had gone, not desiring the usual small talk. "Muffins today, Wynter?"

"Of course, Officer Tom! Let me get..."

She was interrupted by Silas's hand on her shoulder. He had come up behind her with a bag already in hand.

"I've got it, Wynnie. Whole grain pistachio, right, Officer?"

Tom took the bag he offered with a curt nod.

"Got a minute? I need to talk to you." Silas frostily requested.

"Sure. Thanks, Wynter, I'll see you tomorrow. What's the special?"

"Protein chocolate chip. It's new, you'll love it. See you..." Wynter's chipperness was diminished. She met Silas's eyes warily as he took off his bright green apron.

"Be right back, Wynnie. After you, Officer." He invited Tom with a wave of his arm.

Tom took his coffee from the counter and strode out the door, Silas following close behind. They walked around the side of the building, where Tom had parked.

Silas wasted no words. "I saw you leaving the other day. That was beyond tacky."

Recalling the state of undress he'd walked out of the building in brought a flush up the back of Tom's neck. "I'm sorry, Silas. You're right, I wasn't thinking."

"I also saw the ring. I gotta say it, bro. *If* you love my sister, you shouldn't be using her like that. It's not right. She's not cheap trash. She's a good woman."

Tom allowed the sting. "I know that. My intent was to ask her to marry me. I let it get out of control. It's my fault, not Sunnie's."

"It's not the first time." Silas's eyes narrowed as a thought presented itself. "Was this the first time? The only time?"

"I could tell you to blow, but I won't." Tom said brusquely. "Yes, this was the only time."

Silas wasn't prepared for such blatant honesty. He scanned the ground while Tom sipped his coffee. When Silas looked back to Tom, he saw he looked as pained as Sunnie.

"Did she say yes?"

I wonder if this is how perps feel during an interrogation? Tom thought before he answered.

"She said nothing. I told her how I feel, but I'm not sure she's ready. I don't know what it is that she's afraid of. I hope you know she never has to be afraid because of me." It was sincerely spoken, the love behind it plain.

"I'm praying for you—both of you. She needs a good man in her life. I thought it was you. So long as..."

Tom held a hand up, easing Silas out of a tirade. "That will not happen again, Silas. Sunnie has my word. Now, you also have my word."

Silas let the anger go, satisfied that Tom was speaking truth to him. He offered his hand, "See you tomorrow. Sunnie usually comes down around ten."

Sunnie arrived late for Sunday school class, relieved that the only chair open wasn't next to Tom. Several hard weeks had passed and she was no closer to an answer than the night Tom left the ring on her coffee table. She slipped into the seat as Pastor Paul continued his discourse on the current chapter.

As she got up to leave, Paul stopped by her chair. "We missed you the past few weeks. Is everything all right?"

Sunnie was unsure how to answer. "Sure. You?"

"Blessed, Sunnie. We're blessed. Just checking, since you haven't been here. We've been praying for you."

"Thanks, I appreciate..." Sunnie's answer expired as her hands flew to cover her face.

"Sunnie? What's wrong?" Pastor Paul asked, confused at the deep pink flush that covered her face.

"He told you!" she whispered through her fingers. "I didn't think he...I really have to..." Sunnie turned to flee the room quickly as possible. He realized—too late—what she assumed he meant.

"That is not it, not at all. I'm always concerned when someone misses classes."

Sunnie's expression was an advertisement for disbelief. He went on, swiftly weighing what he could and could not disclose. "Tom did come to speak to me. I know he's hurting over the silence between you. Silence he feels he caused. Sunnie, why don't you come see me, we can..."

Their discussion was suspended by Tom returning to the room.

"Hey Paul, I forgot..."

He stopped short when he realized the discussion Paul was involved in involved Sunnie.

"Ah. Sorry, I'll...it's good to see you, Sunnie." He groaned to himself at the formality of the statement.

Thick tension built before she moved from the spot she stood in. She walked to Tom, and he braced himself for the inevitable; he could see from the betrayal in her eyes what was coming.

She swept from the room, leaving them with an echo of the slap she landed across Tom's face. Paul glanced from the red welt to his watch.

"I'm sorry, Tom. I have to run...if you need me this week, you have my cell," was offered in apology before he gathered his belongings and left the room.

Tom stood in the quiet room alone for a few moments. The terrible hurt in Sunnie's eyes would stay with him long after the sting of her hand on his face ever would. Certain she was lost to him forever, he silently walked out of the church.

Sunnie hurried down the steps of the church and ran to where her car was parked. How she wished she had someone to turn to, but who? She wasn't comfortable confiding more to Silas and Wynter than they already knew. Sammie wasn't an option, not with this. She slapped the roof of her car in frustration.

"Hello there, Sunshine!"

She turned to see Victoria and George walking towards her, arm in arm. *Thank you, Jesus!*

She waved brightly, hoping she didn't appear as false as she thought she sounded. "Hi there. It's funny how we all go here and I rarely see you two. Hey Vic, can I stop by today? I haven't seen you in forever."

"Sure, Sunnie! It'll be great to catch up. I want to know everything you've been up to since you moved out of the gate house! Lunch on me."

"George's chicken salad?" Sunnie asked with real hope as her stomach reminded her it was time for a meal.

George laughed with a polite nod of his head. "Of course, Sunshine! We'll see you in a bit."

This is perfect! she thought. Victoria would help her get her head on right. She got in her car, feeling much better than she had a few moments before.

When George got into their car, Victoria said to him, "Something's not right, George. That was not Sunnie's normal—that was completely forced. Sammie's been telling me for weeks that Sunnie seems distracted. We may need some privacy. Do you mind, love?"

"Of course not. I'm glad she feels she can come talk to you. I can find something to occupy my time, should I need to."

"I swear this driveway wasn't this long before. And where is that stupid mutt?"

Sunnie looked around for Victoria's enormous Irish wolfhound before she exited her car. She never enjoyed being jumped on. She heard him barking in the house as she walked up the steps.

Victoria shooed him into the other room before opening the door. "Come in, Sunnie! It's so good to see you after so long."

Purple lipstick appeared on Sunnie's cheek. "Tell me everything. How's your building? Silas's coffee shop is adorable, as is Wynter. Do you get along well? Honestly, I feel like I haven't talked to you in months!"

Sunnie shrugged off her sweater while laughing at Victoria's barrage of questions. She missed their mornings together, drinking tea and talking about anything that came to Sunnie's mind. They argued Sunnie's passion for yoga, biblical merits of vegetarianism, free will, traditional hymns versus contemporary worship music. Sunnie was sure she could tell Victoria what was on her heart today.

If I can accurately explain it, she thought as she rubbed the lipstick off with her thumb.

George joined them for lunch, before excusing himself to peruse the Sunday newspaper. Victoria brought Sunnie a large mug of her favorite citrus flavored tea.

"How is that nice policeman you've been dating? Isn't he the mayor's son?" Victoria held an innocent air while she sipped her hot, black coffee.

Sunnie tried to ignore the slight nauseous feeling she had. "Vic, you know he's the mayor's son. Didn't you have an hour long discussion with him one day after church about his father's budget?"

Victoria waved her hand. "Well, really, he's far too generous in areas he should be more conservative in. My father would have never...well, that was long ago. But, that doesn't answer my question."

"You do have a way of cutting through the bull. Truth is, I don't know how Tom is. Vic, this may sound crazy, but can we sit somewhere else? The smell of that coffee is killing me. Maybe I've been smelling it too much at home, at the shop, or something."

"Certainly, Sunnie." Victoria answered with an unobserved glance of scrutiny.

The fresh air did alleviate the queasiness Sunnie related to the turmoil her life had become. They settled into comfortable wicker chairs and sipped their drinks in silence as Sunnie gathered her thoughts. Finally, she blurted out, "Tom asked me to marry him."

To Sunnie's annoyance, Victoria did not seem the least bit surprised by this news. "I take it you said no? Why? He's delightful."

"I don't know, Vic; that's the problem. Delightful. I wouldn't have said it that way, but yes, he is. I am so comfortable with him. We always have fun together. I could spend the rest of my life with him."

"I think you left something off of that list, dear. Don't you love him?"

"Of course I do." She wasn't surprised how quickly she admitted it; it had been deeply etched in her heart for months. "Vic, it's so hard to get over that 'if I give him my whole heart, he'll destroy me' thing. I could never be in love with anyone else. I know I can—I am—but after watching my father walk all over Mom time and time again..."

"You know, I fought with your mother plenty over John. I understand, Sunnie, what you are saying. I watched that happen to her also. You have to remember something. At that time, he wasn't a saved man." She held her hand up at Sunnie's sputtering protestations.

"No, Sunnie, you listen to me! I am not giving him a pass. He hurt all of you. It seems that not all of you have released that hurt, though. Your mother—bless her heart—has a tremendous ability to forgive. Those last years, your father really was a changed man. He never hurt your mother again, the way he did before."

Loathe to admit it, something in what Victoria was saying made sense in Sunnie's mind. "Go ahead. Where are you going with this? How does it relate to Tom?"

"Sunnie, dear, it relates to how you keep Tom away from your heart. Your mother released the hurt. Your sisters, they both made good marriages. Silas should have the same struggles according to your assumptions, yet he has a wonderful relationship. Here is a man who loves you—who you claim you love. What's stopping you? John? You told me yourself that you forgave him."

Sunnie sat back a moment, recalling the day she stood by Jackie's gravesite. "I know what you're going to say. That because I forgave him, I need to forget. I understand that in my head, Vic. I'm still so afraid to love that way. So totally. The way Mom and Rob are. You and George. Heck, even Wynter and Silas, although they border on nauseating."

"Well, Sunnie, I think you need to. Yes, I'm sure he will hurt you at some point. If you want to make sure you don't get hurt, you're going to be very lonely."

Sunnie's eyes widened. "Vic, Tom said the same thing to me. That he would never intentionally hurt me. That he probably would, though. That staying 'safe' would be lonely."

"Well, it's true. Even your mother will hurt you. Does she want to? Of course not! But, it will happen. He's a smart fellow. So, you know that forgiving means you can set aside the hurt. You want to open up to Tom. There's some piece of this puzzle you haven't shared with me. What happened?"

"How do you know something happened?"

"I knew at church that something was on your mind. Your mother has been concerned about you the past few weeks. My guess would be that you've had a huge disagreement with your policeman."

Sunnie threw her hands in the air. "Vic, I'm an idiot—that's what happened. Do you remember when we had that chocolate cake talk?"

"Oh yes! How once you taste the cake, you will never be happy again with just one bite. Fondling the wrapper on a chocolate bar isn't fulfilling. I remember you didn't think much of that as an example. Has your view changed?"

"Tom took me on the most wonderful date at The Parkington. We had a wonderful night...dinner and dancing. When we got back he wanted to talk. He was going to ask me to marry him. Instead..." Sunnie's face flushed.

"Instead you decided the chocolate was too tempting."

"Too much so. It's not the first time we almost...ugh! Why is this so hard, Vic? I know what the right thing is!"

"Aren't you in the Romans class at church?" Victoria asked. Sunnie's flush deepened. "So you understand the principles involved here. Our flesh always wants what is contrary to the Spirit. Answer me this, Sunnie. Was it forced?"

Victoria was taken aback by the look of anger that briefly crossed Sunnie's face.

"Of course not! What is it with you and Silas?" She took a self-containing breath. "I threw myself at him. In the morning, he apologized. He apologized to ME, Vic. What was he supposed to do? I was practically naked."

"He should have left you, even if you were completely naked. Would you have been angry? Probably. I give him credit for taking the responsibility. He is correct. In the eyes of the Lord, he is responsible. He's the man—he should have been your protector. Now, what does your brother have to do with all of this?"

"Silas saw Tom leave in the morning. He came up by me in an uproar, like some sort of overprotective father. He wanted to know if Tom forced himself on me. It was freaky how much he reminded me of Jackie." Sunnie shook her head at the memory.

"Well, you both bear a striking resemblance to your father, Silas more so than you. Does he know about the proposal also?"

"He saw the ring. Si and Wynn have been great. I wish I knew what to do! Today I was late for class and Tom...well, he didn't even look in my direction."

"Have you even called him, Sunnie? Don't be unduly hard on him." Victoria saw the veneer beginning to crack.

"No, I haven't. I've seen him a few times in the coffee shop. Just a nod and a quick hello. Paul came over and asked how I was after class. I took it completely out of context. Tom came back in the room while Paul and I were talking. I was so upset...I slapped him in the face."

Victoria's jaw dropped. "You what? Sunnie!"

Sunnie shot off the chair, pacing like an irritable panther. "Vic, I know, I know. I lost it, again. I'm telling you, I'm surprised he hasn't called me to get the ring back. Maybe he'll just transfer to another town, where crazy people don't live. Who would want to deal with me?"

Victoria laughed aloud. Sunnie stopped pacing, placing her hands on her hips. "Hey, thanks, Vic. I appreciate that."

"Oh Sunnie! It's just that I had a similar conversation with your mother before she married Rob. She was wondering if Rob wanted to stay around when she was obviously insane."

"My mother? She was afraid that Rob didn't love her? He was crazy about her, anyone could see that. I didn't even live here and I knew it."

"Sounds similar. The times I have seen you together, it's obvious how you feel about each other. It's easy to read you, when one knows you. Why don't you call Tom and tell him that you'll marry him?"

"I don't know. Why don't I?"

Sunnie stopped pacing and faced Victoria. "I think I'm going to go home and pray. Listen to some praise music and stretch. Possibly pick up the phone. Thanks so much, Vic. For everything." Sunnie hugged her before gathering her sweater and bag.

Victoria patted Sunnie's back. "You are welcome, Sunnie. Please do me a favor on your way home."

"Sure. I think I'll stop anyhow and grab some onion rings. I've had a crazy urge for them all week."

Victoria nodded, suspicion confirmed. "Stop at the pharmacy, dear. Get a test."

"A test? What kind of..." Sunnie's mouth formed a silent O.

"Yes. That kind of test." She led Sunnie to the steps. "Just to be certain, of course."

Events of the ride home blurred in Sunnie's mind as tears blurred her eyes waiting to read the results. The few moments stretched into eternity; when she was certain of what it said, she lay across the bed and cried herself to sleep.

Chapter 20

"Here we go, Lord." Sunnie said as she pulled up to the log house. Victoria had been right on all accounts. It took two more weeks of searching her soul before she finally made the call. She breathed deeply a few times before stepping from her car.

Stuart exited the front door before Sunnie was at the steps, his ever-present cigar clenched in his teeth. "Sunnie girl! I was beginning to think I'd never see you again! How have you been?"

Stuart's warm greeting set her at ease. At least he was happy to see her.

"Good to see you too, Stuart. I've missed coming by. Sorry that it's been so long."

"I know Tommy was happy you were coming. He's with Beau, in the stable. Would you like to wait here, or go out there?"

A wave of relief flowed. Sunnie did not have the wherewithal to hold a coherent discussion with anyone else at the moment.

"I think I'll meet him there, Stuart, thanks. I will be back, though."

She breathed out a prayer on the way, "Lord, please, please, please give me whatever I need to talk to Tom...humility is probably good. Help me to accept his responses, no matter what they are. Thank you."

Tom heard the car pull up. He rubbed Beau's nose, whispering to him, "Here we go, boy. Hopefully later, we'll be riding into the sunset, eh?"

Beau tossed his head, snorting.

"Yeah, sorry. That was corny, even for me." Tom leaned his forehead against the horse, saying his own quick prayer for God's blessings. He left the stall, not sure of what to expect from Sunnie.

They turned the corner of the stable at the same time, colliding into each other. Tom instinctively reached out, keeping Sunnie from toppling backwards. They stared at each other before they burst into waves of laughter.

"Are we always going to have to run into each other, Sunnie?" Tom finally managed, wiping his eyes with the back of his hand.

"Is it bad to say that I hope so? It seems to be the only way the Lord can get anything through my thick head."

She didn't miss the hopeful look in Tom's eyes. "Well, I can live with it, if it's part of the package." He smiled, sensing Sunnie's hesitancy. "Do you want to say hello to Picasso? He's been missing you."

"Love to. Thanks."

Tom grabbed a handful of sugar cubes on the way to Picasso's stall. He handed them to Sunnie as she reached the door. Picasso's head was peering over the edge, excited to have company. Sunnie stroked his soft nose, murmuring to him while she fed him the cubes one at a time. She wiped her eyes after he consumed them all before turning back to Tom.

"Sorry, I'm emotional these days. I did miss him. Can we walk a bit? I have so much I want to say to you, Tom. Thanks for seeing me."

Tom stared at Sunnie for a minute. *Would this be good?* She looked so serious— but resolved, peaceful.

"Sure, Sunnie. Let's go by the creek. Would you rather drive over there?"

"No, walking is fine."

As they left the stable, Tom threw caution to the wind and reached for Sunnie's hand. She eagerly entwined her fingers into his. A silent thank you reached Heaven from them both. They walked along a bit without speaking, enjoying the fact that they were together again.

"Tom, I need to apologize to you. I was manipulative and selfish. I was very unfair." Sunnie paused on the trail, turning to face Tom. "I'm so sorry for putting you in the position I did. Would you forgive me?"

"Of course, Sunnie girl. Can you forgive me for using you like...well, like I did? I violated more than your body; I violated your trust. I am so sorry."

Both felt the restorative work of forgiveness begin as they nodded to each other. When they resumed the walk, their hands were still clasped.

"I'm sorry that I slapped you. In front of Paul, no less. I jumped to a terrible conclusion that I should have known better not to." Sunnie hoped she would never again embarrass this man she loved in public. "I am sorry for assuming the worst about you. Can I explain something to you?"

"Of course. I want to hear everything, Sunnie. Everything."

They stopped by the creek and Sunnie sat on the flat rock. As she gazed over the water, she started to pour out what she always kept so tightly locked in her heart.

"Physical relationships were always easy for me. When I was younger, it was a way to show affection without having to deal with feelings. At Weston, they were a way to power." Sunnie faltered a bit, expecting some reaction from Tom. A firm, clenched jaw was all she collected.

"When I moved back home...started to go to church...I thought that would all be behind me. I couldn't allow myself to tell you I loved you. It was easier to offer my body rather than my heart."

Tom sat on the ground, unsure of what his reaction should be. "Sunnie, I should not have..."

"No, Tom. *We* should not have." Tom conceded with a quick nod, eager for her to continue opening up to him. She said she loved him, yet he felt something was being held back.

"I wish I would have had the courage to tell you that morning. I shouldn't have let you leave. Si saw you leave, you know. He almost decked you." Sunnie snickered at the thought.

"I did see him a few days later. He had every right to be angry with me. I don't care that he's younger; he's your brother. He probably would have decked me good."

Sunnie snorted. "Please, Tom! You held me in those arms. He would have hurt himself, not you."

Her face flushed pink, and he hid a grin at the comment. "Well, I would have allowed him the free punch, okay?"

"Anyhow, he came up after he saw you. He was in my face about you taking advantage of me. He saw the box on the table. He told me not to let my father stop me from marrying you. Those were the first words that sunk in. I thought I forgave him, but I was still holding on to the easy excuse."

Sunnie pulled the ring box out of her bag and held it out to Tom. He looked at it, but did not move to take it from her.

"Are you giving this back, Sunnie? Do you not want to get married?"

"What I'd like is for you to put it where it belongs, but I need to tell you more. I'm so afraid that it will make all the difference." Sunnie's voice quavered.

Tom felt a wave of apprehension. What could they possibly have left to discuss?

"Sunnie, whatever this is, it won't change a thing. I told you I wanted to ask you to marry me for weeks. I'm happy that one mistake didn't change your heart about me. Now please, whatever this is, tell me."

Sunnie attempted to control the trembling her hand insisted upon. She was sure he'd be happy, but the timing—well, wasn't it all in the Lord's timing? Sunnie took a deep breath, and stated it flat out.

"We're having a baby." It seemed to echo across the creek, into the trees—out into space. Sunnie's heart sank when Tom took the box from her hand without a glance. He continued to stare at the box when he spoke.

"Is that what changed *your* mind, Sunnie? How long have you known?"

The tension in Tom's voice rattled Sunnie's nerves. Remembering she laid it all in God's capable hands, she answered him.

"Almost two weeks, now. Of course, it helped. I don't want to be a single parent."

Tom's head snapped around to look up at her and she groaned. Her head dropped into her hands as she fought tears of frustration. "That was terrible of me. I want to marry you, Tom, and not just to get through this. I need you. No matter how asinine I behave, you let me be me. I'm sorry."

"I know that's not how you meant it. It's okay to say you need something." Tom got up from the ground and sat on the rock next to Sunnie. He pulled her to him, breathing in the scent he didn't realize he missed so much. "I want you to need me. It's normal."

"I don't know how to do normal. That's what I've been trying to tell you. I may end up—no—I WILL end up saying dumb things—like that—all the time. I may not wash your socks or something."

Tom laughed with relief, hugging Sunnie closer.

"I can deal, Sunnie. I told you I've been in love with you for a while, now. I'm not walking away from you. I knew you needed some time to think. I'm just glad I wasn't waiting long. Is this how life with you is always going to be? Always unique, unexpected situations?"

"Honestly, I'm afraid. To start life with you, without really being with you. I'm afraid that all we'll have to hold us together is the kids. Like mom. My father was so cruel to her for so many years. I don't know why she stayed, except for us. I don't want to feel like I trapped you. Or that I'm trapped. Am I making any sense at all?"

"Sunnie, this is the first time you've ever made *any* sense."

She pulled back to look at him. His eyes—the ones she loved—were alight again, with humor. When she relaxed against him, he pulled the ring from the box. She held up her hand after he slid it onto her finger, admiring the sparkle. The happy countenance she held was worth waiting on, just as Stuart had assured him.

"Is it all right to kiss you today? Or should we wait?" Tom's serious tone took Sunnie by surprise.

"Really?"

"No." Tom hesitated. "Only if it will cause you to stumble, Sunnie. I don't ever want to cause you to stumble again. I won't even hold your hand till we're married if that's what you want."

Sunnie considered that. It was sweet and romantic. "How about a compromise? Kiss me now, just to celebrate, of course."

Tom chuckled. "But? I know it's coming.You *will* marry me right away? This isn't the start of an extended engagement?" There was an air of panic in Tom's question.

Sunnie giggled. "No, we'll get married right away. As far as this kiss, though, let's celebrate now. It shouldn't be too long to wait. How hard can that be?"

All that existed for several minutes was her heart beating in time with his.

"Okay. Harder than I thought." Sunnie said once she had a voice back.

"Harder than *you* thought? Thanks, Sunnie. I'll remember this. Let's go tell Picasso and Beau. Then we can go tell Pop and your mom."

"No! First we need a marriage license. Unless you want to wait longer than we need to. We can tell whomever in whatever order we decide to AFTER."

"That sounds better. Okay, let's roll. Give me your keys."

She handed the keys to him as they stood. He held her hand a moment before they left the rock. "You're sure about all of this, Sunnie girl?"

Sunnie looked into Tom's eyes, with a smile that set Tom's heart at ease.

"I've never been more sure about anything in my life, Officer Jacobs. Never."

They nearly jogged back to Sunnie's car so they could get into town as quickly as possible.

"I'm nervous," Sunnie admitted once they pulled up Rob's driveway.

"Sunnie, it's your mom. She'll understand." Tom took Sunnie's hand to give it a squeeze of encouragement. "I'd kiss you again, you know, if you didn't institute the 'no contact' law. You know I must obey the law. That was evil."

"I believe it was your idea, Officer. Now, come on. Aina is looking out the window, so they know we're here." When she turned to leave the car, Tom tugged her hand. She turned back to look into a most serious expression.

"What's the matter?"

"Let me handle this. Just trust me."

She hesitated before nodding. Tom winked and kissed her hand. "Don't worry,

Sunnie girl. Just leave it to me. You can tell Pop."

She grumbled something about him having the easier task when they stepped from the car. Tom followed her up the deck steps envisioning a long lifetime of Sunnie's exaggerated annoyances. He looked forward to every one of them.

Before she opened the door to her mother's kitchen, Sunnie glanced back at Tom. Overwhelmed with a surge of emotion, she reached out and hugged him tightly.

"I love you, Officer."

Tom returned the hug before remarking, "Copy. Unless you want to continue to break that 'No Touching' law, open the door."

Sunnie snickered, and wiped her eyes quickly. They entered the kitchen to see Sammie and Aina at the table finishing their lunch. Sunnie greeted them both with a hug before asking about River's absence.

"He's napping with Daddy. Hello, Tom, good to see you again." Sammie welcomed, wondering if his presence meant she was about to hear good news. She'd been praying Sunnie would overcome the things that were keeping him at a distance.

Tom's warm smile gave Sammie some hope. "Thank you, Mrs. Revell. Nice to be here." Tom turned to Aina, "How's Aina Bug?"

"When me ride Casso, TomTom?"

Tom chuckled, squatting to be eye-to-eye with Aina. "How about Sunday? If Momma and Daddy say it's all right, I'll take you on Picasso."

Aina, clapping, turned to Sammie. "Me ride Casso!"

"We'll see, Miss Aina. Now, finish this sandwich. Sit down, you two. There's coffee."

"I'll get you some," Sunnie offered. The rich aroma from the hot beverage rose to her nose before she could get the cream from the refrigerator. A violent lurch in her midsection made her place the cup on the counter and hastily excuse herself.

Wonderful, she thought. *Perfect timing.*

Sammie stared after her in curious worry as Tom finished fixing his abandoned cup. Rob called a hello to Sunnie as she passed him in the hallway. Aina dove off the chair and into his arms.

"Good to see you again, Tom," he managed while Aina covered his face with kisses. Rob shook Tom's hand before placing her back down in front of her lunch remnants.

"So? What's going on?" He looked to Sammie expectantly.

She shrugged, looking at Tom with a smile. "I'm not sure yet. I think you're done here, Aina. You go watch something now; Momma needs to talk to Sunnie and Tom."

Satisfied with the promise of riding a real horse, Aina skipped to the living room. She sat quietly by the television while men in brightly colored shirts sang songs.

Sunnie returned to the kitchen, the color in her countenance restored.

"We couldn't watch that much television," Sunnie teased her mother before offering Rob a hug. She placed herself on a chair next to her mother.

"At that age, yes you could. So, tell us. What's going on?"

Sunnie twirled the brand new ring as she looked to Tom. Sammie caught the action before she had a chance to hide her hand. She suppressed any commenting on the bauble and turned her attention to Tom.

After placing the empty cup in the sink, he moved to stand beside Sunnie. He rested a hand on her shoulder as he made their announcement.

"I asked Sunnie to marry me several weeks ago. She needed some time, and today she agreed. We came right away. I'm very blessed to finally be able to tell you."

Sammie and Rob glanced at each other, not quite startled by the turn of events. Rather, by the reserve they were both showing. They silently communicated a moment before Rob nodded and looked to Tom.

"But, there's something more, Tom. What's the problem?"

"Well, sir, it's not a problem. Not to me. We both hope you'll be happy. You'll be grandparents in April."

Sunnie wasn't expecting balloons and confetti, but she was unprepared for Sammie's reaction.

"Rob, take Tom out on the deck, please. I'd like a word with Sunnie alone."

Tom followed Rob out the door after squeezing Sunnie's shoulder. Hoping to escape a long, detailed inquisition, Sunnie offered to go and check on River. Sammie placed a hand on her daughter's.

"Sunshine, you tell me all of this. I'm not unhappy. I want to know how you really feel. About everything."

It was a great relief for Sunnie to pour out the whole story starting from the moment she knew her feelings for Tom were more than she wanted to admit. They laughed and cried through the telling of their wonderful date and the pitfalls they failed to avoid.

When Sammie rose to rescue a fretful River from the confines of his crib, she embraced her eldest child. Sunnie soaked in the always comforting love before letting go.

The same tale was being told to Rob, with apologies from Tom for his indiscretions. "I hope Mrs. Revell isn't upset," was the only hint of uncertainty heard.

Rob deliberated quickly and decided to share a confidence with Tom. "You know, Sammie and I had our own close call. We did take steps to assure it didn't happen again."

Tom shrugged. "I wish we would have done the same. I'm not unhappy, Rob. Baby or no, I'm happy Sunnie agreed to marry me. Hindsight is 20/20, they say."

"I understand how hard this was for you. If Sammie and I were younger, I don't know that we would have been able to keep it together. I think you've handled it as well as you could. That says a lot about you, Tom. And your relationship with the Lord."

Tom scrubbed his face with one hand, releasing the last of the tension he was experiencing. "These have been the worst weeks of my life, Rob. I cannot believe I allowed it to happen. I appreciate your understanding."

Rob clasped Tom's shoulder. "The road is never easy, Tom. I'm happy for you both."

"I don't think anything involving my bride-to-be will ever be easy, Rob. I wouldn't have it any other way, though."

When they all were gathered back at the table, Tom relayed the remainder of their plans. "We're planning to be married on Sunday at our—my father's. We're going to talk to Pastor Paul when we leave here. He's an old friend and he's been a big help to me the past few weeks. I'd like for him to marry us."

"That only gives you a few days to plan. Can we do anything?" Rob offered.

"Thanks, but I'm sure we'll have it covered. I know it's short notice for Pop, but he won't say no. He thrives on challenges. He may be upset that we're not going to live there right away."

132

Sammie glanced up from River's noisy nursing to Sunnie. "Oh! Sunnie, are you going to sell the building?"

"It's a possibility, Mom. The shop is doing well, so I'll offer Si the opportunity to buy me out. We haven't decided on living with Stuart or building a house just yet. It's all so much to think about." Sunnie took Tom's hand in hers. "I'm glad that Tom is willing to give me time to make all of these decisions."

Tom and Sunnie shared a private look that melted Sammie's heart.

"There are two other things I need. Mom, would you stand with me? I can't think of anyone else I would rather have by my side."

Sammie fished a handkerchief from her pocket to swab her eyes. "Of course I will, Sunnie! Thank you for asking."

"Don't go crazy, Mom, no new dresses or anything. Church dress is fine." Assured that Sammie would not go on a wild shopping spree, she turned to Rob.

"Rob? Would you...well, give me away?"

Rob bowed his head, emotion catching his words. "Of course, Sunnie. I'm honored. Thank you."

Sunnie leaned across the table and embraced him. "Thanks. I appreciate it."

She felt the emotions welling again, and she released Rob. "Now, before we all become blubbering idiots, we better go see Paul." Sunnie glanced at Tom.

"Sunnie's right; we better get to him before he finds a pick-up basketball game to join. Thank you, Rob. Mrs. Revell. Sunnie will call later with more details."

"Do you want me to call your sisters? Tell Jude when he gets in?" Sammie offered.

Sunnie gratefully accepted. "Thanks, Mom, if it's no trouble. Tell Storm I'm sorry she can't be here. I'll see Silas later to fill him in. Oh! Please, Mom...call Vic? I bawled on her shoulder two weeks ago; I want her and George to be there."

Sammie watched them from the door, praying over their future together. They paused to talk before Tom opened the car door, and Sammie saw the peace on Sunnie's face, a peace that she had not seen in many years. She was barely aware that Rob had taken River from her arms.

With a sudden motion, she turned from the door and dashed to the living room. She collapsed in her rocking recliner with a laugh. "Grandparents!" she said aloud with awe.

Rob chuckled from his spot on the floor where he was playing with Aina and River. "Samm, you already have grandchildren. Four, I believe the count is up to."

"I know Rob. I just never thought Sunnie..." Her mind cataloged through the many hard years and hours of prayer. Rejoicing had replaced the tears.

"She's got a good man there. He apologized to me, you know. For not having enough strength to wait. I told him about our close call. I admire him, Samm. He's exactly what Sunnie needs."

He turned to his children and clapped his hands together. "Now, what is everyone going to wear on Sunday? Aina, do you need a new pretty dress?"

Sammie left them to their shopping plans to make the necessary phone calls. There was no telling Rob that Aina had scores of pretty dresses already.

Chapter 21

"Tom, please? It won't be long and it's on the way."

"Sunn, we really need to go talk to Pop before someone from Town Hall calls to congratulate him! There are drawbacks to your father being mayor, you know."

A bit more adamant insistence brought them to Sunnie's. Unsure why she needed to stop, Tom followed her into Wynter Delights. Silas and Wynter were at the counter going over menus, and they both looked towards the door when the bells announced the arrival of customers.

"Hey guys! Listen, Si, I need a few favors from you."

"Sure, why not? Will I get a break on rent?"

"In your dreams. First of all, Sunday. We need a wedding cake. Possible?"

"Oh Sunnie!" Wynter bounded around the counter to hug the couple and Silas offered a handshake to Tom. Wynter settled back behind the counter, an enormous smile on her face.

"Of course that's possible! Just tell me what you want; I'll make sure it's ready!"

"Thanks, Wynn. Whatever you think is fun. Just make sure it's chocolate cake." Wynter nodded, pulling an order sheet from beneath the counter.

"How many people?"

Sunnie looked at Tom, her face blank. "I don't know. What do you think?"

Tom tallied family and the few expected guests.

"Let's be safe and say thirty-five."

Wynter nodded, scribbling numbers, designs, and writing the word chocolate in large letters.

"Si, I need you to come upstairs with us for about, oh, fifteen minutes. I need to show Tom a few things, and I need you to be there."

The guys exchanged bewildered looks. "I guess he's getting the grand tour?"

Sunnie huffed, took Tom's hand, and started for the door leading upstairs.

Upon arrival, Silas found the remote for the stereo and plunked himself on the couch. "I could be sitting at the counter downstairs you know. You take the Weird Award, Sunn."

After tossing a small pillow at him, Sunnie pulled Tom into her room. Sunnie glanced at her bed before focusing on him. She attempted to tell him what she needed to.

"I need you to know, Tom. I...when I was living in the city...well, none of the men I was dating at that time...ugh." She dropped her head to his shoulder.

He lifted her face to his. "Sunn, what is bothering you? Just tell me." Concern that she was having second thoughts lingered in Tom's mind.

Sunnie's eyes filled with tears. "Oh, this is so stupid! I'm sorry that I have a past to deal with. I did not bring my past here. I need to know that you believe me and that you are really all right with...me."

Tom pulled her close. She snuggled into him and allowed the last of the emotions to flow. When he was certain she had purged them, he loosened his hold.

"Sunnie girl, stop worrying. I love you, and that is that. It's behind us."

Sunnie smiled, tears clinging to her lashes. "I feel like I should apologize to you right now for all the things I know I'm going to do that will make you miserable. Right now is a perfect example. I'm going to try hard not to. I know that I love you, too. And I've never been more sure of anything. I'm not sure what I did to deserve you, Officer Jacobs. I'm glad I crashed into you."

They laughed quietly together, forehead to forehead until the comfortable aura around them was broken by Silas calling from the couch, "Sunn, just exactly why am I here? I need to get back down to close out the shop."

Sunnie stepped back from Tom and wiped her eyes. "Oh, if he only knew. I have to get you out of here before I don't let you leave."

"I could be easily persuaded to stay, but we know that's not in our best interests. We better get going anyhow. Let's release Si from PDA Patrol...for now."

When they returned to the living room, Silas gave them both a cursory look. "Okay, no rumpled clothing...I assume that's what I'm supposed to watch for?"

Sunnie hit him in the head with a couch pillow. "Sort of but, eww, how gross it sounds when you say it. Thanks Si. We need to get to Tom's. Go make me some muffins. Oatmeal cookies. Maybe some breadsticks, too."

"Hungry much? You know, you never request anything more than a muffin. You barely finish that. What is this, wedding jitters or something?"

Sunnie glanced at Tom. When her cheeks bloomed the slightest pink, Silas began to piece the puzzle together.

"Wait...wedding cake for Sunday. THIS Sunday. Are you..." His inquisitive gaze turned to Tom. He winked as confirmation.

The look Silas shot back to Sunnie could only be attributed to the gleeful torment in which siblings delight.

"Growing a rhino in there?"

Tom laughed as Sunnie chased Silas out of the door, managing to land three more blows to his retreating back.

The news of Stuart's expected grandchild trumped MacAfee dropping the charges against Sunnie. It stilled the blustering he had started over the short amount

136

of time Tom informed him he had to plan a small reception. He promptly demanded Roy and Maisey's presence for a toast before bustling to his study to look through his files for caterers. The plans were well under way by the time Sunnie departed.

"I am not driving anywhere alone again until this baby is born!" she vowed to herself before falling into bed, exhausted from the eventful day. She thanked God for the favorable reactions of the family before falling asleep.

On Sunday, Sunnie was awakened by the silly ring tone she had chosen for Tom. Wondering what he'd think of the choice, she reached to answer.

"Hey there, Officer." Sunnie swung her legs over the edge of the bed and stretched.

"You sound like you're still in bed. Aren't you up on the roof doing those heathen exercises?"

"No, I was enjoying one last morning of sleeping in. I assume tomorrow I'll have to be out of bed at the crack of dawn, making you eggs, sausage, bacon and biscuits or something."

"Not for me. I'll be down by Si, grabbing a muffin and coffee. Do you even have a coffee pot?"

His father bellowing orders at people decorating the house disrupted their conversation. Tom laughed. "You should see him! He's so in his element."

"Go tell him I said to calm down. Yes, I happen to own a coffee pot. I know how you cops love your coffee, so I better learn to make it."

"That is so cliché, Sunnie girl. Are you making it out to church this morning?"

Sunnie laughed. "Are you crazy? I can't let you see me! Bad vibes and all that nonsense. I'm going to go with mom, then get dressed there. I'll see you at two o'clock."

"Well, I won't lie—I'm disappointed. I'll just have to wait until two to see you. Enjoy the time with your mom, Sunnie. I'll see you later."

"I'll be there. Love you."

Never one for mushy emotions, Sunnie felt that expressing her feelings to Tom on an hourly basis would never be enough. A giddy, un-Sunnie-like giggle escaped as she prepared for her wedding day.

The blue satin dress she had chosen—the shade reminded her of Tom's eyes—hung by the door. She calculated the hours before she'd have it on as she went down the stairs.

Tom caught sight of Stuart, gesturing wildly about something or another when he hung up the phone. He smiled, enjoying watching his father a moment before getting himself ready for the morning. When Tom walked out on the deck to leave for church, he found Stuart relaxing. The cigar in his mouth was unlit and thoroughly chewed, a sure sign he was in charge and relishing every moment.

He smiled at his son after he finished what was left of the coffee before him.

"Have you intimidated the whole staff yet? It's not even nine. That has to be a record, even for you."

Stuart's deep laugh resonated in the morning stillness. "Son, if you had given me a bit more time on this, I wouldn't have to. Where are you off to? Church? Meeting your bride-to-be for coffee?"

"No, Sunnie is going to church with her family this morning. I'm hitting the early service. I'll be back to make sure you don't shoot any of the help."

"Tommy, you go, you come back, and you get ready to say, 'I Do.' Everything will be fine." Stuart took the damp cigar from his mouth, looking squarely at Tom's. "You're a good man, Thomas Stuart Jacobs. I'm damn proud of you. I'll miss you being around here. Even if it is only for a year or so."

Tom felt his throat tighten. Stuart rarely showed raw emotion. For Stuart, this was as raw as it got. Tom hugged the stout man, choking back his tears.

"Thanks Pop. I couldn't have done it without you. I'll be home in a bit. Don't tear off too many heads while I'm gone."

Stuart made a gruff grumbling sound—some incoherent thought—as he dug in a pocket for a worn bandana. Tom left Stuart on the deck loudly blowing his nose. He was bellowing again at an unfortunate young girl who was carrying flowers into the house as Tom drove away.

Sunnie walked in on a spirited discussion at her mother's house. Aina was weeping as though a favored pet had died. Sammie and Rob were standing by the sink, a half-dressed River dangling from her hip.

"She cannot wear pants to church or the wedding. Further, I will not allow her to ride that horse if she doesn't start behaving as she should. I need to finish getting River ready. I'm not budging on this, Rob."

Sammie looked around Rob's broad back, smiling to Sunnie. "Hi, sweetheart! We'll be ready in no time. I'll be right back down."

River waved his chubby hand at Sunnie as he was carried away by Sammie.

She walked to the living room and draped her dress over a chair. She listened as Rob soothed Aina's weeping, listing the reasons she needed to honor God by honoring Momma. Aina agreed that she should look beautiful for Jesus and for Sunnie.

When Sunnie entered the kitchen, the tears were subsided. A final, sweet, "Yes, Daddy," followed by a hug made Sunnie smile. She could imagine Tom having the same calm demeanor with their children.

Aina hopped from her chair, hugging Sunnie's legs before scooting up the stairs to find her shoes. Sunnie heard a warbled "I sorry, Momma," float back down.

"Women. Even the little ones." Rob had a faint smile on his face as he watched Aina disappear.

Sunnie reached for a glass. "What was wrong?" she asked, opening the fridge.

"Aina insists that she cannot ride Picasso in a dress. She must wear pants. It wasn't enough that your mother packed her a change of clothing; she wanted to make sure she was ready."

He winked before finishing his coffee. "Your mother and I sometimes differ in our parenting."

"You and Mom seen to have a good system, Rob. It wasn't that way when I was..." Sunnie bit her lip and offered Rob a smile. "Sorry."

Rob gracefully waved away Sunnie's embarrassment. "It has to come down to what's best for the child, Sunnie. Not for either parent to 'have their way,' so to speak. You learn as you go. In our case, your mother has far more training with the troops than I do. It's not such a big deal for me to defer to her. I see how you all turned out, and I approve."

Sunnie smirked. "You missed my early teens, Rob. You may not have said that if you witnessed them live."

"Well, Sunnie, we all have a wild spot or two."

Sunnie turned at the sound of Jude's deep laughing. "Yeah, Sunnie had a wild spot for all of us. Nice belly, by the way."

She glanced down, not seeing any obvious bulging in her waist area. She looked back at Rob.

He held up his hands. "I am NOT commenting. You look wonderful, and that's all I'm saying."

Sunnie rolled her eyes before finishing the juice. *This is going to be a long day*, was her thought.

Chapter 22

"How many people are here?" Sunnie asked nervously.

Aina was chattering about the horses as they drove down the long lane toward the house. Sunnie counted several cars she wasn't familiar with as well as Silas's ugly work van.

Sammie patted Sunnie's arm. "Don't worry—as soon as you see Tom, you won't know any of us are even there. Do you see Vic's car?"

"No. I really thought this was going to be no big deal, Mom."

"Stuart is the mayor. He knows how to throw a party, even a small one. After all, Sunnie, it is his only son's wedding. Come, now. You'll be late." Sammie stepped out of the car, opening the back to extract Aina from her car seat.

Aina pointed excitedly and whispered in awe, "Horsies! Sunnie, where Casso?"

"Picasso is in the stable right now. We'll see him later. Tom won't forget."

Aina nodded with wide eyes, mesmerized by Beau's appearance. He was prancing about in all the excitement, showing his best to the guests.

Praying for calm, Sunnie turned to see Stuart hurrying towards them. She thought his pinstripes looked quite regal, though surprised there was no cigar protruding from somewhere on him.

"Sunnie girl! You are a vision, my dear! Tommy may faint when he sees you, yessir."

Sunnie bent to place a kiss on Stuart's smooth cheek.

"Let's hope he gets through the vows first. Stuart, thank you so much for everything you have done here." She smiled to him before making introductions. "This is my mother, Sammie Revell. And my youngest sister, Aina. Mom, Aina, Mayor Jacobs."

Stuart waved his hand. "Now, now. This is family...Stuart, please. It's my pleasure to meet such charming women. This must be the young lady who wants to ride Picasso."

Aina bounced in her dressy shoes.

"Yes sir!" Her tiny voice squeaked. Stuart scooped her up in his arms and walked towards the corral.

"Well, Miss Aina, you will. Would you like to say hello to Beau before the wedding?"

Rob walked up behind the women, staring after Stuart with a light scowl. He had River in his arms and a diaper bag hanging from a shoulder.

"Who is that man, and where is he talking my daughter?"

"That's Stuart. You've never met him?" Sunnie had been certain the men must have met. Rob had owned a successful business in town for years.

Rob shook his head.

"He's only taking Aina to see the horses. Come, so I can introduce you." Sammie smiled with indulgence as she took Rob's arm in hers.

Rob looked back at Sunnie, "Remember what I said about differing parenting styles?"

She giggled at Rob's comment. Unsure of what to do, she closed the car door and walked to the front of the house, wondering where Tom was.

A whistle stopped her progress to the door. She turned her head in the direction it had come, to see Tom hanging out of a large window at the far end of the porch. She smiled, her heart soared and she hurried across the porch.

"What are you doing? You're not supposed to see me before the wedding." She did her utmost to appear annoyed. It didn't work. It never had.

"Sunnie, did you forget how we met? How much bad luck can we have?"

"This day has lasted for.ev.er. already, Tom!" She stated with a dramatic flair. "Let's leave as soon as the vows are said."

"It may be considered rude, Sunnie girl. Besides, I was looking forward to that whole 'smashing cake in the bride's face' deal. It'll probably be the only time I can get away with it."

"No, it won't. Because you're not." Sunnie saw something mischievous bloom in his eyes. "I won't come in there unless you promise me."

"Maisey taught me how to lasso. I'll get you in here. Hog-tied, if I have to. You know, I think you're getting a bump, there." Tom pointed to Sunnie's still-flat stomach. He laughed when Sunnie smoothed the blue satin with her hands.

"There is not, Thomas! Jude said the same thing this morning! Stop making me self-conscious."

"Well, it's my privilege to see it. Jude has some sort of sibling torment thing to call on. Now, get in here, it's nearly two. I have to go tie my tie." He paused, waiting on Sunnie to meet his eyes. "You look beautiful, Sunshine Young *Jacobs*."

"Sunshine *Ellen* Young Jacobs, thank you. See you inside."

The transformation inside the house took Sunnie's breath away. Flowers decked every possible surface, including a beautiful bough across each fireplace mantle. Out on the deck were balloon bouquets as well as the floral garlands gracing the railings.

Sunnie's hands covered her mouth as she prayed in thanksgiving for Stuart's generosity and love. When she contained her emotions, Silas was standing beside her. He was dressed in a smart suit and his long hair was neatly arranged instead of the shaggy style he preferred.

"Who are you and where is my brother?"

"You look terrific, Sunn. It's my pleasure." He made a quirky bow, then smoothed the hair that had flopped over his forehead before holding out his arm.

"You are quite the gentleman, Silas. Thank you."

"It's a clever ruse," he quipped. They laughed as Sunnie hooked her arm in his.

They strolled into the living room, greeting several people before Sunnie noticed Storm, Steven and their sons standing across the room. Victoria was trying to coax her younger grandson into her arms.

"Si! How?" Another detail God worked out for their special day.

"Do you think Vic and Mom would have let them miss this? They got in early this morning. Let's say hi."

Just past two o'clock, Paul made his way to the massive fireplace. He called all to attention with a shrill whistle he usually reserved for the courts. "For a small crowd, you're a feisty bunch," he wisecracked. "Where are the bride and groom? Come up front here, please."

The small crowd parted, allowing them through to the mantle.

"We all know how Tom and Sunnie became reacquainted, don't we? I believe it was at the toy store?"

Sunnie's face flushed as their guests politely laughed. Tom took Sunnie's hand and gave it an encouraging squeeze.

"Yes, it's been smooth ever since. Their road won't always be easy, as any of us who are married can attest to. Marriage is not a golden road to pure peace on earth. Though it is, most times, a slice of heaven on earth. My wife may not comment."

Laughter spread through the room again. Once the snickers faded, Paul went on. "The road Tom and Sunnie are embarking on will be filled with fender benders, no doubt. It will be much easier to bear together. Solomon spoke of this in Ecclesiastes, chapter four. He states that two can stand against one who is looking to overpower. He goes on to say a threefold cord may not be broken."

"Unless I have lost the ability to count, I only see two standing here. Yet, both Tom and Sunnie have that third element, their faith. Christ stands with them, to strengthen them, to bind them together stronger than standing alone! When things get rough—as they surely will—they have an anchor to hold them steady. When they stumble, they will brace each other. If they fall, as they will, they have each other to pick them back up."

Paul paused, now focusing on the couple. "Tom, Sunnie, who will stand with you?"

Stuart stepped forward, his chest puffing with pride. Sammie handed off Aina to Victoria and stood next to Sunnie.

"Who here gives Sunnie to be joined together with Tom in the sight of God?"

Rob stepped forward, "I do."

Sunnie leaned to hug him, whispering a teary thank you in his ear.

Paul asked Tom, "Rings?"

Tom produced white gold bands from his pocket and handed them to Paul.

"Thomas Stuart Jacobs, my longtime friend, will you take Sunshine, the woman next to you, to be your wife?"

Tom smiled, answering, "You bet."

"Sunshine Ellen Young, will you take this man, Thomas, for your husband?"

Sunnie smiled back to Tom as she answered through tears, "Absolutely."

"Do you, Mayor Jacobs, or you, Mrs. Revell, know of any reasons this marriage should not take place?"

Sammie and Stuart both answered with the more traditional, "No, we do not."

"Thomas, do you promise to abide by what Scripture speaks of, as well as the laws of the land, in all you do to take care of your wife?"

Tom solemnly nodded. "I certainly will."

"Sunshine, do you promise to abide by what the Scriptures say, as well as the laws of the land, in all you will do to be the best helper possible for Thomas?"

Sunnie nodded, "I will do my best."

"Tom, please place this ring on Sunnie's finger, repeating after me. *Word for word* this time," he requested with a grin. They both repeated their vows after Paul, sans ad libbing.

"Thomas Stuart Jacobs, you now have a wife to hold and cherish till Jesus calls you home. Sunshine Ellen Young, Thomas is now your husband, in the eyes of God and this state. You may now kiss your bride, my friend."

Tom and Sunnie stood overwhelmed, captivated by each other's eyes. Stuart finally gave Tom a shove on the back. They kissed to peals of laughter as Stuart commented, "I never thought I'd have to *make* him kiss a fine woman like that!"

"Everyone, I present to you Mr. and Mrs. Thomas Jacobs. May I be the first to say congratulations? Thank you for the most unusual wedding I can tell people about for years to come." Paul hugged them both before stepping aside so they could be congratulated by the remainder of the family.

"I find this highly unfair. I stay dressed up, and you can be comfortable."

The ceremony was through and they were enjoying plates laden with the catered buffet Stuart contracted. Tom changed from his suit to horse-riding gear.

"At the rate you're finishing that plate, you'll be busting out of that dress. I have home court advantage. In two weeks, you'll have clothes here too. I'm rather enjoying having the finest looking woman here." Tom leaned closer to whisper in Sunnie's ear. "You know, our time is up."

Sunnie grabbed his wrist to look at his watch. "Barely, mister. You still have about thirty-four minutes."

"Like I've said before. Pure. Evil. That should be on your driver's license. I'm taking Miss Aina Bug on a ride. Where's your mom?"

Sunnie pointed in the direction of the family room, where Victoria and Sammie were attempting to get all the babies to play with each other.

"When I'm done, we're cutting that cake and leaving. See you in a few." With a wink and a quick kiss, Tom was off to collect Aina for her promised ride on Picasso.

After Aina's ride, Tom and Sunnie cut the wonderful cake that Wynter had created for them. Much to the dismay of both Silas and Jude, Tom kept his promise to not smear any in Sunnie's face. After the delicious confection was consumed, they started saying their goodbyes.

Before they departed for the apartment that was now their home, Stuart placed an envelope into Sunnie's hand. "You take good care of him, now. Don't stay away too long. Picasso will miss you."

Sunnie was moved to tears by the heaviness in Stuart's voice. "We'll be back, Stuart. Don't you worry." She embraced him tightly. "You enjoy the house empty for a while. Soon you'll have a squalling baby here."

Stuart guffawed as he pulled a fresh cigar from an inner pocket. "I'm looking forward to that, Sunnie girl."

He waved the hand-rolled Don Alberto under his nose and sniffed appreciatively. He glanced back to his new daughter-in-law with a wry grin.

"I suppose you'll be banning these around my grandson?" He assumed his put-upon politician stance.

"Yes! We'll have that talk later, though. I can see that it'll be a rough one."

Tom clasped his shoulder as he walked by. Stuart lit the cigar once he watched them drive away. "Can't smoke in my own house, eh? We'll see," he muttered, going back to enjoy the party.

Tom pulled the keys from Sunnie's hand as they approached the door. He dropped his bag on the floor and faced her with a questioning look.

"Tom? What's wrong?"

"Are you going to allow me one small tradition? After all, I did keep my word about the cake."

"Depends on which one. I don't have a garter on, so you can't pull it off with your teeth." She laughed at his exaggerated eye roll. "Oh, so sorry! I assumed that was the top of your list."

Tom unlocked the door and pocketed the keys. He swooped his startled, delighted bride up into his arms. "You, Mrs. Jacobs, are being carried over the threshold. I knew you'd think it was corny since you already live here."

Sunnie's merry laugh echoed in the hallway as Tom carried her in and set her down on the couch. He nodded with satisfaction before retrieving his bag and shutting the door.

"Now, we can say we had ONE traditional custom."

"That was perfectly sweet. Thank you."

She was still holding the envelope Stuart handed her. Tom plucked it from Sunnie's hand when he sat.

"What's this?"

"Oh, I forgot. Your dad handed me that before we left. Let's see..."

Tom held the envelope away from her with a grin. "I think not."

The envelope was forgotten about until morning.

The aroma of coffee enticed Tom from bed the following morning. A wave of disappointment in not finding his bride with him passed as he pulled on sleep pants. He found a steaming container of Silas's finest residing on the kitchen counter, but not Sunnie. With a glance at the unused coffee pot, he added cream to the cup before heading back to the bedroom.

Just as he was beginning to become concerned, Sunnie appeared looking pale. She sat gingerly next to him and quickly held a hand to her mouth after a good morning kiss.

Tom laughed, rising to remove the offending paper cup. "Way to shoot down your new husband. I'm glad I know it's the coffee and not me."

"M sry. M shr ll be ver iss snn," came her muffled reply.

Tom drained the last sip before setting the cup next to the pot. He questioned Sunnie about the unused coffee maker while pulling fresh clothes from his bag.

Sunnie's face turned from pale to pink. "Well...I forgot to buy filters."

She listened to him laugh on his way to the bathroom, deciding this married thing was pretty terrific. She jotted a note on the pad on top of her Bible to buy filters before making the bed.

After an inventory of the cabinet contents for breakfast foods, they decided a trip to the store was in order. When Sunnie went to the bedroom for her bag, she spied the envelope from Stuart protruding from beneath it. She took it, along with the note about coffee filters, back to the kitchen.

"Tom! We forgot about this again!" She waved it at him before impatiently tearing the top. "I hope your father wasn't expecting a phone call last night."

"I think he knew better than to expect a call last night, Sunn. So, what's in it? We're stopping downstairs for more coffee and a muffin before we go...what's wrong?"

She seemed spellbound by the sheaves of paper in hand. She held them out to him in speechless amazement. He looked them over carefully as a grin spread across his face.

"Unless I read these wrong, we have two hours to get to Philly and catch a plane to California. Followed by a connecting flight to Hawaii."

A moment of silently absorbing the news passed. Tom tossed them in the air and grabbed Sunnie by the waist. After whooping and swinging her around once, they hurried to pack. They stopped long enough to let Silas know they were on their way to the honeymoon neither of them thought they would have. Silas and Wynter waved to them as the cab drove up Maple Street.

Chapter 23

The glow—as well as the tan—of the honeymoon was evident as Tom strode into the building two weeks later. He was greeted with congratulations and handshakes from everyone he passed on the way to clock in.

He stopped by Chief Malloy's office to thank him for the unexpected time off. With promises of pictures, as well as covering for anyone over the next six-month time frame, he headed to the garage. It was looking to be a fine day in Lakeville.

Penzi met him as he walked to his car. Tom afforded him a cool nod, attempting to go about his business.

"Whoa, Jake! I came to offer congrats, man. I guess the best man won, eh?"

"It was never a contest, Penz."

Penzi smirked. "Whatever you say, Jake. My invite to the wedding must have gotten lost in the mail. Anyhow, best wishes."

He thrust a hand at Tom, who shook it with little enthusiasm. When they broke, Penzi leaned against the fender of the cruiser. "Yup, best man. So tell me, Jake. When's the baby due?"

Tom looked at him through narrowed eyes, "Say again?"

"C'mon, Jake! Quick, hush hush wedding, flown out of town for two weeks. As only *the mayor's son* could manage. Give it a rest, man. We all know."

A quick sweep of the garage showed Tom that the people there were largely ignoring Penzi's rant. The tensions between them over Penzi's misguided ideas regarding Sunnie were well documented.

"Penziotti, I am not answering a question like that." He turned to face the few lingering to catch snippets of the discussion. "You all can think what you want. You will anyhow."

Tom turned back to Penzi. "I'm sorry that you can't be genuinely happy."

"Let's hope your wife is happy. Think you can keep her happy, Jake? I know I could. I told you that long ago."

The clear challenge was stated. As the normally bustling garage hushed, Tom made the two steps to Penzi. Toe to toe, both men looked lethal.

"Penziotti, I'll accept an apology. Only this once." Tom growled. It was more a demand than request.

Penzi sniggered. "Fat. Chance."

The stare-down lasted only moments before Penzi spit on the floor. He stalked from the garage to the station. The people in the garage made themselves busy once again, avoiding the normally friendly face that was now flush with anger.

Tom started the cruiser and slowly pulled from the garage, attempting to pray some order into his mind. He occupied himself by quoting every Bible verse he ever memorized; so much so that he missed Penzi screech from the lot just seconds behind him.

The Firebird roared up Maple Street. Penzi whipped into an open spot opposite Wynter Delights. He stormed across the busy street, stopping to advise the driver that narrowly missed hitting him with a string of profanity and hand signals.

Wynter looked up from the cash register at the sound of the screeching tires and shouting. She did not like the look on Officer Penziotti's dark face when he shoved the door open, causing the bells to ring violently. She excused herself from the register to locate her husband. She found him in the freezer, looking over inventory.

"Si Bear, that creepy cop is out front. Can you come out, please?"

Silas looked up from a ten-pound box of strawberries, frowning. "Who, Penziotti? Is he on duty?"

"I'm not sure, Bear, but he doesn't look happy. He nearly tore the door off."

Silas set his paperwork aside and joined Wynter in the front of the shop. He greeted customers warmly as he walked to the stool Penzi planted himself on.

"Officer," he nodded. "What can I get you?"

"How about your sister?" he snarled. "I wanted to congratulate her."

Silas's guard went on high alert. "She's not available. I'll be sure to pass along your message, though. Let me know if you need anything else."

Back at the register, he scribbled a note and handed it to Wynter. "Babe, go check to see if we have this. I'll watch the register."

Wynter glanced at the paper in hand, reading "CALL SUNNIE". She nodded and dashed to the kitchen, only to hear the bells announcing Sunnie's untimely arrival in the shop.

Flourishing a brilliant smile, Sunnie greeted her brother and sister-in-law before she sat at the counter. Oblivious to the brooding man on the other end, she beckoned to Silas.

"Si, we had the most delicious something or another with coconut and macadamia nuts. Do you think you can use that in a muffin? You can even name it after me; how's that? Sunshine Special." Sunnie framed her splayed hands around her face and smiled a cheesy smile. "Sounds great, right?"

She turned to the person who tapped her shoulder. The happy mood vanished when she realized she was trapped on the stool. She was unable to back away from the proximity Penzi put himself in or the smoldering gaze that was fixed on her.

"What do you want, Penzi?" Sunnie brushed at her shoulder, as though something atrocious was stuck there.

"I tried to wish Jake my best, but he wasn't accepting. I thought I'd stop by and offer you regrets instead. Sorry he saddled you with a kid so soon. He should have enjoyed you a while longer. You can get my number from him in case you need a real man to take care of things. You know, I won't...slip—" his disgusting intent was made clear by the sweeping leer "—and make a baby."

As shocked as she was at Penzi's speech, Silas's arm shooting past her from behind was more surprising. Penzi's collar filled his fist, pulling him tight against the counter.

"Listen, you slime bag—this is my sister, and you *will* apologize. Then, you will no longer patronize my business. Unless you have an apology to spit out, get out."

All eyes were focused on the normally sanguine shop owner. Sunnie tried to pry his hand from Penzi's shirt without success.

"Si, calm down," she whispered.

He looked to Sunnie, then reluctantly released Penzi's collar. "Leave."

Penzi smoothed his shirt meticulously. With one last lingering look that caused Sunnie's nausea to come rushing back four-fold, Penzi left the shop. She slumped in the stool, shaken to the core by the bizarre confrontation.

Silas hopped over the counter, unconcerned about his customers' wide-eyed stares. "Sunn? Are you okay?"

She nodded, using her yoga breathing techniques before answering. "Yes, Si, I'm fine. What in the world is his problem? He's a freak." The adrenaline was subsiding, and Sunnie's voice shook. "I need to call Tommy."

"No, Sunn. No use bothering him on duty; I'll tell him tonight." Silas nodded toward the door. "He won't be back."

He turned to the few customers still goggling. "Hey, coffee on the house. Please. Sorry about the bad reality show."

Several laughed, none took Silas up on his offer, and the tip cup seemed abnormally full once the crowd had dispersed. Sunnie stayed around the shop until she received a text from Tom saying he'd be home in the hour.

Sunnie was stirring a large pot of pasta sauce when Tom walked through their door. She tried to mirror his smile after he kissed her in greeting.

"Great to be home. I'll be out in ten," he assured her before leaving the kitchen. She informed him of their company's imminent arrival when he returned from showering.

He looked crestfallen, casting an exasperated glance at the door when Silas's knock sounded. "It's our first night back. Couldn't it wait?"

Sunnie attempted to lighten the mood as they all sat around the table in stilted silence. "Silas is really the one who makes the best sauce. His is even better than Mom's."

Tom prayed before the pasta and salad were passed. Wynter opened dinner discussion asking about Hawaii, and Sunnie jumped to get her camera. Some of the tension left the room until Sunnie turned to Tom, intending to tell him about the muffin suggestion. The look on his face silenced any idle chatter she planned to make.

"What happened today? I know something did."

"Oh. Well...Tommy..." Sunnie looked over to Silas.

"Tom, we had an incident in the shop today. I wanted to let you know what went down."

As he relayed the story, Tom listened with quiet intensity. When it was over, Tom turned towards Sunnie with eyes that had turned an angry, steely gray.

"Did he touch you?"

"When he tapped my shoulder. I hate that this is trouble for you at work! I wish he'd just leave me...us...alone!"

The outburst of emotions unsettled her stomach, and she dashed for the bathroom. Wynter watched after her and Silas turned back to Tom.

"I didn't want to crash your first night back. I thought it better that I told you. If I overstepped here, I apologize," Silas offered.

Tom waved a hand. "No apology needed, Si. I'm glad that you were there. He must have come right after he saw me in the morning." He rehashed the incident at the garage.

"Do you think he's...ya know..." Silas tapped his head and Wynter shuddered at the thought.

Tom balled his napkin in hand, manifesting his tension. "No. He needs to get over it. I'm not happy that it's turning this way." He sighed, scrubbing at his chin.

"Be right back. I'm going to check on Sunnie." He tossed the ball into his pasta bowl before rising from the table.

He knocked on the bathroom door. "Sunn? C'mon out. Are you okay?"

Sunnie met him at the door with puffy eyes and a tired smile. "Sorry. I guess the baby isn't enjoying pasta tonight. Can you put water on for tea? See if Si and Wynnie want to stay. I'll meet you on the roof."

Tom nodded, "Sounds perfect." He kissed Sunnie's forehead. "Relax, all right? I'll take care of this."

She kissed his cheek before shutting the door.

Wynter had the table cleared of dinner dishes, and Silas was pouring sauce into Tupperware. Tom picked up the salad bowl as he extended the offer.

"Sure, Tom. Sounds good. Tell me all about windsurfing. I am so trying that at the shore this year."

Wynter laughed. "Hear that? He thinks we'll be able to *have* a vacation this year!"

They took the water sports discussion to the roof once coffee was ready for consumption. Sunnie eventually joined in, squeezing into a hammock chair with Tom.

"Now, how am I supposed to drink my coffee? I highly doubt this chair was made for three."

Sunnie ignored Tom's complaint, settling back against his chest."I think it's just right. So, what about that Sunshine Special? Who doesn't like coconut and macadamia?"

Following a spirited exchange over the culinary delights of coconut, Silas and Wynter said goodnight. Sunnie and Tom stayed in their spot as he rocked the chair slowly with his foot. The sky was slightly overcast, several dark clouds drifting past the waning moon.

"I wish we were still in Hawaii," Sunnie sighed.

Tom positioned a hand across Sunnie's stomach. "I don't think we could afford to have stayed another day, Mrs. Jacobs. You spent a boatload of money. I need to go over the books with you."

Sunnie applauded, to Tom's surprise. "I hate accounting, Tom. I happily relinquish all but my business card to you. I'm even happy to let you run that account. I have a ton to do this week, don't I? Do we even use the same bank?"

"Who cares? We can open our own account in a new bank. Everything new for us. New house, new car..."

Sunnie sat up, peering at Tom. "I ain't giving up my car. Are you getting rid of the Jeep?"

Tom laughed over Sunnie's attachment to her Miata. "No. Are you planning on being some hot babe-type of mom? Desperate Housewife of Lakeville?"

"You are deranged, husband-of-mine. Can we just...well, just enjoy being us for a little while before we have to make all these huge decisions?"

Tom pulled Sunnie against his chest. "Of course, Sunnie girl. Well, house has to be soon if we want it ready in time for the baby. But not tonight. Let me know when you're ready. I promise; we'll enjoy being Mr. and Mrs. Jacobs. Do you think you'll be all right to ride for a little while longer?"

"I need to call Mom's doctor and make an appointment. I don't see why not. I'm not jumping fences, right? I barely get Picasso to a trot."

"I should ask Pop how long Mom rode before I was born. Knowing Mom, she probably went into labor on Confetti."

Sunnie loved how Tom's voice changed when he talked about his mother, the affection softening him.

"Where did Confetti come from? That's such a neat name." She snuggled into Tom's chest, enjoying the swaying of the chair and the peace she now felt. The afternoon's upset forgotten, Sunnie closed her eyes and listened to the story.

"Confetti was my father's wedding gift. They courted—very old-fashioned Irish family my Mom had—for almost ten years. They wanted to make certain he had a solid job, good prospects, etc. I thought I would go out of my mind the weeks we didn't talk, Sunnie. I don't know how he lasted ten years," Tom commented. Sunnie sleepily giggled.

"In any case, when Confetti was born, Pop gave her to Mom. He said she really took to horses and life here with him. Her family moved here from the Lower West Side of New York City when she was only fourteen or so. Total city girl. He says that she was afraid to ride, but got up on a horse with him anyhow. That's when he knew how much she loved him. She completely embraced life with my father on that land. Are you still with me, Sunnie girl?"

Sunnie's even deep breathing told Tom she had fallen asleep. Swaying softly under the stars, Tom prayed over Sunnie, the baby and everything they needed to accomplish in the coming months. He prayed for God's help and strength to be the best husband he was able to be before he fell into a light sleep.

Chapter 24

As the days passed, the need to confront Penzi grew. Knowing he could be found at The Corral, Tom stopped in at the end of his tour. The stench of stale alcohol filled his nostrils long before his eyes adjusted to the dim light.

Penzi looked up from the pool table when he heard the door. A nasty grin emerged, and he aimed the cue, shooting with ferocity when Tom approached the table. The white ball sailed through the air, beyond its intended target. It hit the top of the bar before rolling to a stop at someone's foot.

"What do you want, Jake?" he asked vehemently, nearly knocking his drink over instead of picking it up. "Go run home to the wifey. This isn't the place for nice married boys."

The drink sloshed onto the table when he put it down, staining the green felt. Someone replaced the ball and quickly left the officers alone.

"Penz, I have no idea what your current problem is, but it better stop being *my* wife. Stay away from her."

"Oh, Jake, stop! You scare me, man. Get the hell out of here. I'll talk to who I want, when I want. Just what are you going to do about it? I know you too well. You aren't going to do anything."

"You're right, Penziotti. It stops now. You *will* stop hassling Sunnie."

The interest of the patrons grew as the volume of their argument rose. Artfully appearing busy, the bartender did not miss a single word as he hovered close to the house phone.

"What's the matter, Jacobs? Afraid Sunnie will wake up one day and realize you trapped her? Boy, I should have thought of knocking up some dopey broad! I thought you were way too holy for that."

It was to his misfortune that he turned away. Before he could grasp his drink, Tom was around the table and they were colliding with the far wall.

Penzi swung the pool cue, clipping Tom's face as he ducked. They wrestled over it before Tom pulled it from his hand and tossed it aside. The bartender picked up the phone and dialed the number for the police garage as the fight continued to clear the tables around them.

In minutes, more officers came through the doors, separating Tom and Penzi with some difficulty. They escorted the bloodied men out the back exit to whispered speculation of who would be suspended or fined.

Chief Malloy was stunned to see who his two bar brawling officers were. Neither had much to say during their on-the-carpet interview except that the fight was mutual. With the promise of a reprimand letter in each of their personal jackets that would include orders to attend an Anger Management course, he sent them on their way. The Chief wondered how to keep this piece of information from making its way across the complex to Mayor Jacob's office.

Once Tom received his new tour—the one he hated—he stopped in the locker room to wash the blood from his face and hands. *Nice move*, he chided himself as he examined the cut over his eye. Scrapes on his knuckles stung in the hot water, draining the anger from Tom's mind.

He returned to The Corral to apologize and offer restitution for any damages incurred. The owner waved him off, desiring no further patronage from Officers Jacobs or Penziotti. It was an uncomfortable visit that was scrutinized by most of the patrons.

Tom called Sunnie, offering to pick up dinner on the way home. The four flights of stairs to the apartment seemed to have increased ten-fold. When she greeted him at the door, she gasped in surprise at his injured face.

"Tom! What happened? Are you all right?" When he placed the bags on the table, she threw her arms around him. Nothing this day had hurt so bad, yet felt so good.

"Penzi and I had a disagreement. No big deal. Let me go wash up. How about we go sit out on the roof? It's a nice night." He walked to their room to change from the dirty uniform pants and bloodied shirt.

"Oh no you don't! Do you really think that I accept that blasé attitude?" Sunnie followed him to the bathroom. "Where did this happen? Did he start again?"

Tom winced when the hot washcloth hit the open wound. "No, I started. Make you feel better?"

He walked to their room, Sunnie following closely, expecting an explanation. He pulled loose clothing from a drawer and continued. "I told him to leave you alone. He wasn't agreeable to the idea, so he tried to clock me with a pool stick."

Sunnie's eyes widened.

"I'm sure he'll need a nose job tonight." Tom ended without apology. He painfully pulled the shirt over his head.

"Tom, this is so unlike you. Are you sure you're okay?" Sunnie inspected the gash over Tom's eye. "You should let me put a butterfly on that. I wish you didn't fight with him."

Sunnie went to the bathroom, returning with a box of bandages. She dumped half the box on the mattress before finding the butterfly. Tom was amused with her ministrations until she squeezed the gaping cut closed and secured the bandage over it.

"That was unpleasant," Tom breathed when she was done.

Sunnie sniffed as she put the extra bandages back in the box. "Serves you right. Do you know how many times I watched my mother patch up my father after a bar fight? Big, tough Jackie. He would moan like a baby when Mom cleaned the cuts and bruises. I hope this isn't going to be a normal thing, Tommy."

"Please don't think this is some new behavior for me. One thing led to another, and I wanted to beat him senseless. I don't enjoy that feeling, Sunn. Power trips are not my thing. Getting reamed by the Chief is not a fun way to end the day." He relayed the order for Anger Management to become part of his weekly routine.

"We need to pray that he leaves us both alone, Tommy. You can't punch him out every time you see him. I'd like you to," Sunnie added with a wink. "But you can't. It's just not...well, it's not the Tommy that I fell in love with."

Tom reached to Sunnie, caressing her arm. "I know, and I promise it won't happen again. I'm just hoping Pop won't get wind of it."

They walked back to the kitchen, and Sunnie readied their dinner plates. When she brought them to the table, she asked, "Would he? I mean, is it very gossipy down there?"

"I guess," Tom shrugged and dug into his dinner. "I never pay attention. Once in a while I hear something in the garage, but I usually ignore it. I know the guys yak. I know he hears things. He'd come home asking me about something or another and more often than not I'd have no idea what he was talking about."

"Well, expect him to call. I'll bet it's worse than junior high. Seriously, men are such old ladies when it comes to gossip. The men at Weston were more into what was happening in the office than the women were. Inter-office email is the bane of business. I'm so glad I'm not in that environment anymore."

They ate in silence, each reflecting on the incident. He retrieved his remaining cartons once he cleared his plate. Sunnie made a face as he mixed everything together, not on his plate, but in the largest carton.

He grinned, "Don't bother with plates, Sunn. It's just extra work."

"I hope the kids don't eat like you...fast and furious. You need to enjoy your food. And I like dishes, especially when it's your night to wash them." She laughed and put her tongue out before resuming her meal.

"You eat slow. I'll bet that's not even warm any more. Further, even though I'm sure it's your night for dishes, I will do them. Will it make up for my childish behavior?" Tom winked over the carton.

"I'll think about it. Depends on what we do after dinner." Sunnie afforded him a huge, cheesy return wink, and they laughed.

They cleaned up the kitchen together and enjoyed a movie before heading to bed. By that time, the incident was forgiven and forgotten.

The last week of September Sunnie came home from a property showing to a giant vase of sunflowers on the coffee table. She laughed out loud when she removed the card featuring two crashed cars.

Sunnie struggled into her last pair of jeans that she deemed publicly acceptable to wear. She had questioned Sammie days before the doctor's appointment about her sudden rounded appearance. Assured by her mother that all was well within the bounds of normalcy, she shrugged an oversized sweater over her head to conceal the fact that the jeans would not zip. Shopping for maternity clothing seemed to be in order.

She studied the mirror as she reflected on her wardrobe needs. Always slender, her new fuller-figured form was taking some getting used to. She turned from the mirror with a shrug, pleased that her husband held no complaints in that area.

Apprehension made its unwelcome appearance when they pulled into the parking garage at the medical complex. In a way it hadn't before, it was all becoming a reality. In several months, she would be a mother.

Tom took her hand and prayed before they left the confines of the Jeep. She held the same hand tightly as they ascended the elevator to Doctor Zander's floor.

Doctor Zander looked Sunnie over with a professional eye as she explained the paperwork. Leaving the couple in the capable hands of the office staff, she walked to the ultra sound room.

"Radar? Are you in here?"

Kyle deGroot—AKA Radar—emerged from his office. "I am, Doc. Are you in need?"

"I think so. I wasn't planning on it, but the dates aren't lining up with the body, if you catch me."

Radar nodded. "I surely do. Chart?"

Doctor Zander disappeared a moment, returning with the chart. Not given to sudden outbursts over patient information, he cried out in surprise when he read the name. "No way!"

Doctor Zander was intrigued by his reaction. "Radar, you didn't even see her yet."

Radar waved the chart at her. "I know her! She was in the first yoga class I taught! Her husband's name is familiar, too. What a trip!"

"We'll be back in about thirty minutes. You can have a reunion." Doctor Zander walked back to the examination room Sunnie and Tom were in.

The usual medically informative questions were asked. Doctor Zander was not content with the responses garnered.

"Sunnie, are you certain of your last known period? You have it listed as late June."

Sunnie nodded. Doctor Zander was not convinced.

"Tom, can you please stand up here at the top of the table? Sunnie, feet here, that's right. So, do you see your younger siblings often?" They continued the light discussion as she went through the steps of the basic examination.

"We see the little ones fairly often. Tom takes Aina horseback riding. Since I'm just learning, I don't. Is it alright for me to continue?"

The doctor nodded absently. Things were not lining up properly.

"Sunnie, I need to make sure of this date. Are you absolutely certain of the last week of June?"

"Absolutely!" the couple answered in unison.

Doctor Zander looked between them. "You both seem assured of the date. Please follow me to the ultrasound room. I'd like a more definitive answer."

"Is something wrong? Sunnie's been doing great, she eats well, does yoga. No more throwing up," Tom asked as he helped her from the table.

Doctor Zander shook her head. "Oh no. I don't think anything is wrong. Tell me, do you have a family history of twins? I know that Sunnie doesn't. Not that it comes through the father's family line. I'm just curious."

"Sure. Cousins, uncles, and grandparents. Ow, Sunn. What's wrong?"

"Twins?!? Tom...twins? You never tell me anything! I think I'm going to faint."

Tom assumed it would be a toss-up as to who fainted first. The grip of Sunnie's fingers on his arm began to cause circulation issues.

Doctor Zander smiled to them. "I have another surprise for you, Sunnie. Our tech, Radar, is a friend of yours. Of course, I'm sure you know him as Kyle."

He greeted them brightly upon entering the room. "Sunshine Young! So good to see you after all these years! You never show up at any reunions. How have you been? Still keeping up on the yoga?"

"Well, right now I'm a bit stunned. Do you remember Tom?"

Radar turned to him with an outstretched hand.

"Name is familiar. Football?" Tom nodded. "Good to see you again, too. We should get together sometime. There's a terrific vegetarian restaurant next town over..."

Doctor Zander interrupted the reunion. "Yes, Radar, I'm sure there is. Right now we need to see if my suspicions are correct. As I tell all my patients, Radar is the best there is. I prefer him to do the initial ultra sounds, but if you have an objection, I can do it myself."

"No, it's fine by me. I'm pretty nervous...if you think there's more than one baby here, I want the best to be looking for it. Is that okay, Tom?"

Tom nodded. "I'm anxious as you are. Let's get it going!"

In the dimmed lighting, Sunnie watched Radar glide the wand back and forth, pausing here and there in concentration. A smile broke as he commented, "There's one!"

Both Tom and Sunnie became mesmerized by the tiny image on the screen.

"Here's the other. Hiding behind each other. They do that. Do you want to know?"

"Know what? There's not more?" Sunnie's voice rose in panic. Doctor Zander patted her hand assuringly as Tom and Radar shared a laugh.

"No, Sunnie. There are two, only two. But, most certainly two. They look wonderfully healthy. What Radar meant was do you want to know the sex?"

Radar continued to point and click in silence while the couple decided.

Sunnie could see the excitement in Tom's eyes, even in the dim light. She felt the wonderful assurance of his love swirl around her as sure as his arms would have held her. Joy replaced the anxiety that had briefly welled up.

"Whatever you want, Tommy. You make the call."

He leaned down to kiss her forehead gently. He said to Radar, "Go ahead. Give us a full report."

Radar pointed out hearts, lungs, eyes, the smallest noses. Finally, with a whoop from Tom, the boys were in clear focus.

"You're fifteen weeks, three days, Sunnie. Everything looks great on this end, Doc. Two sacs, two placentas, two of everything. I'll make a few copies of things here for you to take. It's been a real pleasure to see you again. I'm very happy for you both."

Back in Doctor Zander's office, they listened to all she said about nutrition, exercise and horseback riding. Sunnie was particularly disappointed over the news that the doctor preferred she stop.

"I normally—even with twins—wouldn't consider a woman your age and health to be high risk. However, horseback riding poses its own dangers. You have my best advice. I will leave that with you and your husband to decide. Continue your yoga. I'd like you to up the protein in your diet. Fish or chicken, rather than soy. Thank you, Radar," she said as he popped his head in with copies of the ultrasound on disc and film for Sunnie and Tom.

"I do have to say, we normally aren't so exuberant here. It's a very nice change of pace. I'll be seeing you again next month, unless you have a concern. Convey my congratulations to your mother, please. I'm sure she and Rob will be happy with your news."

Sunnie stared at the pictures while Tom guided her through the hallways to the garage. Once in the Jeep, they both gazed at the pictures of their baby boys.

"Tommy, tell me one thing," Sunnie said in a whisper. "Are you still glad I'm so *unusual?*"

Sunnie watched the smile break over Tom's face. This was a tremendously happy man. She was content to be the vessel of his happiness.

"Sunnie, I would have been surprised if there was *only* one. You do tend to do things in a big way."

They drove to the Ranch to share the news with Stuart and ask him where they could start building the house they would need by April.

Chapter 25

On Christmas Eve, Sunnie made a pot of chili and a batch of cornbread. While their delicious aromas filled the apartment, she wrapped and placed Tom's gift under their small tree. When everything was ready, she laid down on the couch with a book, waiting for Tom to come home.

Tom ran late; he stopped at Stuart's to pick up Sunnie's gift. He chuckled at the vision that greeted him when he opened the door. As quiet as a mouse he put Sunnie's gift next to the tree. He removed the book from his sleeping wife's hand and put it on the coffee table.

Tom set the table as the chili reheated. Once everything was ready, he went to the couch to rouse Sunnie. She looked so peaceful that he contented himself gazing at her a few moments. He brushed random curls from her face before calling to her.

"Sunnie? Hey, wake up, Sunnie girl."

"No, go away," a sleepy mumble insisted.

Tom smiled softly as he gently shook her shoulder. "Love you too, Sunnie. It's time to get up."

Ten minutes of coaxing later, Sunnie was sitting up wiping sleep from her eyes.

"I can't believe how tired these two make me already! Help me up, please, so I can get dinner heated up."

"Don't worry about dinner. It's all ready to go as soon as you are."

She kissed his cheek after he helped her to her feet. "You are so good to me, Officer Jacobs. I'll never understand why, but I'm glad that you are." She left him with a smile as she headed towards the bathroom.

After dinner was consumed and kitchen gleaming, they watched a holiday movie. When the credits started rolling, Tom clicked the TV off and handed her the brightly wrapped box.

"Please don't tell me you like to peel tape," he teased and was rewarded with torn and crumbled paper in his lap. The delighted squeal when she realized what was in the box made the evening.

She placed a silver riding helmet on her head. "I'm sleeping in this. It's not coming off until I can ride Picasso again."

"It's time you had your own. I debated a top hat like Pop's, but that one seemed to be more you. It's the same color as the Miata."

"Truly, only Stuart can ride a horse with a top hat on. Thank you so much, Tommy. Here," Sunnie handed Tom the box she had wrapped earlier. "I hope you like it."

Tom unwrapped his gift, opened the box, and lifted a simple frame from the tissue paper trappings. The emotions washed over his face as he read through the prayer that had come with his angel. Sunnie had hand-written it out on heavy parchment paper and framed it.

The simple prayer had been the first expression of the feelings Sunnie held for him before she was ready to commit to them. Tom replaced the frame back into the tissue and put the box on the coffee table. She went to his open arms and they sat for some time before Tom was able to speak.

"You'll never know how much that means to me, Sunnie girl. Thank you."

New Year's Eve brought below freezing temperatures in a crisply clear night for Lakeville's annual fireworks. Bundled in layers of coats, hats and gloves, Tom and Sunnie observed them from the roof before scurrying down the spiral stairs to watch the New York City insanity known as The Ball Drop.

While Sunnie's head rested securely on Tom's shoulder, she prayed in a whisper for their new year together. She prayed for Butch and Sundance—their nicknames for the twins—the house construction, even for Penzi. Sunnie wasn't surprised when Tom joined her in an amen at the end. Many nights when Sunnie thought Tom was sleeping through her prayers he would finish with her.

"You could have told me you were awake," Sunnie said quietly, rearranging the twins against Tom's side.

"I like to listen. I love to listen to you pray." He reached to give the boys a soft rub; he felt them settling into the new place Sunnie moved them to.

"I never did learn to pray silently, besides those quick 'Help me' type things." She kissed his cheek and rested her head against him with a languid sigh.

"I hope you never do." Tom answered, pulling Sunnie as close as possible before they both fell asleep.

Sunnie peered through the bedroom blinds to be greeted by a sloppy mix of snow and rain. She sighed at the sky before turning away. Seven months along and feeling every move the twins made, she was beginning to reap the emotional effects from lack of sleep.

She glanced at her husband, envious of his ability to drop into an instant and deep slumber. Although he attempted to enter quietly when he was on the 3-11 tour,

Sunnie still was roused before the benefits of REM introduced themselves.

Meandering from her room to the stove, she put water on for tea. All she desired this dreary morning was to sit quietly while Butch and Sundance were content to do the same.

Plodding to the office, she punched the computer's power switch to be entertained by the lazy flashing of lights as it awoke. She lowered herself into the chair to watch the screen brighten. It seemed the world, including her every move, had slowed to an incremental pace.

"Of course!" she groaned at the screen when the email opened. A note from their contractor with yet another delay in the building of their home topped the Inbox list. Sunnie pushed herself from the desk to answer the whistling tea pot before its persistent call woke Tom.

The sale of the building between her and her brothers–already in process–would have to be suspended again. Of course Silas wouldn't evict them, and her mother certainly wasn't pushing Jude out the door. The benefits of a private sale through family were not outweighing the annoyances of the delays.

Tom's assurances of living with Stuart did not assuage her ire with the situation. It was an option she stubbornly refused to consider. The subject was a frequent source of perfecting patience with his temperamental—and lately, irrational—bride.

"I should eat...something," she muttered as she shut the flame under the tea pot. She searched the fridge as the tea steeped. Yogurt and granola were the only appealing sounding choices. Placing the yogurt on the counter reminded her to set up the coffee pot. She pulled a jar of granola and the can of coffee from the cabinet.

After spooning grounds into the basket, she turned to run the water before she pulled the pot from the maker. Her hand grazed the jar of granola, sending it sliding from the counter to crash at her feet. The sounds of shattering glass brought a dazed Tom from the bedroom to find her in the midst of brown bits, nuts, raisins and glass shards.

"Are you all right, Sunn?" Tom asked, scrubbing sleep from his face.

"Do I look all right? I should just go back to bed." She swiveled the faucet handle off. "Why are you up?"

Tom overlooked her snappish tone. "Because my wife is throwing jars of granola about the kitchen. Go inside; I'll clean that up before I shower. Can you turn the coffee pot on?"

Sunnie poured water in the coffee maker and punched the button with more force than required. She stepped over the mess of glass and granola and went to their room. After struggling into the first pair of jeans that she found–ones that refused to button–she stalked back to the door.

"I'm going to Silas's for something to eat."

"Great, grab a muffin for me." Tom called. The mess was gone and he was enjoying coffee by the time she came back up. She tossed the bag on the table as she sunk into a chair across from him.

"What's the matter, Sunn? No sleep again last night?" He pulled the bag across the table and took his muffin out.

"Of course I didn't sleep well!" she snipped. Once she evened out her breathing, she complained over the contractor's message.

"Sunnie girl, I told you we can stay with Pop. It's not the big deal you insist it is."

Her closely boiling temper erupted. They argued at the table longer than Tom would have liked until he finally pronounced, "You are far too intense over this. I know you can do this rationally."

Sunnie was unimpressed. "I'd rather do it now when we have the time and money. I think you need to speak to them."

Tom finished his coffee and made a silent plea for patience. When he rose from the table, he looked down at her. "I think you're determined to fight with someone today, and unfortunately I happen to be available. Put on some praise music and do some yoga. You'll see things in a whole new light once your head is clear."

"Of course, I can deal with them," she assured herself after he walked away. "I know the codes better than they do! And they think I can't add, either."

She completed the thought with a sharp nod and went to the office. She framed six different versions of an email before she pressed "draft" instead of "send." Giving it all up for the moment, she heaved herself from the chair and went to their room.

Tom was still rubbing a towel over his damp head when he entered behind her. "What's on the agenda today?"

Sunnie closed her eyes, counted to twenty. "Not sure. Right now, it's the shower."

Tom caught her in his arms as she attempted to walk by. "Why didn't you come in? We haven't had much time together this week. That would have been a very nice treat."

On an ordinary day, being playfully captured melted Sunnie's resistance as well as any attitude. Not this day.

"I'm really not in a treat mood, Officer Jacobs," Sunnie specified, extracting herself from the embrace. By the time she was out, toweled her hair, and dressed, Tom was ready to leave.

"Where is that number? I'll call once I get to the station. I'm leaving in ten. Paperwork that I haven't gotten to needs my attention."

Expecting anything but the caustic tone, Sunnie stammered, "But...your lunch..."

"No time. The number?"

Angry tears threatened to spill as Sunnie turned from him. She printed out the morning's email while he stewed by the counter as the coffee maker spurted out his to-go cup of brew.

She thrust the paper at him when she returned. "The number is in the signature."

He stared at her a moment before taking it from her hand. It was deliberately folded into quarters and carefully tucked into his wallet. Keeping a measured tone, he asked, "And what should I demand of them, Mrs. Jacobs? That we require his head on a spit if we cannot be in by the day originally promised?"

Sunnie answered in the defensive. "Of course not, don't be stupid. Just find out what can be done to get us in as soon as possible."

"Stupid," the unintelligible retort sputtered from him. He pushed the wallet into his back pocket and seized his coffee. "See you tomorrow." He whisked past her without a glance back.

Sunnie realized she had trampled the line of tolerance he held for her erratic mood swings. She followed him to the door, hoping to placate him with a smile.

"Kiss?"

It didn't take long to contemplate the request. He always kissed Sunnie goodbye, even if she was sleeping.

"I'm not really in a treat mood, Mrs. Jacobs." He yanked the door closed behind him.

Shaking herself from the spot she seemed rooted to, Sunnie went to their bedroom. She gathered dirty laundry before stripping the bed of its sheets. After piling it all into a wicker laundry basket, she decided to call Sammie.

"Mom must be home. I think I'll do laundry there." She picked up her phone and ignored speed dial. She swiftly punched out the ten digits, drumming her fingers on the dresser before Sammie answered.

"Hi, Mom. I was wondering if I can come by with laundry? Since I have to lug it downstairs anyhow, I thought I'd visit."

"Is everything all right?" Sammie always asked, concerned about the health and welfare of her grandsons. Satisfied all was well with the babies, she offered, "Of course. I'll make some lunch. Did you eat yet?"

"Thanks, Mom, I didn't."

"Is Tom joining us?"

The impatient sound on Sunnie's end signified he was not. "He went in early today... something about paperwork. I'll be there in a few." She hung up to avoid further explanation.

Sammie prayed through lunch preparations. Their adjustment to married life appeared to be going well. Pondering what lay beneath today's uproar–if there was one–could wait until she saw her face to face. When her daughter's car pulled up the driveway, Sammie was prepared to greet her with both spiritual and physical sustenance.

Chapter 26

"Hi, Mom." Sunnie breathed when she opened the kitchen door. The forced smile did not alleviate the fatigue on her face. Sammie called for Rob as Sunnie plunked into a chair and tossed the bag from Silas's shop on the table, along with her keys.

Sammie placed a glass of cold water in front of her, pushing some unruly curls behind her daughter's ear. "You look tired, baby girl. Not sleeping?"

"Not this week. Tom's on 3-11. It's always been hard for me to adjust to, and it's even harder now. Hi Rob."

Rob appeared in the kitchen and leaned down to kiss her cheek. "Hey there, momma. How's the babies?"

"Keeping me up. Where's Aina? I have a cookie for her. It's even better than a flower—it's a horse."

"I'll get her in a minute, Sunnie. She's playing quietly while River takes a nap. Samm, what did you need?"

"You mean, besides to see you?" Sammie winked. "Could you get Sunnie's laundry out of her car?"

Sunnie started to rise from the chair protesting, but Rob's gentle hand and light laugh kept her in place.

"No, it's fine. She always makes me do the hard work. I think that's why she married me, Sunnie. To carry laundry and reach the high shelves in the grocery store."

He took Sunnie's keys from the table before pulling the hood of his sweatshirt up to avoid rain before he went outside.

"I made some egg salad and a nice green salad too. Are you getting enough protein in a day? I know Doctor Zander said that this vegetarian thing is fine, but I'd feel much better knowing you at least had some chicken."

Sunnie snickered. "Have you been talking to Tom? He pesters me about it daily. You all know I eat chicken and fish."

The opportunity to speak to Sunnie alone appeared with Rob as he walked back into the kitchen carrying Sunnie's laundry.

"Rob, how would you like to treat Miss Aina to lunch out? This may be one of the last chances I have for a good long visit with Sunnie before the babies are keeping her attention."

"I think that's a fine idea. I'll just put this by the machines for you. Do we need anything while I'm out?"

"I don't think so; I'll call you if I think of anything. Thank you."

Rob brought the play yard into the kitchen before he left for his date with Aina. She kissed her mother and sister goodbye and admonished River to be a good boy. The baby happily played as the women enjoyed their lunch.

The report on the screen offered no insights to the officer staring at it. He always played the part of patient peacekeeper in their frequent tiffs. Normally, they'd talk through the issue and make the necessary adjustments. This morning had been off for both of them.

"I shouldn't have left things the way I did," Tom pointed out to the screen. He glanced at the time, calculated how many hours it was until he'd be home again and purposed to call Sunnie at the first opportunity his tour allowed.

Sunnie ranted to her mother about the house—and Tom's attitude.

The contractors—and Tom's lack of help with them.

Her lack of sleep—and Tom's waking her up when he was on the midday tour.

Sammie absorbed it all, nibbling her sandwich and praying over her response.

"Then he just...left. Do you believe that?" Sunnie sputtered when finished with her detailed accounting.

"Yes, you seem to have had quite a morning." Sammie placed the uneaten portion of sandwich on her plate and pushed back from the table. "I'll be back in a minute."

"Sure, Mom."

Returning moments later with her Bible, Sammie placed it on the table.

"What you are going to do, Sunshine Ellen, is open this to the book of Hosea. I will start your laundry. Do not leave this table until you read it—all of it. We'll talk more about your—*troubles*—when you're through."

Sunnie pulled the thick book towards her. She recognized her mother's tone; she was going to have some instruction on her attitude.

As Sammie busied herself with laundry, changing River and clearing lunch, Sunnie pored through the story. When a piping hot basket of laundry was placed at her feet, she closed the book.

"Okay, Mom. Why did you have me read that?"

"If it's not obvious, I'm concerned. Don't you think you are being unfair to your husband?" She brought refreshed iced tea to the table.

"I get that, Mom, but comparing me with a prostitute? Isn't that harsh?"

"Not at all, Sunnie. We all sell ourselves to things other than God and His best for us. Especially those of us who don't need to be very concerned about where our next meal is coming from. Whose husbands have good, steady work. Having been on both sides, I find it's harder being secure. I don't think that you have given a whit of thought about how your relationship with Tom is perceived outside of your family. Tom put his own reputation on the line by marrying you quickly. I'm sure his fellow officers have their own ideas about things. How easy can it be for him at work to begin with, having his father in such a high position in town? All these things I'm sure play into his stress on the job, Sunnie. Adding stress over ridiculous things at home is very unfair of you. Your lack of compassion is surprising."

A wave of contrition rolled over Sunnie, quelling the argument that had swiftly come to her mind. She lowered her eyes and concentrated on the laundry basket.

"You fold socks and underwear; I'll take shirts. Your linens are drying now."

Sage advice imparted, Sammie hummed as she folded. The basket was almost empty when Sunnie asked, "Mom, do you really think that Tom has a hard time at work? He's never indicated that."

"I think more than he might say. Vic has told me about some of her childhood here. As a child of the mayor, they had to be above things. Similar to the children of the pastor in your church. Do you know who they are?"

"Of course, everyone knows who his kids are. One of them is always..." she stopped, realizing she made assumptions that were not always correct.

"Do you see now what I'm getting at, Sunnie? No matter what Tom does, he's watched. Did you notice how Hosea obeyed God, no matter what the people said? A prophet, married to a whore? Yet, he loved her because God commanded him to, no matter how his own people perceived it. Tom loves you. He married you because he loves you, no matter what others thought. The babies aside, he accepted you. Even if God hadn't brought the babies into the picture, would he have married you?"

"Yes," she whispered.

"Sunnie, you need to think beyond yourself. Think of all that Tom has given up for you. Maybe he wanted to have a nice, traditional wedding? Perhaps, he preferred to build the house on a different site? I'm certain he would have enjoyed a touch of affection from you today, before he went to put his life on the line for the citizens of Lakeville."

Sunnie sighed, tipping her head back a moment. "You're right, Mom. I've been so wrapped up in my own self. It's so hard." She ceased examining the ceiling and looked back at her mother. "Is it always going to be so hard for me?"

"When you are letting God have it all, it's easier. Yes, you'll struggle. But it gets easier as you grow. Now, let me help you with this basket. I'll bring your sheets by later. Go home, make your bed and, well...you know best how to make up with him."

Sammie laughed when Sunnie blushed. "Sunnie, what's wrong?"

"Mom! Eww, it's just like Silas talking about our rumpled clothing. Never mind, I am not explaining that. Thanks so much, Mom."

Sammie helped her pack the laundry into the small sports car. She brushed some flakes from her bangs as she waved Sunnie from the driveway after extracting a promise to consider purchasing a new, larger vehicle. She thanked God for her own husband as she finished straightening the kitchen.

The chatter on the scanner kept Tom company through the streets of Lakeville. He drove by the spot that his mother-in-law's house formerly stood on. He recalled the stories heard after the fact; he was not on duty that day.

Sunnie's recount of Rob's heroism–saving Sammie from the flames–produced awe and amazement until Tom thought of Sunnie in a similar circumstance. He understood.

In an uncanny coincidence, a text message from Sunnie sounded. Happy to see her name on his call screen, he pulled to the side of the road before reading.

HEY OFFICER, YOU'RE INVITED TO A ROMANTIC LATE-NITE DINNER: STEAK SMOTHERED IN ONIONS, PEPPERS AND MUSHROOMS, BAKED POTATOES AND RED WINE. I'M SORRY ABOUT THE MORNING. HOPING YOU'RE STILL IN THE MOOD FOR A TREAT. ILU, SUNNIE GIRL.

The heavy tenor vanished. Tom quickly replied.

SKIP DINNER, I'LL HAVE THE TREAT. I'M SORRY TOO. SEE YOU LATER, LOVE TOMMY.

Tom resumed his path, wishing 11PM to arrive swiftly. Cruising down Lamar Road, he caught sight of two young men ducking behind an abandoned farmhouse. Neighbors frequently complained of activity in the form of keg parties and strange odors. Searches turned up empty cold medicine packages, quickly discarded drug paraphernalia, and piles of garbage.

He reversed to see where they had gone. Nothing suspicious appeared, so he pulled into to the overgrown drive of the neighboring house. He pressed the switch of the mic on his shoulder. "Lakeville, this is Jacobs. Suspected activity on Lamar. Request backup." Tom provided the address.

COPY. ASSISTANCE ON THE WAY.

"Keep your shirt on; I'm coming!" Silas called to the impatient pounding on his heavy security door in the back of the shop. He tactfully held in the snickers at the sight of his sister's dripping curls.

"Can I help you?"

Sunnie thrust her car keys into his hand. "PLEASE carry my laundry up. I don't think I can make two trips."

He retrieved the wicker basket and followed her up the steps. He placed the basket down on the top floor landing with a puff of breath before handing her the keys back.

"I think I'm going to put a laundry room up here. I can't imagine doing this every night. Does Mrs. Butler know we're taking over next month?"

"Sure she does, Si. I told her to have a wild kegger when I leave." Sunnie chortled at her image of elderly Mrs. Butler with a party hat and brightly colored plastic cup of beer in hand.

"You're the best, Sis. Seriously." Silas looked about the hallway. "Tell me again; why didn't you put laundry in up here?"

"Because I knew I'd have strong, handsome men at my beck and call when I needed them. You can put something over that way," Sunnie pointed toward the front windows. "That's where all the pipes come up. Plus if you have some sort of leak, it won't be in anyone's apartment, only the hallway."

Silas walked over to inspect the area while Sunnie dragged the basket into the apartment.

"Good plan, Sis. I'll talk to Jude about it. Do you need anything else? Got garbage to bring down? Maybe floors to mop, a toilet to scrub?"

"Tomorrow." Sunnie hugged him, snickering at the face he made. "Thanks, Si. I'll see you later. I should have a definite move date by the weekend. Are you guys packed?"

"We're moving up the stairs, Sunn. Pack what?"

"Good point. I guess my stuff is going in storage for a month or two." She pushed a stray curl from her eyes. "Oh well. See you later."

Before making the bed and putting laundry away, Sunnie put some soft music on the stereo. She spent the balance of the day sorting paperwork, boxing books and clearing her office of old files.

It was well beyond dark when she went to the kitchen to start prepping vegetables for the late-night meal. When she clicked on the police scanner, she realized that Tom did not discuss much of what happened on his job. Thinking of the conversation she had earlier with her mother, she made it her business to change that.

Chapter 27

Their romantic dinner was far from Tom's mind. He relayed the appearance of two more men ducking into the window of the house. Assured back up was on the way, he intently watched for signs of activity.

Within minutes of his second call, he saw headlights on the road. They slowed before pulling into the spot next to him. Penzi rolled his window down.

"What's up, Jake?" He looked at his watch, clearly wanting this to be nothing so he could go onto whatever his plans happened to be.

"Four potential perps inside. Two late teens, two older. I doubt they're remodeling. I didn't see them carrying anything in."

"Armed?"

Tom shook his head. "Can't be sure. Plenty of room in those baggy pants for anything."

"Let's take a look. Why does this crap always happen at the end of the day?"

Penzi got out of his car, flashlight in hand. Tom followed, keeping pace quietly. Once they reached the property line, Penzi turned to Tom.

"Where did they go in?"

Tom pointed to the right side of the house. "Lower level, first window on the side. Perimeter check before we go in."

"I'll take the right." Penzi was moving before Tom had a chance to confirm.

Meeting again at the front of the house, Penzi said, "I saw an open door on the right side. Hopefully they're just having a smoke party and we can chase them out of here."

As he turned to enter the house, Penzi was delayed by Tom's hand on his arm.

"What do you mean, chase them out? If they're having a smoker, we're arresting them!" Tom looked into the face he'd known for a lifetime, seeing apathy there. "Penz, we need to do the right thing, here."

"Jake, who gives a rip if a bunch of losers are in here stoning? We chase them out with a warning and get home before it's too late. I'm sure Sunnie would appreciate that."

Tom insisted, "Penz, if there's crime happening, we're arresting them."

He shook Tom off with an exasperated grunt. "Whatever, Mr. Rogers. Shut up, or they'll hear you."

Penzi turned, heading for the open door on the side of the house. Tom took a deep breath and followed once he extracted his gun.

Sunnie turned the music up in the living room before setting the table. She hummed as she placed dishes on the funky throw serving as a tablecloth.

Too bad I didn't get a bouquet of flowers. She looked over the table, nodded satisfactorily and went back to the kitchen.

She pulled down two seldom-used wine glasses. The scanner crackled while she washed them, reporting officers searching an abandoned house.

"That's the old party house," Sunnie blurted in surprise. Amazed it was still standing after so long, she recalled many nights hanging there. She left the kitchen to place the glasses on the table, then stood back to regard her efforts.

She snapped her fingers and hurried to the linen closet. Returning with a fat candle, she set it in the middle of the table. Sunnie glanced at the time—just past 9PM.

She bustled back to the kitchen to prep the steaks. Coating them with olive oil and minced garlic, she left them on the counter to soak in the flavors. When she placed the enormous potatoes into the oven, she remembered candles for their room.

Once the votives were strategically placed, she turned down the fresh bedding. Her mother had been correct. She knew best how to make things right again. She smiled, walking out of the room to answer the knock that sounded on her door.

Tom and Penzi heard activity in the back room. Penzi pointed to himself, then pointed up.

Tom shook his head, motioning with his gun to the rear of the house.

Penzi shook his head, making it clear that Tom should stay put while he checked the upper level. Tom shook his head furiously. Penzi responded with a different hand gesture and started silently up the steps.

He winced at every creak the steps made, but the people in the back room didn't notice. Tom advanced closer to what he realized was a large kitchen. The counters were littered with pots of all sizes. Without a doubt, they stumbled onto a shoddy meth lab.

He could hear the rumble of conversation; they were unaware of the officers' presence. A glow was emanating from the doorway. Tom silently waited for Penzi to return.

Too many minutes later, he descended the steps. "Empty," he said faintly. "You go to the right, I'll take the left. *Don't* be a hero."

Tom's jaw clenched involuntarily. He could smell the drug cooking, the acrid odor permeating the air. He brushed off the uneasy feeling as he crept around the corner, his weapon in front of him.

Tom saw four of them when he rounded the doorway. He wondered how they weren't high from the fumes alone. One of the teens lifted his eyes from the bubbling pot over the propane camp stove.

"Bust! Bust!"

The shout penetrated the quiet of the scene. He jumped away from his cohorts and bolted for a back window as Tom shouted, "Hold it! Police! Do not move!"

The three remaining started when they heard Tom's voice. The pot was kicked over–the hot liquified mess spilled on the garbage strewn floor. Tom was horrified when it ignited, the flames creeping along the floor with the liquid. Tom shouted a warning again, getting ready to fire.

A large dark man with a shaved head pulled a gun from the waist of his baggy pants, swinging his arm towards Tom.

Shouting.

Gunshots.

Penzi was suddenly there, throwing himself in front of Tom.

More shots rang out.

Tom felt white-hot pain in his knee.

The fire spread to the brittle cabinets.

Penzi was down and not moving.

One perp was down. Tom was desperate to get out of the house before the fire spread further. Fighting the pain in his leg, he half crawled, half scurried across the garbage to Penzi.

Blood. Soaking the floor under him.

Tom pulled at the uniform shirt, exposing an entry wound above the Kevlar. He compressed the site with one hand and pressed the radio switch with the other.

"Lakeville! OFFICER DOWN! Fire! Need assistance!"

The only way out was the window. The flames blocked off the way through to the front of the house.

"Penz! Can you hear me?" Tom shouted in Penzi's face.

No reply.

How can I drag Penzi across this room and out that window with this insane pain in my leg?

He couldn't stem the flow of the blood and carry Penzi at the same time. Hooking arms under his, Tom dragged him toward the back window while watching flames devour the walls. The room filled with an eerie orange light. Tom prayed fervently that their charred bodies would be able to be found.

Sunnie smiled at her mother. She had stopped to deliver the sheets left at the house earlier.

"Thanks so much, Mom. Do you want to come in a while?"

"Not now, baby girl. I'm on my way home from Vic's Bible study. She started that twice a month accountability group, remember? Of course, I was in it without volunteering."

Mother and daughter shared a laugh. That was a very Victoria-esque thing to occur.

"Okay. Thanks for bringing these by. And thanks so much for listening before. I'm sorry I'm so dense."

Sammie hugged her daughter. "It takes time, baby. You're doing great. And it looks like you have a nice evening planned. I won't hold you up. Let me know how things work out. With less details than this morning."

Sunnie kissed her goodbye and closed the door. She heard the frantic chatter on the scanner as she walked past the kitchen to the linen closet. She couldn't imagine what had Lakeville dispatch in such an uproar.

I must have taken a bullet, Tom's mind tried to inform him. He panted from the effort of getting Penzi to the window.

Why is there so much blood? His hand was covered, as was his right leg.

Tom struggled to regain calm before he called over the radio.

"Lakeville, this is Officer Jacobs—Officer Penziotti is down—I'm hit—We're in the rear of the house on Lamar—One perp down—Fire out of control—Repeat, trying to exit rear of house."

At least they'd know where to search for their remains.

He attempted to stand to calculate how they could get through the window. His shattered knee protested by crumbling under him, sending him face first into a pile of garbage against the wall.

Tom struggled to a sitting position. The only thought he had was to get them out of the house before it collapsed.

He surveyed the room again. The miscreant he shot was stirring.

"Hey! Get over here and help me!" Tom shouted across the room.

The man looked startled a moment. In a flash, his face contorted to a mask of fury. He cursed Tom before making a run toward the front door.

"NO! You bastard, get back here!" Tom bellowed after him as he disappeared around the wall.

Sunnie took the potatoes from the oven and set them on plates. She checked the time displayed on the coffee pot; 10:26 PM. Tom should be walking through the door soon. She turned up the scanner before pulling a heavy cast iron skillet from the cabinet.

OFFICERS DOWN! I REPEAT, OFFICERS JACOBS AND PENZIOTTI DOWN ON LAMAR! HOSE TRUCK ON ITS WAY ALONG WITH PARAMEDICS.

SOMEONE BETTER INFORM THE MAYOR.

The pan clattered to the floor, chipping the tiles underneath. She bolted to her room for her keys, and hurtled down the four flights to her car. Silas was working late in the shop and heard the commotion on the stairs. He looked out the back door to witness her leave the parking lot at breakneck speed. Thinking it had something to do with the babies, he called her cell phone; it rang in the empty apartment.

Trapped.

He pulled Penzi's limp body across his legs and held his colleague tightly in his arms, waiting for either rescue or Jesus.

"Jake."

He barely heard the whisper above the roaring of the fire in his ears. Fresh blood trickled over Tom's hand. He bent close to hear.

"Get the hell out of here, you dumb ass. You have kids coming. Sunnie can't raise them alone." A ragged breath stopped him from saying more.

"I'm not leaving you here, Penz."

Tom saw a glimmer in his old friend's eyes before he closed them against the pain. One that hadn't been there in many months. Penzi shuddered in Tom's arms. When he opened his eyes again, a half smile broke on his dirty face.

"Stubborn Irish. Name one of them twins after me. I'm sure Young won't mind."

"Just what we need...Tony Jr."

The rumble of large vehicles caught Tom's attention.

"Listen! I hear them coming. We'll be fine, Penz. Just fine."

No response.

"Penz?"

Tom waited for a smart aleck remark that would never come.

The firemen swarmed around the house, one calling to another for an axe. Tom held his friend tightly, weeping in both grief and relief that they had gotten to him in time.

Chapter 28

Sunnie accelerated across town. Tears were blurring her vision before coursing down her face. Almost to her old street, she could see the glow of the fire rising above the trees in the night sky. She drove until she was stopped at a roadblock.

She bolted from the car. A female officer caught her by the arm. "Oh no, Mrs. Jacobs! You cannot go back there."

"Let me go! I have to get back there. Tommy is back there!"

"No, ma'am. I cannot allow that. Officer Jacobs is being taken to Chester County Hospital. Mrs. Jacobs, I suggest you calm down. You won't be doing him, you, or that baby any good this way."

The officer kept a firm hand on Sunnie's arm while she sobbed out her hysteria. Ensuring she was back in control, she escorted Sunnie to her car. As she pulled away Sunnie heard her radio call.

"Mrs. Jacobs en route to the hospital."

Forty-two minutes later, Sunnie parked near Stuart's car. She ran to the doors where a flood of local news people were clamoring for information about a dead officer.

"Oh no! Please, let me through!"

Her chest tightened as she fought through the crowd to a wall of security personnel.

"Please let me by! My husband...Officer Jacobs...I need to get by!"

They insisted on identification. Sunnie realized she left her purse at home.

"I'm Sunnie Jacobs. Officer Tom Jacobs is my husband. Mayor Jacobs is here...he knows me. Get him. He'll tell you. Please."

One security guard nodded and went inside the sliding doors. Sunnie paced for an eternity before he returned with Stuart.

"Come, Sunnie girl. Tommy will be fine. He's in surgery right now."

Stuart pulled her past the guards. One balked and was subject to the wrath of Mayor Jacobs.

"This is my daughter-in-law! You'd be better to guard Officer Penziotti's family from that!" He stabbed his finger out at the paparazzi. "They need you more than us."

A sudden stillness fell when they entered the doors, akin to the silence that follows the bang of unexpected fireworks.

Stuart hooked his arm protectively about her waist and led her to a small, sterile waiting area. Sunnie glanced at a nurse Stuart brushed past. She cast a sympathetic look at them before she went back to her job.

"Stuart, what happened? Why is Tommy in surgery? Where is Penzi? Is he in surgery too? Why are those reporters out there asking about..."

Sunnie made the awful connection. Stuart nodded sadly, as he navigated her into an uncomfortable chair. He stroked her head while fresh sobs wracked her body. He kept his eyes on the door to the surgical rooms.

Rob grumbled about the late-night call as Sammie reached for her cell phone. Still sleepy, all she could discern was muffled sobbing.

"Is anyone there?"

"Yes," a familiar voice answered. It broke again after uttering, "Momma, it's me. Sunnie."

Sammie bolted up, disturbing Rob's arm around her waist. "Sunnie, what's wrong? Where are you calling from?"

"Hospital. Tommy..."

Stuart sympathetically took the phone from his daughter-in-law. He succinctly explained the situation at hand and assured Sammie all was under control. Their eyes met when he ended the call.

"Your mother...she said she will pray," he managed before he turned away—not soon enough to mask his own tears.

Close to four in the morning, doctors arrived to confer with Stuart and Sunnie. Their top surgeon was available and surgery had gone smoothly. Tom and his new knee were in recovery. They walked along a dim corridor to see him.

Sunnie allowed Stuart to enter first, taking a moment to pray. She wiped at her eyes before walking through the door. Stuart positioned himself to one side, giving Sunnie room to come alongside the bed. New tears spilled over her lashes as she bent over to speak to Tom.

"Hey, Sunnie girl." he mumbled.

Tom's hand was punctured with IV lines. She took it gingerly in hers. "Hey, Tommy. I'm here, baby. I'm here." She wiped away a tear that had splashed onto his arm. Stuart exited to allow them privacy he understood they needed.

"Did you bring that steak?"

"Just the treat," she answered before stroking her hand across his forehead. Tom closed his eyes, cherishing his wife's touch. Emotion started welling: he was certain it wouldn't be contained once it finally erupted.

"He saved me."

Sunnie placed a hand on Tom's chest. "Tommy, you don't have to..."

The floodgate had opened. Tom grasped her hand. "That gun was pointed right at me, Sunn. Penzi—out of nowhere—he dove in front of me. I didn't realize it. Sunnie, he—oh Lord, Sunnie!"

A wail of anguish over the loss broke through as Tom pulled her to him. They clutched each other, desperate to drive away the pain. A nurse entered the room and gently pried them apart.

"No more of that now. You cannot disturb these tubes, Officer Jacobs. We'll be moving you to a private room in the next few minutes. Please behave," she admonished as she checked the various attachments.

Tom rested his hand on the twins as the tears abated. They gifted him with several kicks. The feel of life was balm to their wounded hearts. The nurse—as promised–returned with orderlies to move Tom to a private room.

Morphine fogged Tom's mind, for which he was grateful after the uncomfortable bed change. He was aware of Sunnie sitting at the edge of his bed.

He murmured, "I dun thing a bed to two."

She brushed a kiss on his forehead. He scowled.

"What's wrong? Are you in pain?" Sunnie asked.

Tom reached a bandaged hand behind her head and pulled her face to his. He was more relaxed moments later.

"Mush buttah," he sighed.

Sunnie stroked Tom's face as he fell into the drug-induced sleep. Rearranging his tubes and wires, she carefully snuggled beside him. She cried silently when he sighed in contentment.

At 6 AM, a nurse goggled at the couple. She checked the machines and the lines. She closed the door to go about her rounds; they both needed rest.

Sammie arrived at the hospital in the afternoon with Sunnie's bag, phone and charger and a change of clothing.

"It's a good thing your brother has a set of your keys. He put your steaks and potatoes in the fridge. Have you eaten anything? Doctor Zander will not be pleased if you don't take care of those babies, especially under stress like this." She scrutinized Sunnie, looking for signs of anything that seemed atypical.

"I know, Mom. I'm going to go down to the cafeteria once I'm cleaned up. Thanks for bringing me clothes. Let Si know that he can take the steaks or wrestle Jude for them."

"I didn't know if I should bring Tom anything, but I took both toothbrushes from the bathroom."

"I'm sure he doesn't need anything today. I'll go home tomorrow for a while."

They both looked to the bed where Tom lay quiet, the sounds of medical machinery filling the room. Sunnie's chin quivered and fresh tears began to fall.

"Mom...if I hadn't come by yesterday. If this would have happened and we...if I

179

were still mad..." she whimpered.

Sammie hugged her tightly. "Hush now, Sunnie Day. God knows all about it, and He is in control. Go wash up. I'll sit with him while you do. Even though I'm a poor substitute." She smiled to her distraught daughter, producing a handkerchief from her purse before sending her to the bathroom.

"Thanks Mom." Sunnie sniffled.

She washed as best she could, glad to be able to scrub her teeth. Sammie was carrying on a quiet chat with Stuart when she returned.

"Sunnie, I'm going to get back home. If you need anything, you call me, no matter the time. Stuart, always nice to see you."

Stuart bowed slightly to Sammie. She kissed Sunnie once more before leaving.

"Now, there's a fine woman. Your step-father is a lucky soul," Stuart said after the door closed.

"Yes sir. He is. We all are. Stuart, I need to talk to you, but first I need to apologize."

"What could you possibly need to apologize to me over?" Stuart asked roughly; he had held a 7AM press conference to quell the curiosity of dozens of reporters. They hadn't been the only ones who stayed at the hospital overnight.

"Well, I've been rather selfish. I've been giving Tommy a hard time about moving. I wasn't really ready to... Well, I didn't want to have to move in with you."

Sunnie felt her face turn scarlet, but she went on. "Not because I don't love you to pieces..."

He took her hand in his. "Say no more. I understand. Nothing to forgive. Now, what's the boggle in your mind?"

Sunnie swallowed the lump in her throat. She had laid it all at God's feet; it was the only thing that made sense.

"Tommy's not going to be able to make the stairs at our place. We're so close to the moving date anyhow. If we put everything in storage for a month or two..."

The pesky tears started again. Sunnie broke off, dabbing at her rebellious eyes with her mother's handkerchief.

Stuart's gruff visage melted away in a surge of love for the headstrong woman his son married.

"Sunnie. Nothing would make me happier. Of course. Roy and Maisey would be happy to help you get packed up. It'll be good for Tommy to be near Beau."

Relief rolled over Sunnie's face.

"Stuart, thank you so much. I'll try not to drive you out of your own house."

"I'm not eating tofu, Sunnie girl. So long as we're clear on that," he offered in his stern political tone.

"Okay, Mayor Tough-As-Nails. No problem," she agreed with an exhausted laugh. They discussed moving plans as Tom peacefully slept.

Chapter 29

"Tommy, please let me help you."

Tom blanched as he struggled to get dressed. Only two days home and four days out from surgery, he was stunned to find that all their belongings were moved to the Ranch. The combined efforts of family and friends had them settled before he signed the hospital release papers.

"I'll be fine," he grunted, swaying with the effort of tucking his shirt in. "The pain is good; I need to work through it. I just want you to stay by me."

Knowing how adamant he was about becoming mobile as soon as he could, Sunnie handed him a crutch. She watched him as he hobbled to the dresser.

Aware of the storm it would cause, she mentioned, "I think you're pushing too hard too soon."

As predicted, Tom scowled at her in the mirror, his eyes going gray as they always did when he was upset. Sunnie offered, "Use the chair."

"I WILL NOT pay my respects to the man who saved my life in a wheel chair, Sunshine. Stop nagging me on this." He returned his attention to adjusting his tie.

Sunnie put her hands up, surrendering to her husband's desire. "Okay, Tommy. I'm sorry. I just don't want you to strain your knee. I'll tell Pop to take the chair out of the trunk."

Satisfied with the tie, Tom turned to Sunnie with a wry grin. "Pop? You're not here a week, and he's Pop already?"

"Not to his face–yet. That may take me another week." She modeled her outfit. "How's my dress?"

"Sunnie, you look fine. You always look great. Why are you so worried?" Tom sat on the corner of the bed.

"I want to make sure I don't...well, that you can be proud of me. Always." Sunnie commented softly. The hard discussion with Sammie remained vivid in her mind. She wanted no one to look askance at Tom due to her behavior ever again.

He patted a spot beside him, reaching for her hand when she hesitated. When she was comfortably installed at his side, Tom put an arm around her shoulders.

"Why wouldn't I be? You love the Lord, you're brilliant, and it doesn't hurt a bit that you are drop dead gorgeous."

Sunnie flushed a pleasant shade of pink and muttered about his pain medications. Tom chuckled and tightened his hold, losing himself a moment in the scent of her hair.

"You know," he added in her ear, "when this day is out, I'm going to need lots of nursing care. Around the clock, I'm certain."

"Really? I may be able to find someone who will fill all your needs."

If the intensity behind their next few private moments was indicative of recovery, Tom would be walking fine by the afternoon. Stuart's knock reminded them there were other pressing matters to attend to. Sunnie quickly smoothed her dress as Tom rose with difficulty and help from the abandoned crutch.

"Do you need the chair, Tommy boy?" Stuart asked anxiously, brushing past Sunnie as he entered the bedroom.

"No, Pop, thanks. I may need it later, though...after the church." Tom acquiesced to his wife and father. "We'll see. Are you ready?"

Solemnity descended on Stuart's demeanor. Naturally, as mayor, he was asked to speak at the funeral.

"Yes, Tom. I am unfortunately prepared. I doubt I'll ever be ready to perform such a task, though."

Stuart turned, his thoughts back on his duties. Tom's request stopped him from moving further.

"Hey, Pop? Please stay and pray with us?"

Stuart bowed his head. Tom took Sunnie's hand and closed his eyes. They prayed for the Lord's blessing on Stuart when he spoke to the gathered people; for the comfort of the Lord on the Penziotti family, and for the Lord to be glorified by all on this day. Stuart clasped his shoulder before they left the room. Tom hobbled slowly. Sunnie followed both men, carrying her husband's dress coat and hat.

The sensational circumstances surrounding Officer Anthony Penziotti's death had local and national news crews stationed across the street from the church. There was an air of both grief and insanity in the crowd that gathered behind the barricades.

"Vultures." Sunnie was disgusted with the carnival atmosphere.

Stuart pulled into the drive and around to the back entrance of the church.

"Sunnie girl, the media is a strange mistress. As soon as they love you, they'll sell you for the next buyer. They'll dig into anything, stop at nothing, and report very little truth. You just ignore them. Tommy, you're sure about the chair?"

"I'm sure. Just let us off by the door, I'll see you inside. Is Father Crawford saying the Mass?" Tom had fond memories of Father Crawford, who had been a young new priest when Tom had been in the school.

"I believe so, son. Let me help you."

He bounded around the car to help Tom extract himself from the back seat. Once Tom shrugged into the heavy jacket, buttoning the gold buttons with Sunnie's help, he donned the rigid hat. With Sunnie at his side, they entered the back of the church. Tom pointed the way to the nave.

They had discussed the course the Mass would take as well as some of the terminology Sunnie was unfamiliar with. She would have enjoyed visiting the ornate church for any other occasion. Tom ushered her to a pew in the midst of a sea of uniformed officers from as far as New York City.

Sunnie spotted Jude standing in the back of the church, looking mature and handsome in his dress uniform. She waved him up the aisle to join them. He greeted Tom with a salute and then slid into the pew to assist Sunnie in positioning him for maximum legroom.

The casket sat in front of the communion rail, gleaming in the sunlight streaming through the windows. A large portrait of Penzi in uniform was placed on an easel next to it. The mountain of floral arrangements surrounded the stand and flowed over the few stairs.

Ensconced with the grieving family was Chief Malloy. Stuart soon joined them, offering the weeping mother condolences and a shoulder to lean on. People stopped by Tom to express both sorrow and hope for a quick recovery. His hand tightened in Sunnie's each time.

The crowd rose when the music swelled from soft background to signify the procession was starting. The sweet aroma of incense filled the church. The participants performed their assigned tasks as Father Crawford took his place in the pulpit.

Sunnie listened to Tom intone the responses with most of the gathered mourners. Determined to honor Penzi in every possible way, he grappled with the kneeling, sitting and standing as Sunnie and Jude offered their arms for support. The pain was nearing unbearable.

Father Crawford called for Mayor Jacobs to honor his fallen officer. From the lectern, Stuart praised Penzi's service record, his camaraderie with his fellow officers and his work with the Big Brother organization. He sought Tom's face as he moved to his closing remarks.

"Officer Penziotti made the ultimate sacrifice. Officer Penziotti gave his life that another might live. The family of that officer..."

The crowd hushed as the formidable Mayor's voice caught with emotion. He paused, gripping the lectern until his knuckles whitened. Father and son nodded in understanding as their tears freely flowed. Tom's arm around Sunnie's shoulder tightened; their fingers entwined.

"The family of that officer will never forget the gift of life that Officer Penziotti gave them. May God bless Tony, and the whole Penziotti family now and in the future. I am proud—very proud—to have had such a fine officer in my police department, to have known him as a personal friend. Thank you for the honor of allowing me to speak here today."

Several Lakeville officers rose when Stuart finished, to place a flag over the casket. As the altar servers stepped down from their duties, Sunnie was moved by the sound of the bagpipes from the front of the church. Strains of *Amazing Grace* drifted in as the officers lifted the casket to be ushered down the aisle, followed by the family, officers, and friends. Outside, police motorcycles from the surrounding towns held the traffic at bay.

Jude accompanied them to Stuart's car, conveying regrets from Rob and Sammie. After he helped Tom into the back seat, Sunnie hugged him as closely as she could manage with the twins taking up space. She allowed him a hello rub before they departed.

The ten-minute drive to the cemetery passed in tense silence. Tom sank into the seat, willing the throbbing in his leg to cease.

The reality that this was part and parcel of being the wife of an officer chased 'what if' scenarios around and around in Sunnie's mind. She sent mute pleas toward heaven that she would never be at the head of a motorcade.

The procession flowed through Lakeville to the adjoining small town where the Catholic cemetery stood. On the way to Penzi's gravesite, Tom pointed out a small marble sepulcher adorned with a Celtic cross. His mother's grave.

Stuart popped the trunk open to remove the wheelchair, but Tom refused its use. They walked slowly to the line of seats at the gravesite with the aid of the crutch. The fringe of the green awning fluttered, and all was quiet as the family assembled.

Tom's face was tight with pain and sadness when he struggled to stand as the final respects were to be paid. The only sound across the vast graveyard was the snapping of the canvas as the flag was folded.

They placed their flowers on the casket before greeting Penzi's parents. Mrs. Penziotti threw her arms around Tom's neck, thanking him for being there. Thanking him that her boy wasn't alone in his final moments. She hugged Sunnie intently, making her promise to take care of Tom and the babies. Mr. Penziotti's handshake and thanks were hollow.

When Sunnie glanced back, she saw Mrs. Penziotti collapse into her chair, the flag tightly clutched to her chest, her only remaining link to her beloved son. Shielded in the privacy of Stuart's car, Sunnie buried her face in Tom's chest and wept.

Chapter 30

The people in the foyer of Lakeville Town Hall quickly parted as Stuart thundered past them, leaving a trail of cigar smoke in his wake. Everyone in the building knew he was on a mission and were not going to be blamed for its delay.

Arriving at his destination, he slapped the letter clenched in his fist onto Chief Malloy's desk. The chief jumped from his seat to shut the door as Stuart's voice sounded.

"What the devil is this, Jim? An inquiry? Who is making these insane charges?"

"Stu, you know very well I cannot do anything about this. One of our officers was killed in the line of duty! Of course, there's an inquiry. I *especially* cannot do anything about this since your son is involved. How is that going to look? The son of the mayor is untouchable? Leave it alone, Stu. It will look worse than it already does."

"What are you talking about? Tommy and Tony were childhood friends! That boy was at our house more than his own through grade school!" Stuart fumed. An inordinate amount of smoke wafted through the office toward the open window.

"There's been tension between them. I have it from several of my officers. Tom clocked him in the jaw almost a year ago, and there was an incident just after Tom arrived back from his honeymoon. It looks bad, Stu—especially since we can't find this scum who shot them."

"What are you talking about, Jim? When did Tommy and Tony have problems? Why didn't you tell me?"

Chief Malloy pounded his fist on the desk in frustration. "Damn, Stu! First of all, I am the police chief in this town!" He poked a thumb into his chest. "They are MY officers, no matter whose kids they are! I am not obligated to scurry across the foyer if your son stubs his toe. He's a man and an officer, and when he's on duty, he's MINE. If you don't like the job I'm doing, too bad!"

Both men glared across the desk, Chief Malloy huffing after his outburst. Stuart started pacing, causing another cloud of smoke to waft out the window.

"They had a brawl at The Corral. Neither one would say what caused it so I chewed their butts and ordered them both to Anger Management. JUST LIKE I WOULD HAVE DONE NO MATTER WHO IT WAS!"

Stuart stopped short, pulled long on the cigar and glared at the man he usually worked seamlessly with.

"You doubt Tommy's report?" He released a cloud with the question.

"No, I have no doubt it went down just like the report reads. They both have exemplary service records. It's the personal that looks bad. If Tom would have come to me about it..."

Stuart pounded the desk again. "Tommy wouldn't do that and you know that damn well. Reporting a fellow officer and close friend? It was between them, whatever this idiocy is. For what—**exactly**—should he have reported to you?"

The unpleasant task of informing the mayor of the tensions between his officers soured in Chief Malloy's mouth. It was beyond comprehension that word had not reached his office by now. Steeling himself for an explosive response, he answered evenly, "Sexual harassment. Against Sunnie."

Stuart blanched, his eyes wide with bewilderment.

"I'm sorry, Stu. Do you see—now—why I cannot step into the middle of this?" He held his hands out, wrist to wrist. "My hands are tied. I can't stop this."

The two most powerful men in Lakeville held the other's eyes across the desk. Understanding the way it must play out, Stuart exhaled a great breath. He stood straight and adjusted his jacket.

"When will Tommy be notified?" The question was framed in quiet dignity.

"Today. He's officially on paid leave until it's resolved. You know he's looking at required counseling, too."

Resigned to the system, Stuart nodded and took his copy of the charges from the desk. Chief Malloy sat heavily in his chair as soon as Stuart closed the office door. He did not look forward to the inquiry. *If only the shooter could be found*, he thought as he stared out the window.

It was an unusual occurrence for a stranger to be knocking on the door of the secluded home. The uniformed officer escorting the business-suited man startled Sunnie. With all persistence, he explained the envelope in hand could only be presented to Officer Thomas Jacobs.

"You'll have to wait one moment," she requested tartly before closing the heavy door on them. She walked through to the family room where Tom was executing therapy exercises.

"Tommy, there's an officer and another man at the door. He insisted he can't give me whatever blasted paper he has in his hand. He needs you."

Pausing to wipe the sweat from his face, he glanced to her. "So? Let them in, Sunn. What's the issue?"

"They won't tell me," she replied before turning on her heel to allow them in. Tom stood as they entered the room, the tension that swept in with them tangible.

"Officer Thomas Jacobs?" The man in the suit and the expressionless face ventured.

"Yes. And you are?"

An envelope was thrust in Tom's direction, his question ignored. "This is from the Office of Inquiry, County of Chester. You are summoned to appear before the county judge for questioning regarding the death of Officer Anthony Penziotti. Thank you."

Leaving Tom in a cloud of apprehension, the men exited the room as soon as the envelope was in his hands. Sunnie hurried back once they were gone to share whatever this brought. Tom's eyes were wide as he read the contents.

"Sunnie! They don't believe me! They claim I purposely put Penz in danger! That I let him die. Incredible. I can't believe this. I'm suspended, with pay—big freakin' deal—until they are satisfied. Satisfied? Can't these idiots read?"

In utter frustration, he balled the notification and hurled it into the fireplace. Sunnie experienced a sense of déjà vu, having watched the same scenario play out when Tom's Honorable Discharge arrived a week earlier.

"Why haven't they found the shooter? They have the bullets. Why aren't they out there looking for him? He's a damn cop killer! This is just great. Just terrific."

Sunnie retrieved the letter from the grate. She smoothed it as best she could, to read it herself. "Oh no, Tom! It says..."

"I KNOW WHAT IT SAYS!"

The sharp interruption forced Sunnie to cringe. He violently jerked the towel from his neck, leaving an angry red welt. That flew across the room to land on the couch.

"I'm taking a shower, Sunn. Do me a favor and find out what's going on across the way, huh? You haven't mentioned the house in at least a week. Are you planning on us staying *here* now or what?"

"Of course not! We've been busy, with therapy, and having to see Doctor Zander. I'm sure it's going fine..."

"Sunnie, do you hear yourself? The day I was shot, you wanted me to call them and send heads rolling. Now you don't care? It's not fine by me. I want to know what's going on. It's one thing left that I have control over. So you—" Tom pointed her in the direction of the house, "—get over there and find out."

He partially limped, partially stalked from the room. Sunnie breathed deeply before walking out the back door to inspect the construction progress.

Reflecting on his ill temper during the shower, he did pinpoint the cause. Since the funeral, Sunnie had been by his side almost continually. She went to physical therapy appointments. She was generous to a fault. Non-argumentative. Pliant to the wishes of all around her. It was driving Tom out of his mind.

If he believed in such absurdities as alien abduction, he would assume that's what had happened. Even at their most intimate, the strong, independent woman he married had all but disappeared. He understood the 'why' behind her changed behavior; he now set his mind to turn it around. Today.

She found him on their bed, reading the latest crime novel. He listened to her forced, yet upbeat report with no comment, mentally noting at least four things she normally would have been ballistic over. The indifference, where it would have produced a fight, was Tom's line in the sand.

Sunnie ducked as the book left his hands and hit the dresser. It skimmed across the surface, knocking several things loudly to the floor before it joined them.

"Enough!" Tom rose from the bed and stiffly worked his way to her. "Sunnie, you need to stop! Can't you see what's happening? You can't leave me now; I need you. I can't go through this alone."

The tight grasp on her arms gleaned a frown, but she quickly shrouded it.

"Tommy, you need to calm down. I'm not going anywhere. Let me clean up that mess and then we'll..."

Patience took a holiday at the Jacobs home. In an attempt to provoke her, Tom shook her–hard.

"Sunnie! FIGHT BACK. Yell at me, roll your eyes, kick me. Do something other than agree with every. Single. Thing. I say! The woman I fell in love with–the one that agreed to be my wife–has disappeared somewhere, and this person that looks incredibly like her is in her place. *That* is what I'm talking about. Sunnie, please," Tom cradled her face gently. "Please don't let fear take you away from me. You almost let fear keep you away before. I can't stand that it's taking you away again."

In shock that he was manhandling her, that he raised his voice, she looked into his eyes. The desperation she found opened the floodgate and the tears she'd been holding back for weeks flowed. Tears of tension, distress, the ones she'd been afraid to allow him to see.

Tom's arms, loving and tender, were about her as she purged them all.

"I miss you, Sunn. I need you...now more than ever."

"Oh, Tommy. If I ever lost you..." She voiced the raging fear that held her heart locked. Tom put his finger to her lips.

"Don't. Don't think it, Sunnie. You can't. It's part of the package. You can't allow it to kill the passion."

She responded to his kiss with the fire fear had been holding at bay. He left her arms long enough to shut their door, locking the troubles away from them. It was mutually agreed it was long past time for a true reunion.

Prepared to bolster his son and daughter-in-law from the bad news of the day, Stuart was stunned to find a holiday atmosphere in his kitchen when he arrived home. The tantalizing aromas of beef stew, buttermilk biscuits, and cinnamon rolls filled the house. Anxiety had evaporated.

"Well, what are we celebrating tonight? It smells divine in here. Sunnie girl, did you really make something that required beef?"

A laugh echoed when Sunnie greeted him with a hug. "Yes sir, and if I may say, it's darn good. I made cinnamon rolls too. We went across the way, lit a fire under those deplorable workmen, and said hello to Beau and Picasso. I need to ask Doctor Zander how soon I can ride after the twins come."

"Ha!" Tom laughed from his station, where he was icing the cinnamon rolls. "It better not be before I can, or I'll lose my mind! I can't wait to take the boys on a ride. Pop, how old was I when I first rode?"

Stuart was befuddled by the complete change of mood in his household.

"Tommy, did the letter of inquiry come?"

The couple looked to each other and laughed. They laughed even harder as Stuart's eyebrows disappeared into his hairline.

"Tommy, are you back on those painkillers?"

Tom laid the frosting-laden knife on the counter and walked to Stuart, bestowing a bear hug on the unsuspecting man. He kept one arm about his father's shoulder when he turned toward Sunnie.

"Look at her, Pop. Isn't she gorgeous?"

Sunnie rolled her eyes at them before getting back to tossing salad, a blush blossoming on her face. Tom turned back to his father.

"I am not going to worry over this. No way. God is in control. I told the truth and that will have to be sufficient for whomever is questioning it. My leg is getting better by the day; the twins will be here soon. So long as Sunnie is with me, I'm not concerned."

Tom walked back to the counter. "I promised Beau I'd be riding again soon, but I'll bet he would love to get out. By the time you're back, dinner will be ready."

Stuart looked between the two of them a moment. A large grin started to break across his face. "I told you, son, a fine woman by your side makes all the difference. I don't know what you said to him today, Sunnie girl, but it worked. Don't enjoy that stew without me!" Stuart walked out of the kitchen, chuckling. Tom went back to frosting the cinnamon rolls.

Sunnie placed the salad on the table and walked to Tom. She scooped some frosting from the bowl with her index finger.

"I'll bet he suspects," she teased Tom.

He pulled her close and relished a long, lazy kiss. The wonderful ice blue eyes were dancing again.

"He'll certainly guess if he sees that love bite on your neck. Keep your hair down the next few days."

He quickly scooped frosting from the bowl and deposited a dollop on her nose.

"Consider that compensation for our wedding day," he stated, chuckling when she put out her tongue before utilizing abundant paper toweling.

Stuart walked back through the kitchen, after changing to his well-worn riding gear. He picked up the alleviated mood, whistling cheerily as he walked out the doors to the deck. Sunnie watched him, then said to Tom, "You know, I may miss him. Does he change diapers?"

189

Chapter 31

The day dawned bright and beautiful, yet Sunnie remained lying in bed. She listened to the muffled voices of Stuart and Tom discussing the inquiry in the kitchen. She and Tom stayed up long into the night discussing his meeting with the PBA appointed lawyer. His report was straightforward; the lawyer assured him there shouldn't be anything to worry about. Between concern and discomfort, Sunnie had slept little.

Tom grumbled at his reflection, unable to fumble his tie into place. Sunnie stepped to the dresser, speaking softly as she deftly knotted it. "I know that you can do this, Officer. I've seen you tie a tie."

Concern painted Tom's face. She laid her hands on his chest.

"Everything will be fine. Stupid, but fine."

Tom pulled Sunnie's trembling hands into his. "Are you sure you can make it? It's going to be long and uncomfortable. I understand if you want to stay home."

"As if. You couldn't keep me away. You are stuck with me, Officer Jacobs. Through anything and everything."

They looked into each other's eyes intently before praying.

Awaiting arraignment for over thirty hours, the rank man rolled over on the stale cot. The precinct was bursting with major crime busts, as attested to by the noxious air quality.

He cursed the day that he had to flee from Lakeville. If only Manny hadn't taken a shot at that cop. He could have laid low for a while before moving on to better places than the streets of North Philadelphia.

Hours after the house on Lamar went up in flames, he and Billy hooked up. Billy relayed the fact that he left the blaze to eliminate the two officers. After days of scanning public trash bins for newspapers, they read the news of Officer Anthony

Penziotti's death, as told by Officer Thomas Jacobs. They left Lakeville that morning.

The larger concern was putting distance between them and Manny. Neither had any desire to be the object of honing Manny's knife skills; those who were did not live to tell about it. Philadelphia seemed a good distance to travel.

The flow of money and all that followed along with it went well for a while. The makeshift meth lab was proving lucrative; life seemed good on the North End. Until a S.W.A.T. team broke down the door at Dark O'Thirty the other morning.

All he recalled was his girl du jour wailing from the front room when the barrel of an assault rifle appeared before his eyes. He thought it was meth ghosts taunting him until they bodily carried him to the stairwell and tossed him down.

He was hungry, dirty, possibly had a dislocated shoulder, and worried about what the charges would be. If they were severe enough, he would play the Manny card. After all, giving up a cop killer could save him from a harsher sentence. His mind started formulating how to play the court appointed attorney who had finally arrived at his cell.

The old-time courthouse in Chester County was a wonderful historical site, its clock tower soaring above the columned entryway. It spoke of majesty and justice, a testimony to the founders of the country.

It scared Sunnie out of her wits.

Tom gently pried his hand from her grip.

"I do need this to swear in, you know. I think I need to stay far from you during the birth."

She smiled in apology. Determined to be strong, she shrugged away the tears. "I will be so glad when this day is over."

"They don't have anything to argue about. It will be. The worst that'll happen is that you won't be calling me 'officer' any more. Maybe we can move out West after all, and I can become a cowboy."

Stuart interjected his opinion into their discussion.

"Tommy, they will not be stripping you of your badge. Stop worrying about that. The most they will do is suspend you pending further inquiry."

Tom was resigned to the fact that they would never catch the shooter. They proceeded silently inside the courthouse.

"You're looking at twenty to twenty-five, Max. That's the best I can do for you."

Amy Vander Wall wrinkled her nose at her client. Even though she was a fierce believer in the system—that all men should have representation—there were times her high ideals didn't seem so worthy to keep. Exhibit Number One was sitting before her, scratching himself rudely while he pondered her offer.

Thinking her years of schooling were for naught, she snapped the portfolio closed and stood.

"Call me when you decide, Max. And please, make them allow you a shower."

She signaled at the two-way mirror to be released from this version of prison, a dingy room that was a level above the unpleasantness of the holding cells. When she reached for her bag, Max's hand shot out, gripping her wrist.

Although she had the security of knowing fifty officers would come if she glanced to the mirror again, she recoiled from his touch. He grinned at her obvious discomfort.

"I ain't doin' that much time over nuthin', pretty lady. I got some info. Good info. You willin' to listen?"

Max caressed her fingers. Amused by the look of abject revulsion on her face, he released his hold before sitting back.

"I can't promise anything until I hear it."

She prepared to walk away. Nothing that this disgusting, filthy meth head had to say could be remotely interesting.

He barked out a laugh before the story of shooting Officer Anthony Penziotti from Lakeville spilled from his lips. Recovering her composure, Ms. Vander Wall returned to the hard plastic chair and signaled for coffee.

Chapter 32

The random buzzing of security arches and the clip-clacking of heels on the marble floors all pounded into Sunnie's head with relentless insistence. As the security officer pulled someone aside to be wand searched, Sunnie and Tom placed their belongings in the appointed bin for scanning.

Satisfied guards allowed them to collect their belongings. With Stuart leading the way, they boarded the elevator and found the courtroom. Chief Malloy and the PBA lawyer were conferring quietly in a corner. Tom kissed Sunnie's forehead and shook Stuart's hand before joining them.

The seats Stuart and Sunnie occupied were surprisingly comfortable. The table in the center of the room had several chairs on each side, one already taken by a stenographer.

They all turned their heads to the sound of someone entering the room. Penzi's young partner bee-lined to a seat away from all, inspecting his shoes once he landed. Tom raised his eyebrows to Chief Malloy. Having no explanation to offer, he shrugged.

The judge entered by a side door, followed by a young, smarmy looking man whose dark hair was slicked tightly away from his face with an overabundance of styling product. Projecting a large desire to prove himself, he sat with exaggerated importance to the right of the judge, arranging notes.

Outside the small room, Amy Vander Wall and Assistant District Attorney Martin Cho stared at Max though the glass. He arrived as Max's third accounting of the shooting was being told. She turned to him, her eyes still wide with amazement.

"What do we do with this?"

Martin Cho ran his hand over his close clipped hair. "We make this loser a deal and call Lakeville."

"Make him what deal? We can charge him as an accessory to the murder of a police officer!"

Martin Cho raised his eyebrows. "How progressive for a defense attorney. He'll have to testify at whatever future trial there is *if* we can find this Manny. If. Can we get the ballistics report on that?"

"You're the ADA here, not me. You do whatever it is you need to do. This is one guy I won't be happy to see lose his case."

They nodded to each other. She turned to the door of the room, working out the exact phrasing of the offer. Martin Cho walked back to the squad room to locate the number for the Lakeville Police Department.

Tom raised his right hand and placed his left on the Bible the clerk held out. Once sworn in, he sat next to Sheila Jackson, PBA attorney. Her posture was confident. It was a clear case, or so they all believed. Andrew Wilson established the fact that he disbelieved Tom's incident report immediately.

"Officer Jacobs, is it true that you and Officer Penziotti dissolved your previous friendship?" He did not bother himself to look up from his paperwork.

"No. We did not dissolve our relationship." Tom answered in a voice clear and steady.

Andrew Wilson peered at Tom.

"I see. Please answer my questions, Officer. Do not twist what I asked. I asked about your previous friendship. Was it not, at the point in which the incident occurred, dissolved."

"By mutual agreement."

A veiled cough from across the desk intimated Wilson's disbelief of Tom's statement. Ms. Jackson gave him a nod, and Sunnie's pulse quickened.

"Why was that, Officer Jacobs? Why, after knowing Officer Penziotti since childhood, did you decide—*mutually*—to dissolve your friendship?"

Determined not to satisfy whatever callous need Andrew Wilson had, Tom sat a bit straighter before he answered

"We had a disagreement that we could not overcome."

Wilson attempted an intimidating stare-down, which ended by Judge Caldwell's pen tapped on his sleeve. He studied his collection of papers a moment longer, before raising his head to continue his assertions.

"During the end of August, did you not have a fight with Officer Penziotti? In fact, two other officers from your squad were called to a place—" he looked down again, and back up quickly, "—known as The Corral to break up a fist fight between the two of you."

Sunnie shifted in her seat as she watched the color creep up the back of her husband's neck. Tom was doing well in restraining his outrage.

"Yes. That is all true." The answer came out tighter than Tom intended.

"What was this fight about? I see here that you refused to discuss it with your Chief, and you now have a reprimand in your jacket. How very understanding of him. I've seen how small towns run their police forces. Slipshod. Added benefit for you is

196

the prestigious position of your father. He is the mayor, correct?"

Sunnie could not restrain Stuart from projecting himself out of the seat and across the room. He stopped behind Tom's chair and bellowed, "That fact is completely irrelevant to this hearing!"

Judge Caldwell's small gavel hit the table twice. Stuart turned away, grumbling about incompetence as he burrowed in his pockets for a cigar. He returned to the seat to chew irately on the end.

Andrew Wilson smirked before looking back down at his paper work. The man was working hard to prove something; it was obvious he chose the ruination of Tom's law enforcement career to build his reputation on.

"Thank you, Mayor. Officer Jacobs, is it possible that due to your...ties..." He paused, sliding his eyes to Stuart before he continued. "To higher positions allowed you to be insubordinate to your superior officer? Would you have allowed that in your own *former* Guard unit, Officer Jacobs?"

"Judge Caldwell, are you going to allow Mr. Wilson to continue to badger Officer Jacobs into an outburst? I would like it noted that he is being treated as hostile, even though he's done nothing but answer truthfully the questions put forth."

Ms. Jackson received satisfaction from the judge, who quickly jotted something on her own legal pad.

"Noted, Ms. Jackson. Mr. Wilson, stick with facts, not speculation. Mayor Jacobs, please do refrain from further commenting. You may answer, Officer Jacobs."

Tom nodded his thanks to Judge Caldwell.

"I don't see how that is relevant," he said to Andrew Wilson. "Officer Penziotti and I agreed to what Chief Malloy required of us. What the difference was about was between us."

"I strongly disagree, Officer Jacobs. I assert that due to your continuing disagreement you allowed Officer Penziotti to confront a dangerous situation while you did nothing to back him up."

Andrew Wilson looked pointedly at Sunnie. "It wouldn't be the first time one man killed another over a woman."

"Judge Caldwell!" Sheila Jackson protested.

The judge held her hand up. "Mr. Wilson, do not try my patience. Officer Jacobs, go on."

"I did not shoot Officer Penziotti. A highly paid and intelligent man such as yourself can understand a simple ballistics report, I assume."

Sunnie squeezed Stuart's arm, containing a cheer that was bursting to be released. She was certain she saw the corners of the judge's mouth quirk into a smile before returning to her stoic demeanor.

"Of course. Officer Jacobs, the fact remains that you were in a situation that caused Officer Penziotti's death. You wrote in your report..." Andrew Wilson pulled a copy of Tom's incident report from his pile of papers.

"*Officer Penziotti surveyed the situation from the left side of the room. Once the gun was raised, Officer Penziotti stepped in front of me.*"

"I stated Officer Penziotti *threw* himself into the line of fire." Tom corrected.

Andrew Wilson frowned. "You seem very sure of yourself, Officer Jacobs. I would like to introduce testimony from Officer Peter Dolan. Officer Dolan has witnessed several altercations in the past year between you and Officer Penziotti. Officer, please step forward."

The room was silent but for Officer Dolan being sworn in. He sat uncomfortably next to Tom.

Sheila Jackson raised a hand. "May I say, Judge Caldwell, we were not informed that Mr. Wilson was producing witnesses. I could have provided a room full of people who can testify to Officer Jacobs's excellent character."

"So noted," she replied, jotting again on her pad. She turned a steely gaze to the prosecutor.

"Stick to the facts, Mr. Wilson. You also, Officer."

The young officer seemed cowed by the whole affair. He focused his attention on Mr. Wilson.

Andrew Wilson cleared his throat, his pompous manner grating the edge of Sunnie's nerves.

"Officer Dolan, you were partnered with Officer Penziotti?"

"Yes. It's Chief Malloy's policy for new officers to partner part of the time with more experienced ones. Officer Penziotti was next in rotation." His voice cracked apprehensively.

"Tell me when you witnessed the discord between Officer Penziotti and Officer Jacobs."

He leaned back smugly in his chair, awaiting the damning evidence to pour from the young officer's lips.

After pondering his response over an agonizing moment, Officer Dolan turned to Judge Caldwell. The arrogance quickly faded from Mr. Wilson's expression.

"Tony was my friend. I won't speak ill of him when he cannot defend himself. The disagreements he had with Officer Jacobs were personal. He made some off-handed comments to Mrs. Jacobs before she married Officer Jacobs. Tony was a ladies' man. He meant nothing by them."

He glanced apologetically in Tom's direction before continuing.

"I believe that they agreed to disagree. I do not believe that Officer Jacobs purposely put Tony in danger. Tony was the kind of friend and officer who would take a bullet for you."

Officer Dolan collapsed after Judge Caldwell's curt nod. He took a deep breath. He chanced a glace to Tom, relieved to receive a grateful nod of thanks.

Andrew Wilson slammed an open hand on the desk. "Officer Dolan! When I questioned you in Lakeville you relayed several incidents that you witnessed between the two officers. You said you witnessed Officer Penziotti make lewd comments regarding Mrs. Jacobs. Are you retracting what you told me?"

"No, sir. You must have misunderstood my meaning."

"A ten minute recess is in order," Judge Caldwell announced with a bang of her gavel.

Once the room emptied, she strode to the door, shutting it with a firm, yet quiet, hand. She turned sharp gray eyes on Andrew Wilson.

"Mr. Wilson, I don't understand why you are making a mountain out of this molehill. When I am done with my cigarette, I expect you to have some sort of evidence that Officer Jacobs was derelict in his duties—*in the extreme*—or this inquiry is over."

She punctuated her request by sweeping past him in a swirl of black robe.

He stared after her as she exited, his dreams of a cushy corner office becoming ashes as fast as the cigarette she'd placed in her mouth before closing the door.

"Lakeville PD, how may I direct your call?"

Millie's rote and monotone greeting conveyed the fact that exciting events did not usually happen in Lakeville. Not in the twenty-something years she worked dispatch.

"This is Martin Cho. Assistant District Attorney, Philadelphia. 26th District. I need to speak to Chief Malloy immediately."

"I'm sorry, Chief Malloy is out of the office today. You may speak to Lieutenant Williams."

The ever present nail file dropped from Millie's hand at Martin Cho's curt reply.

"I need Chief Malloy, and I need him now. We have a suspect in the murder of Officer Anthony Penziotti in custody. I suggest you page him. I will wait."

"Oh, umm...yes, let me find his cell number...I'll be right with you, Mr. Cho." Millie almost disconnected the call as she searched the cluttered desk for the chief's cell phone number.

Tom and Sunnie returned from the restrooms to the group huddled in the hallway. Stuart was looking confident, working the cigar down to nothing. The Chief and Officer Dolan were confabbing while Ms. Jackson checked vital emails on her Blackberry.

Tom placed his arm around Sunnie's shoulders; he seemed more relaxed than earlier in the day.

"Sunn, I think this is going to end up a wash. He can't prove what he wants–I can't prove against him. I guess I'll be home a while. You sure you won't get sick of me hanging around?"

"You're joking! With newborn twins, you may never be allowed to leave the house!" She attempted to keep his mood light.

Chief Malloy's phone rang. He pulled it quickly from his jacket and excused himself from Officer Dolan. He groaned to himself at the number showing on the ID screen.

"Yes? I told you not to call unless it was damned urgent."

"Chief! I'm sorry, I wouldn't have called..." Millie fumbled, knowing that Chief Malloy was irritated. He did not take kindly to direct orders being ignored. "There's an ADA from Philly on the phone for you. He says he's got a suspect in custody."

Chief Malloy put a hand over his eyes. Leaning against the wall, he briefly considered hiring another dispatcher.

"And this is urgent how, Millie? What does an ADA from Philly need me for?"

"It's about Penzi."

He cast a sidelong glance at the crowd before turning his back to them. "Say again?"

"He says he has a suspect in custody and it may be the shooter. Should I give him your cell number?" Her voice squeaked over the phone.

A dozen roses seemed the better alternative to unemployment. "Yes! Please give him this number. I will be expecting him immediately!"

Judge Caldwell commanded their presence in the courtroom. The chief lingered in the hallway and ignored the icy stare he received when his phone started to ring.

Chapter 33

Chief Malloy put some distance between himself and the door lest anyone overhear his conversation.

"This is Malloy."

"Martin Cho. 26th District, Philly. I believe I have someone you would be very interested in."

"Is it our shooter?" Chief Malloy held a breath.

"Not quite. He named the shooter. He's an eyewitness willing to testify. We have an all points out for a Manfred Vilellas. Your officer isn't his first murder."

"Hopefully, it'll be his last. I'm sorry you aren't closer to Chester County. My other officer involved is on inquiry right now. Wilson is like a dog with a bone–he won't leave it alone. I'd love it if you swooped in and saved the day, as the old saying goes."

As relieved with the news as Chief Malloy was, the next was better.

"Andy Wilson? Skinny, greasy haired kid?"

Chief Malloy snorted on the other end of the phone.

"Find me a fax number. I'll have a copy of this to you in minutes. I suspect Wilson flunked out of police academy and humanities."

Promising a call back, the Chief slapped his phone shut and bolted to the elevator. Ten minutes later, he was heading back to the courtroom, perusing the arrest report and confession of Maxwell Hodges.

Stoney silence filled the conference room as Judge Caldwell expectantly looked for Chief Malloy to materialize. Her gray hair, severely swept back and held with pins, glistened in the light of the room. After five minutes, she waved for the proceeding to continue.

Resorting to unadulterated gossip, Andrew Wilson made his final stab at tearing down Tom's character. "Officer Penziotti made many attempts at winning your wife's affections, did he not, Officer Jacobs?"

"Judge," Ms. Jackson started to protest, but Tom waved it off.

"So it would seem. My wife—at that time a good friend—refused a date with Officer Penziotti on several occasions."

"I maintain that she was seeing him; that this was the friction between the two of you. She was seeing you both."

Tom's eyes became stormy gray, but he did not rise to the bait.

"I trust my wife, Mr. Wilson. She did not, on any occasion, date Officer Penziotti."

"Can you be so sure? I looked into your wife's career at Weston Acquisitions. She seems to have a penchant for older men, dating several at one time. Charles Weston himself included."

Tom gripped the arms of the chair, preparing to rise. Outraged that this was paraded about, he was certain Sunnie was melting in mortification. Thoughts of his hands about the man's thin neck sounded appealing at that moment.

Sheila Jackson placed an alarmed hand on his arm. Assured Tom was staying in his seat, she turned to the judge.

"Judge! Mrs. Jacobs is not the one on inquiry here! Her past holds no bearing on the events that occurred. Are we going to allow this smear tactic to continue?"

The judge looked Mr. Wilson in the eye. "I'm astonished that you hold a law degree. I will personally see to your disbarment if you do not contain yourself. Is that understood?"

He ignored the judge's warning, hurling one last desperate question. "Are you planning on DNA testing, Officer?"

General chaos erupted from the small crowd. Officer Dolan managed to stay out of Stuart's path, which was direct to Andrew Wilson. Ms. Jackson was loudly protesting the whole proceeding, and Tom was attempting to wrestle his enraged father away from the table.

Judge Caldwell reached the limits of her patience. She pounded the small gavel on the desk nine times before she was satisfied that everyone would be quiet.

"Mr. Wilson, that is quite enough from you. If all you have are empty accusations, you have wasted this court's time. Mayor Jacobs, while I appreciate your ire, I expect you to behave as a gentleman in my court."

Stuart bowed to Judge Caldwell. "My most abject apologies, Your Honor. I will remain silent for the duration of this hearing."

Before he turned to console Sunnie, he saw a slight gleam the judge's eyes. He pondered the attractive look as he took his place and patted Sunnie's hand.

"Thank you. Officer Dolan, do you stand by what you have said here today? That things were misconstrued?"

She noted his affirmative nod on the legal pad and reviewed her copious notes. As she was about to pronounce her opinion on the hearing, Chief Malloy threw the door open. He strode to the table and triumphantly handed her the faxed arrest report.

She reviewed it carefully over several tension-filled moments. Satisfied, she placed the report on the table in front of Mr. Wilson.

"Mr. Wilson, here is your 'missing link.' The police have a suspect in custody who witnessed Officer Penziotti's murder. The account is remarkably identical to Officer Jacobs' report. Officer Penziotti sacrificed his life for a fellow officer and friend. Do you have any reason, at this juncture, to refute this?"

The defeated man stared sourly at the report, collecting his voluminous amount of paperwork.

Judge Caldwell graced him with a look that would have withered a full-bloomed rose bush. Unabashed, he offered Tom a somewhat rehearsed sounding apology. Another pointed look from Judge Caldwell extracted an apology to both Sunnie and Stuart. Andrew Wilson hurried from the room, lest he should have to offer apologies to anyone else.

"I must remember to call Martin when I get back to my office." Judge Caldwell commented. "Sheila, it was good to see you again. We'll do lunch very soon. Officer Jacobs, I am very happy things worked out for you. Please do inform me of the birth. Mayor Jacobs, it was a pleasure."

Stuart's face flushed pleasantly.

"Chief Malloy, should you ever seek higher aspirations, I believe you would make a fine county sheriff."

Chief Malloy shook the judge's hand. "Thank you, ma'am, but I am quite happy in Lakeville. I have fine officers."

She looked at both Tom and the young officer and smiled. "Yes, you do. Officer Dolan, thank you for your testimony. Your devotion to your fellow officers will serve you well through your career."

She turned to leave, unbuttoning the top button on her robe. She glanced back at the group, her eyes resting on Stuart. "There's a lovely cafe not two blocks from here. Should you feel the need to celebrate before your ride home."

She left him a brilliant smile as she swept from the room.

Tom pulled Sunnie into the crook of his arm before shaking hands all around. When he had his father's undivided attention, he grinned.

"See Pop? I told you it would all work out fine."

Stuart clapped Tom on the shoulder, his wide smile firmly in place.

"You did, Tommy. That you did. Well, Jim, young Officer Dolan, would you like to join us for a celebratory lunch? My treat, of course. Ms. Jackson, would you join us, also?"

Stuart herded them out of the room, happy to be back in charge of his little corner of the universe once again.

Chapter 34

The Sunday after Easter, Stuart bustled about his room, preparing for his day away from Lakeville. He looked out the expansive window that allowed him a view of the corral and much of the back property. A warmth rose in his chest, knowing his son would soon be raising his own sons on this land he loved so well.

Downstairs, he found Sunnie lying on the couch, a wastebasket strategically placed at her head. Tom was sitting at her feet, sipping coffee as they watched the live simulcast of their church service.

"Someone ill today?

"I'm sure these two have no more room, and I'm paying for it. No sleep and nothing is staying down. Sorry, Stuart. I was hoping to be miserable on my own couch by now."

His forehead rumpled. "You know, the day Tommy was born, Claire felt much the same way. Ill almost non-stop until labor kicked in. Have you called the doctor?"

Tom waved Stuart off as he rose to replenish his mug. "I doubt it, Pop. We still have a week to go. It's probably the extra ice cream Sunnie ate last night when she couldn't sleep."

Stuart followed him into the kitchen.

"Tommy boy, I think you best call that doctor. If there's anything I remember about that day, it was the look on your mother's face. Sunnie has that same look about her. I know she's adamant about getting to the birth center."

"Pop, if Sunnie feels worse, we'll call. Promise. Where are you off to so early?"

"Mass, then I have some business to take care of. I'll be out most of the day. Sunnie girl, you take care, now."

He waved over his shoulder as he hustled out the door. Sunnie giggled to Tom when she heard the sound of his car pulling out of the driveway.

"He's been going more lately. That's great." Sunnie voiced before a wave of sickness had her hanging over the edge of the couch.

Tom held her hair back through the worst of it. Sunnie leaned back, an arm across her forehead.

"I haven't felt like this since I stopped drinking," she moaned when he returned with the basket rinsed and dried. "I wonder if eating all this beef is making me sick? Can you help me up? Maybe if I take a hot shower, I'll feel better."

When she pulled herself from the couch, the twins readjusted themselves. Tom saw the movement they made, as well as the wince on his wife's face.

"Already fighting for position," she breathed.

"Well, someone has to be first. Maybe we should call Doctor Zander. Come; take a shower. I'll sit with you."

"Ahh, this is just what I needed," she called through the curtain as the hot water beat on her back. Tom toweled and combed through her mass of curls after he helped her dress comfortably.

"Do you mind if I lay down a bit?" Sunnie asked, stifling a yawn unsuccessfully.

"Why would I mind? I know soon you won't be lying around. Do you want the bucket?"

"No. I think that passed. It must have been that ice cream."

She fell asleep within minutes. Tom cleaned the kitchen from the breakfast dishes. After a quick check on Sunnie, he retreated to the family room to do therapy exercises. He wanted the infinitesimal limp gone before he returned to work. Involved in his thoughts on the upcoming birth, he didn't hear Sunnie enter the room until she spoke.

"Tommy, I can't get comfortable. My back is killing me. I can't find my phone; where's yours? I want to call Mom."

He pointed to the kitchen, continuing with his routine. Hearing a television theme song warbling from the couch, he abandoned the elastic strapping and excavated Sunnie's phone from beneath the cushions. Sunnie walked into the room, wearing a sly grin.

Tom walked over to hand her the phone.

"*Bad Boys*?"

She snickered as she scrolled through the call list. "I was annoyed with you one day. It seemed like an ideal choice."

Tom listened as Sunnie ran down her list of morning ills to her mother. She listened to Sammie's advice, thanked her, and assured her she was fine. She carefully worded what she relayed to Tom once she saw the concern in his expression.

"She thinks I should call Doctor Zander. Really, Tom, I don't think I'm in labor. I'm not in any real pain, my back hurts. I've had cycles worse than this. I think I should go back and lay down a while."

After he scowled, she amended, "What do you want me to do?"

He took stock of Sunnie's exhaustion and the determined look on her face that screamed, "I am going back to bed." He was not as confident as she that this was not the start of labor.

"Go lay back down a bit. The birthing place isn't that far from here; first babies usually take a while, right?"

Sunnie shrugged. "Maybe I can sleep in the recliner. I can't lie down on that bed again."

Relief washed over her face as she settled into the enormous leather chair. "Oh, this is so much better. I should have been sleeping here. Can you get me a drink, please? I should have gotten it first."

"Sure, Sunn. Here's the blanket." He laughed when Sunnie tossed the heavy chenille blanket back at him. Hormones had not allowed sleeping under blankets in weeks.

"Okay, no blanket. Here's the remote. I know you want control."

Returning with drinks and a large bowl of snack mix, Tom relaxed on the couch. They spent the afternoon between auto racing and basketball; Sunnie was no less animated at home as she had been at the track.

Stuart returned home early in the evening bearing bags from the Asian restaurant. They thanked him enthusiastically for the wonderful meal, and Sunnie inquired about his afternoon. Both she and Tom laughed aloud at the flush that crept up his face.

"Town business, that's all. I have some paperwork that needs to be in place for the morning. If you need anything, just holler."

He bustled from the room, leaving them with stunned expressions and no satisfactory explanation of his day. They extrapolated all sorts of wild political situations he could be involved in.

When Stuart returned to the kitchen later in the night, Sunnie was curled as well as she could in the recliner. Tom was sprawled on the couch, snoring. He covered them both and switched off the television. He reflected on how much he enjoyed having them in the house as he climbed the stairs to his room.

Eleven on the clock brought a sharp pain to Sunnie's side, waking her from the sleep she'd fallen into. The realization that readjusting her position did not help made her mentally upbraid herself for not listening to her mother.

"Tommy?" she tried once before another contraction took her remaining breath away. Before another pain rumbled across her abdomen, she called out again. "Tom!"

He started from his sleep and stumbled to the chair.

"Please help me up, Tommy! Oh, I should have called."

Tom helped her to the bathroom. He called Doctor Zander in time to share the event of Sunnie's water breaking. She gave him strict instructions to meet at the birthing center.

He slung her bag over his shoulder and helped her to the car. With each moan of pain, his eyes strayed to the clock on the dashboard. He started calling up his class on emergency childbirth during the short ride.

Sunnie's contractions jumped in intensity as they pulled to the door of the birthing center. After a cursory greeting, Doctor Zander whisked her to the rooms as Tom parked the Jeep. He returned quickly and was shown to the comfortable room.

Tom felt the calming atmosphere of the muted color scheme and soft music. Sunnie was situated in the birthing chair; he refrained from commenting how similar it looked to one found in a dental office.

Doctor Zander handed him a gown when she walked by to be in her expected position.

"It's a good thing you didn't wait any longer. You would have had a home birth. I'm sure you are both ready to meet these boys!"

He walked to the chair after mastering the gown. He swiped damp curls from

Sunnie's forehead.

"Ready?"

Her eyes shut, and she breathed deeply through the pain of a contraction. Tom held his breath, releasing it when she looked into his eyes.

"I hate being out of control, Tommy. This hurts so bad. Don't you dare leave me."

He wiped the tears from her cheeks. "I'm not going anywhere. Look at me and concentrate. It'll all be over sooner than you think. I know it hurts. It'll only be a little while."

She gripped his arm, and he coached her gently through the next contractions. He encouraged her not to cry, assured her she was doing a fine job, and promised he would soon be crying with her in joy.

Doctor Zander's melodic voice explained every stage of labor Sunnie quickly went through. She made some minor adjustments to the chair.

"Sunnie, you'll feel a burning sensation. It's commonly called the ring of fire. It will be intense. It's your body preparing for the baby to emerge. It will only last a moment; try not to push until I tell you. You're doing great. Baby Sundance will be here in no time."

Tom saw the panic welling, and he gripped her hand.

"Sunn! Look at me."

His strong voice soothed her. She looked from Doctor Zander to him.

"He's almost here. Breathe deep. You can do this..."

"No...Tommy..."

"Sunn! You'll be fine, and you'll be holding him in a minute. Now concentrate! Breathe, don't push until Doctor Zander says."

She labored through several more contractions before Doctor Zander gave the order to push. To the cries of his parents, Colin Thomas appeared in her waiting arms. Sunnie fell back, exhausted by the emotions and anxiety rather than the actual process of Colin's arrival.

The attending nurse swaddled the infant before handing him to Tom. As Doctor Zander focused on the afterbirth and cord cutting, Sunnie watched Tom's face transform to pure joy. His tears, as promised, flowed freely, washing some of the residual birthing mess from Colin's face.

His small, smushed face brought the same joyful tears to Sunnie's eyes. She oohed softly over the reddish fuzz on his head, his small pouting lips. The couple kissed tenderly, sharing tears before the contractions announcing his brother's imminent arrival had them hand the baby to the nurse. While Colin was being cleaned, weighed and measured, dark haired John Anthony entered the world with a wail.

When all was quiet and Sunnie was comfortably resting in a fresh bed, Doctor Zander recalled the birth statistics along with a piece of interesting news.

"This is a first for me in over two decades of practice. The twins have different birth dates. Colin was born at three minutes to midnight; John Anthony followed at twelve-o-nine."

Tom laughed deeply, startling John Anthony from his first nap. "Only you, Sunn. Only you."

Tom picked up the squalling baby from the basinet, kissing him before handing him to Sunnie. Colin was peacefully sleeping after his first nursing session, ignoring the brother who was giving exercise to his lungs.

208

"You told me a long time ago, Officer, that you enjoyed my *unusualness*. Don't think I'll ever allow you to forget that. Ow!" she exclaimed suddenly as the baby traded squealing for nursing. "Does he have teeth already?"

Doctor Zander laughed. "No. New borns have strong suckling muscles, as well as the need. You seem to be doing fine, Sunnie. I would like you to stay a while longer, till morning. So long as everything is fine, you can go home at that time. Tom, you are free to stay or go home a while. I'll let you two have a bit of privacy right now. I'll be back in about an hour to do some annoying pressing on your abdomen." Doctor Zander winked, closing the door on her way out of the room.

"I don't think I've ever seen babies with so much hair." Tom commented, getting up from the chair to lean over the basinet. His finger lightly traced his son's brow. Colin seemed to sigh happily at his father's touch.

Tom walked to the bed, leaning over to kiss Sunnie's forehead. "You were amazing. I'm so proud of you."

The brilliant smile he knew belonged to him alone appeared. "I was so scared, Tommy. I couldn't have made it through without you."

John Anthony interrupted the intimacy between his parents with a grunt. Sunnie handed him to Tom. He was lovingly placed next to his brother and the parents observed their contrasting faces.

Tom sat on the bed. "You need some rest; you did all that work."

Sunnie rested her head against Tom's chest. Listening to Tom's soft prayers over her and the boys, she drifted into a light sleep.

When Doctor Zander returned, the new family was all sound asleep. She left the room, allowing them some time to rest.

Chapter 35

The rumble of continuous thunder greeted the Jacobs family the morning of the twins' dedication. Instead of the snit it would have put her in, Sunnie praised the Lord for the abundance of her newly finished home to house their guests planned for the afternoon.

She faced the window to watch the pouring rain as she worked through her morning yoga routine. Tom arrived back from an early morning bed check on the twins, coffee in hand. He paused at the door to observe his wife work the graceful movements.

"I don't know how you can stand so still. You look terrific doing so, however. It's going to be a busy day. I was hoping for a game."

She smiled at him as he walked past to look out the window. The new backboard and hoop installed two days earlier was being baptized in the downpour.

"Maybe it'll clear up. I know you...you would play in the rain. Rob probably would, too. The boys are still sleeping?" Done with her routine, she started towards the bathroom.

"Yes, they were five minutes ago," he answered as he watched the horses tear across the corral, his eyes on the mysterious new arrival.

"You know, I'm still not clear who Thunder belongs to. Pop keeps giving me the most lame answers."

The sounds of a twin waking up reached them. "I hear one of them fussing. I'll get him so you can shower. Is there a bottle ready?"

She offered a brief hug when he walked past. "I pumped last night. There should be two. That sounds like John Anthony. I won't be long."

Tom walked into the room and lifted a wide-awake and hungry baby from the crib. He spoke soothing things to him as they walked to the kitchen. The bond he was grateful he had the chance to form in his time home was present in the eyes John Anthony shared with him. Tom smiled down on him while waiting for the bottle to warm.

His mother-in-law shed a few tears over this twin's name. For her, it was proof that her daughter had dealt with the stormy past. Tom reflected on how much Sunnie had grown the past year, how much they both had. Their relationship was far and above what he hoped and prayed for.

"Sunn, do we really need so much stuff?"

Sunnie grinned at Tom's frustration with the collection of baby gear that was classified as essential.

"Yes, we do. Get used to it. Just wait till we're carting around Little League stuff. It just gets worse, not better."

Certain the babies were secure in their car seats, Sunnie closed the door. She looked up to the sky as the clouds over Lakeville started breaking. Tom joined her, placing his arm around her shoulder. What seemed to be a thousand beams of sunlight streamed from behind the dark edge of the storm clouds.

A large swath of brilliant blue sky emerged, and with it a rainbow in colors more vivid than either of them imagined or had seen before appeared. Sunnie gasped, pointing to the spectacular arc's point of origin beyond the stables.

The strength of the sun faded the illustrious vision. Tom pulled her a bit closer, to quietly ask in her ear, "Do you feel like I do?"

Gratitude and joy so overwhelmed her she could only nod.

"God gave that to us. Only us." His voice was laden with the same emotions she was feeling.

"I have the feeling that no one else in Lakeville saw that rainbow, Sunn. His promise to be with us always. It looks as though it's coming from the tree house."

"Exactly, Tommy!" Her agreement sounded in an awed whisper. "That's exactly what I thought."

Sammie's tears were freely flowing—as always—as she observed the dedication of her grandsons. The years she prayed and shed tears over her daughter made the moment all the sweeter for her. Pastor Paul's prayer over the family ended, and the couple stepped down from the platform.

Sunnie handed Colin to her mother before sitting next to Tom. Stuart gladly relieved his son of John Anthony. They glanced at each other with a smile; it was the first time since their birth one of them did not have a babe in arms. They clasped hands and rose as one to join the congregation in worship.

The end of the service brought many to congratulate the couple and politely oogle the twins. Sunnie's eyes searched out her mother.

"Mom! Can you and Rob hurry on over to the house? I doubt we'll get out of here before people start showing up. Everything is ready to throw in the oven or take out of the fridge. We'll be there as soon as we can."

"Of course. So glad the weather changed for you. We'll see you there." Rob and

Sammie collected their children and disappeared into the crowd.

Tom's conversation with Stuart was ending as Sunnie turned her attention towards them.

"I'll be there in just about an hour. Ronnie is meeting me in town."

Stuart waved to Sunnie before hurrying from the row of seats.

"What were you laughing about and who is Ronnie?" Sunnie asked him as she buckled John Anthony into his car seat.

"Judge Caldwell."

Sunnie raised her eyebrow. "No way! He's *dating* the judge?"

Tom surrendered Colin to Sunnie. "Yes, he is. I knew all those trips to the county seat weren't all Lakeville business."

Guests were milling on the deck and in the yard when the hosts pulled down the drive to their home. Before they pulled in the garage, Sunnie noticed Stuart with Judge Caldwell by the corral fence. They were encouraging Aina to feed Picasso some carrots under Rob's watchful eye.

There was no shortage of arms for the twins to repose in. After caring for their guests, the couple finally sat down to enjoy a plate of food together. Aina was soon at Tom's knee, begging for a ride. He gladly set aside dessert to take Aina across the road to the corral.

Sunnie was almost jealous to get back to riding. She hadn't had the time, between the house and the twins' care. Her brand new helmet sat unused on their dresser. Watching as Tom slowly walked Beau around the corral with Aina sitting in front of him, she breathed an envious sigh.

Sammie observed her daughter from the table. She saw the impatient stance, one she'd seen many times through the years. She rose from her spot by Victoria and walked to stand by Sunnie.

"The house is coming along beautifully, Sunnie. Your master bedroom is especially wonderful. I love how it's set up and away from the rest of the house."

"Thanks Mom. I wanted it to be a getaway. Tommy needs a quiet place once he gets back to work. I miss my closet just a bit, though."

"You know you could have added an office or made one of those bedrooms an office."

"Well, I'd rather not have to give up an office when the next baby comes along. Tommy would love a houseful. We'll see how the Lord works that out. In the meantime, Steven and Storm have a room to stay in when they visit. Maybe we can have some missionaries stay over. It's the Lord's house, not mine."

Sammie returned her daughter's smile. Sunnie turned back with a wistful eye to the corral. Each time Aina passed Rob, she leaned over to high-five his waiting hand.

Sammie gently took the monitor from Sunnie's hand. "Why don't you go on over? I'll take care of him," she motioned to the sounds emitting.

Sunnie sighed, but smiled. "I can't, Mom. I need to go get him. He really shouldn't be hungry yet, though."

"You never did hide disappointment well, my Sunnie Day."

"Mom!" They laughed. Sammie patted her shoulder.

"Sorry. There's plenty of people here to handle the twins. Please go enjoy some time with Tom. And Picasso."

The urge to bound across the road was hardly curbed.

"Are you sure?"

At Sammie's nod, she threw her arms around her mother's neck before dashing inside to obtain her as-yet-unused helmet.

From his seat on Beau, Tom saw Sunnie hurrying from the deck across the road. A great smile broke across his face when she waved to him before climbing up the corral fence. Once he deposited a disgruntled Aina into Rob's arms, he continued the circuit of the fence to the spot Sunnie was perched on.

"Looking for a ride, ma'am?"

"I was hoping to go on a hunt...for the end of our rainbow."

"Picasso isn't saddled. You'll have to ride with me."

The smile he first fell in love with appeared. He situated Beau so she could climb on easily.

"Don't forget a blanket," she whispered before leaning against the broad shoulders. Her arms slid intimately about his waist, and she heard the deep chuckle.

"Isn't it tacky to leave our own party for...to hunt a rainbow?"

"When will we ever have another opportunity? No one will notice if we're gone. Not too long, anyhow."

"Whatever you say, Mrs. Jacobs."

Delighted that Sunnie was with him, he drank in her touch and the scent that was now a part of his life. Reminded of the first time he brought her to his home, he thanked the Lord that it was a place they now shared. The place they would raise their family—together.

No one did notice they had been missing. Walking across the dirt road to return to the party, Sunnie reflected with happiness that she had, indeed, finally found her rainbow.

FINIS

The Song behind the Story

Naturally, Sunnie has not only one, but two songs that I played during the writing and editing process. The first was "I Will Worship You." As Sunnie grows in her relationship with the Lord, she desires only to worship Him. Her frustrations at having to learn hard lessons, as most of us do, are voiced. Towards the end of the story, I switched to "The Stand." As Tom and Sunnie stand together as one, they stand firmly in their Savior. I hope you enjoyed their journey.

There is no known author of The Policeman's Prayer, quoted in Chapter 13.

If you have need of a Bible, please email me. I will be sure that you have one in which to meet the wonderful person of Jesus Christ. He is the Way, the Truth and the Life. dhbarbara1@gmail.com

Look for these current books in print and upcoming novels by D.H. Barbara

Seasons Of A Life
A soon-to-be empty nest, a broken down car, and a chance meeting steers Samantha Young's life down a highway she never dreamed of traveling. The foundational Lakeville novel. Available on Amazon.com

Upcoming:

Loaves and Fishes
Everything Silas Young has dreamed of, he's accomplished: but one. Will he allow disappointment to plant a root of bitterness in his heart and mar his two most important relationships?

Restoration
The last of the siblings to get out on his own, Corporal Jude Young stretches his wings in directions he knows better to follow. He soon realizes he needs to call upon the Master Mechanic to repair the wreck he's responsible for causing.

Wild Flowers
Autumn Young dreams of the day she'll have home and family of her own. She puts her own plans on hold due to her father's unexpected death to help her mother through those first hard months.

Called To Serve
On fire to serve God from the first time she called upon His name, Storm Young longs to do just that at the side of the one man she's loved since grade school. The only thing standing in the way is that his plans are not the same.

Officer Jacobs' Triumph
He is living the life he always dreamed of; a loving and beautiful wife, a growing family, known as a well-respected officer in Lakeville. Tom Jacobs' adamant insistence that "all is well" with his life is severely tested. When he fails that test, he must rebuild all he's destroyed by one foolish choice.

Other Novels by D.H. Barbara:

Angels Unaware
A battle unseen rages around us. For Moriah, this battle will become real. A superstar entertainer who has run from God her whole life, she comes face to face with the reality of eternity. Have you ever entertained an angel, unaware?

Park Bench
The Kennedy assassination. The moon landing. Watergate. The Gulf War. September 11. Follow as history unfolds from different perspectives as seen through the eyes of people who occupy the same bench in a park over the span of 40 years.

The Petras Project: The Beginnings
Jesse Petras moves to Harrington at the behest of his friend and fellow pastor Sam Jordan, to help start an inner city mission. He builds more than a ministry when he meets Celia McCann. Sam's past life holds a surprising secret that threatens all.

14744583R00116

Made in the USA
Lexington, KY
17 April 2012